THE DRAGON'S REVENGE

CONOR KOSTICK

Published by Level Up in the United Kingdom in 2019

Cover by Claire Wood

ISBN: 978-1-912701-82-7

www.levelup.pub

A big thank you to Mike Virtue, Russ Liley and especially Patrick Reed.

PRAISE FOR CONOR KOSTICK

"The most important Irish novel of the year." Celia Keenan, the *Independent* reviewing *Epic*.

"Just as *Saga* (2008) exploded beyond opener *Epic* (2007), this third volume ratchets up this science-fiction gaming series to a whole new level." Kirkus reviewing *Edda*.

"Contemporary and futuristic fantasy can provide a powerful critique of dehumanisation and help explore ideas about identity. Conor Kostick's *Saga* falls into this category." *Sunday Independent* review of *Saga*.

"It is a rock 'n' roll, helter-skelter time, a journey not for the faint-hearted but bound to enthral wired-up skateboarders, the mathematically literature and those who just enjoy a well-written narrative. This is what happens when Hal from *2001: A Space Odyssey* meets *A Clockwork Orange*." *Village Magazine* review of *Saga*.

"Irish author Kostick's powerful debut imagines an agrarian world where violence is illegal, except within a massive computer game that provides the economic and governmental structure for society." *Publisher's Weekly* review of *Epic*.

"A gripping first novel... A surefire winner." *Kirkus* review of *Epic*.

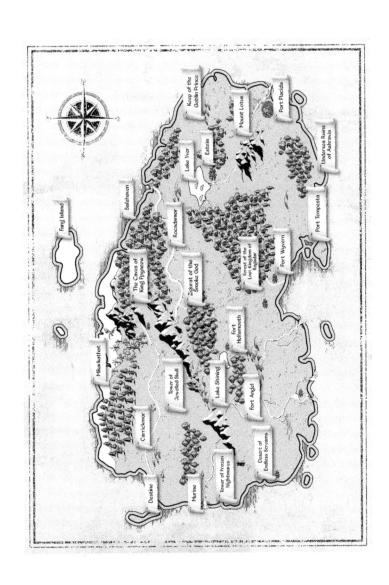

THE
DRAGON'S
REVENGE

CHAPTER 1
DRAGON ATTACK

'Let's try again,' I spoke patiently.

It's not easy getting a heal rotation to run smoothly, especially if the clerics are relatively new to each other. The *Restore* spell is a complete healing spell but takes eight seconds to cast. Far too slow for a dragon fight. So you have to recruit eight high-level clerics for the raid, each of whom begins to chant one second after the other. That way, woosh, woosh, woosh…there is a continuous series of powerful heals landing on your tank. It works like kids singing 'Frère Jacques' in the round in primary school and is just as messy to get it going properly.

'And go!'

'One.'

'Two.'

'Three.'

'Four.'

I was sitting on a rock - well, my warrior avatar, Tyro, was - with the clerics all gathered around me, calling out their number as they began to cast the spell. The curious thing about the scene was that even though all avatars can be fully customised in the world of *Epic*, these players looked pretty similar. It was like I was circled by clones. That's because they all had the same quest gear: Neowthla's Breast Plate, a shield of warding and Mov's Hammer of the Elements. Top ranking cleric items, representing years of effort. Nothing but the best for my raids. Except.

'Five.'

'…'

The sixth cleric just stood there. No raised arms to cast a spell. Nothing but a blank stare into the distance.

'Oh, come on Triggle. Where are you?' This time I couldn't keep the exasperation out of my voice.

'Sorry, man, pizza arrived just at the wrong time.'

And that encapsulates the challenge of organising a big raid. One hundred and twenty-three avatars, all logged in to *Epic* in the hope of making history. Some were just kids, maybe waking up in the middle of the night to join a raid, the way I used to. Others, perhaps, were middle-aged, hot-shot lawyers, closing their office door and lowering the blinds for an hour of *Epic* play. And everything in between. I felt responsible for their time and was very conscious of the need to keep everything running to schedule.

'Start over please. And go!'

Now the rotation was established properly, the clerics twitching in order, landing their spells about a second apart. I let it run through five cycles and called a halt.

'Good. Go over to your starting places behind Braja.'

As the clerics obediently trudged past me up the hill, I swapped my communications from local to the raid channel, which I'd earlier defined as 'Dragonattack' and made an announcement. The pizza incident had caused me to worry.

[Channel Dragonattack] 'Ten minutes to start,' I announced. 'This is your ten-minute warning. Eat, drink, go to the toilet. We begin in ten.'

Then I took my own advice, raising my foot off my little tracking pad and unclipping from the gloves and helmet. It was always a little disconcerting phasing in and out of *Epic*. The game was this huge fantasy environment, with extraordinary landscapes and incredible skies. There are two moons in *Epic* and whether by design or just the way the game had evolved, you could get breath-taking evenings, like the one I'd just stepped away from, where the sun was setting on one horizon and the moons had risen from the other, to glow as though burnished with copper.

By contrast, I unclipped from the game to see a dingy room barely wide enough to fit my bed. My clothes were strewn on a floor whose faded brown carpet had a well-worn path from door to bed. It was dimly lit, my bedroom, mostly because my curtains were nearly always closed: who wanted to look out at the grim walls and barred windows of a factory on the other side of the alley? I had put shelves in myself and these ran around high up, above my poster-clad wall (two trance-metal bands featured, but the majority of the posters showed scenes from *Epic*, including one of the dragon Mikarkathat).

If there was one feature of the room that did not look typical for a teenager's bedroom in overcrowded Dublin, it was the high-tech gear on top of the shelving. Black boxes there had small blue and green LEDs, blinking in and out of phase. Thanks to my sponsors, I had enterprise-grade computing and online access. No lag for me.

On entering the bathroom, I was met with a waft of warm, moist air and a strong scent of flowers. The glass panes of the narrow shower stall were covered in droplets. Evidently, Mum had just been in here.

'Mum?' I shouted downstairs. But there was no reply. Her new cleaning job was in the Bartlett Private Hospital, over an hour away on the south side of town. She'd probably just left. And I wouldn't have heard her call goodbye, not while in *Epic*.

Refreshed, I clipped up again.

And a whole new - far better - world rushed upon me.

Even clipping up is an intense, addictive experience, let alone fighting dragons. You place one foot on a tracking pad, a foot that becomes adept at spinning it in whatever direction you need to move your avatar; you place the helmet over your head, seeing the login screen and hearing an ambient theme music, and you slide your hands into the gloves.

Then, the moment I lived for. A gesture with your index finger and a sinuous line of pastel colours surges over you like a crashing wave, accompanied by a rushing sound like that of an aeroplane taking off. As your heart beats fast in expectation, the colours turn kaleidoscopic before crystalizing into the environment in front of your avatar.

With a quick flick to bring up and then slide away one of the game settings menus, I checked the time. [Channel Dragonattack] 'Six minutes, thirty seconds to start. We start on time. No delays for anyone. Long duration buffs on.'

It was crucial to start on schedule. There were people in the raid from all over the world who were making sacrifices to be here. For those from India and further east, the timing probably wasn't too bad, unless they were skipping work for the afternoon. For those west of me, on the other side of the Atlantic (we had a lot of Brazilians in this raid), it was about four in the morning.

No delays for anyone. Except Raitha. I signalled I wanted to speak to him in private chat and he accepted, the flashing red chat bubble beside his name turning green.

[Channel Tyro/Raitha] 'You there? All good?' I asked.

[Channel Tyro/Raitha] 'I am more than good, thank you, I'm PUMPED!'

Raitha was from Kerala in India and was usually softly spoken. This declaration, however, was nearly a shout and it made me smile.

Back my early days, Raitha and I had found each other and liked what we found: commitment, determination, drive, good skills. She - I say 'she' but I had a feeling it was a 'he' behind the avatar, not that I cared - was a warrior too. Two warriors are not normally a good combination. It works for one fight, after that you have massive downtime as you recover without the help of magical healing.

Raitha and I smote our way through the mobs of the Kastrival Desert, recruiting healers to join us when we could, but pushing on together regardless. Hours and hours. Days and days. And yes, years too, four years. Fighting. Recovering. Maybe chatting a bit, mostly about tactics, although Raitha also had a taste for philosophy. Then fighting some more. Grinding out the levels and sharing everything that dropped without the slightest rivalry. By now, it felt as though Raitha was my sibling. Probably my older sibling, even though I was more of a raid leader than her.

[Channel Tyro/Raitha] 'Let's do it then,' I said and changed channel to make the announcement. [Channel Dragonattack] 'Form up.'

I was pleased to see an immediate response from the avatars all around me.

[Channel Dragonattack] 'Where do the druids go?' an adult female voice asked. I didn't recognise her. Then again, half the players in the raid were unfamiliar to me.

[Channel Dragonattack] 'If you are not sure about anything: where you should be, what your priority is, ask your section leader. Keep this channel clear for my voice and for emergencies.' I tried not to sound like I was delivering a reprimand. We were all raid noobs once. Not that anyone here was less than level sixty. Most were at the game's cap of seventy-five.

By contrast with the main body of raiders, my section leaders were pretty much hand-picked and even the newest had raided a dozen times with me. Eighteen of them were veterans of the first time we fought Mikarkathat, the ice dragon. That had been a closely fought encounter. Close enough to give me the belief that victory was possible. [Channel Dragonattack] 'Two minutes. Short-term buffs on. Electricity resistance on the tanks.'

By now our formation was established. It was the one some gamers called the bull's horns. Side by side in the centre of the formation were the raid's two main tanks: Raitha and me. Curving forward to my left was half the army and to my right the other half. The reason for this formation was that when engaged, we'd envelop the dragon and once the warriors at the base had firmly gained the dragon's attention, the rogues and backstabbers at the tips of the horns would run around behind her and do their worst.

Not everyone was in line. I had two sections of hunters out of formation, behind me. Also, both Raitha and I each had a paladin immediately at our backs. These guys were doomed. And of course, the eight clerics were off to the side, to Raitha's right. They had to get close enough to be able to land their heals but it was imperative that the clerics stay out of the way of the forked lightning that Mikarkathat would breathe against us.

5

I raised my sword. [Channel Dragonattack] 'Advance, walking pace.'

The pleasure of leading an army of heroes against the most powerful dragon in *Epic* is hard to describe but I'll try. In part, it was visual. When, in the real world, would you ever see anything like this? A windswept, heather-covered hill, a purple and navy sky, with two large, near-full moons ahead and a setting sun behind. With the darkest of our three shadows stretching ahead of us towards the crest of the hill, a hundred and twenty-three comrades in full battle-mode marched to the toughest battle of their game lives.

Each one of us had already been on a journey of several years to arrive at this moment. Everywhere I looked was a figure to make me proud of being part of this army. Near me was Grythiss, a Shadow Knight lizardman. Wearing shimmering black plate mail, he walked tall, a lance in his hands with an emerald pennant. That had been his reward for completing the Serpent of the Golden Spire quest. I'd organised the final raid for him and, ever after, he'd never failed to turn up when I needed him. Right now, his forked tongue was flicking in and out of the gap in his polished helmet. It was as though he were nervous and excited, although surely the game's animations were not smart enough to pick that up?

Across to the right was Sapentia, an elven sorceress with turquoise hair and a gold-lined cloak to match. In the real world, she was well known for her hosting and writing Japanese dating sims. Here, she was a level seventy-five specialist in the art of elemental summoning and utterly disdainful of any attempt to flirt with her or mention her other role. Here, in other words, she was Sapentia and there was no other world.

Everywhere I looked, whether I knew the person's story or not, I saw resolute, skilful champions striding towards battle. And it made me proud to be leading them. A seventeen-year-old Irish kid from Cabra, one of Dublin's most deprived and neglected areas.

In case everyone wasn't feeling the intensity of the moment enough - we all were, of course - I called up my *Epic* playlist and broadcast *Ride of the Valkyries* in the raid channel. It was something of a trademark of my raids.

[Channel Tyro/Raitha] 'My friend,' said Raitha immediately, 'this is what I live for.'

[Channel Tyro/Raitha] 'Me too.'

With a glance at my comrade, I took a moment to appreciate that life was great. It really hadn't been. Only in the last few months, when Mum had seen that I was becoming a celebrity and was able to earn some money from sponsorship, did the constant battle between us ease up. Naturally, she wanted me to concentrate on schoolwork. Equally naturally, I wanted to concentrate on *Epic*. Our conflict and the need for lying and secrecy about how much I was playing the game had made me utterly miserable at times. Her too, I'm sure. And even when Mum and I had been getting on together, there was still our grim, tedious battle with poverty to put me off the real world.

It was all good now though.

Raitha and I were the last to march over the curve of the hill and there in the rocky dip below us was Mikarkathat, staring right at us of course. She knew we were coming; she'd probably been waiting ever since that last raid when she had feasted on our bodies.

This was the queen of the dragons. Mikarkathat was enormous. Her size alone made you feel your cause was hopeless. With her wings spread out, she'd have covered half a football field. Her head soared ten metres or so above the ground. And in her monstrous way, she was beautiful.

Those outspread wings were an amazing opalescent colour, shot through with blue veins and a purple that began deep at her shoulders and faded to violet at the tips of her claws. A colour so dark a blue as to be nearly black ran along her jagged spine, while the underneath of her body was that opal-white again. The contrast between dark and light was so strong that Mikarkathat looked more like a snake than many dragons do. Her head, too, was serpentine, flat in shape, with wicked, black eyes and a wide mouth which you could see was full of sharp curved teeth when she dropped her lower jaw, as she was doing now to hiss at us.

There was a lot of murmuring and swearing in the main

channel from those who had never seen Mikarkathat before. And also from those who had.

[Channel Dragonattack] 'Stay at a walk,' I instructed and the voices immediately ceased, at least in the raid channel; probably they were swearing away in their sections, which was fine. 'Our right flank needs to edge away more.'

Mikarkathat was on the rise, it seemed as though the whole hillside was lifting up. An incredible, deep *whomp* sound swept over us as she beat her wings. You could feel it in your body. And another. And another. The dragon was airborne.

[Channel Dragonattack] 'Warriors: charge!'

It seemed as though the dragon was looking directly at me with her wicked eyes and perhaps she had singled me out (did she even remember me?), for with a huge roar she plunged downward and from her fearsome jaws blasted lightning at me and those immediately beside me. On our previous attempt, this initial, shocking pulse of purple and white electricity had knocked out about a third of the raid and even though we resurrected the dead as fast as we could, we never caught up.

This time, only two of the dozen warriors who had run slightly ahead of the rest of the raid were dead. Admittedly, all of us had suffered significant drops in our hit points, but this was still a good start.

[Channel Dragonattack] 'Move in to position but wait until Raitha has the aggro before attacking.'

We didn't want the dragon spinning around taking out characters left, right and centre. Not at all, we wanted her focused on Raitha (and me), the toughest warriors in *Epic*.

In the past year, when we had started to organise raids in earnest, Raitha and I had decided to diverge in our priorities for character advancement. I'd gone for pure defence; she'd gone for the ability to hold the monster's attention with aggro-creating abilities and gear. So now, Raitha was triggering every means she had of building hate in the dragon.

Streams of black vapour poured towards Mikarkathat from a mace that Raitha was brandishing. This was a quest reward, *Oveade's Mace of the Pit*. It was a crappy weapon to hit with, but you could target a creature and draw its rage upon you with the mace's *Demonic Taunt* effect, one of the best aggro-creating spells in the game. I knew too that Raitha would be mashing her *Taunt* ability as fast as she could. I had a macro for that and it was constantly pushing *Taunt* for me so that I was building up aggro too, that way, if Raitha died the dragon would attack me and remain facing in its current direction rather than turn on someone else.

Thud! With a ground-shaking landing, Mikarkathat swatted at Raitha with her front claws and drove her open maw onto Raitha's figure. Dizzy with the lightning - that caused blobs of dark afterimages to swirl over my vision - and also with the shaking terrain, for a few seconds all I could see was an impression of fang and claw. I could, however, view the translucent raid screen I had pulled up by rolling both my eyes rightwards and it showed me that Raitha was nearly dead.

Suddenly, her health bar was back on full. The paladin behind her had used *Holy Intervention*, the once-a-day full heal that high-level paladins obtained. That was why they were there, generously sacrificing themselves, because there was no way either of them could stand this close to the action for long.

[Channel Dragonattack] 'Go, go, go! All in. Heal rotation go.'

Now an extraordinary welter of confused sound competed with the angry roars of the dragon. Accompanied by dramatic rushes of noise, like a succession of waves hitting the shore, dozens of spells were being cast and streams of colour were flowing from the fingers of the spell casters towards the dragon. Many of the spells wouldn't take hold, but those that did would slow her, DoT her (damage over time) and remove some of her buffs.

It was crucial to slow Mikarkathat. Otherwise, even with *Restore* landing perfectly on her every second, Raitha could still be taken out by a flurry of attacks from the raging dragon. A surge of elation shot through me when it was apparent that some slow spells of ours had worked. We were off to a great start. Although Raitha's hit points dropped alarmingly, by as much as three-quarters in a second, they were back up to maximum before the next hit.

[Channel Tyro/Raitha] 'I believe we have a chance of victory,' said Raitha, with intense excitement in her voice.

[Channel Tyro/Raitha] 'Maybe.'

[Channel Tyro/Raitha] 'Thou art going down, dragon!' Raitha sounded as enthusiastic as I'd ever heard her, despite the alarming drops in her hit points.

And what she had said rang true, the dragon's hit points were noticeably declining. Still over 90 per cent though.

Because my actions were all pretty much automated (*Taunt* and *Attack* were on macros; I only needed to concentrate in order to trigger some gear effects manually and watch for ability opportunities), I had the mental space to study the raid screen that overlaid my vision as a near-invisible translucent veil whose constituent boxes brightened as I turned my eyes to them and faded as I looked away.

In front of me, filling the whole sky with its presence, was a slathering, bellowing, ferocious dragon. The fiercest in the game. Despite its furious roars, its beating wings and the constant battering I was taking, I was barely giving the dragon any attention.

Mikarkathat radiated some kind of electrical field that drained you of hit points and spirit. Judging by the raid screen, a lot of us, much more than half, were on less than a quarter hit points. I knew this would happen and had assigned the druids, once they had tried to DoT the dragon, to heal the non-tanks. As for spirit, I'd made it a condition of participation by caster classes that they each bring a *Major Potion of Spirit Restoration*. Plus, I had all my section leaders carry spares.

[Channel Tyro/Braja] '*Restore* please.'

[Channel Tyro/Braja] 'Yep,' replied Braja. During downtime, Braja could be a non-stop talker. On a raid though he was focused, clinical, all economy of word and deed.

And eight seconds later, I was back to full hit points.

Clerics were in high demand in *Epic*, it was kind of a boring class and hard to level solo. In groups, however, well, you were everyone's friend. About three years ago, Raitha and I had called for a cleric to join us in the *Halls of the Amber Palace* and Braja had come over. First thing he'd said was, 'You better be good because I'm high-grade awesome.' Then he'd given us his terms: loot was randomly distributed unless a cleric item dropped; if it represented an upgrade, he got it, no arguments. Secondly, we had to listen to heavy metal from Finland while we battled.

'Bring it on!' Raitha had laughed and soon we were rocking the zone. The three of us had been a team ever since. Braja had the same dedication to the game as Raitha and me, playing it even more than me, somehow fitting in the time around a job as a postal worker. You could tell from his conversation that Braja had read a lot. Whatever he had studied in the past, it was *Epic* that he had mastered.

Right now, Braja was somewhere to my right minding the clerics in the rotation, the extra cleric who kept topping their hit points up as the dragon's AE (area of effect) caused their health to sink. But he also kept his eye on me.

[Channel Dragonattack] 'Stand by to rebuff *Protection from Electricity.*' This alert was especially for the druids and sorcerers.

Last time, when Mikarkathat was reduced to 75 per cent hit points, she cast a really strong debuff and stripped our front row of protection, then she did her second lightning breath attack and that had blown Raitha to pieces: think smouldering boots and nothing else. Everyone nearby had taken a massive hit too. It was a cruel trick from the game and, at the time, one we'd all complained about in the subsequent forum discussions about the fight. How was anyone supposed to survive that combination of debuff and nuke? After analysing the recording of the fight, however, I could see there was just time to restore the crucial protection buff.

Exactly the same happened now. With a surge that raised her head high, Mikarkathat screamed and all my buffs disappeared.

[Channel Dragonattack] 'Now!'

Triumphant, vengeful, fearsome, the dragon drew itself up again, judging where best to blast its lightning breath. A moment before a shocking pulse shot through all of us grouped at

11

the front of the dragon, a small square appeared on my translucent buff list. The icon was a picture of a purple ball, with lightning all around it on the outside. While I could feel the spine-tingling rush of electricity all around me, my hit points only dropped by a quarter. Our two paladins were wiped out by the attack, but Raitha was going strong, already back on full.

[Channel Tyro/Raitha] 'Oh, my goodness!' shouted Raitha. 'I rode it out this time.'

I was too busy checking out the status of the other players to reply. This was going well. Over a hundred of the team were still battling hard and the dragon, slowly but surely, was being taken down from 75 towards 50 per cent, which was my next worry. Last time, we managed to get to 50 per cent, only to see the dragon do a trick with its wings, beating them hard, increasing our hit point drain and slowing us. At that point, the raid had become a wipe. This time, I had a plan, but I was still sweating over it.

Hack, hack, hack. *Taunt, Taunt, Taunt.* My avatar was chopping away at the dragon (with a *Longsword of the Moon*). Whenever the dragon shifted - which it did a lot, jumping up to claw Raitha or give a mighty cry - I could see dozens of my comrades crowded around it, all chipping away with weapons that in any other circumstance would have been impressive-looking but which here looked small and ineffective.

55, 54, 53, 52…I watched the bar representing the dragon's hit points drop.

[Channel Dragonattack] 'Hunters!' I called out.

And over the rise came ten hunters, all fully buffed, full hit points, held in reserve for this moment. The hunter class, when it reached level sixty and did the appropriate quest, could trigger an *Undeviating Flight* ability that allowed them ninety seconds of double damage with a bow. Now the arrows rained in hard upon the dragon's flank. Even though Mikarkathat leapt backwards at 50 and the effect of her beating wings kicked in (my blows felt as though I was hitting her through a wall of glue and I could see from the raid UI [user interface] we were all losing health) the dragon's own hit points were rushing downwards.

At 40 per cent, the dragon dropped back to the ground and we were restored to normal speed.

[Channel Dragonattack] 'Well done the archers!'

I was speaking largely to dead characters, who would be waiting for news from their respawn point. If the strength of the hunter class was its ability to do massive amounts of damage quickly, its weakness was poor armour and hit points. Most of them had not lasted much longer than the ninety seconds of their ability. One was still going strong, I made a note of her name: Roisina.

The raid UI showed at least half of the participants were still alive, their names were still written in green. Crucially, the *Restore* rotation was working with only one gap (cleric number three was down). Now we were into uncharted territory, but if the previous surprises had come on Mikarkathat's being reduced to 75 per cent and 50 per cent, there had to be a new challenge at 25.

28, 27, 26…

Boom! The skies opened and twenty demons looking like whirlwinds (wide, dark open mouths, angry eyes, bodies of fast spinning mist) poured down on the raid.

[Channel Dragonattack] 'Air elementals!' someone shouted in the raid channel but I forgave this at once. This was an emergency.

The problem was, the new arrivals weren't tied down, so they rampaged wildly, killing with glee. As fast as I could, I targeted those nearby and as well as tossing axes at them to get their attention, did my best to *Taunt* them. At the same time, I spoke to the raid channel, hoping I sounded calm and confident, rather than as rattled as I actually felt.

[Channel Dragonattack] 'Root and kite classes, try to take the adds away.'

Damnation. My eyes held tears and a cold sweat rushed over my body. Most of the clerics were dead and the raid was near wipe. Only now that I could taste failure did I realise how much this victory meant to me. We were so close. Focus. It wasn't over yet.

13

There were four elementals attacking me. No, three, Grythiss was on my left and had taken one.

While I smashed into the elementals, triggering my *Slash* ability so that I could hit all three simultaneously with great sweeping blows of my longsword, I anxiously studied Raitha's hit points. They dropped by a quarter every second, came up a bit, but then dropped still further. At least the surviving healers were doing the smart thing and casting quick heals, there was no time for a *Restore*, Raitha would be dead before it landed.

[Channel Tyro/Grythiss] 'Can you get these elementals off me? I'm going to be up against Mikarkathat soon.' Again, I strove to keep my voice calm.

[Channel Tyro/Grythiss] 'Certainly, oh mighty leader. Thsssss.'

There was a time for role playing, I thought, but this wasn't it. Ignoring the elementals, I targeted Mikarkathat once more. And all of a sudden, she was on me.

Raitha was gone.

[Channel Dragonattack] 'I'm now the main tank. All healers on Tyro!'

Even as I shouted, and this time everyone would have heard the panicked screech in my voice, I triggered all my defensive abilities: *Wall of Stone*, *Diamond Shield*, *Unbowed Heroism* and even a dozen minor ones that I'd hardly used after level fifty. It didn't matter that I wasn't hitting the dragon much. Someone had to keep the aggro while the raid re-organised and that someone was me.

Bring it on then, dragon.

I stood right up to her: toe to claw; face to maw.

Mikarkathat was on 17 per cent. My hit points, having fallen instantly to 32 per cent were now rising slowly as some of the heals landed. It was impossible to see what was happening elsewhere, what with a dragon the size of a house in my face, but I could tell the air elementals I'd drawn towards me were gone. Whether Grythiss had killed them or was running around with them chasing after him, at least I wasn't flanked.

[Channel Dragonattack] 'What's going on? Was it a wipe?

Is someone going to resurrect us? Or do we set off for the nearest portal stones?' Some idiot thought it was finished.

[Channel Dragonattack] 'Still going,' I replied. 'Dragon on fifteen. Eleven of us standing. Stay off the channel, this is tight.'

[Channel Tyro/Raitha] 'Go! Tyro, go my friend! Win it for us.' Raitha was in my ear.

It was heartening to be cheered on by my fallen comrade, but I didn't reply, I was too busy dividing my attention between fighting and the raid screen.

Among the living were: Braja, who I knew had my back for healing so long as he had spirit left; Sapentia, seeing her alive gave me hope; Grythiss; and that hunter, Roisina. We also had a druid, a shaman, a rogue and three other warriors.

[Channel Dragonattack] 'Spirit check.'

[Channel Dragonattack] 'Sapentia here. I'm on zero. I've four elementals parked with *Root* on staggered timer. If I med, I just get enough to cast *Root* again in time to keep them off me.'

[Channel Dragonattack] 'Braja. Twenty-three.'

[Channel Dragonattack] 'Roisina here, hunter. Thirty-nine. One elemental snared.'

[Channel Dragonattack] 'Grythiss. Zero, two elementals in train.'

The druid answered with eleven and the shaman six. I hadn't asked for a report on the elemental situation but they had been right to raise it. That was a big consideration.

[Channel Dragonattack] 'Any spirit restoration potions left?' I asked.

No answer.

Both *Wall of Stone* and *Diamond Shield* were in their last thirty seconds, I could see the timers running down at what seemed an incredible speed. When they were gone, I was going to see my hit points slide fast. The decision I had to make was this: all in on the dragon, who was on 13, ignoring the elementals? Or would we fall short if we did that? My intuition said it was too soon for a do or die call.

[Channel Dragonattack] 'Grythiss, circle to Sapentia and

take her mobs as they break the *Root*. Sapentia, med up for a nuke. Healers, stay on me. Either when I'm killed or else when the dragon is on six, go all in. Stop healing, ignore the elementals. To repeat: everyone in when she's on six, with whatever you have left.'

[Channel Dragonattack] 'Yessssss, oh brave human. The lizardman obeys.'

Blood and thunder, that guy was a character. I was so tense, I could barely speak coherently, let alone play-act. A lot depended on Grythiss too. His hit points were below 20 per cent, so he wouldn't manage for long against several elementals, but I figured that shadow knights were good at getting aggro and I knew he had a nightmare for a mount. That was fast, faster even than the elementals, so with some skill, he might be able to tag the ones that Sapentia had rooted and keep them chasing him as the roots broke. If not, we'd get six elementals rushing back to the fight and we'd wipe.

My two best abilities dropped and immediately I saw the effect on my hit points.

Mikarkathat on 11, Tyro on 46.

Mikarkathat on 10, Tyro on 29.

Mikarkathat on 9, Tyro on 32, three heals had landed during that second: cleric, druid and shaman. Was there anything else I could do?

Mikarkathat on 8, Tyro on 17.

Mikarkathat on 7, Tyro on 2. Damn. Damn.

Mikarkathat on 6, Tyro on 7.

I probably didn't have to say it but: [Channel Dragonattack] 'All in!' There was an extraordinary flash of red light that left me dazzled for a moment.

Mikarkathat is dead. You gain experience.

[Channel Dragonattack] 'We win. I'm not sure how,' I announced; doubtless I sounded amazed. I really was, had we truly won? No more surprises? There it was. A massive dead dragon sprawled in front of me and the summoned elementals had all gone.

I heard giddy, high-pitched laughter coming from Sapentia.

[Channel Dragonattack] 'Critical hit with *Fire Strike.*'

One hundred and thirty odd voices couldn't contain themselves. A party began in the raid channel as - with a good dose of swearing - the raiders all started to voice their sense of achievement.

We'd just made *Epic* history; Mikarkathat was dead.

CHAPTER 2
GREED

This was easily the highpoint of my playing experience. I'd led successful raids before and victory always brought a wonderful glow along with a sense of achievement that lasted for days. This, however, was against a monster that no one, not even the most powerful guilds, had managed to kill. My sense of achievement was a high no drug could have taken me to. Physically, my body felt like it was filled with energy and this visceral delight was constantly being reinforced by all the messages I was getting. Dozens of private channel requests were flashing.

[Channel Tyro/Sevora] 'You are the man! Seriously, I've been on a lot of raids and this was the best organised I've ever seen.'

[Channel Tyro/Desmoulan] 'Inspired leadership, bro, any-time you need a rogue in your raids, I'll be there.'

[Channel Tyro/Sapentia] 'Respect.'

[Channel Tyro/Grythiss] 'Lizardman say you good human. You brave and smart. Me your ally for life.'

And fifty more of the same.

I replied, modestly, to as many as I could, until the moment came to calm everyone down.

[Channel Dragonattack] 'Quiet in the channel please, loot time.'

Immediately, everyone stilled. Surely there were some ex-traordinarily rare treasures on the dead dragon, not to mention items that would help complete the most challenging quests in the game?

I'd been watching the raid screen turn green as, one after the other, the dead were brought back to life by *Resurrection* spells cast by clerics (or by rogues from a wand). You'd see almost-naked characters appear over their own corpse and quickly bend down to pick up and equip their gear, then the body would disappear. Once everyone was present, I placed my hand on the head of the dead dragon. A list of about twenty items popped up and I flicked the *Link All* option and dragged the resulting box into the raid channel.

Now everyone could see all the loot and the stats on the items. At first glance, it looked very good indeed.

In a guild raid, the guild leader would divide up the loot according to what would further the goals of the guild overall. My raids, however, were pick-ups. Myself and my friends always formed the core officers, but a lot of complete strangers were present. There was only one fair way to do this.

[Channel Dragonattack] 'We'll keep it simple. Everyone rolls once in this channel, random 1000. Highest picks, then the next, until there is no loot left.'

The game had a random number generator. You just had to type /roll 1000 and everyone would see your name accompanied by a result between 001 and 999. Soon the raid channel was full of these rolls. Irritatingly, a female shaman rolled in local chat instead of the channel and even though she got a 734, which probably was enough to win something, I had to insist she rolled again.

The rules were clear, I told myself, and if you start to make exceptions, you create a lot of ill will instead of disappointing just one person. I sincerely hoped she'd do as well with her roll in the raid channel but, sadly, she only got 460, which wasn't going to be enough.

Having left my own roll until last, I hesitated and then did something I knew at the time was utterly wrong and equally stupid. The highest roll by a warrior was 811. Among the loot was a shield with amazing stats and the *Diamond Shield* ability as a triggered effect. It was absolutely made for Raitha, but she'd only gotten a 303. So instead of rolling, I triggered a macro that was completely illegal and I chose my score. The number 813 appeared in the channel by my name.

[Channel Tyro/Raitha] 'Whoot nice!'

I was amused to hear such enthusiastic slang from Raitha, who was usually extremely articulate and well-spoken.

[Channel Tyro/Raitha] 'That's a new shield for you, my old friend,' I told her.

[Channel Tyro/Raitha] 'This cannot be. You must pick something for yourself; you deserve it.'

[Channel Tyro/Raitha] 'It's yours.' I put all the insistence I could into my voice. 'This is exactly what you need. We can take any boss now, with you geared up with this shield.'

There were plenty of whoops and congratulations for me, but I already felt sick. My cheating was crazy on so many levels. Firstly, I might well have rolled a win, fair and square. Or I might have asked the raid to award the shield to Raitha and probably everyone was so fired up and delighted with the result, they would have agreed. Instead, I'd let greed get the better of me.

Of course, I had my justifications: it had been my raid; the shield would be wasted on some pick-up warrior we might never see again; it was only a game; smart players outsmarted the rules. That kind of thing. But cheating the loot role was wrong and already it soured the sweet taste of victory I had been experiencing.

Suddenly, I wished I could turn back time just ten seconds. Just to let me make another choice. Let me roll fairly.

It was stupid to even own that macro to tempt me. I should have deleted it years ago. I was never very good at resisting temptation. Ask my mum. She'd long ago learned not to keep any treats around the house. If I found a bar of chocolate or some crisps, I just couldn't help it, I devoured them at once, even though I knew they were hers. And I always felt bad. But this was a thousand times worse.

I'd made a bad choice. Now I knew how it felt to have cheated these wonderful people who had fought so well as a team, I would try never to do anything like it again. This, I resolved with complete sincerity and resolution. And even while calling out the names of the winners, I deleted the macro and then cleared it out of my computer's bin. It was gone for good.

We had reached my turn to choose.

[Channel Dragonattack] 'I pick the *Shield of the Dragonslayer* and I invite Raitha to loot it.'

Again, there were cheers at this, cheers that did not lift me as they should have.

Most of the items in the dragon's treasure were *Fastened*. The good news about *Fastened* items was that you could never lose them. If you died, they remained on your body to be reclaimed after resurrection. If you were a victim of PvP combat, the item would never be available to the winner to loot. The bad news was you couldn't trade or sell *Fastened* gear. So whoever picked up a *Fastened* item got it and that was that. When it was no use any more, all you could do was delete it or, if you were sentimental, as I was about some items, keep it in your game bank storage as a souvenir.

That's why I didn't just loot the shield and toss it to Raitha, she had to obtain it herself.

[Channel Tyro/Raitha] 'I'm choked, my dear friend. I really am. This is the best day ever.'

With the new shield on her left arm - gleaming silver, with a dragon emblem in purple - Raitha came and stood before me, clasping my shoulder with her right hand. [Channel Tyro/Raitha] 'You're the best comrade anyone could want.' Her soft voice, nearly a whisper, was tearful.

[Channel Tyro/Raitha] 'You too,' I replied.

With the rest of the loot distributed, people were leaving the raid and unclipping from the game. It was time for me to go too, if I was to make it to school for English.

[Channel Dragonattack] 'Later all. See you on the next one.'

This prompted another round of congratulatory messages, but I just unclipped with a tightness in my chest and stomach that made me feel a little nauseous.

From muscled warrior to angular, skinny teenager: I was

back in the real world. A world that seemed greyscale in comparison to the vivid colours of *Epic*. Even though I'd timed the raid to allow me to make it to class on time, I was behind schedule. Perhaps, deep down, I hadn't expected to win, because it was the assignment of loot that had caused me to spend a bit too long in the game. At least my satchel was ready; I'd prepared it last night.

As I jogged past the rows of red-brick terraced housing, keeping an eye out for dog dirt on the cracked paving stones, I groped inside my satchel and pulled out a breakfast bar. That, plus my water, would have to do until lunch.

St Dominic's Secondary School. It had a picture of the saint on the gable end, which faced all those (like me) who hurried towards the school from the west. With arms wide and a welcoming smile, the saint seemed to want to gather in all the young men and women of the community. Lovely. And utterly deceptive. Inside the building there was no sense of community. It was a Hobbesian nightmare of all against all, with the authorities encouraging our divisions out of fear we'd otherwise turn on them.

Mind you, the adults did have genuine concerns. The bigger boys wouldn't hesitate to strike a teacher. They didn't care about reports and exam results. They had nothing to lose. And when the kids did unite, which happened from time to time around some grievance, well, we would be pretty good at challenging the staff. Like when some of the Sixth Year took the wheels off Mr Jameson's car and left it standing on bricks.

I had Jameson now for English and just got in the door ahead of him. As quickly as I could, I took my seat and pulled out the books and biro that I'd need.

Beside me, a friend of mine, Jules, leaned in close. 'Well done!' she whispered. 'You took down Mikarkathat?'

The question brought back the positive feeling I'd gotten from this morning's events and I found my blood was still liquid gold. 'Yeah. How did you know?'

From a flash of her phone, before Jules hurriedly put it in her desk, I could see that a video of the raid already had over ten thousand views. When I put up the official recording with my commentary, I'd be disappointed with anything less than a million in the first week.

'You were awesome.' Jules gave me the thumbs up just as Jameson called us to order.

'Lower Sixth, you are fortunate today we have a visitor.'

This announcement was greeted with a few cheers, signalling the pleasure of some that we wouldn't have to wade through any of *Moby Dick* today. Unfolding himself from his official teaching pose, Jameson stood up and stepped towards the door, which he opened. Our English teacher wanted to be considered as elegant and sophisticated. Why else would he wear a waistcoat every school day? And move around with such studied motions? And have unnecessarily large round glasses?

'Mr Watson has come from Yuno Industries to talk to you about entrepreneurship.' The way that Jameson said the word 'entrepreneurship' made it clear he despised the term. But I was wide awake and scrutinising our visitor attentively. Yuno were the designers, manufacturers and administrators of *Epic*.

A moment later, Mr Watson rolled in through the door and across to the front of the class. He was one of those overweight, middle-aged men who worked out. So his upper body was strong and his muscled arms swung out wide from his sides as he walked. Broad face, made broader by a red, orange and white beard; blue, penetrating eyes looking at us over a pair of rectangular, somewhat racy, purple spectacles; white shirt; jeans; and casual shoes. It was impossible to guess where he stood in the company hierarchy. Not at the bottom. The sales reps all wore ties.

'Over to you, Mr Watson.' Resuming his chair, Jameson gave a vague, disapproving wave of his hand and turned his attention to an envelope from which he extracted a piece of paper.

'Hello.' Mr Watson had an American accent. This was surprising. I bumped him up a bit more in the company hierarchy. 'Young men and women, please indulge me.' He smiled with what seemed to be real warmth and peered around the room. 'Write down something you'd really like to own. Please, pick up your pens and write something. Anything. A Ferrari? A horse? A house? Please, write it down.'

What did I really want? A chance to go back in time and roll for raid loot properly? A better house for my mum and me? There was no way I was going to write anything that would make me embarrassed if it were read out. At last, I put down 'A *Sickle of Entropy*'. This was an ugly-looking *Epic* weapon with a strong *Slow* effect. There were only two in the game and both in control of guild players. I'd love one for my raids. While Raitha was building up aggro on the boss mobs, I could keep them slowed. The weapon would have made Mikarkathat a much easier kill.

'All done?' asked Mr Watson. 'Let's hear a few.' He pointed to a boy in a Liverpool kit: Seanie Howlin. Bad choice. 'What did you write?'

'A Glock Seventeen, Gen Four.'

'The gun?'

'Right.'

At his table, although still concentrating on the letter in his hands, Jameson shook his head in dismay and disapproval, either at the mention of guns or at the sniggers that broke out.

Mr Watson did not seem troubled. 'Thank you. And you?' It was Amy Pringle's turn.

'A washing machine.'

'About time,' muttered Conor Pearson, our most hurtful wag. He got his giggles, but not from me. The fact that Amy often came to school in stale, unwashed clothes was no reflection on her but the desperate state of her home. I'd been there.

'Perfect,' Mr Watson ignored the unrest and, having failed to learn anything about the hazards of asking questions of members of my class, looked directly at me. 'And how about you, young man?'

Slowly, I crunched up the paper and shook my head. 'Nothing.'

'A boy who has everything?' Now he looked straight at me through his fashionable glasses with eyes that were surprisingly blue. Two of my class chortled, which was annoying. They'd rather put me down than unite against this stranger.

'Well, moving on.' Mr Watson began to walk back and forth, gesturing with his arms as he talked. 'You all – most of you – have your goals. The crucial question is how are you going to get them? Some of you might have written down items that can be bought after a period of work and saving. That's fine. But for serious ambitions, like a house, you just aren't going to get there by work alone.

'This is where being an entrepreneur comes in. Now, being an entrepreneur is all very well if you go to an expensive school and your parents can get you started in whatever market you have in mind. Right?'

Now he had our attention. We were acutely aware of the fact we were bottom of the heap. But we weren't used to people saying so. In fact, the line from the teachers was that we were all just as talented, smart and so on as anyone else. It was just that our disadvantaged backgrounds meant we didn't perform as well academically.

That was the line. The truth was, what talents we had were in the direction of subversion, troublemaking and petty crime.

'Well, I'm here today to tell you that you all have the opportunity to be entrepreneurs. Because *Epic Two* is only weeks away from launch and we've done something that we think is quite profound: we've linked the game currency to Blackcoin. Anyone can earn Blackcoin by playing the game and we anticipate that the early players, especially those who concentrate on crafting and trading, will not only earn fortunes in the game, but that these will be transferred here, to the real world.'

Several hands went up. Mr Watson paused, looking pleased, and pointed to Jules.

'You mean, your gold, or whatever, can be traded for Blackcoin? Like, if you loot a boss mob, how much Blackcoin will that be worth?'

'I do mean that. Let's face it. Whether we at Yuno approved or not, we know that some players would farm gold and sell it for real money. That happens in every online game. In *Epic Two*, we are going to embrace that fact and control it. You'll be playing for cash. The exact exchange rate will fluctuate, of course, but I imagine if you kill a top boss, like Mikarkathat, that would be worth at least two Blackcoin.'

Blackcoin was a crypto currency, each unit of which was trading for about two-hundred and fifty dollars. My raid would have earned five hundred dollars by this new system. Not bad. But why had he mentioned Mikarkathat? That could not have been a coincidence.

While I thought about this and studied Mr Watson for any clues, Jules was looking insistently at me from under her cap, as if to say, *Wow, this is awesome news.* She was into *Epic*; we'd often talked about it. But her parents managed to keep her off the game and her druid was only in the thirties. I gave her a nod.

The class now turned into something of a free for all, but in a way that must have surprised Jameson. In the whole year he'd been teaching his English lessons to us, he'd never seen so many hands up and so many of us wanting to know more about a subject he was teaching. Mr Watson was fielding questions left, right and centre, as my class tried to figure out the angles and whether it really might be worth their while to get in early on *Epic 2*. Even the non-gamers were interested in Blackcoin.

Of course, I knew all about the coming game and as a raid leader and high-level character, I'd been offered an account in *Epic 2* as a beta-tester. Most of us who were at the top of *Epic* weren't interested. Truth be told, I'd been hoping *Epic 2* would be postponed or even scrapped altogether. It had taken me four years of intense play to reach the place I was now, at the top of *Epic*. And still there were zones far too dangerous for me to adventure in. I wanted time to enjoy my status as an elite player. Not only would the launch of *Epic 2* spoil that by requiring me to grind up to the top all over again, but I'd risk losing my game friends. And some of those friends, Raitha especially, were the best I had.

My attention began to wander as I began to consider the options for my next raid. Probably, it would be the castle of King Ragnok the cloud giant. There was something of a logjam with that raid, both clerics and paladins needed drops from King Ragnok for top-end item quests. And I owed those clerics and paladins who turned up for Mikarkathat, big style.

Then I heard my name. Jules, grinning broadly had just told Mr Watson that I'd just killed the toughest dragon in *Epic*.

'Oh, I know.' Watson smiled, looking right at me. 'That's why I'm here. If someone from this school can succeed at *Epic*, anyone can. It's Tom Foster that has earned you all a free invite to beta-test *Epic Two* and get a head start in making some Blackcoin.'

Everyone turned to look at me, which I hated. From the heat in my cheeks, I knew I must be blushing. At home, safely protected by the anonymity of my avatar, I could address hundreds and even thousands of people without a hint of embarrassment. Here, I couldn't stand the attention of thirty. At least my classmates were all signalling respect and approval. Even Matt O'Keefe, who was always trying to pick a fight with me, was giving me the thumbs up. With a deep breath, I allowed myself to enjoy being praised for success in *Epic*.

CHAPTER 3
THE CONTRACT

I was walking home at the end of the weirdest day in school. Lads who you knew were heading for a career among the crime gangs of Dublin and beyond had sought me out in the breaks, wanting to know how much outlay was needed for a decent *Epic* rig. The idea of earning Blackcoin had grabbed them. Explaining what they needed, writing everything down for them, had been a pleasure, for two reasons. One, because these were guys you wanted to be in with. Not too far in. But enough that they considered you one of their own. A fellow sharp, not a flat to be chewed up and spat out.

Secondly, it felt good to be appreciated in school. In the virtual world or in the comments on my video channel, I'd become something of a star. There at least, I was treated with respect (at least, up until now. Damn, I shouldn't have tampered with that loot roll). In school and on the streets of Cabra, I was no one. To my peers - and I knew how they thought - I was just a gamer kid, a bit on the small side, with slanted eyes and a freaky blue haircut. The fact that I might have given the whole school a head start in *Epic 2* seemed to have impressed everyone, not just the other gamers. And by everyone I even mean the girls of my class, who otherwise had no interest in anyone their age.

Today, therefore, my journey home was a cheerful one. Well, apart from that nagging regret about the loot roll. It was with real anticipation I looked forward to getting home to Mum and trying to explain why I was happy.

A car drew alongside, the shaded rear window of an expensive Mercedes winding down with a purr as it pulled in to the kerb. It was Watson, being chauffer driven. Who was this guy?

'Tom.' He leaned forward to catch my eye with his blue stare. 'Could I have a word please?'

'You want me to get in?'

'Yes please.'

I laughed aloud. 'You must be kidding. The number of times it's been drilled into us: never get into a car with a stranger.'

'I'm not a stranger, though,' he said patiently, smiling. 'You know me from school.'

'All the same. I have to get home.' I started forward again and was surprised to hear a car door open. With a glance back, I could see Watson on the pavement.

'Does the number eight one three mean anything to you, Tom?' There was steel in his voice.

That stopped me, mid stride, with a shiver that brought out a cold sweat all over my body. What did he know about my loot roll?

'I hate to bring this up, Tom, but we could ban you from *Epic*. You broke the EULA when you used that macro. And your *Taunt* macro.'

Damn. Damn. Damn. Holy swords of Mov. I was in trouble. The joyful world I'd been living in a moment earlier was suddenly impossibly far away.

'What do you want?' I managed to say, but I don't think I hid the fear in my voice.

'A chat.'

I shook my head.

'What will the community say if we release that log?'

I hated Watson and I hated myself.

'Come on,' his voice was gentler. 'I've got an offer for you and I think you'll like it.'

My mum is something of a dissident, a rebel. Getting pregnant with a Vietnamese man, for instance, was a bit unorthodox for someone living around our way. And so too was dumping him before I was born. That streak is in me too. As I stood on the pavement, my mind vacillating between two very different courses of action. I nearly walked away. Sod Watson. Sod his threats. No one blackmailed me. I'd done bad; I'd take my lumps. There were other games.

The problem was, there really wasn't anything else as immersive as *Epic*. The next best games felt like lame cartoons in comparison. And then there were my friends. My fans. I didn't want to disappoint them or lose them. I might even be banned before I had a chance to talk to Raitha. If I could only talk to her (him) Raitha would understand.

Despite my anger and a fierce desire to just take off, I found myself in the car. To be fair to him, Watson seemed to understand. He didn't make any patronising remarks but gave me a moment.

The car smelled new. My seat was reclined and the air conditioning was cool. 'Well?' I asked at last.

'Yuno Industries have got a problem with *Epic Two*.'

'Oh?' Whatever I had expected him to talk about, it wasn't this.

'The game is supposed to be launched next month, as you know.' Watson looked at me earnestly over his glasses. 'But we're in deep trouble.'

'Go on.'

'We made some of the top bosses AI. Well, one of them, Mikarkathat, has gone completely off script. I mean, way off. She's organised an army of her own and has conquered a third of the world. Newhaven has been sacked and wiped out of the game.'

Newhaven? That was a city that most players started out from in *Epic*, especially those playing a human character. I had begun there. How could you destroy such a city? It was packed full of high-level guards and NPCs.

'How is that possible?' I asked. 'Won't the guards and merchants and guild masters respawn?'

'It seems not.' Watson shook his head. 'Not when the buildings are all gone. And in any case, the dragon has stationed a part of her army there, four hill giants. If someone does manage to log in, they will be taken down at once.'

'So where do newbies begin now?'

'There are several alternative towns. But we are worried they might not last for the coming year, not with the progress Mikarkathat and her army are making. And that's not all, not by a long way.'

'Go on.'

'We can't rewrite the dragon.'

Watson paused, as though to check he had my attention. He certainly did.

'Did you try shutting down the game? Or just taking her out of the code?'

Watson blew out a disconsolate breath. 'Sadly, *Epic Two* is a distributed computing project. It's running on millions of computers all over the world. Someone thought this was a smart move, creating huge redundancy and computing power from volunteers so as to ensure the game never crashed and that wherever you were in the world, there wouldn't be much lag.

'The difference in the AI was amazing. When the game was just on our own servers, the NPCs were either fully scripted, or, if they used Natural Language Processing to try to understand what they were hearing, got it wrong about half the time. By contrast, when we drew upon the network of millions of users, well, they scored nearly human accuracy, even when talking to sarcastic or deliberately misleading players.

'I was there when our engineers made the pitch, so I'm to blame as much as anyone. Marketing loved the idea, because it created a massive community behind the game, even before launch. Accounts loved it too, of course, all that free computing power. No one asked the obvious question: what if we need to take the game offline? It just didn't occur to anyone that we might have a problem so big we needed a restart.'

'Interesting.' It had never occurred to me that a huge company like Yuno, with its reputation for being smart, could make such a howler of a mistake.

'You could say that,' muttered Watson dryly. 'Or you

could say enormous, sodding disaster. We are a month from launch and a rogue AI is taking over the game.'

'And you want my help?'

'Right. You've killed her in *Epic*. There are differences. Mikarkathat is an ice dragon in *Epic Two*, but basically the challenge is the same and I believe you can kill her again.'

'That Mikarkathat raid took place after four years playing the game and I needed the help of a hundred and thirty other players.'

'Right again. You've good social skills. That's also why we want you to be part of the solution.'

'But you've only got a month.'

He knew that, I knew that. So what was the plan?

'How often did you actually play the game? On average, over those four years?' When Watson was getting down to business he didn't smile so much.

'I don't know, four hours a day.'

'Three and a half. We have the figures. If you were to play for fifteen hours a day, that would speed progression up by a factor of at least four.'

'One year then.'

'We can give you a guide. We know all the quests, their solutions, the best drops. That kind of information, we reckon, could accelerate your progress by a factor of six.'

'Two months.'

'Right.' Watson nodded earnestly. 'Two months of intense play and you'll be capped at a hundred.'

'Not seventy-five?'

'*Epic Two* is capped at a hundred, but the time investment is about the same. Players love the sense of achievement in levelling up so we gave them more of it.'

'And you are recruiting, what, a hundred players for this project?'

'Three hundred.'

I whistled. 'You know, maybe you are looking at this all wrong.'

'Maybe…?' Watson waited for me.

'Maybe you should make it public. This is an exciting challenge. Why not come clean? I bet you'd get millions on board with a challenge like this. To level up and defeat the dragon and her army. It's exciting.'

Watson drew a deep breath and let it out contemplatively. 'We've thought about it, of course. And I'm not closed-minded about the idea of going public. It's a plan. But the finance and legal people don't like it. It's impossible to know what kind of experience we are offering players with that dragon on the loose. If your respawn point gets run over by the evil army, is that it? Is your favourite character gone forever?

'And there's another issue too. The "AI have rights" crowd would be all over us.'

'All right. So, what's your offer?'

With a deep-throated chuckled from his large body, Watson rummaged in a compartment to his right and passed over a contract of about twenty pages. He ticked off the main points.

'First, you sign the non-disclosure. This remains private, always, or you can be sued for all monies paid to you plus damages to the company. Second, you come to San Francisco for three months to play *Epic Two*: we'll pay your travel and living expenses and three thousand dollars a month. If anyone kills the dragon in those three months, all the players get a ten thousand bonus. If you are on the raid when it happens, twenty thousand.'

Funny, the money. Because I'd have done this for the thrill alone. Imagine: San Francisco and a dream team of game players on a dragon hunt. I ought to be paying him. Still, I tried not to show too much eagerness.

'Is this what everyone is being paid?'

'No. Some of the players are staff members, they are getting their usual salaries, plus the bonuses.'

'What's the most that one of the other non-salaried players are getting?'

'Five thousand a month.'

'I want that.'

'They didn't cheat at *Epic*.'

'Sod you, Watson.' All at once a veil of rage and shame dropped over me and I reached for the door handle. He could go sort out his problems without me.

'Wait. We'll pay you four thousand a month.'

'It's not the money.' I turned towards him and he pulled away, obviously seeing something in my expression that surprised him. 'It's the blackmail. I'm not going to live under that cloud, Watson. If I sign up, you have to fix those logs. Delete them. I'm not having you or anyone else come back to me time after time with that stupid mistake.' I could feel tears coming, tears which I fought against. As steadily as I could, I continued. 'Put that in the contract. And you can make it four k while you are at it. And something else. If I'm raid leader when we kill the dragon, I get a million bonus.'

'Five hundred thousand.'

'Seven fifty.'

'Six is maximum.'

My laughter surprised him. 'Watson, you are just making this up as you go along. You're high up at Yuno. You probably have a free hand and a large budget to make this happen. Don't tell me there's some kind of maximum on the raid leader bonus. We are in new territory here, right?'

His look was cold and unresponsive. 'Six, but I'll throw in sweeteners. One trip for your mum to come visit. A car while you are in San Francisco. A phone with plenty of credit.'

'All right, put them all in the contract and I'll sign tomorrow.'

'Tonight.'

'You want me on the plane tomorrow, huh?'

'The project has already started,' said Watson sombrely.

'Have you already got all the three hundred players?'

'No. Just our staff members at the moment.'

'There's one more thing then. I'd like you to make the same offer - four thousand a month - to my team in *Epic*. Raitha, Sapentia, Braja and Grythiss.'

Watson nodded. 'Makes sense. I'll contact them.'

'Are we done then?' I pulled on the handle to open the door.

'I'll call over shortly with the revised contract.'

It was a little Big Brother how they seemed to know so much about me, well, my address, my route home and my game logs. Still, I fairly skipped back the rest of the journey.

'Mum! Mum!' I slung my bag over the knob at the bottom of the banister rail and hurried through to the kitchen, from where there was a delicious smell. Tomatoes and garlic cooking in oil. The table was ready: bread, a glass of milk for me, water for her, knife and fork each and an old, wooden salt shaker.

Taking my seat, I watched my mum stir the frying pan. As so often when she was back from work, she looked tired. In fact, I associated the dark green nurses' uniform with my mum in poor form. At the weekend, in her jeans and hoodie, she was always better company.

'I've been headhunted by Yuno. They are going to pay me four thousand dollars a month to play *Epic Two* at their headquarters in San Francisco.'

'San Francisco?'

'Yeah! Isn't that amazing.'

'You're only seventeen.'

'Don't worry. They'll look after me. And it's only for three months.'

'Three months?' She gave me a sharp look. 'What about your exams?'

'They don't matter. They are only mocks.'

'Tom!'

'You know what I mean. It's not like they count for any-thing other than practice.'

'Three months is a lot of work to catch up.'

'Only six more weeks of school though. And I will catch up, I promise.'

Bringing the frying pan over, she scooped some of the mix onto my plate. Then, catching my eye, gave me a rueful shrug.

'Two days until my pay comes through, we'll get something nice then.'

'It's fine, Mum, thanks.' And honestly, it wasn't bad at all. With a bit of salt and a slice of bread to soak up the juices, it tasted delicious. I just wished there had been more of it.

'This guy from Yuno, Mr Watson, came to school today.' And as she efficiently devoured her own portion, Mum listened and nodded while I told her about my day. 'Matt O'Keefe came up to me at lunch and told me I was a smart kid.'

'Matt O'Keefe, huh? What would he know about being smart? That bollix normally makes your life a misery.'

'Exactly. That's what I'm telling you; everyone loves me now. And all because of *Epic*.'

'Three months.' Mum shook her head. 'That's a long time, I'll miss you.'

'I won't miss you.' I tried to joke, but as soon as it came out I felt terrible. 'I'll be too busy.' Mum looked sad. 'Anyway, they are throwing in a trip for you as a sweetener, you can come at the halfway stage.'

'I'd love to see San Francisco.'

'Take a holiday then. Yuno will pay for everything. Come for a fortnight.'

'I couldn't take that much.'

'Nine days then, two weekends either side of a week off.'

'Maybe.' She smiled. 'Maybe that would work.'

There was one piece of bread left, the crust. That's all we had until Friday. I eyed it.

'Go ahead.'

'No, you,' I protested. 'I'm fine, that was great.'

'Go on.'

Picking up the crust, I drew my knife across it a couple of times until I could tear it neatly. Then I gave her half. She smiled at me then got up and brought the frying pan over. After I'd soaked my piece of bread in the remaining - tasty - oil within the pan, I gave the pan back her and she did the same.

'The money is good.' Mum rested her elbows on the table.

'But it's not as important as your education.'

'You're going to let me go, right?' In fact, she wouldn't be able to stop me, but I'd rather not have to do a runner. It would upset us both too much.

'I suppose so. Remember your promise though. You'll catch up over the summer, even if it means cutting down on your gaming.'

'It won't. Anyway, I do promise, honestly.' And I meant it. Six weeks wasn't so bad, I could probably do that in three, given how slowly we got through the curriculum as a class.

Our doorbell rang. With a look of surprise and a gesture towards her hair, Mum stood up. Normally, she wore her hair up tight in a bun at the back, partly for work and partly because she didn't like how the dark roots in between her thick blonde - almost peroxide white - tresses looked when her hair was down.

'It's all right, Mum, you look fine. It's only the Yuno people, they said they'd be around with the contract.'

And it was. Well, just the one.

'Mr Watson, my mum, Stacy Foster.' I did the introductions.

'I'm delighted to meet you, Stacy.' Through his beard, Watson gave a smile so charming you'd never imagine him capable of the steely tones I'd heard when in his Mercedes. 'You should be very proud of Tom; he's a remarkably bright young man.'

Watson suddenly became interesting to me and not because I took his flattery at all seriously. It is probably obvious to everyone but the very young that people are not always what they seem. Or rather, they act according to motives that they are not always aware of. This thought had struck me like a revelation last year. I'd been talking to Mr Smyth, who used to employ me as a paper boy. He'd really barked at some kid who he suspected (probably rightly) of stealing a handful of Percy Pigs. Then Mr Smyth had turned to me and was instantly kind and solicitous about my progress in school. The difference? It was my mum! She was outside and I suddenly realised from a glance he took towards the window that Mr Smyth fancied her. His politeness to me reflected his feelings for her. Feelings that he might not have even been aware of.

Ever since then, I'd studied the people around me: the other kids in my class; my teachers; my mum. And I prided myself on the fact that I could tell the difference between the kind of person they believed themselves to be and the kind they actually were. In my mum's case, for instance, she thought she was a bad mother. That she should do more to help me with school, feed me healthy food, stop me playing too much *Epic*. But the truth was, she was a very, very good woman, trying her best in tough times.

Watson, however, had me stumped. I had absolutely no idea what manner of man he was. When I'd seen him in front of the class, I'd thought him a flat. A bit of an oaf. A cuddly rabbit in front of a pack of wolves, trying to entertain its way out of trouble. In the car, or just before, when he'd blackmailed me, I'd seen he was actually a sharp, ruthless. You wouldn't see that now though; he came bumbling into the house, thanking Mum, apologising for intruding, saying he wouldn't be long.

There were three chairs, all battered looking, around our rectangular wooden table. Once we were each sat down, Watson delved into his black satchel and produced two wads of paper.

'Yuno's contract with Tom Foster. I'm sure Tom's told you all about it.'

'Well, a little.' Mum folded her arms. I hoped she wasn't going to be difficult. 'But he hasn't been home long.'

'I've brought this too.' Watson hadn't stopped smiling. 'It's a non-disclosure for you. I'd like you to sign it - you are promising not to talk about this with anyone else - then you two can speak freely to each other and also you can come to San Francisco to see Tom.'

'Have you got some sort of ID?' Yep, for some reason, Mum was definitely hostile.

'Well, let me see.' Watson, who filled our kitchen with his bulky body, had to stand up to produce a wallet from his pocket. 'These are my business cards.'

Mum read it and passed it to me, without catching my eye. *Jeff Watson, CTO, Yuno Enterprises Ltd.* 'What's a CTO?'

'Chief Technology Officer.' Watson nodded at his own answer.

Jeez Louise. He was right at the top. What was he doing over here? In our house even. I looked around the room. What did he make of it? A man who must be comfortably a millionaire. What did he make of the bars over the window, which we'd put in after a break-in (which missed our valuables but left Mum without her box of old music; it must have been kids)? Or the remnants of our meal, on plates that didn't match? Sod him anyway if he was judging us, I had nothing to be ashamed of.

'Anyone can make cards. How do I know this isn't a child-kidnapping scam of some sort?'

'Oh, it's not a scam. No, not at all. It is, however, an emergency. We are supposed to launch a new game, *Epic Two*, in a month's time. Our investment in this game is enormous, larger than the GNP of most countries. If the game collapses, Yuno might not survive. The company will crash along with the game. We need a team of talented players to go into *Epic Two* and fix it as soon as possible. And every day we delay the problem gets worse.'

I was glad Watson hadn't mentioned dragons. That level of explanation wouldn't really work with Mum. Best keep it very general.

'Here,' said Watson. 'A three-month open return ticket to San Francisco in your name. Travel whenever you want, just let us know and we'll meet you at the airport. And here'—he put another ticket on the table, along with a boarding card—'for Tom to travel tomorrow. There will be a taxi at six in the morning. Our team will collect him and take him to the Belvedere Hotel, where he'll be staying for this project.'

'And here.' He placed a slim smartphone on the table. 'This is for Tom. You can ring him as often as you like, we'll pay the bills.'

Mum had a few more questions, but I could see she was convinced that Watson was for real. I could see too, that

Watson wanted to cut to the chase, get the contracts signed and get on with his job. But he masked his impatience well. He even agreed to a cup of tea, which he hardly drank. At last - as far as both he and I were concerned - Mum went and got a pen.

Before I signed, I looked through the paperwork for the important point. They'd phrased it well, no one would understand the significance of it. Clause 20.iii: *Log of character Tyro will be deleted from GC2025 to GF8112: 07:28 – 07:32.*

As I read this and looked up at him, Watson gave me a slight nod of his large head. Good. I'd made a horrible mistake. But it looked like I was going to survive it. And I'd learn from this.

After we'd shown Watson out, I went upstairs to pack. I could get some new clothes in San Francisco with my first pay transfer and in the meantime, the hotel probably had a laundry service. So I travelled light, stuffing underwear and T-shirts into a backpack, which also had my toothbrush and a new phone. With that done, I felt like opening the window and shouting, 'I'm out of here!' I wouldn't miss the place, nor my class, nor my teachers. I'd always been happiest when in *Epic* in any case. I would miss my mum though.

When I went downstairs, she was still at the table, head in hands. Looking up at me, I could see tears in her eyes.

'Are we doing the right thing? You don't have to get in the cab.'

'Jeez, Mum. San Francisco; *Epic Two*; plenty of money. It's just amazing. We're so lucky.'

Letting out a deep breath, Mum stood up. 'You're right. But I'll find it lonely here without you.'

I laughed. 'You're always complaining about the mess I make, or the noise when I play music. But you love it really.'

'I won't miss picking up your clothes, I know that.'

Surprising her and myself, I came over and gave her a hug. We didn't normally do hugs. My mum is small, even smaller than me, so it was her in my arms, rather than the other way around.

CHAPTER 4
EPIC 2

San Francisco. The air smelled different. The trees looked different. And I felt happy. My hotel was amazing. I had imagined it would be a hi-tech place, with a lift up the outside of a huge tower block or something. But it was an old wooden building, painted blue and red on the outside. My room was old too, with creaking floorboards beneath a thick carpet; a bronze framed mirror on the wall; pale ceramic women holding up the beside lights; a chandelier for the main lights; and wallpaper that had a red velvet design set in it. It was like a bedroom prepared for an aristocrat two hundred years ago and preserved until now (with the exception of a blisteringly fast internet connection).

My window was open and I woke up to a blue sky, the call of birds that I didn't recognise, and the smell of freshly ground coffee. Right then, there was no one in the world, I mean no one at all, that I would have exchanged places with. Shower (hot and powerful), clothes (jeans, Moomintroll T-shirt), breakfast (unbelievably intense fresh orange juice, two thick waffles and an apple) and I was ready for the car that came to take me to Yuno.

There was a screen between me and the driver, so we didn't talk. I just sat back, enjoying the cool air conditioning and watching the streets go by. Plenty of traffic, of course, big, slow-moving American cars on the wrong side of the road. Once we got through a few wide junctions, we went a bit faster and the houses changed from wooden ones to taller, stone buildings. And then we were outside a tower that was made of steel and dark blue glass. Yuno Industries Headquarters, with

41

the flashing sword logo high up in white.

Inside, the foyer was spacious, with a lot of green from potted trees and even ivy, working along a trellis mounted on the walls. The receptionist asked me to wait and I took a seat at a table full of magazines about the games industry. From them, you'd think nothing was wrong with *Epic 2*; they were full of screenshots and interviews with the developers. The most anticipated new game for the year, certainly, perhaps even for the decade.

'Tom Foster?' A girl not much older than me was standing by the table: brown hair in a ponytail; pretty, slender build; sandy-coloured top and grey trousers; hazel eyes and a welcoming smile. 'I'm Felicity; it's my job and pleasure to give you orientation.'

'Hi.' I stood up, suddenly unsure, should I offer my hand? I did.

When she shook it, I felt I'd done the right thing. 'You're from Ireland?'

I nodded.

'Awesome. I've always wanted to go. It's supposed to be so green and so friendly.'

Now the funny thing was, I found myself agreeing and telling Felicity that she would love a trip to Ireland. Yet if someone at school had come out with that flat-headed rubbish, we'd have torn them to shreds. Friendly? Only a fortnight earlier, a biker had pulled up outside the nearest pub to our house, gone inside and shot a man. The victim was 'well known to the gardai' as the news put it when they want to say someone was a criminal.

Apparently, it had been quite a scene. The victim, realising something was up when the biker entered with his helmet still on, had thrown over the table and ducked behind it. Everyone else present had scattered. Cool as you like, the assassin walked around, holding fire until: *bang! bang!* And one more for the head. Seanie Howlin told me you don't get paid unless you shoot the target in the head.

This incident had jumped into my mind. But instead of disabusing Felicity, I wanted her to like Ireland, I felt pride in my country. And it was beautiful and friendly, mostly. While we rose up the lift to level fourteen, I found myself talking about extraordinary places in Ireland, which I mostly knew only by reputation. Mum had taken me to Newgrange, though, so I could tell Felicity about that. A structure about five thousand years old.

'Our oldest buildings are only about two hundred years.' She laughed.

Soon I had an ID badge and knowledge of where to go for food and for toilet breaks. Surreptitiously, I sent a text to Mum, boasting of the fact they had vending machines stocked with cold drinks, fruit and snacks, and everything in them was free.

Then, we came to the project floor.

'Does it have a name?' I asked.

'How do you mean, Tom?'

'The project. Our goal, of eliminating Mikarkathat.'

She laughed, as if I'd said something funny and shot me a glance. Then dropped her voice. 'Officially, there is no project. Remember your non-disclosure. Unofficially, though, well, we call this floor the Den: it's where we have our control room. If you tell someone you are going to the Den, they'll know exactly what you mean.'

What a den. Having had our passes scanned, we came through a sliding door to a large open room with a huge table in the centre of it. Blue-tinted light poured into the room from all four walls. We were high above the city, with only a few other towers nearby to obstruct the view to a pale amber horizon. Additional bright, modern spotlights pointed down at the table, on which was a map and figures that were about two-inches high. It reminded me a bit of a massive paper and dice role-playing game setup, or maybe a wargame.

'Let me introduce you to the General. Then I'd better get back into the game.'

There were several people gathered around the board, one of them was a bulky, middle-aged man in a smart jacket and light blue shirt. 'Mr Blackridge. This is Tom Foster.'

'Aha.' He turned his dark eyes upon me. 'The slayer of Mikarkathat. Let's hope you can do that again. We've been expecting you. You don't look Irish though.'

'My dad's from Vietnam,' I replied, a touch resentful at his remark. I did, however, enjoy the curious looks from the other people nearby (a dozen men and women, mostly in their twenties).

'This is the situation.' Blackridge turned abruptly to the map.

As he did so, Felicity touched my forearm. 'It's been a pleasure. I'll see you soon.'

And she was leaving in the direction of a side room. I wanted to say something in reply, something about having enjoyed her company too. But Blackridge was aiming the red dot of a pointer at various spots on the map.

'All this territory, as far as Lake Shining is in the hands of the evil army. They have been held up by Fort Hellsmouth at the end of the lake. The elves there have driven off one amphibious attack. We had a couple of players involved, but it was mostly NPCs who won the battle. They froze the water and when the enemy orcs got out of their boats, fireballed them, sending them down to drown in their heavy armour. Man, you should see the video!'

Blackridge gave me an unwelcome, hearty clap on the shoulder.

'Now, in the north is the dragon herself. She hasn't moved too far recently, I don't think it suits her to come out of the mountains, but her troops are raiding pretty widely.'

'What are the figures?' I pointed to the clusters of plastic warriors and wizards that were mostly in the south.

'That's us. That's your teammates. Over there'—he gestured to a large screen—'you can see who is in the game and what level they have reached. Down here, you can see what regions they are in. The plan is to level up fast, well behind the front lines and when we have a couple of hundred players capped, we should be able to raid Mikarkathat and take her down.'

'And if she conquers the world before we're ready?'

With a scowl made more intense by his jowls and heavy, black eyebrows, Blackridge waved his arm. 'Then this is all gone. The whole company. And we can look for new jobs.' He said this as though talking about the end of the world. It didn't seem quite as tragic to me. There would be other companies, other games. Other jobs for him and his friends. Still, I was looking forward to this challenge.

'You should get started,' Blackridge said.

'In a moment.'

Surprised that I might disagree with him, Blackridge's frown deepened and he seemed about to say something else, but then turned his back on me.

The reason I wanted to stay here a little longer was that I wanted to study the map some more. Not only to relish the excitement of looking at a world with regions like Forest of the Lost Kingdom of Ragadar and The Tower of Frozen Nightmares but also to choose a sensible starting point. Safety was important, but it might also be important to be able to conduct raids into enemy territory. I didn't really like the idea of all the player-characters grinding up miles from the action and letting the dragon's army advance without hindrance. Not that it was my position to say anything about strategy, not while I was level zero and the other players, were what? I turned my attention to the player board. One fighter, Molino, had reached forty-six. Not bad.

'Good,' Blackridge announced, 'Scarlet has reached twenty. She can enter the 'Keep of the Goblin Prince', tell her to join Cathbad's group at the west tower and pull for them.'

I looked around. Was he talking to me? His attention was on the board. 'And you can get Foster started.'

A young man gestured to me from the far side of the board, waving me over. Blackridge never even lifted his head. This seemed to me to be an affection, a pose to say to me that he was too busy to bother addressing me directly. It rankled. But I walked around the map all the same.

I was led down a corridor with a dozen doors, behind each were rooms, mostly unoccupied, with *Epic* rigs. What rigs though. The tracking pads underfoot were huge, like those of gym machines. They were designed to be used with both feet and hanging from the roof above them were harnesses to bear your weight when you worked them. While my guide waited impatiently, I watched a player run fast, expertly spinning the loose surface beneath his feet. The goggles and gloves I recognised. They were top-of-the-range Fecatti's. Like my own.

'You can clip up in any rig along here,' the young man said. 'The General wants you to begin as a human warrior in Mount Lotus. It's easy there, just level up on the bats in the caves to the south and we'll give you more orders when you've reached level five. Collect the furs too. We have tailors who can make basic cloth leggings from them.'

I nodded my understanding and turned the handle to an unoccupied room. The General wanted me to begin as a human warrior, did he? I had a six hundred thousand-dollar bonus to earn and my own plans for how to go about it. There was something else, too. Ever since I'd discovered *Epic*, I'd experienced a taste of freedom. I could choose to be who I liked in *Epic* and live an alternate life, a long way from kitchen cupboards with no food and a school full of people I'd normally stay well clear of. If I let the General tell me how to play *Epic 2*, I'd lose that precious freedom.

Once, in English class, we came across a line in *Jane Eyre*, that really electrified me. It was something about not being a caged bird. About being a free human with an independent will. Yes, I had thought at the time, that's me. That's all I want to be happy. Freedom.

All right. Time to go earn my pay and enjoy myself too. It must feel like this for junkies, preparing for a hit of smack. The expectation of pleasure was a pleasure itself. Especially when you knew you had all you needed to be happy right in front of you.

The harness was new to me and I took a while to get the straps right. Then I hauled on it until I was standing comfortably on the tracks, but I could lift both feet off the ground if I needed to. Then the gloves. Then the goggles.

Epic 2 had a new musical introduction, not too dissimilar to the trance-metal I liked and a magenta button to point a finger towards in order to enter the game. There was a background landscape of a ruined castle, which looked appealing. Just the kind of place I'd want to explore if I was playing for fun. Against this image various menu options floated around. And of course, I couldn't log into the world yet, I had to create my avatar. The focus of my eyes had caused different options for character classes to pop up and by flicking my index finger, I could cascade subcategories. They all looked interesting but I closed them. First, I backtracked to choose my species:

Half-elf

The advantages of the race were good vision in near darkness and improvements on stealth skills compared to a human (although if those skills were your priority, you would be better being a halfling or a full elf). There were disadvantages to being a half-elf but they were all social rather than tactical. Some merchants, for example, wouldn't trade with me out of prejudice against elves; some quests too would never be open to me.

Next, gender. Curiously, *Epic 2* had two more options than the male and female choice of *Epic*. But male was fine and I selected it.

Male

The next menu was all about appearance and I had some fun choosing a face. Was anyone monitoring me? If so, they must have wondered what I was doing, spending time on a detail that, in terms of our mission, was irrelevant, namely the size of my ears. But I would be playing this avatar for months, I wanted him to look good. In the end, he looked a little bit like me, in that his face had slightly oriental features.

All right, now the crucial decision. Class:

Hunter

I'd been mulling over this choice ever since setting out on my journey to Yuno headquarters. I'd been reading up about the options, reminding myself of the more obscure classes. And hunter was one of them. The hunter was a hybrid, somewhere in the middle of the archetype classes of warrior and rogue. Why that choice? I had two reasons, well, maybe three. Firstly, the mission needed me to level fast. Warriors, unless they are grouped, have too much downtime. Hunters got healing spells, which although low-powered compared to the classic healing classes of cleric and druid would make a huge difference to my downtime over the next few weeks. The other reason that appealed to me is that the hunter made for a good solo class. You could *Set Traps* to capture mobs and you also got a whole suite of spells to help with hunting, related to stealth, outdoor speed, tracking and snaring your opponent. Hunters, so the forums said, could tackle mobs several levels above them and kite them. Finally, I was bored with being a tank, even a top-end, elite, raid tank. Essentially, what you did in battle was set your weapons to hit and mashed *Taunt* over and over.

Thinking back to the raid against Mikarkathat, it was the ranger, Roisina, the sorceress, Sapentia and the shadow knight, Grythiss who had to display the most skill in the fight. They managed the arrival of the elementals and we would have wiped if all three of them hadn't been at the very top of their game in controlling the newcomers. When we raided against Mikarka-that in *Epic 2*, I wanted to be a level one hundred hunter, capable of taking control of dozens of adds if necessary and pouring arrows into her if not.

Did I care that I was going against Blackridge's instruction to create a human warrior? Well, in short, no. Sod him. Of course, I believed in teamwork and following a plan. But I hadn't come here to be a cog in the machine. I'd come to build a raid team that could take out Mikarkathat. And there was something about the man that had irritated me. A sense of self-importance that he'd projected when dismissing me without a 'goodbye', 'good luck', or even eye contact.

To my basic starting attribute score of 11 in each of Strength, Dexterity, Spirituality, Intelligence, Constitution and Beauty, I now assigned the three points that the game allowed me in order to start my journey towards specialisation. I put all three into Dexterity, because my chance to hit as an archer was strongly affected by my Dexterity score. The next most useful attribute for a hunter was Spirituality, because this set the size of your spirit pool and when the hunter obtained spells, the more spirit you had the more often you could cast them. Since I wouldn't get my first spells until level 7, I could afford to wait before boosting Spirituality. I'd get a new attribute point to spend each time I levelled up, so I'd probably use the gains of levels 5 and 6 to improve my Spirituality score.

Right, before entering the game, I still had to choose a starting region and a name. I picked Palernia, which was in the north-east of the continent. Not too far away from where the dragon had her headquarters, apparently. The enemy armies all seemed to be operating in the south though. From my - admittedly brief - examination of the campaign map, Palernia looked like a good region for a half-elf hunter. It had a huge forest that stretched all the way to the northern coast, full of intriguing places of interest, like lonely towers or islands off the coast with ancient ruins.

Starting region: Palernia

Name: Klytotoxos

This was the name I'd prepared. It meant 'bow-famous' and sounded sort of elven, right?

That was it. I was all set to begin my adventure. With the same gesture as in clipping up to *Epic*, I triggered my entry to *Epic 2*. An even greater tsunami of sound and colour than I was used to rushed upon me and I was born anew in an unexplored universe. No longer Tom Foster, I was Klytotoxos the Hunter!

CHAPTER 5
THE EYE BEHOLDS

An unbelievably beautiful scene was in front of me. If the game's designers had wanted to get you hooked from the moment you arrived in world, they had succeeded. I was on a sand dune, covered in long-stalked grasses and wildflowers, looking out to sea. In the distance were islands whose stark cliffs and stacks suggested it would be a challenge to reach their tree-covered interior. Yet, was that a flag, flying over the treetops of the nearest island? Or a bird? Definitely a flag. With a slight haze in an otherwise perfectly blue sky blurring their details, there was a mystery about the islands. They beckoned: 'come, explore, discover, possess.'

Behind me (I wobbled as I turned; it would take a while to get used to the new style of tracking pad) was a forest. It was a young forest, in that the trees were slender and well-spaced: ash, elm, oaks and several species I didn't recognise but whose delicate branches and small leaves reminded me of birch. In the depths of the forest, shafts of sunlight picked out a light under-growth and occasional clusters of foxgloves of the most vivid purple or individual, bright yellow St John's wort.

Sounds: soporific, hushing waves; distant, talkative seagulls; from the forest a caw-ing from a species of bird I did not recognize; a background hum of bees; a sudden thrumming beat upon a trunk, like that of a woodpecker.

Turning to the beach once more, where white, dusty sand met a turquoise sea, I realised a woman – an elf – was standing there, looking towards the horizon. She had been so still and her pale cream cloak so similar to the colour of the sand, that I only noticed her when a breeze coming from behind me had moved it.

Before I moved towards her, I checked my inventory.

A knife; two ripe nectarines; a water flask.

Now that was as minimal a beginning as I'd ever encountered. Not even two copper pieces to rub together. Nor was the knife a weapon, it was a small-bladed item, for simple cutting tasks. The damage to speed ratio on it was so poor I'd be better using my fists. No bow. That was disappointing in a hunter. How was I going to start my journey to elite archer?

Oh well.

Allowing the harness to take some of my weight, I ran, pretty successfully, over the sand and as I approached her, the elf turned with a smile that would have caused the moon and the stars to linger in the skies to witness it. I mean she was beautiful. All elves have that fine, high-cheekbone look. With this woman, there was something more, perhaps in the extraordinary, cerulean green-blue eyes she fixed me with, or her cascades of near-white hair that fell to her waist in sinuous curves that evoked the waves of the sea that were constantly coming towards us.

'My son.' Her voice was gorgeously expressive, as was the welcoming gesture she made with the whole of her arm, right down to her fingertip.

'Hello.'

'It's time for me to depart.' Willow seeds were drifting from the forest and she caught one as it passed. 'There is a message in the waves and the sand and the motion of the trees. The members of the Order of Nereids are summoned to war and I do not believe you and I will meet again.' As her smile became melancholy and she caressed my cheek, it seemed as though a cloud had covered the sun, though it was above me, as bright as ever.

'Can I come with you?'

'You must be a pure descendent of sea elves to enter the palace of King Neyus. And your father, as you know, was human.'

'My father?'

She smiled affectionately and the sun shone brightly again. 'It is time for you to find him. Ask for Knegos, in the town of Safehaven.'

You have been offered the quest: Find Knegos.

Accept

'Where is Safehaven?' I asked her.

'Two days' walk along the coast.' She pointed to my right, which I took to be south-west.

While I wondered what else I should ask, the white sail of a ship rounded the cliffs of one of the islands. It had a leaping, dark blue dolphin as a design upon it.

'I leave you with three gifts.'

You learned the skill Set Traps (1).

You have learned the skill Archery (1).

You have learned the skill Bowyer (1).

Aha! Good to have those skills up and running.

'Thank you.'

Before I could say any more, she was gone and a shrieking sea-eagle was in her place, flapping its heavy wings, causing me to stagger back as she became airborne. She flew low across the waves to the boat, which altered course upon her landing on the bow. Soon, the dolphin-marked boat was hidden by another island and having stood up to wave, I now lowered my arm.

Well. Interesting and entertaining. Ten out of ten for the game writers. There was a lot to mull over in that short encounter. It gave me the context for my choice of half-elf as a species and possibly some high-level quest leads in the future.

For now, though, I had only two nectarines. I'd better get walking towards Safehaven.

As I travelled along the beach, I marvelled at the design of the tracking pads, the ground actually felt softer under foot when I walked on the sand than when I crossed slabs of white, cracked stone that lay across the beach like the splayed fingers of a fallen giant.

This was very pleasant. A far cry from the grey skies of

Dublin. But I wasn't here to holiday. How could I level up? Either in my skills or my level as a hunter. Not until level 7 would I get my first spells and I was in a rush to do so. My research had led me to believe that once I had magic at my disposal, I would achieve far more in battle than I could for levels 1 to 6.

Alone with my thoughts, I walked and walked, all the while enjoying the limitless views across the seas and the sight of seagulls sweeping over the waves. Presumably, being a fantasy wargame, there was danger nearby. Wild, predatory animals, or monsters of some sort. Typically, however, the game was designed for new players to get started in relative safety. So while I did check from time to time that I wasn't being stalked, I mostly followed a line of dunes (easier to walk on than the sand) south-east.

What would Mum be doing now? It was about 10 a.m. in San Francisco, so that was what? Five o'clock in Dublin. She'd be finishing work and leaving for a house that probably felt a bit quiet to her without me. Or maybe not. Maybe she had invited some friends round. It was payday, after all. Thinking about this got me excited, I couldn't wait for my first month's pay to arrive in my bank account. I really didn't need much here. The hotel and headquarters took care of the necessities. I would send Mum three thousand dollars. What a difference that would make. She could get new clothes. Fix up the broken shower. Loads of things that make life sweeter.

You are thirsty.

A game message popped up on my IUD. I wiped it away and ignored it, interested to see what would happen. In my real-life body I felt thirsty too, but wanted to go on for a while longer before taking a break.

After thirty minutes, the message came back.

You are thirsty.

This time I drank a quarter of the water from my flask. Getting more water would not be too challenging, I'd already crossed a dozen streams that had dug shallow, sinuous channels in the sand as they made their way to the sea. I'd just have to track them back far enough to get a decent flow of clean water.

Food, however, could be more of a problem. There were a lot of rabbit holes in these dunes. Could I catch one? Tom Foster was a vegetarian, mostly, but Klytotoxos the hunter was definitely going to be a meat eater.

When the elven lady, my in-game mother, had given me skills, they appeared as options in a drop-down menu in the UI. I tried one now.

Set Trap

No joy.

You are missing necessary items.

Of course. On the plane, somewhere over the Atlantic, I had read about this skill. It was a bit like crafting, you had to have the right components in your inventory. And different items allowed for different, more or less effective, traps. I'd have to look up the art of setting traps again in a break. No doubt I'd get the same message if I tried to make a bow.

And I did.

In any case, the landscape was changing, the dunes were becoming irregular and between them the ground was marshy. A buzzing alerted me to the presence of a lot of insects. Here, there were flocks of waders between me and the line made by the sea meeting a dark, muddy land. On a relatively high dune, I paused to plan my route. This could be the mouth of a major river and I wouldn't want to go halfway across it to find my path blocked by water or swamp.

The sun, now nearly overhead, caused the land here to shimmer with thousands of glittering pools. Obviously, there was a lot of surface water around me, catching the light. And it did seem to me that a shining, silver ribbon in the distance was a river, making its way through the fecund landscape. Best to turn inland for a while.

As I walked through bushy clusters of tall grass, mangroves and rhododendrons I could hear my footfall change from a slapping sound when I had trod the hard, crusty sand on top of the dunes to a squelching noise. And the tracking pad felt spongy beneath my feet. This was a whole new dimension of sensual experience compared to *Epic*. I liked it for that, even though I was not moving as quickly through the landscape.

Unexpectedly, there was motion near my feet. I paused. What was it? Something on my right. After a long while, in which I felt hot and anxious, I spotted it. A brown snake, which had rushed away from me and was mostly underwater in a brackish puddle. My goggles had a nice feature, which is that they read my eye position and automatically triggered a targeting of the snake. I didn't have to point with my glove and select the target manually.

There was a readout on the UI: *dangerous.*

Level One then. Damn. No bow. No decent knife. I could hardly fight a snake with fists though. Much as I was desperate to get started on levelling up, I decided that a fight here would be a mistake and that I must get hold of a decent sized, heavy piece of wood at least, to use as a cudgel.

Skirting the snake, reluctantly, I kept on going through the swamp-like environment for what seem like hours but might have only been one. With the need to check ahead in case of another snake, the time passed much more slowly than when I'd been daydreaming about Mum while looking at blue skies and distant, misty islands.

At last, with the shadows of the treeline reaching out towards me, I came to the river proper. It didn't look too bad. About twenty metres wide, shallow enough, rather brown though. Too brown to fill my flask. As I studied the ripples on the water, I made a mental note to get the swimming skill as soon as I could. Hopefully, I wouldn't be out of my depth here. And indeed, as soon as I started to cross (with the tracker ball feeling loose beneath me), I was happy to discover that the river only went as high as my waist.

On the far bank, however, I was less happy.

You feel pain -1hp.

What was it, had some creature from the river targeted me? A snake? I span around and as I caught sight of my legs, I gave a yell of disgust. Leeches, larges leeches all over me. Damn. With vigorous slaps of my hand, I found I could knock them off. Not before another message.

You feel pain -1hp.

Given that a 0-level hunter starts with only 8 hit points, losing two of them was significant. Not a great start. How far away was that town, Safehaven? The name was suddenly very appealing. There was higher ground ahead, south, and I was fed up of this swampy estuary. Pushing myself hard, concentrating on my footsteps, I hurried on until the grass became thicker and less spongy. Satisfied there were no threats in my immediate environment, I decided to take a break and unclipped.

CHAPTER 6
DEATH

Here, the experience of returning to the real world was even more disorientating than leaving *Epic* from my home rig. It took a moment before I could even walk straight, with the ground feeling incredibly hard after the tracker ball. On leaving the toilet, a young woman I hadn't met before greeted me.

'Are you Tom Foster? Please come with me to the control room.' Curiously, her head ducked down at once, shy, or anxious. Probably aged about twenty, she was shorter than me, with a brown bob that was swaying as she avoided my eyes. Her T-shirt was navy with rainbow letters on the chest that advertised *SmartBot* an AI company. She was pretty and hampered by being so much younger than her, I would have been daunted at the prospect of talking to her. Except that the opportunity didn't arise; she hurried ahead of me the whole way.

There were more people in the control room than earlier, maybe twenty of them standing around the large map, Felicity, my chirpy guide to the building among them. These were my comrades, presumably. Most were relatively young (though none as young as me). An elderly man in a smart, pink polo shirt and a middle-aged woman were also there. Gamers? Or company staff. All were looking at me; I smiled and raised my hand. No one responded.

From his post near the centre of the southern edge of the map, Blackridge was staring at me, his heavy face threatening.

'Foster. What the hell are you doing? I told you to start a human warrior in Mount Lotus.' From his right, Blackridge picked up a figurine and hurled it at me with real force. Leaning back, I let it whistle past me to hit the wall and bounce on the tiled floor. 'You'd be level three by now. Instead, you're a shitty hunter. What's that about? Useless on raids. The slowest class to level up. What the hell were you thinking? Delete that crap and start again, properly!'

Very conscious that everyone in the spacious room was looking at me, I felt a constriction around my heart so powerful that I'd never experienced anything like it before. Fear and shame fought to get control of me. Should I do what he said? My initial reaction was to duck and hide from this angry man. No. I had my plan and it was a good one. What did this guy know about killing Mikarkathat anyway? I was the only one who had ever done so. There was something else too. I took a deep breath that shattered the iron bands that had built up around my ribs. I was from Cabra, Dublin, Ireland. And while on the spectrum from murderous headcases to mildly anti-social troublemaker I was definitely an outlier in the direction of polite society, no one pushed me around like this.

In control of myself, although my heart was beating like crazy, I picked up the figurine from the floor and examined it: a skilfully rendered warrior in plate mail, holding a two-handed sword high above his head. Nearby was a bin full of plastic figurines. Crossing to the receptacle, I dropped the warrior in and rummaged until I found an archer. An elf, but it would do: leather armour, bow raised and arrow notched. It was a stretch, but from the opposite side of the map to Blackridge, I reached across and placed the figure on the coastline of Palernia.

Then I met his gaze.

'You think you're smart, kid? Well, I'll give you another chance. Get back in there and start levelling a warrior or you're on the next plane home to Ireland, or Vietnam, or wherever.' He was spitting contempt.

Poker is a game that had always interested me. If it hadn't been for *Epic*, I probably would have played poker online a great deal. Having said that, I was well aware that I needed to learn more about the maths behind the game before playing it for significant sums of money. One aspect of the game that I think I would be good at is recognising when a player is bluffing.

Take Blackridge, huffing and puffing in front of his team. The General. The man in charge. Or was he? There was a fade in the intensity of his shouts when he made his threat. Surely, Watson was higher up the corporation structure than Blackridge? And surely what mattered to Yuno was the result? Could Blackridge really send me home? I doubted it. Maybe I was wrong, but I went all in.

'I've read my contract a dozen times. My mum even more. There's nothing in it about taking orders from you. My job is to kill that dragon and that's what I'm going to do. And I'm going to do it my way.'

'On your own?' Blackridge sneered.

'Of course not. I'll lead a raid.'

'Not with this team, you won't.'

'We'll see.'

I gave him a moment to prove me wrong in my call and send me home. He just stood there, teeth clenched, muscles of his jaw tight.

With a nod to the spectators, I turned back towards the rigs. Before I left the control room I checked the board. There I was: Klytotoxos the Hunter, Level 0, Safehaven. I had a long way to go to prove myself.

Back in the game, I felt a great deal more relaxed than when I'd walked away from Blackridge. I'd rather encounter a poisonous snake here than that bully in real life. Whoever put him in charge of this project made a bad mistake. If I were building a team - and I'd the experience of having done so online - I'd listen to the players, and if someone said they had a plan that involved being a hunter, well, I'd probably let them try it, even if I had doubts. Sod him anyway. Time to rid myself of thoughts about that bruising exchange and concentrate on the game.

One glorious day I'd reach level 20. Then I'd get the spell *Swift as a Panther*, which would double my speed for an hour, by which time the spirit I'd lost casting it would have been restored. In other words, I would pretty much be able to keep the buff on the entire time. For now, though, it was plod, plod, plod. There was plenty to admire as I journeyed: scatterings of white and purple wildflowers across the grass; hundreds of birds; an amazing rendering of the effect of a light breeze on the treetops, utterly realistic. Even so, it was pretty dull. I couldn't think of a better option though. Perhaps I could have tried to find beginner mobs near my spawn point and level up on them. Then search out slightly tougher mobs and so forth. The quest I'd been given, however, was pretty straightforward and it would be helpful to have a town nearby to trade in.

You are hungry.

No kidding. I was starving. After hours of my walking south, keeping the sea in view but not going back to the beach, the sun was descending above the treetops. In real life, I'd been the best part of five hours in the game, with nothing to show for it and an empty stomach demanding I visit the canteen. While my avatar munched a nectarine, I wondered about my plan for the night. Probably, the safest action would be to log out in case of roving monsters.

Given that the gentle hillside I was on was fairly safe-looking, perhaps I should unclip here and go eat. What you had to consider in leaving the game was the possibility of clipping up and finding yourself under attack, having been unfortunate enough to appear in the world close to a monster. Again, this had the feel of a region suitable for new players: I was well away from the forest edge; had good clear views towards the sea and downhill, back to that river I'd crossed.

As I lifted my arms to unclip the helmet I heard an odd sound, like a drum beat. Yes, it was definitely a drum, from within the forest. Lowering my arms again, I stared hard towards the heavily shadowed region past the first line of trees. The sound was getting closer and it seemed to me that the ground beneath my feet shook. What could this be? Realisation came along with the appearance of several goblin archers. It was an army on the march.

To the heavy beat of a marching drum, the forest itself

seemed to be moving as hundreds of deep green, muscular goblins emerged, some of them carrying banners depicting a white, fierce, fanged face on a red background. Their level was 5, minimum, since every one I targeted was labelled *impossible* (in *Epic*, as here too probably, if you targeted a mob, you'd often get an indication of its level of difficulty. One the same level as you was described as *even*, a level higher as *challenging*, two or three levels higher as *dangerous*, four as *very risky* and five or more as *impossible*).

All of the goblins were armoured, with plate mail on the heaviest, a chainmail-plus-leather combination on the archers. And they were heading towards where I thought Safehaven was, on a route that would bring them close to me!

With a feeling I'd already spent too long staring, probably with my mouth open with amazement, I turned and ran. Perhaps I could warn the town. Perhaps I could be the hero who saved them and gain a lot of faction items and even experience. Was this a quest opportunity? If so, it was a strange one, because it wasn't likely to ever recur.

A flicker, as swift as a blink; I flinched and a dark arrow streaked past my right shoulder.

You have learned the skill Dodge (1).

Go me!

The next arrow hit me in the back. Even though my real body was still standing, all I could see was the immense blue sky and a wisp of cloud, high, high up.

You have been hit by an arrow for 6 damage. You are on 0 hit points and unable to move.

A dozen heartbeats later a dark, fanged figure leaned over me, blocking my view with his drooling, grinning face. There was nothing I could do. Unclipping wouldn't help, to avoid people cheating in these situations, your avatar remained static in the game a full minute after you unclipped.

You have been assassinated.

Damn. As a curtain of complete black fell over me, leaving me in silence, I felt something like a mild electric shock from the equipment. Now that was an unpleasant new feature of the game. It wasn't the worst death I'd had playing RPGs, not by a long way. All I'd lose…wait. I was alive again. Back in a sunny, calm glade on the edge of the forest, near where I began. Naturally, I no longer had my backpack, nectarine, flask and knife. Presumably, if I found my body, I'd be able to retrieve them. Although possibly they were lootable items and the goblins had them. In any case, that was trivial. What was far more shocking was that I had a red bar to the right of the 0 on my level indicator. An experience penalty. It was going to take me a lot longer to even reach level 1 than before. Clearly, death was worse for you in *Epic 2* than in *Epic* where there was no experience loss. Would you drop levels? I wondered. Suppose you had just made level 1, then died, would that penalty bring you below 0 and would you lose your recent gains? I didn't remember reading about this. Hopefully, I wouldn't find out from personal experience.

Finding a lump in my throat and tears in my eyes, I swallowed heavily. I'd died plenty of times in games before. This was different. This time I was out to prove something to Blackridge and the others. And what would they see? That after a full day of play I was worse off than if I'd just started. Blood and thunder! This was bad. My appetite was gone. I had to play on some more. How could I get experience though, without a weapon? It had to be through the *Set Trap* skill. And what did I need to use that? Cords at a minimum. A sharpened stick, maybe, to dig a pit. Both could be found.

There was no point trying to race to Safehaven, the goblin army was eight hours ahead of me. The people there would have to manage their defences without my warning. Hopefully, they had strong walls and vigilant guards.

Instead of moving towards the beach, therefore, I set off walking through the forest, looking attentively about me for items I could gather to make traps with. Soon, I had a pretty decent five metres of rope, made of out three strands of ivy I'd plaited together. And I also had a branch whose tip was strong enough to scrape away at the soft soil of the forest floor. The task of finding these items distracted me from my failure to progress in the game, although it was never too far from my thoughts.

Set Trap

Of its own accord, my avatar squatted down and tied the cord to an ash sapling that it had pulled over ninety degrees. Then it tried to lay down a loop.

> You have failed to set a trap.

The tree sprang up, pulling me off balance as I hung on to the cord. Oh well.

Nearly thirty minutes later, after seemingly endless failure messages, I got this:

> You have set a trap.
> You have become better at Set Traps (2).

Good.

With that one in place, I started over. More cord, another trap. And, eventually, another skill improvement. This was quite a different experience to my happy march down the coast earlier in the day. This was a grind.

> You have become better at Set Traps (3).

Rinse. Repeat.

> You have become better at Set Traps (4).
> You have become better at Set Traps (5). You have reached your level cap.

Ahh. Shame. So I'd probably have to be level 1 to be able to advance the skill to 10 and so on. The shadows of the forest around me were dark, although my ability to see tiny details was hardly affected at all. One of the advantages of being a half-elf compared to being human was excellent low-light vision. It was getting late in the game and presumably in San Francisco, since the game clock was also on a 24-hour cycle. And I had something of an appetite. Time to unclip and in the morning I could see if my traps had brought me any luck. Something my avatar could eat, hopefully.

When I had gathered my wits upon entering the real world again, I could see that the building was as busy as ever. All the rooms were lit up and at least ten people were rigged up.

Without meaning to, I gave a heavy sigh. This morning, when I had woken up, the day had been full of promise. I'd really been looking forward to chatting with my teammates and maybe making some new friends, if there were other players around my age. Back home, my interest in *Epic* - at least the level I played it at - tended to cut me off from my classmates, most of whom were much more interested in bands and sport. As a result some of my best friends, like Raitha and Braja, were people I'd never met in the flesh, although I had shared with them intense moments of delight and also of failure.

Speaking of which, it was the knowledge that I had pretty much been a total failure during the course of the day that meant I no longer had the same eagerness to chat to the other players. Also, I found that as I approached the control room my stomach was constricting with tension. Evidently, my body was anxious about Blackridge, even though my assessment of the situation was that I was fine, he had no real power over me. It was Watson I had to account to and hopefully, he would understand my strategy.

On opening the door from the corridor into the control room I was relieved to see that instead of Blackridge, a middle-aged woman I hadn't noticed before was standing on the south end of the map, moving figures with a long stick and sometimes looking up at the scoreboard on the wall. There were only three other people in the room.

'Hello,' I said.

'Hello. Might you be Tom Foster?'

'I am.'

She gave me a smile from beneath her grey fringe. 'Welcome. I'm Katherine Demnayako, please call me Katherine, I deputise for Paul when he takes a break.'

'Oh, then I should tell you this. A goblin army, with banners showing a white goblin face on a red background, is probably attacking Safehaven right now.'

'Safehaven?' She was looking at the wrong part of the map, down south.

'It's on the north-eastern coast, in Palernia.'

'Oh. How many would you say?'

'I don't really know, I just saw them coming out of the woods, about forty or so, but there probably were a lot more behind them.'

'Thanks.' Katherine looked across at one of the others in the room. 'Mark, would you please clip up and check this out. And Ying Yue, can you print a goblin with the banner of King Ppyneew.'

A man in his twenties left the map without a word and walked over towards the corridors with the rig rooms. Meanwhile, a 3D printer started up in the corner of the Den and I watched with interest as it built up a goblin warrior carrying a banner.

'Like this?' Katherine asked. And I realised she wanted confirmation of the image on the banner.

'Exactly.'

'Oh dear. The dragon has a new and powerful ally. The caves of King Ppyneew are a top-end raid region. It just gets worse and worse.'

Listening to the dejection in her voice, I was reminded that for the staff of Yuno, their loss of control over the game was a disaster. Suppose the goblins had conquered Safehaven: then Klytotoxos's father, Knegos, might well be dead and unable to respawn. This would break my crucial quest lead and, presumably, the path to learning more about the game. There's no way you could open such a game to the public. At least, not unless you went for Plan B and admitted there was a problem in order to encourage people to help solve it. That's what I'd do. Give everyone a month's free subscription (since if the dragon conquered our spawn points, you wouldn't be able to guarantee the character could return to the game on death) and hope they got interested enough in the challenge to stick at it.

'We'll get the game back,' I said, with what I hoped was an encouraging tone.

It was only a flicker of her eyes, but I caught her looking at the scoreboard and when she nodded at me, it was with a careworn expression. I knew she'd noted that I was still on 0.

After a pause, I said, 'I'm going to the canteen. Then, I think I'll go to my hotel.'

'Rest is important.' Katherine was looking at the scoreboard, where something had changed. A group had moved region and she turned to the map and adjusted the figures on the board accordingly. After she did so, she turned her tired-looking face towards me. 'You can ask reception to call you a car.'

On the way down the lift to the canteen, I took out my phone. Then I hesitated. I wanted to chat to Mum about my day. But it had sucked. And anyway, it was 3 a.m. her time. So instead, I just sent a message: *Finished my first day. Didn't go too well. Getting something to eat and going back to the hotel. Will try to unclip around 6 p.m. your time tomorrow for a chat but don't worry if I'm late, stuff might be happening in the game.*

There were six people in the canteen, all sat together. Two of them I recognised from the Den. So naturally enough, having made my choices from the self-serve displays (lentil curry and rice, a bowl of ice-cream and a pear), I went over to them.

'Mind if I join you?'

Unbelievably, no one answered. Nor did they meet my eyes. Jeez Louise. What? These were men and women in their twenties and thirties, and they couldn't manage to be polite. Obviously, the issue was that I'd fallen out with the General. And there they were, saying nothing, not even to each other. Just hurrying their food.

'Something wrong?'

A girl glanced at me, pale and anxious-looking. 'You should play like you're supposed to. Yuno are paying you.'

'There's nothing in my contract about how to play. Just that my goal - our goal - is to kill Mikarkathat. And that's what I'm going to do.'

In response, one of the men snorted derisively. A surge of anger gripped me but I said nothing; I just sat in the nearest empty chair and began my meal. There was no point making things worse by picking a fight. Especially when I was still on 0

66

and couldn't really defend myself other than bring up what I'd achieved in *Epic*. And that might sound like showing off. I might have to lead these players in a raid one day.

After an awkward, silent meal, they left as a group. As soon as they were gone, I flung down my spoon. There was no point pretending I was enjoying the ice-cream; right now, I just wanted a good night's sleep. Sod them all anyway.

CHAPTER 7
BACK IN BLACK

That night, I dreamed that Blackridge was making me row a boat. Or perhaps a rowing machine in the gym. Anyway, it was pull, pull, pull, without end. When I woke up I was annoyed at myself for letting him into my unconscious. Later, as the car took me to Yuno's headquarters, I found that a lot of yesterday's joy in my new life had disappeared. Still, *Epic 2* was an amazingly immersive fantasy world and I was looking forward to resuming the story of my alter ego, Klytotoxos the Hunter.

Of course, Blackridge was on duty in the control room, discussing tactics with a group of eight players. It sounded like they were going on a mini raid, as Blackridge was counting off the boss mobs they would face and their related quests on his thick fingers. Jealousy isn't quite the right word for what I felt, but I did experience a pang of loss, that I wasn't part of whatever it was they were up to.

As I left in the direction of the corridor with the rig I used yesterday, Blackridge caught my eye but he didn't stop his briefing.

Right. Deep breath. Back to *Epic 2*. With a hope for a better day.

After I'd clipped up, I flicked the enter world menu and a rush of sound and colour picked me up and deposited me in the forest.

Morning in the forest was pleasant, there was a gentleness in the birdsong and the erratic flight of a dozen dark blue butterflies, who barely alighted on a flower before taking flight again. In the direction of the darker, older trees to the south-west a mist had formed in the night and still lingered, blocking my view of the deep interior of the forest. First, I should check my traps.

A rabbit! Good start. But nothing in the second, third and fourth. The fifth, however, contained a shock for me. A wolf had been raised up by the cord around its right hind leg. It was just able to touch the ground with its front paws and it was standing there now, trembling with the effort, the grass all around having been torn up by its claws.

Wolf: Impossible.

Here was the chance I needed to gain experience and level up. If I could find a sharpened stick, I should be able to kill it. And a level 5+ kill by a level 0 character had to be worth a lot of experience, maybe enough for two levels even with the penalty I had acquired from dying. Mind you, if the cord from the trap should give way at all while I tried to stab the wolf, I'd be dead with another penalty to my experience.

There was another consideration too. Even though I knew this was only a game, I felt a pang of remorse at the suffering of the poor animal. That back leg was clearly dislocated, it was raised at far too steep an angle. The pain the wolf must have experienced – and probably still was experiencing – must be awful. In testimony to that were the signs of a fierce struggle by the wolf to get free. Savage marks were torn into the bark of the tree that had sprung the trap and raised the wolf off the ground.

All the time I contemplated the scene, the wolf had been staring at me with unblinking grey eyes. When I finally moved, it continued to watch me and scrabbled around slightly to try to follow me as I circled: presumably the wolf intended to attack me if I came too close.

'It's all right,' I said as soothingly as I could. 'It's going to be all right. I just have to untie that cord.' Without dwelling on the wisdom of the decision, or I would have talked myself out of it, I'd resolved to set the wolf free. If I could do so safely.

Round and round I went, looking for an opportunity to climb the far side of the tree to the wolf. And although the wolf wanted to follow me, the rope got tighter as it scrabbled to face me, until with a whine of pain and exhaustion, it stopped trying, head against the trunk. Laying my rabbit on the ground, with a deep breath and a test for the firmness of the ground (that is, the rigidity of the tracker pad), I ran and sprang for a branch. Snarling and suddenly overcoming its agony, the wolf whirled back around the tree, loosening the rope. It jumped at me, but was too late.

'Take it easy, friend. You're almost free.'

I climbed to where the rope was tied and with some effort, loosened the knot, allowing the cord to fall to the ground. Immediately the wolf rolled around and around over the ground, as if trying to bite its own tail. As it did so, the howls the wolf emitted were long, loud and awful. But then it stood up, hip back in place, silent. The wolf gave me a long look before limping over to my rabbit, which it picked up with its powerful jaws before moving slowly (on three legs) off into the forest.

'Hey! That's my lunch.'

Oh well.

One day, assuming Yuno didn't go bankrupt and close the game, I knew that Klytotoxos the Hunter would be an absolutely awesome and respected avatar. For now, however, I only had one thing going for me, which was my *Set Traps* skill. It took time to make cords, but that's what I would have to do and try to trap a monster or creature that I felt less squeamish about killing. At least I could explore the forest as I went around setting traps.

Moving towards the south-west, where the density of trees increased, as did the size of their trunks, indicating a much older forest, I was on the lookout for fruit. And sure enough, there was a short, dark tree with pink and white blossoms that looked like it was supporting clusters of cherries. Only they weren't exactly like cherries in the real world. I picked one of the red berries and tentatively nibbled at it.

You have discovered the skill Gathering (1).

Great. Progress, of sorts. Hoping that message meant the fruit was not harmful, I ate a dozen of the pseudo-cherries and picked a dozen more for later, which I had to keep inside my shirt for want of the backpack my first incarnation had carried. I didn't like the forest so much here, the ground began to rise and fall in a series of short but fairly steep hills, which meant I either had to walk in the valleys and feel vulnerable to an attack from above, or walk on top of a hill and be easy to spot, or else on the hillside and feel an uncomfortable tilt of the ground beneath me.

Turning back, a motion on the ground caught my eye. These half-elven eyes were good. Even in dim light I could focus on very small details. It was a yellow snake. I had no remorse about killing snakes. I targeted it.

Fern snake: Challenging.

Right. That meant it was level 1. And I had no weapons. On the other hand, it wasn't moving and it lay, perhaps half-asleep, under a sturdy-looking branch. After a short search, I found a decent-sized (moss-covered) rock, about as heavy as I could manage with one hand. Then I pulled myself into the tree with my other hand and made my way to the branch above the snake.

Somewhat alarmingly, the branch dipped as I moved out on it and if this had disturbed the snake, causing it to move away, my plan would have failed. With delight, however, I saw that the snake had not moved and the fact that I was now only my own height above the ground was a big plus in being able to hit the snake. Aiming for its head, I worked my way to the point I was directly above the creature, then let go of the rock. *Thwamp!*

You have killed a Fern snake. You gain experience.

Happily, about half the red bar of experience penalty had gone!

Although the system alert reassured me that the snake was dead, I was very careful in removing the rock from the body. Snake meat was edible, right? I didn't fancy it though. I'd rather get fruit from trees and bushes, or rabbit from my traps. Snake-skin, on the other hand, would be good for a backpack. How cool would that be? Or a waistcoat. I was feeling cheerful. With any luck the snake would be on a fast enough respawn timer that I could do this again soon. In the meantime, I got a stick and moved the body to a patch of red earth that was visible where the turf covering of the forest floor had broken open due to the sharp rise of the hillside. I also placed the rock beside the base of the tree.

After a circuit of my traps – nothing yet – I came back to the Fern snake. Nothing there yet either. Never mind. A few more traps. A few more cherries. And there it was. A lovely yellow snake. The timer was about an hour. Climb. Go out on the branch. Line up the shot. *Thwomp!*

You have killed a Fern snake. You gain experience.

Hurray, I was back in black: I'd made a little progress towards level 1. Three more of those would do it. This would be a good time for a break. So standing by the tree, safely away from the snake's spawn point, I unclipped.

Stumbling slightly as I adjusted to the – rather dull-looking – real world and actually walking on floors, I exited the room and went down the corridor to a vending machine, where I selected water and a cheese sandwich. As I stood there munching (and worrying about the crumbs, should I try to sweep them up? There was a bin nearby), Felicity, my orientation guide, came out of another of the rig rooms. Clearly, she intended to come to the vending machine, but seeing me she turned around, looking anxious and awkward, and hurried towards the control room instead.

My arm, which had been raised in greeting, fell back to my side. With a loud 'tut', to express how rude I thought this kind of behaviour was, I finished my sandwich and (ignoring the crumbs) set off back to my rig and plan for snake squishing.

Three hours, two rabbits, and three more flattened Fern snakes later I heard a beautiful chime and saw flash of golden stars.

You have gained a level. You are level 1.

At last! The feeling of relief I got from the moment was surprisingly intense. Until now, I hadn't realised just how much I was suffering from being stuck on 0. What had made the situation all the more unbearable was the knowledge that Blackridge and the others could see from the scoreboard that I was still on 0. Probably, they joked about it. Well, 1 wasn't much, but it was progress.

My new attribute point I added to Dexterity, bringing me to 15. My hit points were now up to 16, which made me feel a lot more sturdy. Nothing else had visibly changed, I guessed though that the cap on my skills, which had previously been 5, would have been lifted to 10. That gave me something to do for the hour before my next snake, work on my main skill and main way out of the tough spot I was in. Perhaps due to my improved Dexterity it felt that my rate of success with Set Traps was higher. I'd reached 10 in the skill before it was time to drop a rock on a Fern snake.

One problem with my strategy, quite apart from the fact it was boring and unimaginative, was that the experience reward now that I was the same level as the snake, was a smaller proportion of what I needed to get to level 2. I'd have to kill another 10 or 12 of them. Mind you, since I didn't have a bow or even a dagger, finding a more interesting and rewarding mob to fight was out of the question.

Given that I could potentially level my bowyer skill to ten, surely that would allow me to make functional bows and arrows? What did I need to do so? I decided to take a break and read up on the skill.

With a little less tension in my stomach as I crossed the control room, I noticed that the whole floor, the Den, was noticeably busier with people of all ages. And what was pleasant was that several of the new people smiled at me. I even got a 'hello'. Newcomers, obviously, who weren't aware I was out of favour. But it felt good all the same. On my journey out to San Francisco, I had assumed there would be a sense of comradeship between everyone involved in this project and I'd been looking forward to making new friends. The clash with Blackridge, however, had cut me off from the regular Yuno staff. Maybe the new arrivals would be more open and friendly towards me.

Refreshed and thoroughly informed about the art of bow and arrow making (I could use rabbit gut for the string and wood from a variety of trees, with yew being best, but, sadly, I needed a knife too), I was on my way back to find a rig when a small, dark-skinned young man with extraordinary brown eyes stopped me in the corridor.

'Are you Tyro?'

I nodded.

'I'm Raitha!' he said, with a flash of bright, white teeth as he smiled with delight.

'Oh, I should have guessed from your accent. Great to meet you, man!'

'You too.'

And suddenly we were embracing. So this was my best friend of the last four years. I liked him; he smiled easily.

I took his arm. 'Let's go for something to eat and I'll fill you in. I'm not off to a great start.'

'Certainly. Let us do that. But first, I must say something. It has been in my thoughts for the whole journey.' Raitha looked at me seriously. 'Thank you. The four thousand dollars a month means a lot to my family and me.'

I waited for a moment. 'Is that it?' I couldn't help but chuckle.

'Is it what?'

'Is that your prepared speech? How long was your flight? Surely you had time to come up with something more substantial and heart-warming?'

'Man, you're so unmoved. You suck at being a comrade-in-arms. I will admit that my speech could have been longer and no doubt it would have brought you to tears, but for the fact that *Blade of Reckoning* was one of the options among the movies; I watched it twice.' His dark eyes were full of amiable mischief.

That's something you didn't pick up on in-game, the subtleties of non-verbal communication.

Unlike yesterday, when it was nearly empty, the canteen was busy and had a sense of energy and community. I'd only recently eaten, so just picked up an apple and a bottle of water. Rubbing his hands with a gesture of eager anticipation, Raitha piled up his tray with a burger, fries, baked beans, a bowl of ice-cream and a slice of apple pie.

'America, the land of great food.' He said this with utter sincerity. 'I'm going to avail of it to return home without a trace of my current look of emaciation.'

'You look fine,' I replied. And he did: slender brown limbs, fit and healthy-looking. 'But don't let me stop you piling on the cholesterol.'

'Oh, you could not keep me from this tray of delicious food without a *Forcewall* at least.'

There was a considerable mix of age groups represented by the people eating and chatting at the tables. No one seemed to be as young as me though, which made me feel a little proud, if isolated. Raitha and I sat near a balding, older man who was reading a hard-copy of the *Epic 2* guide, which he held in one hand, while his spoon was in the other, occasionally being dipped into some soup.

'So you're a male,' I said.

'You knew that, though. Didn't you?'

'I suppose so. Should I still call you Raitha?'

I had to wait for an answer while he chewed and swallowed a very large bite from the burger. 'Yes, yes of course. I shall be Raitha in the game and that's where we will be spending most of our time. My birth name is Yatish, but you may call me Raitha. I prefer it. Please, treat me like you did before this meeting. Like I am a female warrior.'

'How old are you?' I hadn't meant to ask the question, in case it sounded rude, it just came out when I studied Raitha's face. It was a kind face, open, but one that could have been that of an eighteen-year-old or a twenty-eight-year old.

'Twenty-two. You?'

'Seventeen.'

'I think I knew that. You are a remarkable young man. When you lead raids, I feel that you are much older than me.'

'Thank you.' I swallowed the bite of apple I had been chewing. 'It's strange that when I enter the game, I really do feel older, smarter. A better person all around.' I gave Raitha a smile to show I didn't entirely believe this. Yet, perhaps it was true.

Leaning forward, I dropped my voice to nearly a whisper, 'Raitha, I have to confess to something I'm really sorry about.'

'What?' His look of puzzlement - as if he could not believe there was anything I could possibly do wrong - was heartening. Just this minute, however, I had decided to bite the bullet. This was a very painful moment and a risky one.

'I used a macro on the roll for the *Shield of the Dragonslayer* to make sure you got it.'

There was a long pause as Raitha's eye's bulged with surprise and his eyebrows shot up. He nearly choked on his burger, then looked wildly left and right before returning his brown eyes to mine. When he had cleared his mouth, he let out a long breath, then lowered his astonished eyebrows and stared at me sombrely for what felt like a very long time.

I could feel myself blushing.

At last, he spoke. 'Tyro, you are my comrade. You meant well, I understand. If you had acted for yourself, that would have been very wrong, we could not be friends. Yet you acted for me, for future raids with our other friends.

'It was still very wrong, yet not so awful when properly considered. You probably need to hear me say this: I forgive you. Now, let us never talk about this again. This is a fresh start. This is *Epic Two*!'

'Thank you.'

Having smiled at me with a look of deep, earnest affection, Raitha now sank back in his seat turning his gaze to his apple pie and giving a roll of his head from side to side. 'You almost spoiled my dessert.'

'Sorry about that.'

'Now, while I enjoy this wonderful apple pie, you must tell me about the game and we shall plan how to defeat the dragon once more.'

With lowered voice, not wanting my words to reach our neighbour with the book, I ran through my experiences at Yuno headquarters, starting with my refusal to obey Blackridge and then detailing the difficulties my hunter faced in levelling. From time to time Raitha paused in his obvious enjoyment of his dessert, to give me an intelligent look, but he didn't interrupt. When I concluded with a modicum of pride in my Set Traps skill, he flashed a white smile.

'What class do you think I should play?' he then asked.

'I was assuming a warrior again, to be the main tank in raids.'

Raitha nodded. 'I thought that would be our approach too. Instead, I have a better idea. Like you, I will create a hunter and like you she will start in Palernia. In fact, in every respect I shall copy you. That way, there is an excellent chance I shall spawn near you. Then I can eat your rabbits. More importantly, you can borrow my knife to make bows and arrows. With these weapons, we shall level up together.'

Reaching across the table, I held his lower arm. 'That's brilliant, my old friend. Twins. We shall be twins.'

CHAPTER 8
TWINS

Walking back through the control room, side by side with Raitha, I felt full of energy and when Blackridge looked across from his busy position before the map, I met his sneer with a confident smile. The building was filling up with players; there must have been twice as many people present now as yesterday. What a project. And what expense, although the cost of running this operation was probably trivial in comparison to the amounts Yuno had invested in creating the game.

It was even difficult finding a room with two rigs side by side, and as we looked in through the windows, a young man wearing shirt and tie - which was unusual from what I'd seen of Yuno Industries - and holding a clipboard asked Raitha for his name.

'Raitha,' my friend answered.

'Would that be Yatish Poathur?'

'It would.'

'Great, welcome to Yuno Enterprises. The General has asked that you create a wizard near Port Wyvern.'

The look that passed over Raitha's face was a delight. He was obviously struggling to control an impulse to give an angry response. In the end, he simply raised his eyebrows questioningly and shrugged. 'I play in partnership with Tyro.'

'Ahh, of course.' The young man gave me an indecipherable look. 'But we are a team here, working towards a carefully balanced raid group.'

'I understand why we are here and I intend to do my best

for the sake of the goal. Your General might be an excellent raid leader, but I have never met him. Tyro, on the other hand, I have stood side to side with in thousands of battles. We have been in every kind of tactical situation from two-person encounters to large raids. And in that time, I have come to know and'—he paused—'it would not be too strong a word to say, I have come to "love" him. Tyro is my comrade. I will not be separated from him.'

With a mock, self-depreciating shrug - *what can I do?* - I opened a nearby door and we both went inside, leaving the Yuno company worker in the corridor looking anxious and shuffling a little from foot to foot. Probably, he did not relish reporting this encounter back to Blackridge.

'My goodness, a harness and a two-footed tracker pad.' Raitha paused beside a player who was clipped up and running, spinning the pads beneath her feet at great speed.

'It does take a bit of getting used to. But after an hour in game, you won't even be aware of it.'

'Very well. Let us clip up.' There was a definite excitement and sense of anticipation in his words.

We did so and just before I put my helmet on I gave my best friend a wave, thinking about how no one - Mum excepted - had ever stuck up for me the way Raitha had just done. As though aware of my thoughts, Raitha saluted, gave a nod and then turned to his equipment.

One of the great attractions for me of playing *Epic* was the sense of creativity it gave me. I was telling the story of Klytotoxos the Hunter and now was the time to add a new chapter to it. Klytotoxos and his twin sister, Raitha. Impatiently, I let the onrushing wave of sound and colour wash over me.

And I was back in game.

Hurriedly, I set off for my spawn point. Knowing it would take Raitha a few minutes to create his character, I allowed myself some slight diversions to check my traps, which brought me a rabbit and a hedgehog, which I felt sorry about. He was still alive, although pretty feeble.

Coming to the area at the edge of the forest where I had

been born, I was disappointed no one was there. Just as I began to doubt our plan and worry that Raitha had begun life somewhere else, he popped into existence. A very lovely, slender, half-elf huntress clad in soft clothes of green and grey. She had long silver hair and sea-green eyes.

'I was not expecting to meet Klytotoxos, where is Tyro?' Raitha sounded surprised. He must have targeted me and seen my name.

'It's me, Tyro, I just wanted something more appropriate for a hunter and Klytotoxos means "famous with a bow."'

'I am disappointed. Still, at least I can call you Klyto, which has a similar ring to it. Well. How should we start?'

'Let's try to make bows and arrows. I think if we are the right distance apart, we should be able to aggro kite mobs.'

'Remember, you are talking to someone who has only ever been a warrior. What is aggro kiting?'

'Kiting is when you have a mob chasing you at a distance, like a kite on a string behind the person who is holding it and running away. Aggro kiting just means if I'm running, you shoot at the mob until it turns to you. Then as you run away, I shoot it. If we have enough room and enough arrows and especially if we are faster than it, the mob shouldn't harm us at all.'

'I understand and am eager to try this. Yet before we do, should I speak to that elven woman on the beach? She probably provides me with an introductory tutorial?'

'Oh, of course. I didn't think she'd respawn. I talked to her and she turned into an eagle and flew away to a boat. But she did give me three skills.' I was surprised to see the figure who was my mother had respawned. It did make sense though, either her or some other NPC was needed for brand new players to get a start.

'Just so.' Raitha set off across the dunes to the white sand beach and I followed. The sky was a little greyer than on the day of my birth, when it had been a glorious blue, and a strong breeze coming from the sea lifted the pale tresses of the woman as she turned to watch us.

'Let's group up,' I suggested, sending the invitation and of course Raitha accepted. Now any experience we gained would be shared and both of us would be able to loot slain mobs. Plus we had group chat available if we were too far away to hear each other in local or didn't want to be heard in local (admittedly, with two people, you could just use private channels, but with three or more, group chat really came into its own).

When we were close enough to see into the woman's extraordinarily vivid green-blue eyes she smiled, and it seemed as though I were bathing in the warmth of the midday sun.

'My daughter.' As had been the case for me, she made a fluid, welcoming gesture, bowing and shaping her whole arm. Her attention was on Raitha.

'Pleased to meet you,' said Raitha.

'It's time for me to depart.' Shading her eyes, the elven lady, our mother, looked at a seagull as it dipped and swerved over a darker patch of seawater. 'There is a message in the waves and the sand and the motion of the birds. The members of the Order of Nereids are summoned to war and I do not believe you and I will meet again.' Even though I remembered this part, I was moved to a sense of sadness from the thrilling and fateful way in which she spoke those words.

'I am sorry you are leaving so soon,' said Raitha politely, and my sense of tragedy gave way to amusement. The NPC was talking in the language of an epic and Raitha had responded like she'd just popped in for a cup of tea but now had to go to the laundrette.

'You must find your father. Ask for Knegos, in the town of Safehaven. He will guide and mentor you.'

'I'm sorry to interrupt,' I said, 'but Knegos is probably dead. The goblin king - Pawnee or something like that - sent an army. I saw the banners with my own eyes.'

Visibly upset, our game-mother turned to look south-east along the coast. My own vision was heightened as a half-elf, but hers must have been more effective still, for a tear rolled down her cheek. 'Safehaven has been burned and the smoke writes the story in the sky. The whole town was destroyed a day ago.'

'What should we do?' asked Raitha.

'I cannot stay and help you; you must look after each other and fend for yourselves as best you can. Raitha, I can give you three skills.'

'Ahh, excellent. I mean, thank you, mother.'

[Group] 'Set Traps, Archery, Bowyer; I presume these would be the same skills as you received?' Raitha asked me this in the group channel, so as not to spoil the role-playing branch of conversation taking place with the NPC.

[Group] 'They are.'

Unexpectedly, our game-mother suddenly began to speak again and with a new branch of script that I hadn't heard before, 'Alas, I cannot replace the skills and wisdom that Knegos would have taught you. There is but one way I can help you further. Klytotoxos, your knife.' As she held out a slender, long-fingered hand, waiting for my knife, there was something determined, yet sorrowful in her expression.

'Here.' Raitha held out his knife, realising that I no longer had mine.

A moment after she had collected it, I was surprised to see our mother cut along the lifeline of her left hand; immediately, it filled with dark red blood. She passed the knife to me.

Fortunately, when I copied her action, I felt hardly any pain, just a tingle. I must have cut deep though:

You have been cut by a knife for 1 damage.

Grabbing my bloody hand in hers, my elven mother pulled me close and as she stared intensely, hypnotically, into my eyes, squeezed hard. Blood, mixed together, ran down our forearms.

You have gained the ability Wolf Form.

Incredible. Unlike a skill, which had to be worked up gradually with a considerable investment of time and which could fail on use, an ability was a fully developed addition to your character's competencies and it was always successful. Abilities were a bit like magic spells, except there was no spirit cost to use one and they were triggered instantly. In *Epic*, no one under level forty had an ability.

'Now give the knife to Raitha,' she instructed me.

[Group] 'You are not going to believe this!' I exclaimed.

[Group] 'What is it, my friend, what just happened?'

[Group] 'Wait and see.'

After the same, short ritual had taken place, our mother turned to look out to sea, where the boat I had seen last time was in view.

[Group] 'This is extraordinary, I have been granted an ability. At level zero. Have you ever heard of such a thing?' I could hear a sense of awe in the shrillness of Raitha's voice.

[Group] 'It's amazing! I haven't come across anything like it. There's a paladin quest in *Epic* that can get *Inspire Bravery* at level forty, I think.'

[Group] 'I believe you are right. Did you get the same ability as me?' Raitha asked.

[Group] '*Wolf Form*?'

[Group] 'No. *Form of the Sea Eagle.*'

[Group] 'Wow! You can fly! That is so useful.'

'Fare well children.' The elven woman walked into the sea, her cream cape spreading on the surface. 'I do not think we will meet again.' With that, her cloak seemed to come alive, enveloping her, turning into the pale belly of a shark whose grey fin rapidly disappeared, hidden behind incoming waves.

Watching her depart, it seemed to me that Raitha's avatar had a mournful expression and certainly his voice, when it came into my helmet was regretful. [Group] 'And thus our mother departs, having bequeathed two-thirds of her soul upon her children. Let us examine our gifts.'

[Group] 'You mean try out our new abilities?'

[Group] 'Most certainly, I do.'

Quickly accessing my UI, I made a hot button for *Wolf Form*, and then pressed it.

The world changed. It became taller, the trees more imposing. Higher still, the grey sky was too bright and I turned my gaze instead to the shadows of the forest. They beckoned: come, there is prey here. Above all there were scents, bewildering scents of all kinds, from the sweetness of honeysuckle and lavender to the heavy musk of wild garlic. Death had a bitter-sweet smell and the rabbit I had caught earlier was enticing. In this form, I need not worry about cooking.

These new rig helmets were amazing. Giving me improved vision for being a half-elf wasn't much of a technical challenge, but releasing appropriate scents for my environment, that was something else. Most of the scents I was picking up I had never experienced before and had no idea what they represented. This feature alone made the in-game experience a whole dimension more immersive than anything that had gone before. No wonder they wanted to save *Epic 2* if they could.

[Group] 'Look up,' said Raitha.

There he was, sea eagle, a distant predator, wings out-stretched, circling far above me. Giving him a bark, that I doubted he could hear, I ran over the sand dunes beneath him.

[Group] 'Follow me.' Leaving off his circling, Raitha flew north-west.

At first I ran to keep up, then for the joy of it. I'd never moved so swiftly, not even when my warrior in *Epic* had been buffed with *Fast as the Wind*, the best movement spell in the game. With a howl, I rushed around bushes, leapt over ditches and sent seagulls squawking into the air with horror.

[Group] 'Where are we going?' I asked, after several minutes of this delightful racing across the dunes.

[Group] 'About a mile away, at that sandstone cliff, I can see a cave complex with human and half-orc pirates. Levels two to five. Perhaps more challenging ones are inside. In the forms we have now, I do not believe we need to make clumsy bows.'

[Group] 'Agreed.'

After some five or six minutes, I detected the scent of humans and a similar smell, which I assumed was that of the half-orcs. Ahead of me, filling the grey sky with its dark presence, a tall sandstone hill, about two hundred metres high, jutted out into the sea where a stack had formed from the action of the wind and waves on the soft stone. As I topped the next dune, I could see the caves Raitha had spotted. Five, no six, pirates were in the vicinity; I ducked down on my haunches and, making my way to a clump of rushes, peered out from them to study the situation further.

[Group] 'I could pull that level two near the tree line,' I offered.

[Group] 'Do so and I shall strike from above.'

Slinking along under the cover of the dune I entered the forest, where it seemed to me I was moving with extraordinary poise and delicacy. Hardly a leaf stirred as I stepped from shadow to shadow. Soon, I was barely twenty metres from the pirate, who seemed to be a bored human, performing guard duty against an attack that he thought would never come. Time to disabuse him.

I whispered to Raitha, even though in group chat the mob couldn't possibly hear me. [Group] 'Ready?'

[Group] 'Ready.'

With a mighty growl that came out with impressive ferocity, I rushed upon the man, who raised a scimitar to fend me off. Ducking low, I raked his thighs with my front left claw and kept running.

You have clawed a pirate for 2 points of damage.

You have discovered the skill Claw (1).

'Come back you wicked cur!' The pirate chased after me and I led him away from the cave he was standing in front of, back towards the beach. In the open.

'Arrrgh! Get off me.'

Even with my heightened senses, Raitha had dived in so swiftly that, until the pirate had cried out, I hadn't realised my friend was already in the fight. Now, I span around and charged back to help him as he gripped the pirate's head in his talons and beat at his ears with his wings.

I made a leap for our enemy's throat.

You have bitten a pirate for 6 points of damage.

You have discovered the skill Bite (1).

The pirate is dead. You gain experience.

A golden glow momentarily engulfed Raitha who, half-fluttering, straddled the pirate's body.

[Group] 'Level one.' I could hear the delight in his voice.

[Group] 'Congratulations! Not bad progress here either, I think five more of these would take me to two.'

[Group] 'Did you take a point of Dex?'

[Group] 'Yeah. I was thinking Dex until five, then two levels of Spirituality ready for our first spells.'

[Group] 'That seems wise. Let us do that.' Raitha began pecking at the dead pirate's eyes.

[Group] 'Come on, Raitha, that is so disgusting.'

He laughed. [Group] 'You are quite wrong. They are delicious.'

When I placed a paw on the body, a menu popped up with a loot list: chipped scimitar; a pirate's badge; 4 copper pieces. The 'Take All' button was greyed out. Nor could I take the items one at a time.

[Group] 'I'm not allowed to loot. We could use that scimitar.'

[Group] 'Not to worry, my friend. Let us level up and if we still need such items, come back in our half-elf form when these battles are trivial.'

He was right, of course, but it was still frustrating to see that loot just lying there, wasted. It would disappear after ten minutes, along with the body. Oh well.

Beating her wings furiously, Raitha leapt into the sky and was soon high above me. It was fabulous that we had these forms.

[Group] 'Hey Raitha.'

[Group] 'Yes Tyro?'

[Group] 'Let's not tell anyone about this.'

[Group] 'Our new abilities?'

[Group] 'Yeah. For a little while at least. Until it becomes important for the project as a whole.'

[Group] 'Agreed. Now, do we believe we can defeat a level three?'

[Group] 'Easily.'

[Group] 'Then I think there is a single pull on the other

side of the cave, near the sea.'

Once more I experienced the pleasure of running as fast as a wolf, low to the ground, using the channels between the dunes to mask me as I made towards the sea. A portly pirate in a black-and-white striped top and holding a boathook was walking along the line of darker sand where it had been moistened by the waves that were rolling gently to shore. When he was about fifty metres from the cliffs, he turned and went back towards them, checking out to sea from time to time. I targeted him.

Pirate: Dangerous.

Very dangerous to a level 1 Hunter with no weapon, certainly. To a wolf with a savage bite attack and an eagle with sharp claws and hooked beak, much less of a challenge, even if we were only level 1. Gathering myself just below the crest of a dune, I waited for the pirate to come back towards me again and - with a quick check that Raitha was above me - I leapt over the sand, rushing silently upon him. My intention had been to engage the pirate with a bite or claw at his leg, then lead him away from the caves while Raitha swooped down from above. Like our last victim. Now I was upon him and he still hadn't turned, I just sprang up on his back and, as he staggered forward, bit at his head, successfully; a big wound opened up from his left ear to jaw.

You have bitten a pirate for 8 points of damage.

You have achieved a *Knockback*. The pirate is stunned.

With the stocky figure splayed wriggling beneath me, I was able to bite again, fastening my teeth on his neck.

Critical Hit! You have bitten a pirate for 16 points of damage.

You have increased the skill Bite (2).

The pirate is dead. You gain experience.

[Group] 'You could have waited for me to join the fun.' Raitha had a laugh in his voice.

[Group] 'You snooze, you lose.'

Despite the fact I knew I could not take it, I had a look at the loot: a boathook (a terribly slow two-handed weapon, without even a decent damage score to compensate, in other words it had a terrible Damage Per Second); a pirate's badge and seven copper pieces. [Group] 'Another badge. They must be quest items. Shame we can't collect them for the rewards.'

[Group] 'The experience was excellent. I am a third of the way to level two.'

[Group] 'Hint taken. I shall spend less time mourning over the loot and more time pulling.'

And we were off on our level grind.

For the next three hours, I pulled the pirates from around the caves and even some inside when we managed to clear the whole area ahead of respawns. Sometimes three would come, so I'd lead them well away from the caves until they lost interest in chasing me. And if one of them lagged behind the others on the return journey, Raitha would come crashing down to start the battle.

This brought me back to when I was just a kid, playing *Epic* for the first time. I'd spent so many hours since, devoted to the one character, my warrior, that it had been years since I'd engaged in low-level fights. The main difference between then and now was that Raitha and I used to have long intervals where all we could do was sit and chat while our hit points crept back up. This time around, with the advantages of our new forms, there was hardly any need for downtime. We really didn't get hurt that much. Usually, Raitha's attacks stunned the pirates and I was able to get my bites in without reprisal. The first serious blow - a hit from a scimitar - didn't land on me until I was level 3, and I had more than enough hit points to absorb it. Then too, as I discovered, as a wolf I recovered my hit points more quickly than I had as a half-elf.

Once we had reached level 5, the pirates outside the cave were providing only a small fraction - less than 2 per cent a kill - of what we needed to make 6. There were pirates deeper in the cave complex who were much higher level (and there were probably quests too). Venturing into confined spaces, however, was not a great idea for a wolf and an eagle.

[Group] 'Time to find a new challenge, don't you think, Raitha?'

[Group] 'I have to agree. I shall always think fondly of these pirates, for giving me such a good start in *Epic Two*. Even so, we must bid them farewell. Let me fly around and try to identify a new hunting ground for us.'

[Group] 'Shall we take a break first?'

[Group] 'Very well. Meet you on the other side.'

It really was disorientating unclipping from the game. Next to me, removing his helmet, Raitha took a moment before his eyes focused and he flashed a white grin. 'Level five. Very respectable.'

'More than respectable, it is awesome. I can hardly believe that only this morning I was stuck, needing to drop rocks on a slow-spawning snake to advance.'

I held out my fist for him to punch in return but Raitha just looked puzzled. 'You copy me, it's like a high five.' When at last he understood and his fist was outstretched, I leaned over and touched my knuckles against his. 'Go us.'

Walking back through the control room towards the canteen, we both paused to look at the board recording player progress. It had been reorganised to put everyone in order of their level. The leading player Molino had reached 55. Nevertheless, because so many new players had just started, even level 5 put us respectably in the middle.

'Look!' With real excitement in his voice Raitha pointed at the board, somewhere just above us.

'What?'

'Sapentia, she's here!'

Was it strange that my heart should leap at the thought that Sapentia was in the building? What were my feelings? Of course I was delighted another staunch raiding comrade was here. Then there was the celebrity dimension. I was somewhat in awe of her online profile as a VR dating expert and script writer, and I was certainly in thrall to her looks. If a cherub had an arrow to aim at my heart and it was magically imbued to attract me to Japanese goth girls, it would be a critical hit every time. Even as I saw the name (Sapentia, wizard, Level 8, Aurigna), I felt a flush of warmth in my cheeks and ears at the prospect of actually speaking to her in person.

'There might be others.' I observed in as neutral as voice as possible.

'Braja!'

'Braja!'

We both called out at the same time. The entry on the board read Braja, warrior, Level 4, Aurigna.

'And Grythiss is really flying! Look already level nine.'

'Grythiss, Shadow Knight, Level nine, Risthrastan,' Raitha spoke aloud. 'This is most marvellous. How shall we meet them?'

'In real life? Or in the game?'

'In the flesh.'

'I have an idea. They will be at that meeting.'

Scrolling along the bottom of the character board, and also displayed on posters stuck to all the doors of the control room, was an announcement:

IMPORTANT.

TEAM MEETING 7 P.M. IN THE CONTROL ROOM.

EVERYONE TO ATTEND.

CHAPTER 9
TEAM TALK

Back in the game, Raitha had found us a new camp. Inland from the sea, the hills beneath the forest grew larger, with wider and deeper undulations of valley and crest. At last, the uneven terrain culminated in a huge hill that pushed high above the tree line and which was crowned with the ruins of a circular wall. Beyond the wall, reported Raitha, was a passage leading into darkness through ominous-looking carved stone lintels. What interested us, however, were the graves on the exposed hillside and the zombies and skeletons standing upon them. It was quite an army that had assembled there, as though a powerful lord of the undead was gathering troops to him. In all sizes, though with a predominance of former humans, the skeletons (whose exposed teeth gave them an air of being amused by something) held a variety of weapons: swords, spears, axes, bows (aha!). The mobs were levels 6 to 9, which was perfect. The pulls were tricky though.

After we'd fought and killed two outlying zombies – receiving only minor wounds – the next-easiest pull looked like it would bring a minimum of three mobs, so clustered together were they.

[Group] 'Here's a thought,' I offered, 'the skeletons are going to be a lot faster than the zombies. There's a group over to the right of two zombies, one skelly. What if we pull them and run halfway around the hill? We should have time to deal with the skeleton before the zombies arrive.'

With a flurry of wingbeats, Raitha landed on a rock near to me. We must have made an odd sight, an eagle and a wolf staring appraisingly at silent, unmoving figures from the grave.

[Group] 'That skeleton is level eight, hard for us. We can try, but if you are mistaken, break off before the other mobs catch up. It would be a shame to die. And my ability button has not reset, has yours? I'm concerned that if we die, we might have a long wait until we can use these abilities again.'

A quick look showed me that *Wolf Form* was indeed greyed out. [Group] 'It has not.'

[Group] 'Possibly, it will reset after twenty-four hours, perhaps though it will be a week, or more. Bear that in mind when you decide whether to fight or run.'

[Group] 'Ready when you are.'

After a short wait, while Raitha beat his wings heavily and took to the skies, I targeted the skeleton in the group of three undead and rushed up the hill. Just as I was considering whether to leap upon him, all three figures lurched towards me, the skeleton raising a short sword. Even after four years of playing *Epic* at a much higher level than this, my heart still jumped at the sight of monsters running fast towards me with the intention of killing me. Swerving sharply, I ran down the hillside to where the first trees grew, then swerved again to my left and ran as fast as I could. It seemed to me that I could hear the skeleton close behind: if so, he was fast. I didn't want to turn to check in case he was upon me while we were still too close to the zombies.

[Group] 'Is it working?' I asked Raitha.

[Group] 'Indeed it is. Keep going though, until I stay stop. In fact you have to go more than halfway around the hill to maximise your distance from the zombies.'

Leaping over bushes and clusters of white flowers that I did not recognise, I rounded a lone, fragile-looking birch tree when Raitha called out, [Group] 'Now!'

Roaring – not that it would have the slightest effect on the undead, but I felt fired up for battle – I halted, turned completely about and, when the skeleton got into range, grinning manically, launched myself at him. Too bad he had no throat; it was a good bite.

You have bitten a skeleton for 4 points of damage.

You have increased the skill Bite (24).

Now, with an unpleasant clacking of bone on bone, the skeleton slashed at me.

You have been hit by a skeleton for 5 points of damage.

As I bit and clawed, while my enemy slashed (far too rapidly), Raitha came crashing down upon the skeleton, rapping vigorously at its skull with his sharp, curved beak.

[Group] 'Peck his eyes out!' I joked.

Raitha came straight back with, [Group] 'Bite his liver!'

Still no sign of the zombies. My hit points were down nearly half, but so were the skeleton's and his or her (hard to tell if it were once a male or female human, I was too busy fighting to count the ribs) life was draining away faster than mine as Raitha clawed and pecked furiously from behind. All of a sudden a shadow fell across me, a pungent, unpleasant smell of rotten flesh filled my nose and at the edge of my vision I could sense something swaying: the zombies were here and with some alarm I saw Raitha's hit points drop fast to below half.

[Group] 'Abort! Abort!' I cried. Without waiting to check - I knew he would do as I said – I broke off from the skeleton who, astonishingly, gave a triumphant laugh. *Epic 2* definitely had more sophisticated AI in the behaviour of the mobs than did *Epic.* Away I went, my small train behind me, this time heading for the forest in earnest. After a few minutes of galloping down the hill, I was dodging in and out of trees, still hearing the skeleton behind me, crashing through bushes and branches as it sought to cut me in half.

[Group] 'You will be pleased to know I am safe,' Raitha announced with a calm voice.

[Group] 'Good. I'm running in the forest, in the direction of the coast, I hope.'

[Group] 'I shall search for a glimpse of you when the gaps in the foliage allow. Don't run into any mobs.'

[Group] 'Excellent advice.' I probably sounded sarcastic,

but I didn't mean to. At the speed I was going, with my perspective so low to the ground, it would be very easy to accidently blunder into an unpleasant encounter.

Ducking under branches, leaping bramble-filled ditches and constantly swerving between trees, I stayed clear of my pursuers. It seemed that the forest was becoming younger here and the rolling ground less steep. Good, this felt like the forest was thinning out. And soon I saw confirmation in a glimpse of grey seas, where a silver sheen seemed to lie like a magic, elven cloak on the restless waves.

[Group] 'Get ready to fight!' Raitha called me away from my appreciation of the landscape.

[Group] 'What is it?' I looked about, wildly.

[Group] 'The skeleton. He's still after you. No sign of the zombies. I think we can take him.'

[Group] 'I agree. Here I go.'

With that I turned and ran back towards the forest. There he was! Still grinning, still wielding a short sword and running, with apparent eagerness, to chop me up. As the gap between us closed to just a few metres and I leapt up to bite the head of my enemy, a streak of brown, of curved claw and hooked beak shot over my head and knocked back the skeleton, whose hit points having fully recovered now dropped by a third.

Soon, we were battling away and I began to feel anxious. Not about the outcome of this engagement. With both Raitha and I hammering away and splintering the skeleton's bones, we were going to win. My concern was that by the end of the battle, I'd be on maybe 10 to 15 hit points. Same for Raitha. And if those zombies turned up…

Looking anxiously in every direction I could without losing my attacks on the skeleton, I could feel my body tensing. Lower and lower went the skeleton's health bar, until, with a rattle of his teeth, he collapsed in a sudden shower of unconnected bones.

The skeleton is dead. You gain experience.

Good experience too, nearly 20 per cent of the way to level 6.

And no zombies. Yay.

Raitha sounded very pleased. 'Well done. Imagine I am holding out my fist towards you.'

'I touch mine to yours.' I raised a front paw and with a chuckle, Raitha wafted a few wing feathers over it.

'What now?' he asked.

'Now we need to rest, let's go to the shore.'

'Meet you there.'

When we were sat, side by side, looking out at the waves and distant islands, I found myself remembering my early days in *Epic*. Evidently, so did Raitha.

'This is like Broomdark Hall,' he said, and I knew exactly what he meant. The regions could not have been more different. Here, we were under a high, if grey, sky, with a silver sea before us stretching to the horizon. Broomdark Hall, on the other hand, was basically a huge haunted house full of mobs and after you'd cleared out the yard trash, it was impossible to avoid pulling at least three or four mobs at a time. After each battle, Raitha and I would sit on a stone sepulchre and wait to heal up. We'd pass the time talking about school and family. While I certainly had an interest in life in Kerala, Raitha was deeply fascinated by what I could tell him about Ireland and his questions always seemed to be exploring whether he'd like to move to my country.

One thing he didn't really understand was how isolated Mum and I were, despite our living in a large, bustling city in a country famous for the friendliness of the people. Raitha, too, came from a relatively poor family. Unlike my solitary upbringing, he had grown up with the children of four other families in a large, ex-colonial house they lived in near the sea. He had been part of pack of more than a dozen kids, who played games of football on the dusty, hard earth in front of the house in one long game that lasted months. Or who hid and sought one another, as they ran through the rooms of the large building. I, on the other hand, spent most of my time hurrying past other Dublin kids in case they were trouble. And whereas Raitha knew everyone on the street and would see nothing untoward in strolling into his neighbour's house, Mum and I never spoke to our neighbours, apart from to argue with them (like when we confronted the couple in the house to our right about them filling a bin next to the wall that divided our yards out front with awful-smelling rubbish and leaving it for weeks). Listening to Raitha talk about his childhood, even though he had very little by way of possessions, I'd have swapped places with him.

Although we were healed up before 7 p.m., the time for the meeting, another pull would take too long, so we went back through the forest, to where we could look up the steep, rocky slopes towards the ominous wall and barrow entrance, then unclipped.

For the team talk, a stage had been set up beneath the player scoreboard. On it was a podium, with a small black microphone curving towards the speaker. There were three chairs: Blackridge sat in one; the elderly woman I'd met, Katherine, was in the other. The third was empty. The room was very full, it was a bit like being at a gig, with the large map a bigger version of the sound desk, around which the crowd parted.

The composition of the audience was interesting. Some would have been Yuno employees and you'd expect a fairly wide range of ages and an even split by gender there. Everyone else, presumably, were gamers recruited from *Epic* for this project. And the people around me did have a certain look. I mean, of course everyone is an individual and there was considerable variation, not least in the nationalities present, but still, definitely more men than women, definitely younger (twenties, I'd say, mostly) than old and a predominance of very casual dress. I fitted right in with my denim knee-length shorts, grey hoody and *Rampage* T-shirt.

And of course, there was Watson. Surprisingly, my heart warmed to see him as he stood at the podium, tapping the mic to obtain our attention. Looking like a top-heavy sailor, in a navy company polo shirt from which emerged thick, muscled arms, he seemed like an old friend in comparison to the self-important Blackridge.

Expectant and silent, the whole room waited for Watson to begin.

'Thank you.' Watson peered through half-glasses at the top of the podium, where presumably he had some notes. 'This is the greatest team of gamers ever assembled.' Smiling, he looked around the room and although it was brief, I felt that he caught my eye. 'How many of you wanted to beta-test *Epic Two*?' A few people raised their hands. 'Go on, please, don't hold back, let me know.' More joined in. Maybe a third. I had been interested, of course, but *Epic* still had a lot of content I'd never seen, plus all my friends. We'd discussed moving over as a group but not enough had wanted to.

'And how many of you have wanted to play *Epic* or *Epic Two* with a state-of-the art rig and ping times of less than a millisecond?'

With a loud rustle, all of us raised our hands and there were a few cheers. Watson chuckled. 'Of course.

'Well, if I were you, I'd be pretty happy. You get to do something you enjoy at the elite level, you get to keep your characters and gear when the game launches and...' His voice rose with incredulity. 'You get paid for it!

'You deserve this. For the hours you put into *Epic*; for the community you created around the game; for the way you carried the storylines into the highest levels.'

Now Watson's voice became deep and serious, the sudden change of tone and volume instantly stilling the room and attracting our attention. 'Of course, you are not here just to have fun. We have a serious task in hand, one that we can only achieve together.

'Yuno has announced to the world that the launch date of *Epic Two* has been put back a month. We have apologised to all our early-bird subscribers and given them all a month's free subscription. That gives us nine weeks to fix the game. Nine weeks, to achieve a goal that we did not believe would be managed in nine months. You have to level up, stop Mikarka-that from taking over the game, and kill her. It is a daunting prospect, but if you collaborate and put the hours in, it can be done. Especially, because you have the advantage of being able to access our developers' notes about the game.

'I'll keep this short, as you'll want the opportunity to ask questions before getting clipped up again. We have installed extra rigs on the floor above, please go there if all those on this level are busy. Mr Blackridge - the General - and the Yuno team will organise you into groups of seven, the optimal amount for the experience-calculating algorithm. Don't bother with trade skills. When you are hitting the seventy-plus levels, we will start raiding for the gear you'll need to face the dragon, especially for gear with cold resistance.

'Now, are there any questions?'

A hand shot up and before Watson could politely call on the speaker, a young-looking goth-type asked, 'Why don't you reprogram the dragon?'

'Oh, we will. Next time she respawns, she won't be AI. For now, however'—Watson sighed and gestured with both arms, as if to say, *What can you do, it was a dumb idea*—'our problem is that to maximise the dragon's machine-learning capability, we let her go and dispersed her code over the millions of computers of our community hosts. Like the game itself, there's no possibility of editing Mikarkathat in a conventional way. She's too dispersed. And she's evolving too.'

Now a tall, brown-skinned woman, wearing a white head-scarf, put up her hand and waited for Watson to nod towards her.

'In a manner of speaking,' she began, 'we *are* reprogramming her and the game. Every action of ours in the game has a code consequence. It is like the premise of Gödel's Theorem. And for Mikarkathat, we are trying to write the G-string.' The woman looked around, confident that we would all understand her point, although I only half got it. Our actions in the game were also changes in the code.

Beside me, Raitha sniggered and sniggered.

'What?'

'She said G-string,' he whispered.

'Who are you?' I muttered back. 'Beavis or Butthead?' Yet all my efforts to project a mature contempt were undone by his continued struggle not to laugh aloud. It started to get to me too. I found myself shaking and tears coming to my eyes. Putting a hand to my mouth, I tried to hide my own laughter.

'Hush. Stop,' I whispered.

Raitha, however, couldn't stop. And now nor could I. What he said wasn't particularly funny, certainly not funny enough to wrack us both with supressed laughter. It was more the wild giddiness in Raitha's dark eyes, combined with a feeling that to burst out laughing now would be utterly inappropriate. For one thing, it might be thought that we were mocking that smart woman. I was glad that the room had people in it from all over the planet; that diversity was something I enjoyed about raiding. The mix. Yet if I couldn't control myself, then not only might I be viewed as the brat who wasn't a team player, but also everyone might think that despite my Vietnamese features I was a racist and a sexist, maybe an Islamaphobe too.

With this sobering thought, I drew a deep breath and rid myself of the waves of giggles that had been pushing against my ribs. And when Raitha saw I was done, he too straightened up as if nothing had ever been amiss and, innocent, he looked attentively at the person asking the next question.

A lot of the questions were dull. 'Where's the best place for a level twelve character to get experience?' That kind of thing. Watson had Blackridge up at the podium now to answer all the in-game stuff. Watson himself just fielded the logistical ones like whether we could sleep in the building (yes, he'd set up hammocks and couches for naps, but it was best to keep a steady routine with at least six hours sleep in bed at your hotel).

Then a grungy person with long, curly black hair waved for attention. Only when he spoke could I tell for sure he was male.

'Are we all getting paid the same?' he asked, which was the first question by someone that in any way went against the, 'we are all team Yuno' spirit of the meeting. I liked the guy at once. Ever since Blackridge had treated me like some kind of pawn to be moved in his great strategy, I'd felt like an outsider and maybe this kid (he was about twenty) did too.

'No,' Watson answered promptly and with a strength that said he had nothing to hide. I admired him for it, I thought he was going to evade the question. 'Our basic remuneration is three thousand dollars a month, most of you are getting that. For some people, especially those of you who had to give up higher paid work to support this project, we had to increase the figure.'

There was a level of restlessness now among the gathering of gamers. With only a perfunctory look across the room, Watson asked, 'Are there any more questions?' His tone suggested that it would be best if there weren't.

When I put my hand up high, Raitha looked at me, half surprised, half amused.

'Yes?' Watson pointed at me and a hundred faces turned in my direction.

'It's more by way of a statement than a question. I'm Tyro; I'm standing next to Raitha. If Braja, Sapentia and Grythiss are here, could you please come find us after the meeting.' I was about to add *so we can form a group,* but I checked myself. No point flagging my intention in front of Blackridge and getting into a row in front of everyone.

'Thank you, er, Tyro. Well, that concludes the meeting. Good luck everyone.'

A round of applause broke out, friendly, comradely, not too frenzied though. This was a cool crowd, not inclined to get carried away.

CHAPTER 10
FRIENDS REUNITED

Braja, it turned out, was an ex-army, now postal worker American from near Chicago. Unlike some people on leaving the army, Braja had stayed fit. He was lean, small – not much bigger than me – and had a light moustache to match his fair hair, which he kept short, army style.

Sitting beside Braja was Grythiss a tall but soft-looking (especially next to the muscular Braja) Swede. Dark hair, heavy-metal T-shirt, black leather jacket, denim jeans, about thirty. The two of them were across the table from Raitha and me.

Having made the introductions, Braja was talking about the crap he had to put up with in his sorting office.

'Whenever it gets busy, they bring in students from the university and while some of them are good kids, there's a lot think that we are dumb dinks. There was this one – and I am not making this up or exaggerating – there was this one guy, couldn't have been more than nineteen, comes in and right off the bat says, "I'm the smartest person you'll ever meet." So I look over at Kevin, who is hauling a massive bag of mail to tip onto the table and he just shakes his head. A while later, the three of us are standing side by side, sorting the mail into a big display of boxes in front of us and I say to Kev, "Have you finished *Being and Time* then?" and Kev plays along and says, "Yeah, I read it on the train to Chicago. Not bad." "I call bullshit on it," I said. "The dialectics in that book are a complete dead end. It's not like Hegel, you know, where they are like, sensuous? It's like eating a dried out old apple instead of a sweet, soft pear." Kev starts laughing. "A sweet pear. You've got it, man, that's just the way Hegel is." And so I turn to the kid and say, "What about you, genius, what's your take on *Being and Time*?" And the kid blushes and says he hasn't read it, so I say, "Anything by Heidegger then." But no, he hasn't read any Heidegger, or Wittgenstein, or Aristotle, or Hegel. "What?" snorts Kev with derision. "You come in here to sort mail and you haven't read Hegel. Jeez, man, let me lend you a copy so you can get up to speed by tomorrow." Well, the kid doesn't come back.'

After checking that Braja was done, Grythiss looked up from beneath a long dark fringe. 'That was very profound, what you said about pears and apples, Hegel and Heidegger.'

'Hah ha! You think so? I know nothing about them. I mean, I tried to read them once. But they are impossible to make sense of. I call bullshit on anyone who claims they have. Right?' Braja looked up at Grythiss and gave him an affectionate smile.

There was a pause. Then Grythiss said, 'I have read *Being and Time*.'

'No way. What's it all about then?'

'To me, it spoke of my existence at the deepest level.' From concentrated eyebrows to narrow mouth, Grythiss looked serious, while Braja was grinning widely now from under his moustache. 'It told me of the emptiness of meaning.'

'Yeah, well, you're Swedish. You're into that kind of thing, like that Munch, Scream, picture.'

Again a pause. 'Munch was Norwegian.'

'Same thing,' Braja came back at once.

'Is Canada part of America?'

Braja shrugged. 'Pretty much.'

All the time Braja was speaking – and he could certainly chat away at speed – I was exchanging amused glances with Raitha and feeling happy. It was a real pleasure to be in the company of these guys, with whom I'd spent hours and hours online.

'Hey Braja, sorry to interrupt your attempts to wind Grythiss up, but how come you are a warrior not a cleric?'

'The guy in charge assigned it to me. And if I get orders, I tend to follow them.'

'Well, it doesn't work for our group. Grythiss can tank, Raitha and I can pull and be DPS. Sapentia will add her DPS too. But we absolutely have to have a cleric. I guess I could try and persuade one to join us, but Blackridge – the guy in charge – is bound to have them all allocated.'

Looking thoughtful for once, it was obvious that Braja was considering this. 'Listen, I know we have a job to do here and they are paying us well. But I also know you guys. We've been through thick and thin, right? I want to be in your group and be your cleric.'

Looking into his earnest face, I felt a wave of relief. With Braja as cleric in our group, we'd fly through the levels compared to having to operate without a dedicated healer.

'That's awesome, man.' Raitha reached out his fist, like I'd shown him, but somehow weak-looking. Still, Braja bumped knuckles and Raitha immediately smiled with satisfaction. 'If you don't mind starting again, that has another advantage too.'

'Don't mind? Of course not. Warriors are boring – excuse me Raitha and Tyro in *Epic* – I'd much rather play a cleric, where the whole group's survival is dependent on my reactions, especially in a crisis. I love that pressure. I love the adrenalin. It's my fix. In fact—'

'You could be a half-elf in the region of Palernia,' Raitha interrupted Braja hurriedly, before his new train of thought could run away with the conversation. 'That way you'll start close to us.'

I nodded. 'Our problem then is just getting Grythiss over.'

'Did I hear a problem? Well here's your solution.' Entering the canteen and walking purposefully over towards us was a Japanese woman in her late twenties with the most extraordinary look about her. Basically, think goth: long black hair with turquoise and blue streaks; dark eyeshadow; exaggerated eyebrow lines; purple lips; a low-cut, black silk basque-corset thing with delicate lacework beneath it that acted as a skirt; black stockings, with a visible line of white skin above their tops – oh, it was hard to tear my eyes away, though I must or she'd

103

consider me a drooling idiot – and lastly, knee-high boots with large heels and an abundance of straps.

'Are you Sapentia?' asked Raitha standing up and offering his hand. 'It's an honour.'

The woman of my dreams ignored his gesture, gave a slight bow and took a seat beside Braja. 'Hai. I'm Sapentia. And you are bunch of anarchists that everyone is talking about. Which one's Tyro?'

'I am,' I said, unable to meet her eye for more than a fleeting moment. My cheeks felt warm and I knew I was blushing.

'Wow, you're young. I imagined you…I don't know. More commanding.'

'Ouch! That's got to hurt.' Braja laughed and, strangely, I actually felt more at ease for him saying it.

'And thought just came to me,' Sapentia went on, offering me a wink, 'that at least you're not that guy with lame moustache. I'd hate taking orders from him.'

'Oh man, burned!' Raitha offered Sapentia his knuckles and then had to withdraw his hand as she looked at him with withering scorn.

Then she turned her attention back to me. 'What's the plan then, Tyro?'

Drawing a breath (be still, my beating heart), I took a tray and turned it lengthways. 'This half is dragon territory. Down here at Port Placida, well away from the action, is where Blackridge is getting everyone grouped. Here is where Raitha and are.' I marked the spot with a potato. 'Palernia. Raitha and I are hunters; Grythiss is a shadow knight; Braja is going to start over as a cleric and you are a wizard, right? Not a sorceress?'

'Right. Go on,' Sapentia answered brusquely.

'We level up to a hundred and cross the mountains, scout Mikarkathat, figure out her defences, then, when we know the route to the dragon and think we have a chance, call everyone in for the raid.'

With all our eyes on her, Sapentia studied the potato as if it were a complex puzzle. Thoughtfully, she cupped her chin in her hand. My stomach felt tense. It was hard, being in the presence of a celebrity who also happened to be overwhelming your body's chemistry. Hard, if you like goth girls, which I certainly did.

'Simple. I like it. And your problem is that Grythiss, being lizardman, is at other end of the world, right?'

By way of an answer, Grythiss gave her a nod. Then, shyly, asked, 'Where were you at the meeting? I didn't see you.'

'Meh.' Sapentia pulled a strand of purple hair back behind her ear. 'I skipped it to keep levelling. I knew I had to get to ten to get *Portal of the Stone Rings* as quick as possible. Which is why I'm wizard, you can see, sorceresses don't get *Portal* until sixteen. Let me guess what I missed: if we all pull together, work hard, be team, we'll get this job done. Right?'

'Right,' echoed Braja, who hadn't stopped smiling since Sapentia had joined us. 'It's like when I was at Fort Benning…'

Cutting him off, Sapentia leaned across the table and picked up a bean from my plate, then, having placed it on the tray, picked up another. 'At low levels you have to be ported from ancient stone circles. There's one down at Risthrastan here and one in Palentia is about here. Grythiss, you'll be fine, mobs are only level six around yours. Palentia is more hard. I haven't been there but guide says not only can you have goblins up to level fifteen, but rare spawn at the stones is a lich, level thirty-four. Only seen at night.'

'If the guide is still valid,' I added.

'True. And it's getting more bad.' Sapentia leaned back, took us all in, then abruptly swung her black-clad legs around and stood up. 'Shall we do it?' Addressing Grythiss in particular, our wizard added, 'Meet you at stones as soon as you can get there. Take leak first everyone, we have hell of much grinding to do.'

'Goodness,' said Raitha, when Sapentia had strode out of the canteen. 'I'm in love.'

'Me too,' I said.

Grythiss sighed. 'As am I.'

'Kids.' Braja laughed at us. 'Take away the garb and make-up and there isn't a lot to love.'

'Oh, but you are wrong,' Raitha sounded offended. 'She is a free spirit. Freer even than Tyro.'

Walking back through the control room, Raitha was at my side, Braja and Grythiss right behind us. It was really busy now and with earnest, eager expressions men and women were running as they went to and from the rig rooms. That was new. Were they genuinely that eager to get on with the game? Or was this urgency a way of displaying your devotion to the cause (while in the Den and observable by Blackridge)? All at once there was a meaty, dark guy in my face, a red-haired girl on his shoulder. Neither was much older than me.

'You're Tyro, right?' Stocky-guy pointed a finger close to my chest. His accent was hard to place, a south American country, perhaps? If I hadn't already figured this lad wanted trouble, his expression gave it away: heavy, flushed cheeks; bright eyes that never quite met mine; sneer.

'I am.' When you've been knocked around by the thin, wiry headcases of Dublin 7, you weren't easily intimidated by unfit wannabe bullies.

'What kind of a scene are you trying to cause here anyway?'

There was a stir and everyone turned at the raised voice of this self-selected guardian of the cause. Even the runners halted.

'You are the one causing a scene.' Raitha leapt to my defence and it warmed my heart to see him − a slender rapier to the hefty battle-axe that was this guy − seemingly unafraid and full of indignation on my behalf. For my part, I felt a kind of relief at the aggressive and accusatory shout. Let's get this out in the open. All the silent treatment; the long stares; I'd had enough of it.

'I'm going to make a scene all right and it will have the corpse of Mikarkathat in it.' I spoke loudly.

Scoffing, the guy shook his head ponderously, the girl behind him doing likewise in uncanny synchronicity. 'You're not going to get anywhere near that dragon. Not without working with the rest of us. And that means following orders.'

'Does it though? What gives one man the right to boss us

around? Since when has one person known more than the collective experience of three hundred?'

'The General wrote a book on *Epic*. He literally wrote the book.' This from the girl, her face reddening now to match her hair; she was grinning too, but it was a challenge, not humour.

'I don't know if you've led big raids…' I began, intending to explain that listening to other people when they offer advice was the key to building a team. That listening to all the expert players gathered here and letting them play with their favourite classes was smarter than forcing them into some rigid schema. Before I could even gather my thoughts on this, however, our troublemaker was leaning over me again.

'Oh, we all know you killed Mikarkathat. Sure, boast away. That's your problem, isn't it? You think you're too bloody awesome to follow anyone else.'

The girl nodded. 'Yeah. You're all ego.'

A glance took in the dozens of faces around me, they were all watching intensely and one or two were scowling and nodding. No one outside of my friends, was with me.

'In my world, leadership has to be earned. And writing a book is fine but putting the hours in is the best way to master the tactics of the game.'

'You shouldn't be here. You shouldn't be taking the company's money if you can't help the rest of us.'

Brushing past me, Braja's hand flashed at speed and the hefty lad's finger was no longer in my chest.

'Ahh.' My adversary was staggering backwards so as to avoid having his finger broken.

'You've made your point. The whole room has heard you.' Braja let him go. 'Now get out of the way and let us back into the game.'

With a heaving chest, the guy clenched his fists, obviously wanting to take a swing at Braja. And equally obviously, even though he was bigger and a lot stockier than Braja, he knew that the lithe man who had driven him back, all the while smiling slightly, would kill him.

'Let's calm down.' Blackridge had pushed through the spectators. 'We're all in this together, remember.' He gave me a look. 'Tyro can do his thing. The rest of us will prove that centralised coordination gets the best results.'

If Blackridge was waiting me to thank him he could wait forever. I didn't need his permission to play the game my way. Pushing through a few resistant spectators, heart pounding with anger, I went down a corridor, checking the rooms until I found one with four spare sets. My friends were right behind me; no one was speaking as we clipped up. I guessed, though, they felt the same as me, that they had something to prove.

It was a relief when the colours and sounds of *Epic 2* rushed upon me.

CHAPTER 11
GROUP KLYTO

Once in the game, I sent group invites to all my friends and almost at once my UI showed that Sapentia, Raitha and Grythiss had joined. Like old times. Good times.

[Group] 'Is that you, Tyro? Klytotoxos?' The voice was that of Sapentia.

[Group] 'Yeah, sorry, I should have said I changed my name.'

[Group] 'I call you Tyro for while, until I get used to it.'

[Group] 'No worries.'

[Group] 'Listen up.' Braja spoke in a whisper. 'We have a problem.'

[Group] 'Go on,' I replied.

[Group] 'I've entered the game in a temple on a hill in Safehaven. There's nothing here but goblins. Some of them are roaming. Oh, sod it. They're on to me. I'll be dead in seconds.'

[Group] 'We'll have to clear the spot, then unclip and tell you when to clip up. What level are the goblins?'

No response.

[Group] 'Lizardman kill hated goblinsss sssoon.'

[Group] 'Hai, we've landed, maybe just fifteen minutes away from Safehaven.'

[Group] 'Raitha and I are headed that way, but if you can clear his spawn point then let me know and I'll unclip and call Braja back in.'

Far, far more quickly than when I'd first tried to walk it in half-elf form, Raitha and I were heading south-east near the

109

coast. I wasn't going to cross that river at the ford with the leeches though, I'd enter it further inland.

Raitha wanted a private chat. [Channel Klytotoxos/Raitha] 'My dear lupine friend, I think it would be best if I flew on to help Sapentia and Grythiss. Do you not agree?'

[Channel Klytotoxos/Raitha] 'Oh. You are right. Go for it. I'm safe enough, this is all newbie territory.'

As I ran on, low to the ground, I once more appreciated the scents around me, a heavy musk from the forest bracken gave way to a fresher, salty breeze off the sea as I left the dense, tall trees behind me and ran through young, more spaced-out saplings. Nettles were everywhere but I didn't need to deviate to find a path through them, I could charge through without feeling a sting.

After about twenty minutes of this enjoying running at speed, Grythiss called out. [Group] 'Goblins are weak. We killsssss.'

[Group] 'Specifically,' added Sapentia, 'level six to eight. You can ask Braja to log in now.'

[Group] 'Who is thissss eagle? A new familiar of some-one's?'

[Group] 'Hah! No, it's me, Raitha.'

[Group] 'How on earth are you doing that at level six?' I could hear the genuine respect in Sapentia's voice. It was the last sound that reached me from the game, as I finished unclip-ping.

Opposite me, Braja was swinging himself around as far as he could in the harness clockwise and then letting straps unwind, to whirl him back anti-clockwise, legs off the ground. When he saw me watching, he just smiled, not the least bit sheepish to have been caught messing around like a little child. 'This gear is amazing isn't it? Makes me want to be a ninja.'

'They've cleared your spawn point.'

'Already?'

'That's Sapentia for you. She doesn't waste time.'

'I'd better get clipped up then. Tell her she'll have to wait. I'm going to create a new character. No point starting with that death penalty.'

'I hear you. I was on negative exp for a while.' Just before I lowered my helmet again, I looked across to where Braja was balancing on his tracker ball and was poised to do the same. Catching his eye, I saluted. 'See you on the other side.'

Woosh! Colour and sound battered my senses until resolving into a light forest where sunlight and shadow dappled the undergrowth. Nearby, a terrified rabbit flashed its tail as it disappeared into a thicket of nettles and brambles.

[Group] 'I'm back.'

[Group] 'Greetingsss,' hissed Grythiss, in a very reptilian voice.

[Group] 'Braja's spawn area is completely cleared,' said Sapentia in her usual brusque way. Then, with a voice expressing rather more curiosity, she added, 'So you've gotten *Wolf Form?*'

[Channel Klytotoxos/Raitha] 'I had to tell them,' said Raitha apologetically in a private message.

[Channel Klytotoxos/Raitha] 'Of course; no worries. These are our comrades. We have no secrets from them.'

[Group] 'Yeah, we got an amazing break. Did Raitha explain?'

Sapentia replied, [Group] 'Sort of. Your starting skill quest was broken by Goblin capture of Safehaven, so NPC, your mother, gave you those instead.'

[Group] 'Hah, that's it, instead of some feeble crafting skills, we got these. It was all she could offer us. I think she kept the water form for herself and gave away the land one to me and the air to Raitha.'

[Group] 'Well,' Sapentia sounded brusque, 'let's get together and make most of this best good luck.'

[Group] 'I'm running towards you now. I'm perhaps just an hour away,' I said.

[Channel Klytotoxos/Braja] 'Group invite please.'

[Group] 'I'm in,' announced Braja a moment after I'd sent him the invite.

[Group] 'Healer. I sssee you. Follow thisss path.'

[Group] 'You are the only one missing now, Klyto. Should we head north to meet you?' asked Raitha.

[Group] 'Maybe stay there and level Braja up a while on Goblins?'

[Group] 'That seems best. Very well,' said Raitha, 'I'll pull to you Grythiss.'

[Group] 'Bring three or four at time,' added Sapentia, 'at least until I'm low on spirit.'

For the next thirty minutes, I ran over hillsides covered in heather and gorse, listening to my friends as they levelled Braja up to 4 in that time. And my twin, Raitha, hit 7, which I cheered. Unfortunately, I was too far away to get a share of the group experience.

Mostly the chat was limited to calls like, 'incoming, a Goblin Shaman' and 'slow up, seventeen spirit'. Then Sapentia asked an interesting question. [Group] 'So, who else thinks set-up stinks?'

[Group] 'What do you mean?' I asked. Did she mean our group? What was wrong with it?'

[Group] 'Yuno Industries are spending lot of money trying to fix problem they should have anticipated. I mean, dispersing code to crowdsourced hosts. And allowing it to evolve. Most extreme big risk. There's something about whole operation we're missing and I don't like it.'

[Group] 'Why are you here then?' asked Braja.

[Group] 'Honestly? Because Japanese boy gamers too lame for me. I wanted to meet Tyro in person and hear cool Irish accent - without headset on. I never think he'd be more young than schoolboy.'

Jeez Louise. What was I supposed to say to that? Outside the game, I'd be blushing furiously and a little bit hurt too. There was a scornful rejection in those ungrammatical words, 'more young'. Here, though, I was group leader and a wolf to boot. [Group] 'Go back to your thought about missing something. Like what?'

[Group] 'I've no idea. And I've been thinking about it long

time.'

[Group] 'Dear me. Please Sapentia, don't spoil my happiness. This is my idea of paradise. Gaming all day, free food, good friends. And being paid for it!' Raitha laughed.

[Group] 'And flying around as an eagle,' I added.

[Group] 'That, indeed, is delightful too.'

[Group] 'I don't have a problem with the set-up,' said Braja, 'do the math. Three hundred times four thousand is a hundred and twenty thousand a month. The total cost for this effort to clean up the game is going to be well below half a million. That's nothing for these guys. If the game tanks, they will be out hundreds of millions, billions even.'

[Group] 'It's an amazing game,' I couldn't help commenting. From scent alone, I could tell I was approaching a muddy estuary full of shore life and wader birds.

[Group] 'More Goblinsss needed for my axe.' Grythiss's mutter contained a strong, disapproving and impatient tone. Grythiss loved to roleplay and immerse himself in the game and our conversations beyond our characters probably spoiled that for him.

Raitha responded at once, [Group] 'I'm flying around looking for more pulls. I believe, though, that we have cleared them all, apart from one commander, who is level twenty-seven.

[Group] 'They are not respawning,' observed Braja.

[Group] 'Not here, at least,' said Sapentia.

After a pause, in which I tried to remember my levelling plan based on my study of the game on the flight across the Atlantic, I recalled the location that interested me most. The others might not like it though. [Group] 'There's an island near the town that should suit us. Mostly mobs twelve to fifteen. Some higher. And a vampire.'

[Group] 'Vampire?' queried Grythiss, probably voicing the concern of everyone.

[Group] 'We will need to leave before dark, obviously.'

[Group] 'Promising,' Sapentia sounded positive, 'how do we get there?'

[Group] 'Any boats in the harbour?' I asked.

[Group] 'I believe so,' answered Raitha and it seemed to me that I saw him, a darker, larger bird among the seagulls near the horizon. 'Indeed, we have a wide choice.'

[Group] 'Pick one and row north to the muddy estuary to collect me. And did any of those Goblins drop bows?'

[Group] 'Dozenssss, oh wise leader.'

[Group] 'Good. Bring me the best please Grythiss and as many arrows as you can; I'll revert to humanoid when I reach you.'

Sending seabirds leaping fearfully into the air, I ran over the mud flats, near to where slow-moving waves were washing over the ground, with a strong sun turning the mud beneath from black to grey before the next wave. There was some group discussion about the best kind of boat and a realisation that none of us had sailing or even swimming skills. In *Epic* I had become an expert swimmer, thanks to levelling in the submerged cathedral Lake Fiackran. That was a level 30+ zone, by which stage various magic spells and items gave the players access to water breathing. In this situation, improving logistical skills like swimming and sailing was a low priority, probably, they wouldn't be needed at all.

Having listened as my group settled on a rowing boat with four oarlocks, I expected them to arrive soon. Raitha, of course, was able to come meet me very quickly and, no doubt terrifying all the birds nearby, circled above me, screeching cheerfully for a while, before flying off towards a headland to the south-east.

At last, a green, slim-looking boat came into view and it did my heart good to know I'd soon be in the company of my friends. Whatever happened with the dragon and Watson and Blackridge, I'd always feel this trip to San Francisco was worth it. The pleasure of being a hunter in the immersive *Epic 2* and of meeting my friends from the past four years was as sweet as anything I'd experienced before. In fact, I don't think I'd felt this happy since my seventh birthday, when, too young to know any better and playing football on a real five-a-side pitch my mum had booked (instead of the usual tarmacked, glass-strewn playground), I thought I was the luckiest boy in the world.

Time to resume my original, half-elf, form. With a slight sense of trepidation (how long until it reset and I could use it again?), I flicked away the icon on my UI that showed a howling wolf. I was tall again, my vision was different too, not quite as able to bring distant features into view, but I could detect the heat signature of the world around me as a yellow-to-red halo. And of course, the scents of the world faded.

When the boat finally reached me, I leapt in and with some clumsy rocking about, got to the spare place at an oarlock, sharing the bench with Grythiss.

'This go better now. Stroke…Stoke…Stroke…' Sapentia called out the beats of our oars into the silver and blue surface of the water.

Looking around as I rowed, I studied the new avatars of my old friends. All Lizardmen appeared pretty similar to me, so with his dark-green reptilian skin and long crocodile face, Grythiss seemed much the same as he did in *Epic*. What was different, of course, was his gear. Because we hadn't much time or opportunity to trade or visit merchants, all of us were wearing only the armour that had dropped from defeated mobs. This meant for a very patchwork appearance. Grythiss wore a pair of iron greaves, a bronze Goblin breastplate and just one bronze Goblin armguard. His other slots were filled with leather armour, all sharing a similar design (patterns of circles and dots for decoration). This must have been the style of whatever mobs he had been fighting before joining us. On the ground beneath his feet was an iron longsword and a sturdy-looking circular shield, studded with metal bolts.

Directly in front of me – her back to me as she rowed – was Sapentia; she was a human female wizard and while I couldn't see her face, it would be plain enough. In fact, there was a good chance that she'd skipped all the customizable facial features and jumped straight into the game with whatever random looks she'd been given with the basic 11 Beauty. All Sapentia's start up attribute points and the ten points from her levelling up would have gone into Intelligence. There really wasn't much point spending them on another attribute. Unlike for clerics (and hunters) it was Intelligence, rather than Spirituality, that was proportional to the amount of spirit available to wizards for casting spells. And how effective she was basically came down to her spell set and the size of her spirit pool.

If she hadn't gone the random route, then Sapentia had chosen to have a dull red-coloured hair, which was tied up in a ponytail, part way down her back. As for her gear, it was again a miscellaneous collection of items. A dirty-white tunic, pale green skirt and old leather sandals. Down at her feet, though, in the shallow layer of water swilling around the bottom of the boat was a useful, gnarled and sturdy-looking staff.

At Sapentia's side was Braja, who had an impressive appearance for someone who'd started just a couple of hours ago. A strong-looking human, with short, sandy-coloured hair similar to his own, he wore a shiny bronze Goblin breastplate and greaves, with rusty iron armour on his other slots. I was amused to glimpse a long moustache, like an iron-age Gaul. Was that what he'd love to grow in real life?

'I don't suppose we have any magic items yet?' I wondered aloud.

Interrupting her timekeeping, Sapentia said, 'I had a *Potion of Healing*, but it's gone now.'

No one else spoke. Magic items were rare in *Epic* and were perhaps even rarer in *Epic* 2. It was with great fondness that I recalled looting my first magic sword in *Epic*. An orc chieftain deep in a burrow complex dropped it, about once per ten kills. Raitha and I had set up camp in the chieftain's cave and farmed him and his elite guards for hours until we both had the *+1 Longsword*. My, we had felt good afterwards, strutting around in the town like hardcore veterans of the game.

There was no talking now, not even Sapentia's calls: she hadn't resumed them after replying to me, as it was obvious that our rhythm remained steady even without her commands. Instead, we could listen to the cries of gulls, the creak of oars in rowlock and the slight grunt of Grythiss as he pulled hard.

Once past the protection of the headland, the waves became much more powerful and it was with some anxiety I felt the boat rock upwards and then fall downwards, plunging into the dark sea and sending salty spray across us all. Soon there was a distinct sloshing around our feet. Nor did the island, which hadn't seemed so far from the shore, appear to be drawing much closer. Could we all drown out here? That would set us back hours given how dispersed our respawn points were and there would be no question of retrieving the gear from the bodies (not a great loss, admittedly).

If anyone shared my concern, they didn't voice it and we continued to pull on through the sea, rising with each wave and falling heavily into the trough afterwards. It was enough to make you feel a bit queasy, even though the motion was only hinted at by the tracker pads and harness.

[Group] 'There's a shingle beach on the landward facing side that should do you. No mobs there at the moment, though there are some appealing dryads among the trees further up.' Raitha, of course, was high above us, scouting ahead.

Rowing on determinedly through the ups and downs of the sea, we reached a stack of scarred, grey sandstone, which marked the tip of the island and not long after passing it, the strength of the waves died away. We were in the lee of the wind now and it felt like we were dashing along as we rowed parallel to a rocky coastline. Even so, the sun was beginning to descend to the west (the celestial physics of *Epic* and *Epic* 2 were similar to those of Earth, except that the game worlds had two moons, which meant for much more variation in the tide) as we found the shallow water with the shingle beach.

Having landed on a rock nearby, Raitha turned a fierce, yellow-ringed eye towards us. [Group] 'Shall I pull those dryads? Two are level eight, one level nine.'

[Group] 'Please,' I responded and we set up: Grythiss half way up the beach ready to catch the aggro, the rest of us back at the boat.

[Group] 'Half-elf hunterssss care nothing for creaturess of the woodsss?'

[Group] 'It's all exp,' I replied. Poor Grythiss, he tried so hard to role play, but all he achieved was to provoke the rest of us into being extra cynical.

[Group] 'Incoming! A dryad.'

From the line of trees up ahead burst Raitha, swerving up into the skies above us. Not far behind her was a dryad, a tree spirit, dressed in bark-like armour, with wild silver hair and holding two long daggers; another one came up to join her and walking behind them, looking like the spirit of vengeance, came the third, unarmed but waving her hands around to cast a spell.

With a blood-curdling roar, Grythiss sent a rusty axe spinning towards the first two and it certainly got their attention: daggers raised high they leapt swiftly and dextrously over the rocks towards him. It was the other, even more fierce-looking one that concerned me. If I could shoot her with my arrows, I might be able to interrupt whatever spell it was she was casting.

You have fired an arrow at a Dryad Priestess and missed.

Raising up her arms the priestess's spell became a scream. 'By the power of root, light and water, I bind you.' And she threw her hands down in a gesture towards Grythiss.

[Group] 'What did she say?' asked Sapentia.

[Group] 'Oh, she was speaking in Dryad. How cool, I understood her. I must have that language. Something about binding Grythiss.'

And I could see the effect already: seaweed was crawling towards our lizardman as though a hundred dark green snakes were attacking him, already it had accumulated around his legs as high as his knees. This definitely would have an effect on his movement, but Grythiss seemed to have no problem swinging his longsword and also chopping down with the edge of his shield. It seemed to me that he had the upper hand against the two level 8 dryads, who were lashing at him with clawed hands, like branches whipping around in a storm.

You have fired an arrow at a Dryad Priestess and missed.

[Group] 'It will take me a while to get up to being a useful DPS class. I'm still at archery one.'

[Group] 'Don't fret,' responded Braja, who was casting small heals on Grythiss, 'that's why we are here. To grind up our exp and skills.'

As I notched another arrow, somewhat heartened by Braja's encouragement, Sapentia began to call out Latin-sounding words and sprinkling the air with dust. Incredibly, I actually felt the pressure around me increase, until with a huge bang, a bolt of lightning smashed down on the priestess, dropping our enemy's hit points by three quarters.

'Life is fleeting for mortals and I will shorten yours even further!' The level 9 dryad charged towards us, skirting Grythiss who obviously had been prevented by the seaweed from taking a step to intercept her.

Screaming, Raitha dived down at her shoulders, claws extended, while I drew a breath, held it, and released my next arrow at the heart of the priestess.

You have hit a Dryad Priestess for 4 points of damage.

You have increased the skill Archery (2).

As our enemy staggered on towards Sapentia, who I feared might be in danger from those flailing arms with their sharp fingers, Braja leapt forward and smashed down upon her shoulder with his rusty mace. A cracking sound, like a branch being snapped from a tree, and one arm was broken. The priestess fell to her knees, glaring at us and with thick pale blood pouring from her wounds. This did evoke in me a doubt. Maybe I shouldn't be killing dryads? Still, as I'd said to Grythiss, it was all exp.

Raising my bow, I shot the priestess in the chest again, the two arrows sticking out, side by side.

You have hit a Dryad Priestess for 6 points of damage.

You have increased the skill Archery (3).

The Dryad Priestess is dead. You gain experience.

Not bad exp either. About 10 per cent of what I needed for level 7.

[Group] 'Archery three,' I announced proudly.

[Group] 'Our enemiesss mussst be trembling.'

[Group] 'Oh, so Lizardmen can do sarcasm?'

[Group] 'Out of spirit.' Braja ran over to where Grythiss was still fighting and began smiting down on the two remaining Dryads. It seemed to me his clumsy-looking mace was ideal for these creatures, whose wooden skin absorbed the sharper blows of the longsword with no obvious sign of damage. When Braja hit them, however, splinters flew everywhere.

No more heals, but Grythiss was fine, one of the Dryads was nearly dead and then, with a tingle running through my body, I felt Sapentia charging up another spell even before I heard her chanting. *Bang!* Again, the lightning bolt fell and with it came the distinct smell of ozone and burned wood.

The Dryad is dead. You gain experience.

The Dryad is dead. You gain experience.

No sooner had Sapentia blown up one of our opponents than Grythiss had downed the other.

[Group] 'Stay here and restore your spirit, I'll find something.' Raitha beat his wings and climbed heavily into the air. Either side of me, Sapentia and Braja settled down to meditate, Sapentia with crossed legs in the lotus position, Braja on his knees, hands folded together.

[Group] 'Tyro, there isss sssomething here for you.' Further up the beach, our Shadow Knight had stepped back to give me room to examine the bodies. On one was a greave labelled 'barkskin' and on the other a barkskin armguard. Both were usable by hunters, both were light and they moved my armour on those slots up to 3 from 0. As an added bonus they looked good: so dark green as to be nearly black, they had a coarse texture of unpolished wood.

[Group] 'Thanks, I hope those Dryads respawn soon, I'd like to get a pair of each of these.'

Although we were protected by higher ground all around the beach and the edge of the forest beyond that, it was a windy day and clouds crossed rapidly overhead, bringing their shadows racing over the sand towards us. Every time this happened, I looked up anxiously, just in case it was some huge creature flying overhead. That was one of the aspects of playing a new game that kept you on your toes. You just didn't know what was in store.

In *Epic*, all the best camps had been worked so often that players knew to the second when the mobs would respawn and what their loot tables were. Here, we were exploring the unknown. The game had evolved so much from its initial conditions, the guides I'd read on the plane were already mostly out of date.

Raitha called out, [Group] 'Spirit check? Do we want a level twelve Griffon?'

[Group] 'Forty-three,' said Sapentia.

[Group] 'Seventy-seven,' added Braja.

I didn't hesitate. [Group] 'Pull.'

[Group] 'Incoming: a Griffon.'

Accompanied by the sound of a large creature forcing its way through the trees, my eagle friend flew from the canopy and very close behind, beating its wings furiously, was a large, grey-and-brown Griffon. Diving behind Grythiss for safety, Raitha laughed. [Group] 'Being an eagle is amazing.'

Even though Grythiss was only level 9, he still had an impressive ability to gain aggro. After a quick cast of some spell that left a trail of purple mist as it enveloped the griffon, our latest opponent swerved to crash upon our tank's shield (held up just in time). A flurry of beak and claw, accompanied by a painful screeching, was all I could see of the mob. Firing an arrow from here was hopeless, worse, I was more likely to hit Grythiss than the Griffon. So I ran past the fight, trusting Grythiss (if the Griffon chose to take me out, I wouldn't have lasted five seconds) and turning I found I had all of a long brown, feathered back to aim at.

You have fired an arrow at a Griffon and missed.

[Group] 'Doesss thisss beasst have ssspecial attacksss?'

[Group] 'Not that I'm aware of. Not in *Epic* anyway,' I answered, Raitha and I having fought dozens of Griffons on the Iron Mountain back in my gaming youth.

You have fired an arrow at a Griffon and missed.

Letting out a sigh, I notched my next arrow. Really, I needed a macro for this Archery skill, to fire as rapidly as possible. That thought, however, reminded me of the dice rolling cheat and I pushed it aside. By the time my next shot was ready, Raitha had joined the fight and the eagle flapping around the Griffon's head was a new obstacle to a clear shot.

Still, a move to my right and I had a pretty good line on the creature's rear left haunch.

You have hit a Griffon for 3 points of damage.

A flash of silver, a stunning peal of thunder and the Griffon was no more.

The Griffon is dead. You gain experience.

[Group] 'Twenty-three.'

[Group] 'Sixteen.'

These were the spirit reports from Sapentia and Braja respectively, who had immediately resumed their meditation poses once finished with casting their spells.

[Group] 'I'll go find another pull, but I'll wait until we are better prepared before bringing it.' Again, Raitha flew off over the tree line. It amused me to hear the eagerness in his voice. My old warrior friend was obviously relishing his new role as our scout and equally his new freedom to roam the skies.

'It's a shame you are so young in real life,' said Sapentia as we sat out the downtime. 'You're kinda cool otherwise.'

'Just kinda?'

'About seven out of ten.'

'Huh. I guess I need to work on that. Did you ever meet a ten?'

'Lizardman iss sssurely a ten.'

'I'll give you eight,' said Sapentia, 'it is cool how you stick to role play, whatever situation.'

'I'm afraid to ask for my score,' said Braja.

'Don't then.'

'Nah. I'll ask. How cool am I?'

'Honestly? I don't know. First impressions not good. A four maybe.'

'Four!' Braja laughed. 'Damn. Still, there was a "but" coming...right?'

'Hai. I think perhaps you smarter than you allow people to see. And if so, I will say six.'

'Six. That's okay.'

'Not yet six. Four. I think you are like typical Japanese man who puts head down, works hard, obeys manager and sees very little outside of route to and from his office.'

I laughed and then said, 'You have Braja all wrong, Sapentia. Do you think he'd be sitting with us now if he was like that?'

'Perhaps not. I hope you right. Because I feel this group is my family and Yuno Industries will soon try divide us.'

'Sister,' even in articulating that one word, I could hear that Braja was offended. 'You can mock my intellect and that's water off a duck's back to me. But don't ever question my loyalty to my comrades.'

'Lizardman isss also loyal to the core.'

'Hah, so. I apologise. Sincerely.'

'Apology accepted. Does that mean I get that six now?'

There was a pause. 'No.'

'Man, you are a tough one.'

Raitha came in on the group channel. [Group] 'Can I please get a spirit check and some advice. I've spotted a sea hag and her cave to the west of you. Should I pull her?

[Group] 'Seventy-eight.'

[Group] 'Ninety-two.'

Sapentia and Braja spoke at nearly the same time. Then there was silence and I realised everyone was waiting for me.

[Group] 'It's a risk. Assuming there isn't much of a change from the *Epic* sea hag, we will kill her in less than a minute. The problem is that anyone who looks directly into her face is stricken as though under a *Fear* spell and while in that condition she can kill you with her stare.

'I've fought one before as Tyro and just looked at her – shockingly ugly – feet the whole time. You'll take more hits than you should Grythiss, but I don't think you'll be in danger if you keep your vision directed downwards.

[Group] 'Lizardman isss ready then.'

[Group] 'Agreed,' added Braja, 'I don't have to look at her at all. I'll use my UI to monitor Grythiss and heal that way.'

[Group] 'Can you look at her back safely? asked Sapentia.

[Group] 'You can.'

[Group] 'How about you and I go behind dune and come out when Grythiss is sure of aggro?' she suggested.

[Group] 'Right.'

It was only a shallow dune that Sapentia had pointed to, so we had to lie down, side by side, to make sure we wouldn't be in view. There was something intimate about the moment. Should I raise my eyes to meet hers in the hope she felt it too?

[Group] 'The sea hag is out of the cave on the rocks again. Can I pull her?'

[Group] 'Pull!' I replied.

[Group] 'Incoming, a sea hag!'

Soon, I heard the angry shrieks of the sea hag coming towards us, from my right. More troll than human, with sharp claws and teeth, I could picture her long streaming hair like seaweed, blowing behind her as she chased the eagle. Not that I was going to peek to check.

The howls were close now and I saw from the group stats on my UI that Grythiss was being attacked. His hit points were going steadily down and Braja wasn't quite keeping up.

[Group] 'Lizardman hassss her attention.'

Even more swiftly than me, Sapentia sprang up and began casting (a *Lightning Bolt* from the feel of the air around me), while I raised my bow. From here, I could see the dark green leathery skin of a monster whose thick, knobbly backbone protruded in an ugly fashion. Able to see the side of her face – keeping my gaze away from the possibility of catching her eye – I felt a wave of nausea and fear. It was extraordinary how the game managed to transmit these effects.

You have hit a Sea Hag for 3 points of damage.

You have increased the skill Archery (4).

Bang! The *Lightning Bolt* hit at the same time. Either Sapentia had gone too early or the sea hag had some electricity resistance for she still had a quarter of her hit points and turned towards us, fixing me with her burning red eyes. Of course, I looked away at once, but not before a stab like that of a severe headache stung me between the eyes.

Beside me, Sapentia looked horrified and, dropping her staff, turned to run. Throwing myself into her, I managed to trip her up and although she was squirming vigorously and crying that we had to get away, I kept her flat, hoping that the sea hag could no longer see her potential victim.

The Sea Hag is dead. You gain experience.

Good experience too. I was nearly level 7. One more cycle of Dryads would bring me past the mark.

'You can let me up now,' Sapentia said in local chat.

'Right.' I stood up and brushed away some sand.

[Group] 'Nothing to ssshow for the fight.' Grythiss had bent over to loot the dead body.

[Group] 'Except a level five cleric,' replied Braja proudly and we all congratulated him.

[Group] 'I'll go check that cave while you restore your spirit levels,' I offered.

I'd noticed before that the vision of the half-elf was superior to being a human and this struck me again as I ducked below a shelf of rock and into a briny-smelling cave. Here, there was a sense of quiet. The sounds of waves and gulls had receded. It was not a big cave, not much bigger than my bedroom at home, with a damp, sandy floor; moss and limpets all over the walls; white fish bones strewn everywhere. It didn't take but a moment for my sight to adjust to the dark and I was fairly sure I could see into every dark crack of the cave walls.

Disappointingly, there was no treasure. If I were a sea hag living here, where would I have my valuables? Dig a hole in the sand? No, because during very high tides or storms, waves would run right up and into this cave, washing away everything on the ground. High up, then? Taking a step up on a convenient protrusion of rock, I looked carefully at the roof area.

And there it was! A natural shelf high off the ground, on which something glinted. The roughness of the cave walls meant I had no difficulty in climbing up and getting an arm onto the shelf and sweeping the contents towards me. The loot consisted of a dozen pearls and a simple silver belt buckle.

Curiously, the buckle showed no signs of wear but even in this very dim light, gleamed as new. I'd have to give it to Sapentia to examine.

[Group] 'My friend, are you safe in there?' asked Raitha.

[Group] 'All done. You can line up the next pull, I'm coming out. Twelve pearls and a silver belt or broach buckle that I think might be magic.'

[Group] 'Interesssting.'

[Group] 'Do wizards in *Epic Two* have the *Identify Magic* skill?' I asked.

[Group] 'They do. Mine, I apologise, is merely level two.'

[Group] 'On my way back to you.'

Outside of the cave, the day felt a lot brighter, even though clouds continued to move quickly overhead. Too quickly for comfort. Out at sea the wind had whipped up the waves to a point that their tops were cascading forward as white foam. Rowing back through those could be really difficult, especially in the unprotected channel between the island and the mainland.

Walking over to Sapentia, who was sat in the lotus position though attentive to me, I handed her the buckle.

After a moment, she looked up from the silver item and passed it back. [Group] 'Definitely magic. Other than that, I could not tell.'

[Group] 'Hurray,' said Braja, 'our first magic item. Shame we don't know what it does.'

[Group] 'I presume we must refit it to a belt,' offered Raitha, from wherever she was.

[Group] 'Using some kind of clothes-making skill?' I wondered aloud. 'Or magic item-crafting skill?'

No one answered and I could sense their shrugs.

[Group] 'Lizardman has belt.'

[Group] 'Well, let's dangle it from there for now, just in case that will allow the magic to work.'

Holding out his reptilian hand, Grythiss walked towards me and I passed the buckle to him. Sliding it on his belt, he studied himself, tried jumping up and down, swept his sword around and then grimaced. [Group] 'Lizardman feels no different.'

[Group] 'It might be a protection or resistance item of some sort?' I suggested, largely to address the downcast tone of his words.

Despite the fact he probably couldn't see me, Raitha backed me up. [Group] 'Perhaps it needs to be set properly in a belt and used in its own right.'

Grythiss handed me back the buckle.

'No, you take it,' I said.

'Lizardman thanksss you.'

With a screech, Raitha swept over the beach, not too far above our heard. [Group] 'Pop! Dryads. Are we ready?'

[Group] 'Ninety-one,' answered Braja.

[Group] 'Full,' Sapentia added.

[Group] 'Incoming! Three Dryads.'

For the next two hours, we settled into a fairly successful grind on the beach. The cluster of the three Dryads spawning every sixteen minutes formed the spine of our efforts between which we always fought at least one Griffon, sometimes two, and Raitha also found a Mantyger (level twelve, which was challenging, but its only weapons were claws) and a pair of Centaurs, who dropped bows and arrows.

Each time the Dryads cursed me accusingly and also when the Centaurs shouted in rage and dismay, I felt a twinge of remorse. If I were role-playing my character the way that Grythiss was, I would treat them as possible friends. Still, there were no 'faction' notices issued after the battles. In *Epic* you would sometimes see: *Your standing with x has improved/worsened.* In other words, my relationship with Dryads or Centaurs more generally was probably not affected. Probably, this was because we were on a remote island where no other members of their communities were witness to our repeated violence.

After seven Dryad spawns, I had a full set of barkskin armour for my limbs (no armour on my chest and back yet) and another complete set had been saved and shared around the group for when Raitha assumed half-elf form again. I'd also upgraded my bow to a *Finely Crafted Composite Short Bow*. Experience wise, the session had been fairly good: I was nearly 8; Raitha was 8; Braja 6; Grythiss 10 and Sapentia 11. If we could sustain a level about every ninety minutes, we'd be on target for 100 inside of two weeks of full-time play. The problem was, however, we'd need time to shift camps every so often as we outgrew the levels and therefore the experience reward of the mobs. And none of us were doing much to improve our non-combat skills or obtain useful gear. Raitha and I, for example, needed to obtain our first spells and learn how to cast them. With Safehaven destroyed (was it recovering now we'd cleared the Goblins?) we'd have to ask Sapentia to teleport us to a place with hunter trainers and merchants.

When thinking about moving camps, I looked anxiously at the sky, which had really darkened. Strong blasts of rain smote us intermittently, even in the relatively protected bowl of the beach. Out at sea the waves looked immense; they were dark grey except where their foamy heads toppled over.

[Group] 'Hold the pulls a sec, Raitha. I'm worried about the journey back. I'm not sure we can cross that sea safely.'

[Group] 'We need to be out of here before sunset and yet it looks like stormy weather is coming.' I could hear the concern in Braja's voice and I shared it.

[Group] 'Or we go vampire hunt.' This was Sapentia. 'We have couple of hours. If no way off the island, then we will log out sunset until sunrise or be killed.'

[Group] 'And miss hours of gaming,' I said heavily.

[Group] 'Exactly. Whereas if we can find coffin before the sun sets, we get nice exp and can keep go to fight.'

Raitha voiced his opinion, [Group] 'This appeals to me. I see his castle every time I fly up above the trees. And it is an enigma. Mute, yet appealing towards me to come and investigate. And there is this to consider too: by going to the castle we do not lose the option of camping out for the night if our time runs out.'

[Group] 'I'm not sure this is wise.' In fact, I was pretty sure it wasn't. 'If we are still there when the vampire wakes, we

128

haven't a chance. Much as fooling around in a vampire's castle while we have daylight appeals to me, I'd rather keep the grind going for two hours and camp if the weather isn't better. Grythiss, what do you think?'

[Group] 'Lizardman doesss not fear vampire.'

[Group] 'Yay. Good for you.' Sapentia cheered him loudly.

[Group] 'Braja?'

[Group] 'I have concerns about what else might be in the castle. Traps and that. On balance though, I'd rather try it than have to log out early for the night.'

[Group] 'All right then, we'll try it so. Let's hurry. Which way is the castle, Raitha?'

[Group] 'Follow me.'

And we all took off, running south-east away from the beach and up over a headland, until the group arrived at a rocky tip of the island. There, just off the edge of the island proper was the castle. If it was solitude you wanted, you could not ask for a more isolated, bleak and careworn residence. Connected to the green, moss-covered cliff by a slender drawbridge, a grey square tower rose out of surging, dark waves. It was as though the sea were an evil monster, licking and slurping at a long, discoloured fang. With only narrow arrow slits for windows, the tower rose some hundred feet or so to a crenelated roof. From the top of the tower, a torn flag stretched out in the stormy winds, falling off then snapping tight again as the wind gusted. The emblem on the flag was a black raven against a scarlet background.

Raitha circled around the top of the tower and then – making me a little anxious – landed on one of the crenellations. [Group] 'Once I was playing a pen and paper fantasy RPG and our referee had spent hours constructing a long dungeon crawl, only for us to use a spell that allowed us to teleport right into the final room.'

[Group] 'I hear you,' said Braja, putting his hand up to shade his eyes. 'You think we should get in at the top.'

Raitha responded, [Group] 'Is this a possibility? For the rest of you to come up here? There is a door, of course, although whether we can force it is unclear.'

[Group] 'I don't think we can, unless Sapentia has a suitable spell. We don't even have rope, do we?' I turned to look at our wizard and was struck by the contrast between her dull, uninteresting avatar (expressionless, heavy face, practical, unadorned clothes) and the real woman we had met earlier.

[Group] 'Apologies. No way up. But I can *Fireball* any doors in our path and blow them away.'

[Group] 'In that case I shall come down and resume my half-elven body. An eagle is not a suitable form for indoor fighting.'

[Group] 'Good idea,' I said.

With a flurry of his large wings, Raitha landed beside us and, after a moment in which she stared at me with her fierce yellow-ringed eye, she began to transform: wings becoming slender, outstretched hands; cruel beak a gentle face; body lengthening to become a female version of my own. Once equipped with the barkskin armour and bow we had been saving for her, she looked great (as great as a Beauty 11 character can look) and we were ready to go.

First across the narrow stone bridge was Grythiss. [Group] 'Don't look down,' he said.

Naturally, I did. It was a dramatic view: a drop of about thirty metres (survivable if you missed the rocks) to a sea seething against the foot of the cliff and generating long pale streaks of foam in the aftermath of the crash of near-black waves over barely submerged rocks. On the far side of the bridge was an arched, heavy wooden door with black iron studs in it. We gathered in front of it.

[Group] 'Does anyone else think this is reckless?' I asked. 'It's not too late to call it off.'

[Group] 'You kid us.' Sapentia laughed.

I chuckled too. [Group] 'You're right. We're going in. How do we get the door open though?'

Grasping one of the two large iron handles, Grythiss grunted as he turned it and pushed at the door. To my surprise it opened and with a big lizardy grin, Grythiss gestured us inside.

[Group] 'Almost as if he wants visitors,' muttered Braja.

Chapter 12
The Vampire's Tower

A carpet (lush and red) dampened the sounds of our group as we made our way into the tower. At the far end of the corridor was a narrow arrow slit, which let in plenty of light as far as I was concerned, but the humans among us seemed to find the castle dark, for Sapentia lit an oil lantern and held it high, causing our distorted shadows to stretch and recede along the bare, stone walls as it swung back and forth. Probably, all of us felt tense as there was none of the usual light-hearted banter.

[Group] 'Look up.' Braja pointed to the ceiling where there was a dark hole I had walked right underneath as I'd entered the building. It was narrow, like a chimney.

[Group] 'What's that?' I asked.

[Group] 'Murder hole. Isss where our enemiesss drop boiling oil on our heads.'

[Group] 'Lovely,' said Raitha in a mutter.

[Group] 'Fortunately, there doesn't seem to be anyone up there.' Braja had borrowed the lantern and was doing his best to peer up the shaft. With a shrug, he stepped away.

We had a choice of four doors, two on each side of the corridor. Grythiss had his reptilian hand on the bronze handle of the nearest. [Group] 'Ready?'

[Group] 'Go for it.' The truth was, I wasn't really all that prepared. A hunter fights best outdoors, not in the narrow corridors of a castle. At this point I should be readying a sword and a spell or two. I had neither, so with an arrow held against the limb of my bow, I peered over our tank's shoulder.

The room beyond was surprisingly large, taking up more than a quarter of the castle. There was light from two arrow loopholes and also from a lit fire. So I could see the man standing looking at us with an expression of surprise. Tall, balding, his clothes included a fine, shining waistcoat with a complex green and yellow pattern for its silk lining. It was hard to tell what character class he was, if, indeed he had a class. Perhaps a wizard.

'Goodness me,' he exclaimed, 'visitors! Do come in. Have a glass of wine.'

One arm extended, he gestured to the seats, which were delicate creations of entwined, pale wood. Or was that bone? From a glass cabinet, he took a bottle of wine and gave us what I thought was a very insincere smile.

Taking three decisive steps into the room, Grythiss brought his iron longsword down with a sweeping blow to the man's head.

'Help! Help!' Staggering, our host glanced towards the fireplace.

'Do you think this is best?' I asked Grythiss. 'I don't know about you, but I was brought up to be more polite when someone offers me a drink. Shouldn't we talk to him?'

'Help! Yes! Polite. Be polite!'

With just a grunt by way of reply, Grythiss kept on smashing into the man, whose life bar was down to half. This was surprisingly high considering the unanswered damage he was taking. As I was getting no data from having targeted our opponent, I had no other way to judge the difficulty of this encounter.

'No one worth talking to lives in castle of vampire,' observed Sapentia from behind me.

'Agreed,' added Braja, 'now step out the way, let me come in with my mace.'

Moving to the fireplace while the two of them struck again and again on the seemingly defenceless man, I studied the mantelpiece (two silver candleholders with melted candles stood on it; between them a painting of a stormy sea). Why had he looked this way?

The doppelganger is dead.

You have gained experience.

If lizards could look satisfied, then this one did. As I moved my gaze from Grythiss to the dead man on the floor I saw he was changing shape, his clothes melting into a grey humanoid figure that was a lot like a shop floor mannequin.

'Aha,' said Sapentia, with a cry that expressed the fact that she was right. 'A doppelganger!'

'Good call.' I had to concede the "punch first, ask questions afterwards" technique was correct. Doppelgangers could be extremely dangerous. They obtained an assassination attempt on a character whose appearance they had adopted. If we'd let this one chat to us, at some point when unobserved it would have transformed and tried to replace a party member by assassinating one of us. Then it would have worked its way through the party.

'Any treasure?' asked Braja.

'Nothing.' Sapentia had bent down over the corpse.

'Did anyone else notice he looked over here when shouting for help?' I asked.

'I couldn't see much at all, you were all in the way,' Braja complained.

Stepping over the body, Raitha came to assist me as I looked all around for a mechanism that could open a secret door. Of course I lifted up the silver candlesticks (and put them into my inventory to sell in the future) in case they were in fact levers of some sort. After pushing, pulling, rubbing my fingers over the wallpaper and around the frames of the painting, I hadn't discovered anything. By contrast, Raitha had ducked into the wide fireplace and immediately cried out: 'Eureka!'

'What is it?'

'An alcove with rungs going upwards. I'm going to climb them.'

'Take care.' There was nothing more practical I could say. Hunters could get some relevant skills for this situation, but we were really supposed to be climbing and tracking in the outdoors.

'Lizard go next.' Grythiss pushed past me and pausing, confused for a moment, looked at the fire. Then he looked up. 'Which wayssss?'

'Examine the left wall, she disappeared into a space there somewhere.'

'Thank you.'

It was amusing that our tank, who had been so brutal to the stranger a few minutes ago, was so polite to me.

'You're welcome.'

'Well, I suppose I should go up next, in case there's healing needed further up.' Now Braja came through, ducking into the fireplace, his light hair catching the brightness of the flames like it was gold.

'And it makes sense for you to guard rear.' Sapentia wanted to follow the others up too. Handing me her large staff, she reached upwards, then turned around surprised.

I had put a hand on her shoulder and pulled her back. 'If there's a trap and they all come tumbling down, I'd rather two of us were uninjured.'

Her human avatar gave a surprisingly authentic shrug, that suggested while I had a point, it was unlikely remaining with me would make any difference. Remain she did though.

[Group] 'I'm up,' came Raitha's soft voice. 'It's a library.'

[Group] 'On my way!' Sapentia had real excitement in her voice and I wasn't surprised. Accumulating a wide-ranging set of spells was essential yet hard for wizards and sorcerers, and if there was any place you might find new ones for your repertoire then surely a vampire's castle was one of them?

For a moment I was alone in the room, my flickering shadow stretching across to the far wall; red and orange light cast by the flames giving the furnishings a warm tinge. Wouldn't it be great to own a castle like this? Full of secret passages and mysteries. It was a shame that even if we found and killed the vampire, we couldn't make this place our base (with each of us having a bedroom and hanging out together in rooms like this one). The problem would be that all the creatures who spawned here would respawn, probably even the vampire himself. Based on how *Epic* worked, gaining possession of property free from respawning mobs was a question of real-life money or completing very rare quests.

Turning my attention to the fireplace, once I knew where to look, I could see the opening: it was a black rectangle in the brickwork surrounding the fire. Bending, nearly crawling, into the shadows, I found I could stand up and see light some five metres up. The feeble, slightly erratic light of Sapentia's torch somewhere on the floor above was creating a square of pale yellow above my head. In the walls, firm iron bars allowed me strong handhold and even with the burden of Sapentia's staff, I climbed easily up to join the others.

As I looked around the room, again I had the sensation that this would be a fantastic place to own. As a half-elf hunter, I mean. Outside the game, I had respect for public libraries and no desire for one of my own. In truth, I didn't read much beyond what I had to for school. My preference being for graphic novels, which hardly counted as reading. The room was a poorly lit (just one arrow slit to the outside world) hexagon shape with bookcases from floor to ceiling on every wall. They were all filled with books encased in dark blue bindings. Picking one at random, I found the letters strange at first; then, they shuffled and reformed into English.

...Mordred laughed: thus do magpies stutter with delight upon stealing; thus do rogues find humour in mocking the man who has entered their domain with no hope of protection from royal authority; thus does the hangman chuckle when the crowd call to him to begin his work. It was cruel, that laughter and I knew at once there was no hope for me...

Lovely. I supposed it might appeal to a vampire. Were all the books like this?

It was strange how the group responded to the library. Taking a random selection of volumes with me, I settled into one of the two, high-backed, midnight velvet chairs. Opposite me, in the only other chair in the room, Braja was doing the same, a huge pile of books beside him. His feet were up on the small table between us.

By contrast, Sapentia was stood before one wall, rapidly taking books down, scanning their contents and throwing them aside, creating a scattered pile on the (intricately designed) carpet. Something inside me winced. Of course, it was efficient of her. Yet I felt it was wrong to harm these books and upset the calm, reflective atmosphere of the room.

Cross-legged, back to another shelf, Grythiss had set his longsword down and was staring intently at a large book with vivid illustrations. Opposite him Raitha was looking out of the one, thin, window. When she blocked the light, I noticed my enhanced vision came over me like a camera automatically adjusting to a change in brightness. For a while there was silence, or rather, no conversation. There was the guzzling sound of the oil lamp; the soft whisper of a page turning and the occasional much louder thump of one of Sapentia's books hitting the carpet.

'We must consider the descent of the sun,' observed Raitha. 'While I appreciate a good book as much as anyone, it would be better to find the vampire first and kill him, then return here.'

'Itss's incredible. Lizardman wonderss who wrote all these books.'

That was a good point. Surely not the game's developers. There was far too much content here for a human team to have generated it. Were they simply scanned versions of real-world books? I asked this aloud.

'I haven't recognised any,' said Braja in response, which caused Sapentia to make a scoffing sound.

'What?' He turned to her, seemingly aggrieved, although I knew him well enough to know this tone was probably something of an act.

She paused in her search for spells. 'How would you know?'

'Oh, now you've let it out. You think I'm a man of little culture. Right?'

'Of certain kind of culture.'

'One that isn't familiar with books?'

She shrugged.

'You should understand something about the army.' Braja closed the book he was reading and stood up. 'Mostly, it's a lot of waiting around. It's very boring for weeks, months even. And then for a few minutes you get shot at. Different soldiers fill that waiting time differently. I read books. Every kind of book. Whatever the others had brought and left around. Romance, history, thrillers, fantasy, biography, sport. Everything.'

'Okay, sorry,' said Sapentia and went back to her task, abruptly, as if letting him know she didn't care whether he was erudite or not.

'Do you have a favourite book?' I asked, slightly uneasy. Probably the two of them sparring was just a bit of play. Possibly, though, there was a real dislike growing between them and of course I didn't want anything to weaken the group.

'What's the one with the captain with the obsession for the whale?'

'You don't know title for *Moby Dick*?' Sapentia was incredulous. 'Wait, do you tease us?'

'Then there was this one about a farmer in Iceland. He was so stubborn: wouldn't let women change him; wouldn't let big business buy him out.'

Grythiss looked up, interested. 'Halldór Laxness wrote that.'

'Probably. I'm not very good at remembering the authors' names.'

These author names didn't matter to me either, I never read the books that people recommended to me. Only if I couldn't log in to *Epic* might I read. Say if Mum and I were on the bus into town. For some reason, however, I was really fascinated by the current one I'd picked out randomly and still held in my hand.

After a while, I said, 'I think we should be pushing on. What time is it?'

'Let me just finish shelf,' replied Sapentia, 'then I'll know what more I have to check.'

What was it that was wrong? So many books on the floor, so little progress made by Sapentia along the shelf? I looked up from my book to remark on this to Raitha, who was staring out of the window as though entranced. There was something wrong too about the sky against which she was silhouetted. It should have been pale, a light grey colour, not a dark sky with a touch of crimson. A sense of alarm surged up in me, but almost at once it was quelled by the interesting lines in the book I held.

'Life,' declaimed Mordred, immediately attracting the attention of the whole room. 'Life. We have all seen how determinedly even the smallest creature will cling to its existence. A wretched insect, injured, strength failing, will summon up the energy to try to move itself to safety. After a flurry of its tiny wings or frenzied twitching of its legs it will cease its activity, seemingly exhausted.' As he spoke, Mordred strolled among the guests, sometimes pausing, as he did now beside the Countess of Lake Sorrow. 'And yet, when you touch the poor insect, it will rally again and do all it can to escape.

'Mortals, on the whole, have the same determination to avoid death. On the whole, I say, because there are some who are entirely careless about death. Perhaps because their own life is so wearing that it would be a relief to cease to exist. Or perhaps because they have reason to believe in a form of afterlife. Not heaven or hell. No, I mean something else.' With a bow, Mordred left the countess and continued his meandering walk. 'I mean, as an undead.'

'Who are you to kill my guests and ransack my home? Nothing but weaklings and fools who deserve the hammer that will now fall upon you.'

Standing in the frame of the library door was a vampire. There was no doubt about that. My shock, however, was twofold. Firstly, far, far more time had passed than I'd realised and secondly, the creature was a human woman (attractive, in an expensive, aristocratic fashion, providing you weren't too put off by the visible incisors and red eyes). Long, auburn hair; dark green leather waistcoat over a ruffed white blouse; black trousers; thigh-high shining black boots.

[Group] 'Damn! We're in deep trouble, what do we do?' exclaimed Braja. 'We can't kill her now she's up and about.'

[Group] 'As soon as I say strawberry, log out and wait until daytime to come back. I'll stall her.'

[Group] 'Strawberry?' There was almost a laugh in Sapentia's voice, despite the crisis that was upon us.

[Group] 'I picked something that I wouldn't say by accident. Now, hush in group chat please. Let's concentrate.'

'Hello, I'm Klyto, what's your name?'

Taking a step into the room, the vampire looked at me scornfully. 'You must know that you are in the castle of Lady Cruoris.'

I bowed low. By now, we'd have all appraised her and seen that she was *impossible*. From what I recalled from reading the guide, she was level 70. 'Lady Cruoris, please forgive us. We are ambassadors from Mikarkathat with an important message for you.'

'The blue dragon? I don't believe you.' The muscles of her powerful jaws visibly flexed and her face, which had been handsome, became more animal-like. 'You've killed my guest and ransacked my library. No manner of ambassador behaves thus and the dragon would not send humans and half-elves to do her bidding.' Now the vampire laughed, but with scorn, not humour. 'She'd eat them.'

'Your guest was a doppelganger who took too much interest in us and your library is enchanted.' I spoke hurriedly, but I could see it was no use, the vampire was looking appraisingly around the room with nothing but malice in her eyes, clearly planning to launch herself on us and deciding which of us to attack first.

'Strawberry.'

'What?' The vampire raised her left hand, nails like claws. 'What did you say?'

'Strawberry.' Curiously, I had a sudden memory of two older lads from the rival St Declan's school back home in

Dublin. They had been shouting at me from the other side of the street and although I put my head down and walked fast, they kept pace and I sensed that when traffic permitted, they would come over and start a fight. Saying nothing is usually the best way to handle grief on the streets, this time though, in response to their call of 'wibble arse' (don't ask me why), I had shouted 'pandas!' at the top of my voice (I can explain that one, a bin company lorry, branded with a panda, had just driven past). For some reason, that bizarre cry meant they immediately lost interest in me. Shame that didn't work here. In fact, the inappropriateness of my speech seemed only to make the vampire's rage more intense.

'In a moment I shall butcher you all and feed upon your blood. Can any of you give a reason why he or she should be spared?'

With a wave at the shelves I hurriedly asked, 'How many times have you read these books?'

Again, my response led to a flare up of anger and a feral expression as she showed me her fangs. With a brief shake of her head, Lady Cruoris growled, 'Many times. The life of a vampire is long.'

'Quite. Well, I'm excellent company and I know hundreds of stories you've never read. *The Lion, the Witch and the Wardrobe*; *The Name of the Rose*; *Jonathan Strange and Mr Norrell...*' I was babbling and I knew it. I just needed her to wait a few seconds more.

'And he's great in bed too! You should spare him and keep him as your lover,' cried Braja.

[Group] 'Ten…nine…eight…' Braja was counting down the seconds until he was unclipped. 'I'm nearly out. Good job Tyro, I hope you make it too.' That was Braja also.

'What impertinence. You shall be the first to die!'

It was quite terrifying having an angry vampire spring for my throat. Even though I knew I was in a game and that my real body was safe, I flinched and cowered. My efforts to block her leap with my arms must have seemed pathetic to her. Feral and immensely strong, she straddled me, pinning me down as I writhed. With one last view of her fearsome incisors, all went black.

You have been knocked unconscious by a vampire. You cannot see, hear, move or communicate. You have been bitten by a vampire for 26 damage.

[Group] 'Anyone still there?' I asked, hoping no one would respond and was pleased that this was indeed the case. Good, my team had all gotten out. My death wouldn't be too much of a setback. In fact, the gear I had on my body was so low level, I might be better off asking them to join me on the mainland and just leave my body here. Speaking of my body, it was odd that I hadn't received the same message as on my previous death.

For a while, I waited in darkness for the vampire to finish me off. Then, presumably, I'd respawn. After a few minutes though, I got bored. Perhaps the vampire was saving me for a later feed, like a spider would its prey. If so, she'd be disappointed. I selected Log Out from my UI and yes, I was sure. Thirty seconds later I was back in the real world. And for once it was more colourful and interesting than the game.

'Did you get out in time?' Raitha asked me. The whole group was gathered around, looking at me hopefully.

'Maybe. I was knocked unconscious but I didn't get a death message.'

'How long to dawn in the game?' asked Braja.

It was Grythiss who answered, with such immediacy it was clear he'd already thought about this. 'Ten hours.'

'Well.' Sapentia put her hands on her hips. 'Downtime. What shall we do?'

Sweeping back his fringe, we got a rare look at the full, pale-moon coloured face of Grythiss. 'I shall catch up with my emails and with sleep.'

'Good idea.' I could ring Mum, just to let her know everything was fine.

'What I would like to do,' said Raitha shyly, 'is play street chess. I believe it's Fifth and Market where the best players are.'

A huge grin crossed Sapentia's face. 'What are you all? I came here thinking you were very cool. Tough guys. Hammer the mobs, be brave. He'—she pointed at me—'is just kid. You'—Raitha—'should be in episode of *Techlicious* and you'—Grythiss—'make meditation class look like wild party. Come on. We are in San Francisco, we have few hours where we can't work. Let's enjoy ourselves.' Sapentia glanced down at her outfit, pulled at the bottom of her bodice to straighten it and then looked up again decisively. '*Two Fat DJs* are playing tonight in Ladybird. I take you all. Meet me in lobby at eleven.'

When all four of us began to murmur our dissent, she shut us up with a sweep of her arm. 'No! You come out. Now I must go get ready.' And Sapentia strode away, her boots clacking determinedly on the hard floor.

Braja rubbed his thumb across his moustache. 'We don't have to go. Maybe it would be good for her to see we can't be bossed around.'

'Sapentia is very insightful.' Raitha smiled. 'I would actually like to be in an episode of *Techlicious*.'

'She's right too,' I said, thinking of how cool it would be if I came back to Cabra and let it be known I'd gone clubbing in the Ladybird. 'We should go out, get some experiences that we couldn't get at home.'

'I hate nightclubs,' said Grythiss. 'They are too loud. I cannot speak.'

You don't say a lot anyway though, do you?' observed Braja giving him affectionate slap on his shoulder.

'Very well,' Raitha said, 'if Tyro wants to go, I shall come. For me, such music is not to my taste. Instead, it will be a matter of sociology. An opportunity to study another youth culture.'

Catching my eye, Braja shook his head in an expression of amused disbelief, but he didn't say anything.

CHAPTER 13
AWOL

I was pleasantly surprised by Club Ladybird. On the outside it had the usual queues of young people, cold in their clubbing clothes, waiting alongside a grimy wall for a smartly dressed bouncer to check their ID (thanks to some Sapentia magic involving us posing as reviewers for various magazines, we were swept in). Inside, however, it was very different to the interior of the clubs I'd seen (all two of them). Here, the venue had the feel of a church, the main room being long and rectangular, with a stage at the far end. The impression of it having a sense of history was reinforced by the large wooden panels of the walls, which were all much scarred. There was a second level and dozens of balconies protruded above us, with fragments of golden paintwork on their exterior.

The balconies were comfortable hang-outs. I knew that, because Sapentia, looking absolutely amazing (purple *Two Fat DJs* tank top, that stopped above a studded belly button; short skirt, glittering with turquoise and light blue patches; purple-and-white striped stockings up to her thighs; white shiny boots; hair hidden beneath a purple wig that cascaded ringlets down her back) steered us through the crowds and upstairs to one that had a 'reserved' sign on the table. Plush, red velvet seats in a semi-circle around a table.

'This is base.' She had to raise her voice over the heavy beats of the first DJ. 'Come back here if you need break and also final end; we'll share cab. I'm going to see friends, do some dancing. Meet you here later.' A final glance at me from her beautiful eyes, made up with thick black eye shadow and she turned away.

A sharp pang of disappointment struck me as Sapentia left, one that must have been evident to Braja, because he leaned in and said, 'She's not your type. And she's too old for you.'

'What is my type?' I replied, annoyed.

'Whatever it is, it ain't her.' And then, seeing as I wasn't laughing, Braja turned to the others. 'I'll get a round of drinks. Beer for everyone?'

Raitha nodded.

'Pernod and black,' said Grythiss, who had sprawled out across the seats. With his heavy boots and baggy black clothes, I very much doubted he had any intention of dancing.

'Pernod and sodding black?' repeated Braja incredulously. 'What kind of drink is that?'

With a rather reptilian gesture (or was that me being so used to his avatar?), Grythiss ran his tongue across his lips. 'A good one.'

'If they don't have it, you're getting a beer, OK?'

Grythiss shrugged.

'Surely, you are too young to drink?' asked Raitha, coming away from the balcony to sit beside me.

'Officially, yes. But where I'm from, we start about fifteen.'

'In Kerala, youth drinking is not so common. For an event like this'—he gestured to the room below—'hardly anyone will drink alcohol. Rather, they will be focused on the music.'

Not that Raitha (or Grythiss) showed any sign of being interested in the trance music that was pulsing through the venue. I, on the other hand, found myself nodding my head and waving my foot from side to side as though conducting the bassline. Maybe I should go downstairs for a dance soon? Even if that meant going alone. I decided to wait for the beer, mostly so as Braja wouldn't be disappointed to have bought me one but to have found I'd left.

We didn't wait long and after he'd returned and set down his tray (three beer bottles and one tumbler with a purple liquid in it), I commented on the fact he was so quick.

145

'Used to be you'd spend half the night queuing at the bars in a place like this. Now though, the kids are all taking E or speed and don't want to dull the buzz with booze.'

'Is there much drug use going on here, do you think?' Raitha stared earnestly up at Braja.

'Oh, my lord yes. I'd say everyone but us is on something, just look.'

'What am I looking for?'

'Zombie faces.'

After watching the crowd below us for several minutes, Raitha sank back into his share of the couch. 'No, I don't really see it. Their faces look normal, happier than usual perhaps.'

'If you could get close enough to see their eyes, that's the real giveaway. Totally expanded. Huge black circles.' Braja was already halfway through his beer and I took a long swig to keep up.

Overhead, the lightshow was sweeping to and fro with excited movements that kept pace with the fast beat of the trance music being played. The volume made conversation difficult so for a while I leaned back and watched the lights play on my friends as though I was viewing them through purple, red, green and blue filters.

Leaning into Raitha, Braja was asking him something about sociology and while Raitha seemed to be replying with great earnestness, Braja's eyes were sparkling with good humour.

Grythiss stood up, towering over us. 'I get more drinks.'

Our tank returned with a tray on which there were three bottles of beer and four glasses of pernod and black.

'There is no way I'm drinking one of those,' shouted Braja, sounding almost gleeful.

'Correct.' Grythiss leaned down to make sure we heard him, black fringe falling forward. 'These are for me.'

Wondering where Sapentia was, I studied the crowd below. The venue was full now and enthusiastic cheers greeted the crescendos in the music. Deciding to go down and join in the dancing, I hurriedly finished my bottle and left. 'Going for a dance!' I called out.

Both Raitha and Braja looked surprised, but neither came with me. That was fine, I wanted to absorb the feeling of the place and, truth be told, find Sapentia to dance with her.

Considering how busy the place was, it was surprisingly easy to make my way through the dancers to somewhere in the middle of the floor. After a while of looking around and catching the eye of strangers (who invariably smiled at me), I gave up and settled in place, enjoying the music. I knew I wasn't much of a dancer, but really, not much effort was needed to respond to this beat. I let my hands trace the cascades of keyboard notes while the rest of me followed the bass drum. Easy. Fun too.

Before coming out, I had wondered about my clothes. All I had brought from Ireland were T-shirts and jeans and my old, warm, navy hoody. If I had wanted to make an effort, I'd have had to have bought something new. But there wasn't time and, in any case, it wouldn't have been worth it. Most people here were dressed pretty casually, although casual in a way that made Grythiss stand out. His dark, heavy clothes were too thick and too sombre in comparison to the light, cheerful designs all around me.

Curiously, being surrounded by people, bathed in swirling lights, inhaling fragrant scents and listening to music so loud I could feel the reverberations in my chest was good for thinking. And what I mainly thought was that I was happy. The grief with Blackridge and the hostility I was getting from some of the other players didn't really matter. Here I was, earning great money for a job that didn't feel like work at all. It felt like an adventure. And I still liked my online friends after meeting them in person. In fact, I liked them even more.

I lost track of time but at last, a good while after the two fat DJs (whoever they were) had taken over, I made my way back to our balcony. Only Raitha was there and he looked up with sadness in his dark brown eyes.

'Are you OK?' I shouted across to him.

'Please look down there, left of the stage about four rows back.'

'What am I…oh.' Astonishingly, Braja was holding Sapentia tight and her arms were around his neck. 'That makes no sense, I thought they didn't like each other.'

'My friend, very much makes sense.' Raitha leaned in close so I could hear him over the music. 'She came here looking for an alpha male who was different to the men she knew in Japan. She was hoping it would be you, but you are too young. I am no alpha male. Grythiss is…well, unattractive, I don't mean to be rude, he's an impressively dogged role player. Braja, on the other hand, is very interesting and most certainly tough.'

'I suppose so.' Had I really hoped to be in the position Braja was in now? Was it ever a possibility? I was a fool if I had believed in something so out of reach. 'And why does he like her? He thinks she's too bossy and shows off too much.'

With that Raitha smiled again, his teeth glowing indigo in the club's UV lights. 'Ah, Braja protested too much, as Shakespeare put it. It is clear now that he was as impressed by her as were we all. And with Braja, there is something else. He is very conscious of being from the working class, which is a matter of pride for him. He wants to taste everything that the middle class enjoy to confirm his belief it is all shallow rubbish. This does not bode well for Sapentia.'

'Oh well. Shall we leave? Get a cab back to our hotels? Get some sleep before a long grind tomorrow?'

'Probably we should, but I think that it would be wise to try to get Grythiss to come with us. He is drunk.'

'Where is he?'

'Leering at American girls. If you look over by the far wall, just right of the middle, you'll see him easily. Not many of the other dancers are so tall or so black.'

As the swirling crimson and purple lights raced over the crowd, I could indeed see Grythiss, facing away from the stage and standing in front of a young woman whose compact dancing gave an impression of self-assuredness. It was hard to see her expression, but I couldn't imagine that the clumsy lurches of Grythiss - whose dark head bent down over her chest from time to time - were likely to make a favourable impression.

'I have an observation about Grythiss's behaviour that I would like to share, may I?' Raitha leaned in, so as not to have to shout.

'Sure.'

'All of us have hidden drives. I believe it very important to understand this and to be self-aware about this.'

Since his pause required a response, I nodded.

'With alcohol taken, we often see these drives, on the surface.'

'Hah! Yes, I see what you mean.'

'Exactly. Now we see lust in Grythiss that normally he restrains. This brings me to a question I think is important. Do we know Blackridge and Watson? Do we understand their drives?'

This was an unexpected but interesting question and I glanced into Raitha's earnest face before replying, 'I would say that Blackridge is like my worst teacher. He thinks he is very important and what drives him is a desire to be worshiped.'

'I agree. You put it very well. And this is why he is troubled by you. And, indeed, by all of our group.'

'Watson. I have no idea.'

'Nor do I. Do you share my belief, however, that Watson is very self-aware and that he is less genial and more purposeful than the impression he gives?'

Again, I paused. 'When I first saw him, stood in front of my class, I thought he was soft and would be slaughtered. But he did OK. When he offered me this job, I liked him.'

'And now?'

'After what Sapentia said I've become a bit paranoid. I can't say. I think I still like him. He's honest.'

'I don't like him and I don't know if he's honest.'

'What about me?' All of a sudden, I felt anxious for the good opinion of my best friend, as though it were in doubt. 'What are my hidden drives?'

'Hah!' Raitha laughed. 'You are like Blackridge, you want to be worshipped.'

'No way!' I felt indignant.

'You are seventeen. For a person of seventeen to want to be a god is a good thing. It means you will not be put on a railroad and sent to your future by other people. For Blackridge it means crushing the independence of others and especially in those who can show up his shortcomings.'

'I'm not at all like him.'

'You misunderstand me.' Raitha placed his hand gently on my arm. 'In India we are less black and white. A trait is not always bad, nor always good. You, I admire very, very much. You listen to good advice and take it, because for you, success for everyone is more important than being the star of the show. Blackridge, I fear, would risk failure rather than concede he does not know best.'

'I can see that.' For a moment, I leaned back into my seat, away from the strain of trying to hear Raitha. Then I tipped back towards him. 'And I like you too, by the way. Though I have no idea what drives you.'

'Oh, just the usual. The desire to be loved.'

Dawn the following morning was a challenge. I'd only had two bottles of beer and had left the club relatively early with Raitha and a very reluctant but ultimately persuadable Grythiss. Still, I hated the sound of my alarm and I felt a distinct tightness around my head as I struggled to get up and silence it. If I was feeling rough, what was Braja experiencing right now? Or, heaven help him, Grythiss?

It was with some surprise, then, that I saw them both standing at the map when I came into the campaign room. There was a distinctly subdued atmosphere in the chamber, one that was not simply due to the fewer number of players who were around at this early hour. People were talking in whispers and the look on their faces was concern. It was the elderly Katherine who was on duty and I came over to her, giving my two group members a nod first.

'What's up?'

'Hello Tyro.' She gestured towards the map. 'An army of dark elves led by the General of Bow and the General of Sword

150

in alliance with a black dragon have conquered Fort Hells-mouth.'

'Wow.'

'Unfortunately, our best characters had their spawn points in and around the city. They can't get into the game any more. Check the board, the trapped players are in red.'

'Jeez Louise.' The highest-level player left in the game, the first green name on the board, was a rogue who was only at 23.

Perhaps surprised at my form of words, Katherine raised an eyebrow and gave me something of a tired smile.

'We've alerted Paul - Mr Blackridge - and he's on his way in. He's asked me to contact everyone for a meeting this afternoon at two. I believe he plans to raid to reclaim the spawn points long enough for our players to clip up and get out of there.'

'That worked for us.' And I explained how we cleared Bra-ja's starting location of goblins so that he could join us.

Shaking her head, Katherine sighed. 'This is a whole differ-ent league than goblins. It's worth a try but the best we can do is draw the mobs away. There's no way we can clear them. The Generals and their bodyguards are all a hundred plus.'

'We have some tricks that might help, but we're a long way off.'

'Better get going then. I'll have someone send you a mes-sage in-game with any news.'

Before I went to find a set, I walked around the board to a very pale-looking Grythiss and a cheerful Braja.

'How are you feeling?' I asked Grythiss.

'Terrible.'

'Heroic performance last night, my friend.' Braja slapped Grythiss on the back then turned to me. 'Fourteen pernod and blacks.'

'Incredible. And expensive,' I murmured.

'It was cheap compared to home. Too cheap. I let myself run away. I'm sorry if I was a problem.'

'No problem at all,' I replied at once. 'Shall we clip up?'

'Yeah, come on mate.' Braja went to guide Grythiss by the arm, but our tank shook himself free. 'Raitha and Sapentia just went ahead, let's find their room.'

After the always-exciting surge of colour and sound of entering the game had died away, I found myself...in near complete darkness. That was very strange. Having prepared myself to clip up to find myself a recently dead character with no gear, I was surprised to see nothing at all. Or rather, a slight hint of an orange glow. Still, my UI was working, so I grouped up the team.

[Group] 'Where are you, Tyro?' asked Sapentia.

[Group] 'Somewhere dark. Are you all OK?'

[Group] 'We are perfect. There is no sign of the vampire, nor even that a struggle took place here. The books are all back on their shelves.' This was Raitha.

[Group] 'She has put me in a prison perhaps? I'll try to find out more. In the meantime, how about you all leave the castle?'

[Group] 'It would be more use of our time if everyone helps look for new spells.'

[Group] 'I'm not sure that would be wise, Sapentia,' I responded quickly, 'remember, there is an enchantment in that room. Let's not fall under the spell again.'

After a long pause, which made me anxious, Sapentia spoke. [Group] 'Very well.'

Good. Now, where was I? Stretching out my hand, I met with resistance and after pushing against it, heard the creaking of wood. As though a light had come on, I could see that I was in a room. Yet the sight was unusual. Everything was dim and coloured in greys, oranges and reds. Since there was no window, no doorframe with cracks around it, nor any lights, I presumed this was what infrared vision was like in the game. Confusingly, half-elves only got low light vision, not full infravision. Had I gained the ability along with my *Wolf Form*? In any case, it was pretty good for textures. Five long wooden boxes; a ladder; a scratched flooring made of planks.

And what had I just moved in order to see this? Some kind of door? No, a lid. I was sitting in a coffin. In a room with five coffins.

[Group] 'Umm. I have good news and bad news.'

[Group] 'What's the bad news?' asked Braja. Simultaneously, Raitha asked for the good news. If I hadn't been feeling giddy from my situation, I'd have pointed out to the two of them how they were opposites.

[Group] 'The bad news is I believe I've become a vampire.'

[Group] 'And?' The question came from Sapentia.

[Group] 'And the good news is I believe I've become a vampire.'

[Group] 'What does that mean?' asked Raitha.

[Group] 'I'm in a coffin in a dark room, I've got infravision. And oh...'

I had been hurriedly checking my UI, looking for alerts, and had just discovered them.

You have gained the ability *Invisibility*.

You have gained the ability *Giant Bat Form*.

You have gained the ability *Cloud Form*.

You have gained the ability *Read Thoughts*.

You have gained the ability *Summon Bats*.

You have gained the ability *Summon Rats*.

You are immune to weapon damage (exception: decapitation or wooden stake in the heart).

You are immune to electricity, cold and fire.

You are hungry and thirsty: you require blood.

You suffer damage in daylight.

[Group] '...Yep. Definitely a vampire. This is...well. I can turn into a bat and go invis. That has to be good.'

[Group] 'Where are you?' Sapentia brought my thoughts back to my surroundings.

[Group] 'A completely dark room, for obvious reasons, with five other coffins in it. There's one exit'—I could see it

153

now—'a trapdoor in the roof. And there's a ladder. Wait a moment, let me open it and see.'

With a leap of astonishing distance, I jumped from my coffin to land beside the ladder. That new agility gave me pause for thought. What were my attribute stats now? Let me see: Strength 23, Dexterity 23, Spirituality 11, Intelligence 15, Constitution 22, Beauty 9. Very nice! And that increased Con had doubled my hit points from 56 (level 7 at 8 points per level) to 112. Every time I gained a level I was getting my class increase (for hunters, that was 8) plus a Con bonus of 8. I was uber!

Feeling confident and cocky even, I threw up the trapdoor with a loud bang, fully expecting to be in cellars of the castle. Just wait until Blackridge found out about this. It would make him green. In my complacency, I made a near-fatal mistake. I must have been just below the roof, because the room lit up with daylight. Unfortunately for me, this was like a fireball going off above my head.

You are damaged by sunlight for 25 damage.

You are damaged by sunlight for 18 damage.

You are damaged by sunlight for 16 damage.

You are damaged by sunlight for 19 damage.

Every second that passed was melting me. Desperately, I grabbed the heavy iron handle of the trapdoor and pulling hard, returned the trapdoor into place with a mighty bang.

You are damaged by sunlight for 20 damage.

After taking a few breaths to calm myself, I spoke. [Group] 'It's the room directly underneath the roof and it opens to the sky. If you can get up top, you'll be able to reach me.'

You regenerate 2 hit points.

Excellent. And what if I lay in my coffin? Would that heal me faster? Doing so, I waited, counting the seconds and making new hot buttons for my UI, so that I could trigger *Invisibility*, *Giant Bat Form*, *Cloud Form*, *Summon Bats*, *Summon Rats* and *Read Thoughts* at need. After eight seconds, I got the heal message:

You regenerate 5 hit points.

Aha! Not bad at all, a little over ten minutes like this and I'd be back to full strength. Laying in my coffin, I listened to the group chat as the others discussed their options and decided to go outside and for Raitha to assume *Eagle Form* (our ability buttons had reset) and take a grapple up to the top. Probably, I had a smirk on my face. With these new stats and abilities, I should be able to level the whole group unexpectedly fast. Especially if I was farming mobs that couldn't actually harm me. Only, it would have to be at night-time...unless we went into an underground dungeon.

[Group] 'We can't find the trapdoor,' grumbled Braja. 'Can you lift it?'

[Group] 'The problem is that the daylight would kill me.'

Raitha gave a response. [Group] 'Even if you could raise it a tiny amount, not enough to let the light in, that would perhaps show us where it is.'

[Group] 'All right; I'll let you know when I've lifted the trapdoor.'

With a certain amount of anxiety – after all, that last experience had been a scare – I got out of my coffin, climbed the ladder and raised the trapdoor a fraction. [Group] 'Anything?'

[Group] 'No,' said Sapentia.

[Group] 'Now?'

You are damaged by sunlight for 1 damage.

You are damaged by sunlight for 1 damage.

You are damaged by sunlight for 1 damage.

[Group] 'Lizardman can ssseee the door.'

[Group] 'Great. I'm going to close it and get back in my coffin while we discuss what to do.'

[Group] 'What do you want to do?' asked Braja.

[Group] 'Go to an underground complex in a passage tomb where Raitha and I were levelling up. The guide says it has yard trash mobs up to level sixteen and a boss who is twenty-four. We could set up in there and it wouldn't matter whether it was day or night.'

[Group] 'I like this plan,' said Raitha, 'the place looked intriguing and there is hardly anything about it in the guide beyond what Tyro has said. There is nothing like exploring territory for the first time to take the grind out of grinding.'

Sounding curt, Sapentia came in. [Group] 'Fine. But we are not waiting all day. The others need us to level faster than we have been.'

[Group] 'There are five coffins in here with me. I haven't checked them, but if they are occupied, that's going to be some nice exp.'

>**You are damaged by sunlight for 1 damage.**

>**You are damaged by sunlight for 1 damage.**

>**You are damaged by sunlight for 1 damage.**

>**You regenerate 5 hit points.**

[Group] 'Umm. I'm guessing you opened the trapdoor.'

[Group] 'Right,' answered Braja, 'now what? Should we all come down.'

>**You are damaged by sunlight for 1 damage.**

The hit point messages kept streaming across my UI. So long as the rate of damage was less than my regeneration, I was fine.

[Group] 'If there are vampires in those coffins, then even with the sunlight to help us, we might be overwhelmed before they die,' observed Raitha. 'I suggest I fly down and try to prise one open with my beak. Should any of the coffins open, I can escape, whereas the rest of you would be trapped.'

Though I couldn't do anything to help while that trapdoor was open, I offered my thoughts. [Group] 'That sounds wise, good luck, Raitha.'

The flutter of wings was loud, even through the lid of my coffin. It was followed by a scratching sound and a creak.

[Group] 'Look out!' shouted Grythiss. 'Coffinsss's open!'

More groaning from wood and a powerful beat and crack of Raitha's wings. It was tempting to peek out. So I did.

My vision instantly transformed from infrareds to normal colours. A block of dusty sunlight marked a large rectangle on the floor. Around the dark sides of the room, all the coffins had been thrown open and five creatures were calling out in pain as they emerged. What were they? Vampires, presumably, although none of them looked at all like the castle's owner. These were withered and emaciated humanoids, brown skinned, wrinkled and frankly, disgusting. It was impossible to tell their gender or even had they once been elves or humans. There was no danger in this situation, for the vampires were caught, unable to advance towards the light but suffering damage all the same.

Dropping the lid back, I checked my hit points: 136 and slowly rising now, by 2 every 6 seconds.

[Group] 'Do you look like that now, Tyro?' asked Raitha.

[Group] 'No, I'm a young, fresh vampire. Just the same as yesterday. Maybe a bit more muscle.'

[Group] 'Hah! Sounds good,' he said.

[Group] 'What's happening?' I asked.

Braja replied, [Group] 'We have them crawling into the corners. They are doomed.'

And almost right away, we all got confirmation of this.

The Vampire is dead. You gain experience.

It took ten minutes and all five were gone, with a healthy boost to our experience that put me a third of the way into level 8. This reminded me, at some point I needed to find a merchant who could sell me hunter spells.

[Group] 'How are we going to get you to the dungeon?' asked Braja.

[Group] 'In this coffin. Let's see what happens when you bring it outside.'

With some lurches and a few complaints, they improvised a harness and began to lift me.

[Group] 'Careful. Don't drop me, if this breaks open I'll be dead in a minute.'

After they put me down, I watched the hit point reports with some concern.

You are damaged by sunlight for 3 damage.

You are damaged by sunlight for 3 damage.

You are damaged by sunlight for 3 damage.

You regenerate 5 hit points

You are damaged by sunlight for 3 damage.

You are damaged by sunlight for 3 damage.

You are damaged by sunlight for 3 damage.

You regenerate 5 hit points

[Group] 'This isn't working, I'm losing about a hit point a second.'

[Group] 'Let's cover it up with our cloaks and blankets,' suggested Sapentia.

Soon, the hit point loss was stable, back to a small gain in fact.

'How's that?' Sapentia asked, her voice near my ear on the right-hand side.

'Perfect!'

Directly above me was Raitha, his eagle had landed on the coffin lid. 'Did you get any useful abilities?'

'Oh definitely: *Invisibility; Bat Form; Cloud Form; Summon Bats; Summon Rats;* and *Read Thoughts.*'

'Wonderful. Perhaps you can make me a vampire too. Do you not think that being twin vampires is a very appealing storyline for our characters? Tell me, though, how does *Read Thoughts* work? I don't recognise it.'

'Good question, I don't know. I have made a hot key on UI for it, let me target you and try. Think of something particular.'

'I really don't see how you can actually read my thoughts.'

'Just concentrate on something.'

'All right.'

Using the Group screen to target Raitha, I triggered the ability.

This ability can only be directed at NPCs.

'Oh, I got the message it can only be directed at NPCs.'

'Interesting. Potentially very useful, depending on the extent of the information and the situation.'

'Raitha?'

'Yes, my friend?'

'What did you think about?'

'Blueberry pancakes. America is such an excellent place for delicious breakfasts.'

'This is the strangest group,' interjected Braja, a laugh in his voice, 'our pullers are an eagle and a vampire stuck in a coffin.'

'I can't wait to get out and do some fighting. According to the alert, I'm immune to all weapons. That should allow us some amazing pulls.'

'So long as vampire can keep mobsss on him.'

'True, Grythiss, we won't be reckless with this gift. I don't have a *Taunt* trained. And there's another downside too.'

'Yesss?'

'I think I'll need to take a drink from your necks now and again.'

CHAPTER 14
GOING UNDERGROUND

Although we made good progress via boat (well, they did, I just lay in my coffin, making smart remarks and laughing to myself) it was after twelve by the time I was told I could come out safely. That only left us a short period before the team meeting.

'Right,' I said brushing myself down, feeling great, 'let's try to get through to whatever boss thinks he owns this dungeon before the meeting.'

'Plan?' asked Braja.

I looked around, my infravision showing me red corridor walls stretching into darkness. There were carvings in the rough stone spirals and symbols that reminded me of my trip to Newgrange. Although I was interested in studying them, I was impatient to get the crawl underway.

'I pull and tank. Grythiss takes adds or mobs I can't hold on me. Sapentia, you are in charge of directions as well as nukes. There was no map with the guide so you'll have to make one. Raitha, DPS when the mobs are below sixty per cent and loot until you are full.'

Looking around, I got a couple of nods and I was off, covering the stony ground at amazing speed. It seemed to be that the corridor was descending slightly. A few hundred metres in and there were alcoves either side with a wolf-headed humanoid in each, some kind of zombie, since the state of the bodies was corrupt. They both held impressively large double-handed axes.

'Hi.' I slowed down to a walk and at about two metres they came alive, plodding towards me, axes raised.

[Group] 'Incoming. Two zombie wolf things.'

To make sure I had at least a minimum of the aggro, I stabbed one then the other with my longsword (doing much more damage than I previously would have, thanks to my new strength bonus). In the time it took to do so, I was struck hard by an axe to my hip.

You have been hit by an Undead Wolfman for 0 damage.

Fantastic! It was true then. I was immune. Feeling a huge surge of delight, I backed off, drawing the mobs after me.

[Group] 'Move up to me.'

These fierce-looking enemies were double my level and rated *impossible*. Yet they had no chance. So long as they continued to try to hit me (and I could see that Grythiss was patiently waiting to let me score a few hits before each time he came in, to prevent his aggro overtaking mine) we were perfectly safe.

'I'm going to use a few *Smite* spells,' announced Braja. 'I'm useless otherwise, you don't need healing.'

'Sure. Just wait until they are down to around fifty per cent.'

Squeezing along by the wall, Raitha, back in half-elf form, got behind the battle and when the Undead Wolfmen were around 60 per cent started hacking at them.

'I've been wondering,' he said, looking over the shoulder of the Wolfman at me, 'what if you do try and turn us into vampires? If you can, then we could all just head on over to Mikarkathat and kill her. No need to level up three hundred people.'

It was an incredible thought. And for a moment I felt giddy about the idea of filling my bank account with the reward.

'Surely it is not possible for players to make vampires,' came Sapentia's voice from behind me. 'Or it would not take long and entire player base of *Epic Two* would be vampires. Yuno are not so dumb.'

'Maybe they are. They've lost control of so much of the game, maybe this is another crock,' said Braja.

'Definitely worth a try,' I replied to Raitha, sticking my sword into the ribs of the Wolfman in front of me.

Our interesting conversation was ended with a flurry of blows from Grythiss and a barrage of nukes from both Sapentia (electrical magic missiles that glowed turquoise) and Braja (a translucent hammer smashing downwards and dispersing in a shower of sparks).

The Undead Wolfman is dead. You gain experience.

The Undead Wolfman is dead. You gain experience.

'Nice, halfway through eight already.'

'Not so much for me. Keep going,' Sapentia spoke, then sat down to increase the speed at which her spirit was restored.

'Come with me, you can rest up closer to the next action.'

After passing the now-empty alcoves, we came to a T-junction.

'Which way?' I asked.

'West is best,' Sapentia replied. 'Go right.'

After a dozen steps I could see a faint orange colour in the distance. 'Set up here, I'll go pull.'

As I advanced down the corridor, I saw I was coming to a hollowed-out room, full of figures. They were horned. Demons? No, undead humanoids again but with antlers and animalistic faces. Other than the fact we had fought our way through hundreds of undead monsters to get here and that these were scary creations, it was a welcoming scene, like that of a feast hall: long wooden tables holding goblets and gaming pieces; dramatic banners on the wall; musical instruments hanging from straps or in the unmoving hands of some of the mobs.

It looked as though some spell had frozen an Iron Age gathering and transformed the participants into these antlered undead. They all scanned *impossible* to me, hopefully meaning for good experience. How to split the pull so I didn't get the entire room? Sixteen of them. There was a cluster of six near the door that might come if I tagged one of them from back here.

Taking out my Finely Crafted Composite Short Bow, I aimed at the nearest figure, a human woman in a long green dress, whose features had been turned into those of a deer.

You have hit an Undead Wild Hunt Member for 6 damage.

You have improved the skill Archery (5).

Nope, the whole room sprang alive and rushed towards me. Oh dear.

[Group] 'Incoming sixteen undead wild hunt members. I'll stop twenty metres from you. Raitha, try and pull singles off for you guys to deal with.'

[Group] 'Sixteen?' Raitha sounded incredulous.

[Group] 'Remind me later to work on some kind of crowd control.'

Just before the mobs arrived, looking like a stampede of angry woodland creatures, I hit *Wolf Form*. If the bow tactic for pulls was going to be no use down here, I may as well be in my stronger, more effective form. And I was curious, what was it like to be a vampire wolf?

A stream of messages poured through the combat box of my UI, too fast to read but all of them presumably saying I had been hit for 0 damage as my hit point bar didn't even tremble. Quickly filtering to just my attacks, I read:

You have bitten an Undead Wild Hunt Member for 26 points of damage.

You have increased the skill Bite (25).

You have clawed an Undead Wild Hunt Member for 12 points of damage.

You have increased the skill Claw (2).

Aha, much better damage, along with more frequent hits and skill ups. Cool.

Raitha's voice spoke in my ear. [Group] 'Incoming. An Undead Wild Hunt Member.'

[Group] 'Did it work?'

[Group] 'Indeed it did, we have just one.'

With my own battle automatically going through the phases (dozens of blows against me to each bite and claw of my attacks), I could concentrate on monitoring my group's hit points. Grythiss was taking plenty of damage but each time he dropped to half, Braja healed him up. The only real issue was that of whether Braja had enough spirit to keep this up for the whole fight.

The Undead Wild Hunt Member is dead. You gain experience.

[Group] 'Seventeen spirit,' reported Braja as though he had heard my thoughts. 'Hold the pull.'

[Group] 'There's no rush,' I came in, 'we have a sweet exploit here, so long as we don't get greedy and you guys wipe.'

[Group] 'It's beautiful.' Sapentia sounded cheerful for the first time today.

[Group] 'Lizardman glad to see hunter doing ssssome work for a change, instead of sssleeping in coffin while we carry him.'

[Group] 'Corpse has a Pink Crystal Shard on it that's *Fastened*,' announced Raitha.

The Undead Wild Hunt Member is dead. You gain experience.

That was my female in the green dress; I switched to a new target.

[Group] 'I suggest Grythiss loot it. That way, when it turns out to be cursed he can wish he'd stuck to dragging my coffin around.'

[Group] 'Wait! If I loot, I can try *Identify Magic* skill.'

[Group] 'Good point Sapentia, go ahead please.'

A short time later she announced, [Group] '"This seems to be part of a much larger item." That's all.'

[Group] 'We might get more of those; you collect them all.'

[Group] 'Spirit is over ninety,' reported Braja, 'pull another.'

And the rest of the group were off again on a new mob. Everyone, including Grythiss (despite the post-drinking effects he must have been experiencing) was in good form now that we had found a way of obtaining a serious stream of exp. And it wasn't just this particular battle. The way this vampire thing was working out suggested that if we were careful, we could use the same tactic over and over. Me pulling and soaking up the hits, them tagging individuals that they could manage. I'm sure everyone in the group had figured this out and was rejoicing in our uniquely favourable situation.

Fifteen minutes later, we'd killed all the undead from the feast hall, collecting six pink shards and levelling everyone at least once: Raitha, who had been on the cusp of 9, was now 10; I was closing in on 10 and I'd also maxed out my claw and bite skill at 45; Braja was on 7; Grythiss was up to 11; and Sapentia led us on 12. Back in the days when I'd gone through the early levels in *Epic*, it had taken a week or so to level up from 8 to 10. This was rocking along and it put us firmly on track to meet Yuno's deadline.

There were also a few armour upgrades for Grythiss and Raitha and a bit of coin. Nothing, however, to redress the fact that we were poorly equipped for our levels. And that gap was only going to widen. It was a problem that I didn't have a solution for. Right now, however, the priority was level, level, level. Questing for appropriate gear was a waste of time, given that we should be able to progress without it and could skip straight to high-level weapons and armour.

Another hour and we'd cleared four more rocky chambers with the same method. I'd pull the room (now in *Wolf Form*, so I rushed in and tagged the nearest mob), then set up with the rest of the team a safe distance away and they would tag singles from the angry crowd who were lashing into me to with no effect. At the end of the fourth such pull our levels were: Braja, 11; Raitha and I, 13; Grythiss, 14; and Sapentia, 15.

[Group] 'We just about have time for one more room,' observed Raitha.

[Group] 'Which way, Sapentia? Out the far side?' I asked, looking at a corridor which left the room from beneath a heavy stone lintel carved with spiral designs.

[Group] 'Perhaps. By my map, this will bring us back to second chamber, we have gone around in circle apart from first.'

[Group] 'Let's check in case they might have respawned.'

A short run down the dark corridor proved Sapentia correct and, unfortunately, that we were killing the mobs faster than

165

they were popping back into existence, assuming that they would do so at all.

Probably, the wisest action we could take was to find a safe place to camp out in good time for the player meeting. But I had one last hope. [Group] 'The inside of the hill is on our left?'

[Group] 'Correct,' said Sapentia.

[Group] 'Let's check this corridor and that last room for a secret passage towards the interior.'

[Group] 'A very wise suggestion.' This was Raitha.

Forming a chain, we worked our way back towards the last chamber, Raitha first, then me, then Grythiss, Sapentia and Braja, one by one, checking the walls, running our fingers across sinuous carvings. As half-elves, Raitha and I had a natural skill in finding secret doors. I couldn't recall reading the exact bonus, but our chance was probably something like 10 per cent each per ten minutes checking, compared to 5 per cent for a human.

It was like looking at a language you didn't know, staring at the twists and curves of the designs on the wall. There was a story here, that was wasted on us. We just wanted the experience. I had a strong conviction there had to be at least one more room, otherwise what was the point of the pink crystal shards?

'Bingo! As I believe you say in Ireland.' Beside me, Raitha had both hands on a slab whose design was one huge spiral.

'We have expression Bingo too,' said Sapentia. 'It is from game with numbers.'

'You've found it?' I asked him.

Everyone crowded around and I could sense an eager excitement in the postures of their avatars, with their raised hands and concentrated attention focused on the wall.

'I had a success message on my UI. Yet, I cannot say for sure this is a door, nothing seems to yield to my pushing.'

'Try tracing that spiral,' suggested Braja. 'Maybe it's magic rather than physical.'

As soon as Raitha placed a finger on the start of the spiral, a faint pink light appeared beneath it. As he ran his finger around the design, crouching to come down to the bottom, then straightening again, the light grew stronger and pale sparks flickered in and out of existence.

No one spoke as Raitha went faster now, working his way towards the centre. At last, with a dazzling flash of pink and silver, his finger reached the final point of the design and the whole corridor shuddered. Chill air fanned my face and with a grinding and scraping sound, the slab sank into the ground, revealing a corridor that ran for about twenty metres to a chamber. This must be the heart of the complex.

Taking a deep breath, I stepped forward. 'I love questing and exploring. If only we didn't have such a grind on, I'd do a lot more quests. This whole passage tomb, undead adventure is just awesome.'

'Concentrate,' muttered Braja, 'there's a lot could go wrong, even for a vampire.'

'Right.'

Even so, it was with a spring in my step that I approached the dark room. My excitement at entering the unknown reminded me of my first few months playing *Epic*, which hadn't been about obtaining elite gear or the admiration of my peers, but simply exploring a massive fantasy world, with its highly varied range of adventures and quests.

'A large rock chamber with just a pedestal, flat topped, like it should be displaying something.' I relayed what I could see back to my friends.

'Safe?' asked Sapentia.

'One sec.' Not until I'd run around the room and also, tentatively, stood by the pedestal and then touched it (cold, rough), did I call them in.

'I have idea,' said Sapentia and she stood beside me, then drew out a pink shard. Having seen her let go of it above the grey surface of the rocky stand, my heart skipped with delight. The shard twisted slightly, as though settling in a magnetic field, and just hung there. Soon, another one joined it and another. It was as though Sapentia was assembling a 3D jigsaw.

In a matter of seconds, the design was clear: it was going to be a long war horn, fashioned as though made from a cow's horn, though in fact, from this magical, pink crystal. The pieces fused together as they moved into position, so the artefact appeared to be perfect and seamless. Did we have enough shards to complete the item? We did. Raitha and I cheered as the last piece fell into place and everyone looked happy, their faces shining pink in the glow from the artefact.

'Now I blow it?' asked Sapentia.

'You do, surely,' I answered.

Without hesitating Sapentia took the crystal war horn in her hands, put the narrow end to her lips and blew hard. Nothing happened, nor was there any sound.

'What's wrong?' she wondered aloud. Then blew once more.

Placing his hand on Sapentia's arm, Raitha murmured, 'Is it possible for you to use your *Identify Magic* skill?'

'Good idea.' Sapentia held the glowing, crystal horn in front of her face and concentrated upon it. We all waited silently. 'I'm told that this is the *War Horn of Nemain*.'

'Sounds good.' Braja reached out for the item. 'Let me try it.'

'Go ahead. But I think Raitha should,' I said.

'Why?'

'Nemain is one of the gods available to half-elf hunters.'

While sorcerers, wizards and their related classes drew their magic and spirit from study and books, clerics, druids and hunters obtained spirit by affiliating to a pantheon of gods. I hadn't yet chosen which pantheon I would join but I had read up on the subject as well as seen the options in the relevant UI menu.

After blowing on the horn to no effect, Braja passed the artefact to Raitha, who held it reverentially.

'Shall I first affiliate to the Ancient Forest Gods?' asked Raitha, referring to the pantheon containing Nemain.

'Good idea, I'll do the same.'

Only cursorily reading the text that popped up to inform me about the consequences of my affiliation (better responses from NPCs of the same affiliation, some new enemies), I returned my attention back to the cavern just as Raitha raised the horn up carefully in both hands and blew gently into it. As I was about to suggest he try harder, a wonderful note sounded: high pitched, sweet and resonating around the chamber with layers of overtones. The whole room now filled with pale pink light and I caught the distinct scent of roses.

You have completed the *Horn of Nemain* quest. You gain experience.

Maybe I was becoming greedy; it seemed that my experience gain had been disappointingly small.

Then we were in the presence of a goddess and I have to say, the game's designers did her justice. Tall, nearly two metres; long, sinuous tresses of black hair; tight-fitting banded and leather armour, mostly of black leather, with glittering silver buckles; a dark-wood bow across her back; sword and dagger scabbarded at her waist; delicate, half-elven features (young, not much older-looking than a human teenager); and extraordinary violet eyes that made my heart skip when she looked at me.

'What are your names? You warriors who have restored the *Horn of Nemain*?'

'Raitha.'

'Sapentia.'

'Grythiss.'

'Braja.'

'Klytotoxos.'

When I spoke, her smile became a frown. Then she looked back up to the others and continued. 'Morc Mac Dela of the Fomoiri will have sensed what you have done and soon he will be here. He will be arrogant and confident, because he knows that no mortal weapon can harm him. The Fomoiri believe me to be in exile from this world and, indeed, my powers are greatly weakened, but I can assist you in the approaching battle. Raise your favourite weapon.'

Should I drop my *Wolf Form*? In order to hold out my bow for whatever benefit the goddess was about to bestow? After a moment of indecision, I remained as I was.

With sombre, unrecognisable words, Nemain gestured at

our group and a flow of golden, sparkling light rushed from her outstretched fingers, to cause the weapons to glow. A rushing noise rose and fell and the light disappeared from the hand of the goddess. Yet it remained in the weapons. While I was delighted for my friends, I also felt jealous and regretful I hadn't acted sooner. These could well be the first magic weapons acquired in the game by any player.

'And you, worshiper of the Ancient Forest Gods.'

Upon being addressed, Raitha dropped to one knee, which was a nice touch.

'You may keep my horn and it will serve you three times. The first blast upon it will give you and your allies greater courage in battle.'

[Group] 'A bonus to hit perhaps,' suggested Braja.

Sapentia immediately whispered back, [Group] 'Hush. This is most great. Listen.'

'The second will remove all evil effects and poisons from you and your allies. The third blast will summon me or, if I am still restrained, I will send what aid I can. After this, you must throw the horn into a forest river. Do you understand and swear to do this?'

'I absolutely do.' Raitha was so earnest I almost laughed. When, however, the goddess turned to look at me again, I instantly felt a cold wave run down my body, as though I had just stepped into a waterfall.

'And you, wolf. I sense evil in you. Do you swear to fight for me in the coming battle?'

'I do.'

'Then I bless your fangs and claws.' The goddess waved her arm. 'They will serve you as if magical until the next moon.'

Not bad, not as good as a permanent magic weapon, but still.

'Mac Dela comes! I must leave. Farewell, you have earned the gratitude of Nemain and that is no light matter.'

The glow dimmed; the cavern felt empty; the goddess was gone.

'Lizardman will worsssship Nemain, though she is not of

our pantheon. She is…amazing.' Grythiss was holding up his longsword and examining it. There was a new, pale turquoise sheen to the metal. 'Do we know what ssshe has done for uss?'

'Plus two,' announced Sapentia.

'Fantastic.' Braja gave a few experimental swipes of his mace, while Raitha put her now-magical bow away across her back.

In the distance came a rumbling sound; the ground shook, dust fell from the ceiling in several distinct streams and then heavy footsteps resounded down the hallways. These effects really did make me feel nervous, as did my concern about the coming fight. We had gotten here with an exploit and might well therefore have arrived at a raid situation with seriously under-powered characters. It was great we had magical weapons but were we up to this encounter, whatever it was?

'It's too late to run, I suppose?' muttered Braja, who was evidently thinking along the same lines as me.

'Let's hope the vampire immunities work.'

Sapentia sighed. 'It would be shame to wipe here; getting our gear back now matters.'

Filling the corridor was a black shadow that emerged into our room and became visible as a creature with a huge, muscular human body and a goat's head, with powerful-looking horns. Quite the demon. In his arms was a massive, two-handed axe.

With a thunderous voice, the giant said, 'Who opposes the will of Morc Mac Dela?'

'I do,' said Grythiss at once. 'I, Grythiss the Lizardman, follower of the beautiful and kind Nemain.'

The monster snarled at this and inhaled deeply. 'You, wolf, undead creature.' He stretched out his axe and pointed the head towards me. 'You belong with me. Fight by my side and you shall have lands, castles and as many humans to feed upon as you need.'

'That's very generous. I accept with gratitude.' I dipped my head by way of offering a wolfish bow and as though eager, I leapt across to stand on all fours beside Morc Mac Dela, facing my comrades, teeth bared.

'Why you traitor, you will suffer for this!' cried Raitha spiritedly.

Sapentia joined in, 'You villain!'

Grythiss just gave a hiss, while Braja, half-heartedly, also cried 'Traitor.'

[Group] 'Now what?' asked Raitha.

[Group] 'I've no idea. Let's play along and see.'

Mac Dela leaned his heavy, horned head down to my ear. 'Which ones have magic weapons? You must fight them.'

'None of them,' I whispered back.

'Ahaha!' shouted Mac Dela with a voice that filled the chamber. 'The *Horn of Nemain* will be destroyed once more and this tomb filled with my followers. Wolf, kill the spellcaster, I will slaughter the rest.' With a confident stride he hefted the axe high and moved towards the group.

'I obey, mighty lord.'

My own leap took me right up onto Mac Dela's broad back and I bit as hard as I could into the flesh of his neck that was visible above the rim of his bronze breastplate.

Critical Hit! You have bitten Morc Mac Dela for 38 points of damage. You are draining his blood.

Encouraged by the message - I hadn't seen the draining result before, which could have been either a vampire skill or a wolf skill that I hadn't achieved earlier - I called out to my friends, hearing the excitement in my own voice. [Group] 'Just stay back for now.'

With deafening roars the monster span around and around, trying to reach me with his sharp horns and prise me off. It was no good: although my shaky vision registered the fact I was feeling some buffeting, I took no damage and my grip on his throat felt secure.

You have drained the blood of Morc Mac Dela for 9 points of damage.

**You have drained the blood of Morc Mac Dela for 7 points of
damage.**

Then he tried swinging his axe over his shoulder, first the
right then left. There was surprising speed in the motion, which
would have led to him cutting into his own body had I not
been there.

You have been hit by Morc Mac Dela for 0 damage.

**You have drained the blood of Morc Mac Dela for 9 points of
damage.**

Yes! My immunity worked against the axe.

**You have drained the blood of Morc Mac Dela for 8 points of
damage.**

It took him some time to realise that although he was landing some very effective blows like this, I wasn't weakening at
all. He must have been down by over 100 hit points before he
changed his approach once more. Dropping his axe, the monster reached around and scrabbled for a grip on my mouth,
failing that (I was embedded too deep and the blood made
everything too slippery for him), he then stuck his fingers in my
nostrils and pulled at them until they tore.

You have been hit by Morc Mac Dela for 0 damage.

**You have drained the blood of Morc Mac Dela for 7 points of
damage.**

[Group] 'Got the axe!' exclaimed Raitha delightedly.

I couldn't see much at this point, with the giant's hands
across my vision, his thumbs, in fact, pressing into my eyes.

[Group] 'Nice, but please keep clear of him.'

Having wasted precious time clawing and tearing at me
with his strong hands, Mac Dela tried again to shake me by
spinning. Additionally, he ran backwards at great speed and
smashed us both into the wall, causing my vision to shudder
wildly and the tracking beneath my feet to slide violently,
reflecting the fact my wolfish rear feet were losing their hold on
his back.

You have been hit by Morc Mac Dela for 0 damage.

> You have drained the blood of Morc Mac Dela for 7 points of damage.

My grip on his neck never weakened, however, and I was quickly able to stabilise my position.

> You have drained the blood of Morc Mac Dela for 8 points of damage.

The monster tried the same trick two more times, to no avail. Then he sank to his knees.

[Group] 'Lizardman sssstrike now? Want to sssee how well my new sssword worksss.'

[Group] 'I don't trust him, it's a trick. Keep away.'

As the combat messages continued to indicate that the monster's hit points were rapidly draining away, Mor Mac Dela spoke in a voice that was slow and with constant interruptions as he coughed blood out onto the floor.

'I'll give you anything you want…I swear…By the ancient gods. I can grant wishes. Nemain can give you nothing…'

Grimly, I held on, watching his hit points run down. How many did he have? We were well over three hundred.

[Channel Oalitha/Klytotoxos] 'Team meeting in ten minutes. Please find a safe place to unclip now.'

[Group] 'I just got ten-minute warning to meeting,' said Sapentia.

[Group] 'As did I,' said Raitha.

Sapentia came in again. [Group] 'We have to finish this.'

[Group] 'Now Lizardman joinsss the fight?'

[Group] 'Okay.'

Personally, I'd prefer not to take any risk here and turn up to the meeting late. My fears, though, were quickly turned into elation. Mac Dela did not rally himself as Grythiss slashed at his legs. In fact, he sprawled full length on the hard floor, groaning, blood pooling around him.

'No. No.'

> Morc Mac Dela is dead. You gain experience.

Excellent experience too.

'Hurry,' urged Sapentia, her avatar standing over Braja, who was searching the body of our slain opponent.

'A necklace, the breastplate and a ring. The breastplate is *Fastened.*'

'Lizardman can ussse?'

'Or Braja.'

'You go ahead,' said our cleric.

'Thanksss.'

While Sapentia moved impatiently to the exit corridor, Raitha straightened up and Grythiss knelt down. A moment later, he was parading around the chamber, wearing the gleaming bronze breastplate, which had a horned helmet design across the chest.

'Lizardman is most handsssome!' he pronounced with evident pleasure.

'Must leave,' said Sapentia, 'I will *Identify Magic* on ring and necklace later.'

'I thought you didn't care for group meetings?' I asked with genuine interest.

'This is different. This is tactical emergency and planning for raid. We must be part of it or dishonour our agreement with Yuno.'

'Fine. Let's run to back to my coffin and camp out.'

We hurried back through the stone chambers, all of them still empty, and into the first stretch of rough stone corridor. There, I lay in my coffin and the others put the lid on it and covered it in cloaks before I unclipped.

CHAPTER 15
ASTRA INCLINANT

More than three hundred of us were gathered in the Den. As with the last time the full team had assembled, there was a stage underneath the scoreboard, only this time there was also a large projector screen standing beside the lectern. Looking at the board, there was a swathe of red, headed by the name Molino, who was a warrior with a very impressive level of 59. About fifty names down came the first green player, Owen, a halfling rogue level 25. Another stretch of thirty or forty players and you came to Sapentia at 15. Then there were a huge bunch of players, myself included, respectably in the middle of the list. I'd come a long way from when I was stuck on 0.

While our last team meeting had been full of enthusiasm and with the delight with which the players were enjoying their work very evident in their expressions, this assembly was sombre. Perhaps, it occurred to me, Yuno now considered scrapping the whole project as unrealistic. Perhaps we were to be sent home. That was a miserable thought. It would be terrible to have this amazing experience abruptly terminated. I was enjoying the company of true friends and the immersive adventure of the game, especially the story of Klytotoxos, the hunter vampire.

Watson, when he stood up, seemed as sturdy and untroubled as ever. Gripping both sides of the lectern in his fleshy hands, he leaned towards us, looking out at the room over the top of his fashionable, purple glasses. 'You will be aware that an army of dark elves and their allies, led by the General of Bow and the General of Sword have conquered Fort Hellsmouth.

This was clearly a move designed to interfere with our project as they have stationed high-level dark elves and monsters at our character's spawn points and it has become impossible for them to survive entry into the game.

'Those of you still able to play the game will raid in order to clear the area, at least long enough for your colleagues to clip up and make their escape. I shall pass you over to Mr Blackridge to explain the details.'

As Blackridge rose from his seat a murmuring began that created quite a considerable volume of noise. There was consternation being expressed on all sides of me. How could players, the majority of whom were below level 20, hope to clear away such difficult mobs? Was the AI really smart enough to have come up with that scheme to thwart our plans?

Having tapped the microphone repeatedly, until he had silence, Blackridge brushed a strand of dark hair back across his forehead and used a pointer with a red dot to direct our attention to the projector screen, which showed a map.

'This is the situation in and around Fort Hellsmouth. We have twenty-one players, including Molino, locked out of the town square here, which is currently occupied by around twenty dark elves of various classes and five ogres. Northwards, at the Temple of Mov, we have five clerics blocked by the presence of eight dark elves and an Iron Golem. Just outside the east gate, at this grove of sacred trees, three druids are being contained by six dark elves and as many Cerebri.

'In the flats outside the great southern gate are over twenty dark elves and, unfortunately, they have a Mind Stealer with them. This is blocking a dozen of our players. A group of seven players is camped out at the nearby village of Middlehampton'—he swung the pointer down southwards—'where about eight dark elves are stationed and three ogres at the Tower of Nalinda are keeping two of our players from appearing.

'When this meeting is over, we will all clip up and join the channel Yuno for the raid. Our assembly point is the ring of stones on Djorjuna Mountain. This is the nearest low-level teleport arrival spot; it will leave us about an hour's march away from Fort Hellsmouth. Our strategy will be to firstly fight and distract the ogres at the Tower of Nalinda. Then the survivors will do the same at Middlehampton. Hopefully, that will release nine players who are all in their thirties and forties.

'We will then reform at the lake for the second part of the raid, a move on Fort Hellsmouth itself. There's no point going into details now, until we see how part one has progressed. Questions?'

Immediately, some twenty hands went up. There were several questions about how to get to the ring of stones that was the assembly point. Not every player was grouped with someone who could cast *Portal of the Stone Rings*. Then, the slender, long-haired young man who had asked about equal pay at the previous meeting was called to speak.

'If this fails, is the deal over? Is the game wrecked? Are we laid off?'

Clearly uncomfortable, his heavy face looking grim, Blackridge took a step back and looked across to Watson, who pushed himself up out of the chair and with his untroubled rolling gait, came up to the microphone.

'We have a plan B. You won't like it though, it's nearly all about trade skills. So let's try to get plan A back on track.'

'Interesting,' whispered Raitha beside me. 'As it happens, I like games with trade skills.'

Gesturing to his colleague, Watson moved to the side, though he stayed up by the lectern, smiling and nodding as Blackridge dealt with a number of tactical questions.

I put my hand up.

Although Blackridge immediately looked towards me, he then quickly turned his gaze around to the rest of the room and, regardless of the fact that my hand had gone up first, invited other people to speak. Finally, lacking any other choices, Blackridge looked sourly in my direction and gave a faint nod of his head.

'My group have a couple of special abilities that will be useful here. Can I ask that we remain grouped together in this raid?'

'Tyro, up until now we have been very tolerant of your

anarchist attitude. At this time, however, we have to work together, everyone, as a tightly organised unit under one direction. You'll be grouped as I see fit. I will be balancing classes and levels and you'll go where you are needed.'

Facing me were scowls of disapproval, couldn't they hear the pomposity in his voice? Evidently not.

'Special abilities?' asked Watson, leaning forward past Blackridge to command the microphone, his voice silencing an upsurge of discontented murmurs. 'What special abilities?'

'Raitha has *Form of the Sea Eagle*, which has obvious uses in a situation like this. And I…I have *Wolf Form*.' Should I have told everyone that I also had the abilities of a vampire? Not while I was still smarting after that last speech from Blackridge, one that could have come straight from the mouth of my worst teachers.

'Very useful. And I'm sure that Mr Blackridge will bear this information in mind when he forms his groups.'

'And I'm sure we won't be in the same group,' I whispered to Raitha.

Fifteen minutes later, back in *Epic* 2, my prediction was confirmed. No sooner had Sapentia teleported us to Djorjuna Mountain (the others carrying my coffin) than we were split up and I was placed in a group with two warriors, a cleric and a druid, all level 12.

[Group] 'I don't see you, Klytotoxos, where are you?' asked the cleric. Her voice was young and she had an American accent, a slow drawl that maybe was from the south-east. All I really knew about American accents was from streamed movies and TV shows.

[Group] 'Can you see a coffin, under a load of cloaks?'

[Group] 'No.'

[Channel Klytotoxos/Raitha] 'Hey, friend, where did you leave my coffin?' I asked Raitha.

[Channel Klytotoxos/Raitha] 'A moment…Sorry, I was just listening to my group leader. Your coffin is resting behind the tallest stone.'

[Channel Klytotoxos/Raitha] 'Thanks. And good luck.'

[Channel Klytotoxos/Raitha] 'You too.' Raitha sounded distant. He was probably distracted by group chat.

[Group] 'Can I ask everyone to meet behind the largest stone please.'

[Group] 'Tyro, I'm the group leader. What's going on?' This was the voice of an older man, our druid.

[Group] 'I'm sorry to say that I get damaged by sunlight. I'll need you to carry me to the action, at least until sunset.'

[Group] 'What the hell?' The druid sounded angry. 'When will this stop? You're always pulling something. Coffin, damaged by light. Are you a vampire?'

[Group] 'I'm afraid so.'

[Group] 'Well, that's ridiculous and makes you completely useless for the next three hours or so. Did you tell the General?'

[Group] 'No.'

[Group] 'I'll do that now. Jesus. You suck; you know that.'

Our cleric, though, spoke in a kinder tone. [Group] 'I could try a *Remove Minor Curse* Spell?'

[Group] 'Thanks, but I don't think it would work. And in any case, I actually think being a vampire will prove useful to the project. At night-time or underground at least.'

[Group] 'How did you get that?' another voice asked, one of the warriors. Although we'd all said hello and introduced our class and level, I hadn't yet learned to associate each voice with a particular person.

[Group] 'A vampire attacked me. She didn't kill me though.' I had been wondering about this myself. When I offered to entertain her with stories she hadn't heard, had that influenced Lady Cruoris's decision? Or had Braja's oafish remark about me being good in bed? Her harem of male vampires stored away in the attic were old and decrepit. Maybe she just wanted a lively companion and a younger lover.

[Group] 'And the *Wolf Form*?' asked the same voice.

[Group] 'My starting quest got nerfed when the bad guys ran over a nearby town. My mentor NPC gave me *Wolf Form* instead, it was all she had.'

[Group] 'You did some quests?' The cleric sounded surprised. 'The General told us not to bother with them.'

[Group] 'Not even for your basic weapons and food?'

[Group] 'The General made sure I was given bronze armour and a mace from the get go.'

The druid came in on our chat, his tones as hostile as ever. [Group] 'Thanks to the General, everything is all very well organised. Those of us who get ahead have to farm gear to help those further behind. You should try being a team member sometime and seeing how it works.'

Then a familiar voice came into my ears. It was Blackridge, whose jolly enthusiasm sounded forced to me. [Channel Yuno] 'That's it. We are all here. Thank you for being so prompt. You have your groups and your group leaders have their instructions. Let's gather just north of the Tower of Nalinda and get ready to create the space for Woan and Oveidio to rejoin us!'

There were plenty of whoops and cheers at this in channel Yuno and a certain amount of banter among players who were obviously familiar to one another. Personally, I liked my raid channels quiet.

[Group] 'I've found Tyro's coffin,' our cleric announced, 'do we carry it?'

Grumpily, the druid said, [Group] 'I suppose so'.

Soon after that, the tracking beneath my feet began to move, making me sway. I was tempted to pretend I was having a snooze, or a read of a graphic novel, while they lugged me down a mountain path. Instead, I kept it civil.

[Group] 'So, where are you all from? Dublin, Ireland here.'

[Group] 'Let's not chit chat,' said our druid, 'there's a lot going on in one-to-one chat and Channel Yuno.'

That was me told. I passed the time checking in on Raitha and Braja. For some reason I felt that Grythiss, who liked to get into role, and Sapentia, who would be busy organising her group, would not welcome an exchange.

After about an hour, we came to a halt and with one last tremor, the ground beneath me steadied. There was then a long, dull, waiting period. From what I was hearing in Channel

Yuno, the General was moving his groups around the tower, more or less encircling it.

With some excitement, our druid suddenly announced, [Group] 'Time to move. Everyone follow me. Tyro, you'll just have to lie there until this is over and we'll bring you to Middlehampton. By then it should be dark and you might actually be of some use.'

Among all the questions and comments - should I buff resistances now? Is someone casting *Haste* for the raid or do I have to arrange it for my group? That kind of stuff - came a voice I didn't recognise which made my heart beat faster. [Channel Yuno] 'There's a hunter in my group who can turn into an eagle. She wants to try pulling the ogres away. Can she?'

The question was lost in the welter of conversation going on in the raid channel. It was really tempting to try to speak up in the channel myself and draw attention to that idea, to reinforce it. Yet I held myself in check. Probably, if the suggestion came from me it would be answered negatively. Clearly, though, Raitha's idea was definitely worth a try. All we wanted from this part of the raid was time enough for the two blocked players to log in and escape. Was it worth all this setup when we were not going to stand and fight? Or were we? Surely Blackridge didn't think we had a chance?

[Channel Yuno] 'What about the eagle? Do we try it?'

[Channel Yuno] 'No,' Blackridge himself answered this time, 'we are nearly set, let's just stick to the plan. Your hunter is to use her bow.'

'Idiot.' I whispered to myself.

It was frustrating, being stuck in a dark box at a moment like this. The sight of the fantasy army creeping through the bushes towards the tower and its ogre guards would be a memorable one.

Calling up the raid screen on my UI, I studied the groups. There were thirty classic, self-contained units, with at least a couple of fighters, a couple of healers and a couple of DPS characters in each. This was the way to organise a raid when each group looked after its own healing. It was a good strategy for a chaotic melee in which there were lots of opponents and no particular boss. Against three ogres, though, whom we only had to keep away from the tower for about two minutes, might it not be better to put all the fast, aggro-drawing characters together into the same groups?

With some satisfaction, not to mention surprise and then amusement, I noticed that Blackridge's avatar, called 'General', was only a level 4 warrior. That was unexpected. He hadn't been putting much time into the game.

Finally (with what should have been last-minute spell-casting and buffing taking so long that I had even begun to hope I might get to participate), they were underway.

[Channel Yuno] 'Go group one,' said Blackridge, like the boss of mission control during an Apollo launch.

[Channel Yuno] 'Group one, on the way.'

[Channel Yuno] 'Go group two.'

And so it continued, Blackridge launching the groups one by one, all the way to the last, number thirty. Mine was sixteen. Not that I could go with them.

Nor could I even watch what was happening, other than follow developments on the raid screen. There I could see the first casualty, a monk in group one. His hit point bar went from full to empty in an instant. These ogres hit hard. If they caught up with you and landed a blow, well, you'd want to be at least level 20 to survive it. Soon the other groups began to suffer losses, bright green bars emptying out and character names becoming grey.

This did not signify a problem. Luring the ogres away from their guard stations was inevitably going to lead to casualties. There was a tone to the - far too many - cries in the raid channel, however, that did not sound promising. From a soundscape made of good-natured, relaxed voices, I was now listening to urgent shouts that seemed to be a good octave higher than when I had joined the raid.

[Channel Yuno] 'He won't move!'

[Channel Yuno] 'We need group six to take over. Group six, now!'

[Channel Yuno] 'Ogre Two is turning back. Repeat, he's turning back and there's nothing we can do.'

Then boom!

A quarter of the raid was greyed out.

[Channel Yuno] 'What was that?'

[Channel Yuno] '*Fireball.*'

[Channel Yuno] 'Ogre Three is a spellcaster.'

[Channel Yuno] 'Ogre Mage.'

[Channel Yuno] 'He's chasing me! He's chasing...Tell Woan and Oveidio to log in.'

[Channel Yuno] 'They just tried.'

[Channel Yuno] 'Try again! Quick he's...'

And so it continued until only about ten players were left alive. As intently as I was concentrating, listening for his orders, I could not hear Blackridge. He was still alive though, his green bar full when I called up the raid screen on my UI.

[Channel Yuno] 'One last try.' At last, Blackridge spoke up again. 'Everyone alive run past the ogres and see if you can shift them.'

Within a minute there were only two green bars on the raid screen, mine and Blackridge's.

Our raid leader spoke with surprising cheerfulness. [Channel Yuno] 'Well done everyone, you tried your best, I can see that. Shame about the Ogre Mage, we didn't have that intel. Please take a short break and then make your way to the nearest stone ring for a teleport. Stay in your groups. We'll get back together and try again.' He paused, then said rather more severely. 'Who is Klytotoxos? Why are you still here on full strength?'

[Channel Yuno] 'It's Tyro,' announced my group leader with considerable venom.

[Channel Yuno] 'What on earth are you doing, Tyro? Didn't you hear my orders?'

[Channel Yuno] 'He's in his *Wolf Form*, lying in a box.'

[Channel Yuno] 'Get out of that box now and take a run at the ogres.'

[Channel Yuno] 'Has the sun set?' I asked calmly.

[Channel Yuno] 'Get out of that box or you are going home tonight.'

At long last, the whole raid channel was silent. What a shame it was to hear me get roared at rather than to pay attention to a raid leader. I could feel them all listening. It was not a pleasant sensation, lying there in the dark, being bullied while three hundred people listened. Sod you, Blackridge. A hundred responses welled up in me, most of them involving swearing. Somehow I managed to sound reasonable, at least to my own ears. [Channel Yuno] 'If I leave the box before sunset, I'll die.'

Blackridge's voice was tired now. [Channel Yuno] 'Just follow my orders. If you die, you die like everyone else.'

No, I thought, dying would not be unproblematic, like it was for everyone else. They could come straight back to their bodies, reclaim their gear and get on with their game. I, on the other hand, would have to log out or I would respawn in the northern forest in daylight and die again. Then respawn and die again. And again. Until my penalty for dying would have created a mountain of experience for me to grind through to start moving forward (I must, I realised while following this thought, move my spawn point to somewhere out of the way of any light).

[Channel Raitha/Klytotoxos] 'It's only forty-two minutes to sunset. Then you can demonstrate to our great leader the value of your restraint.' Raitha spoke with great bitterness at the way I was being treated and my heart warmed to him for it.

[Channel Raitha/Klytotoxos] 'Hi Raitha. Good. Can you unclip and ask Woan and Oveidio to stand by to try again when it's dark? If you can be clipped up then too, I'll let you know when to signal them.'

[Channel Raitha/Klytotoxos] 'I understand. Yet, perhaps this is a better idea. My *Eagle Form* is reset, I could get Sapentia to bring me back to Djorjuna Mountain. By flying from there I can make it to you by sunset and be on hand to help.'

[Channel Raitha/Klytotoxos] 'Great idea, definitely better. All right, then can you please ask Braja to clip in ready to alert Woan and Oveidio.'

[Channel Raitha/Klytotoxos] 'Certainly. See you soon.'

[Channel Yuno] 'Not moving, Tyro? Then you're done at Yuno.'

Suddenly, the raid screen was gone. I was on my own, ungrouped.

I saw a private message request from Blackridge and took the call, even though I knew it wasn't going to be pleasant. [Channel General/Klytotoxos] 'Unclip and go to your hotel. I'll arrange for your flight home when we are done here.' He spoke curtly.

It was understandable that Blackridge was feeling angry and stressed, his job was probably on the line and the raid had failed. Taking it out on me, however, was pathetic. Up until now, I realised, the hassle I'd been getting from Blackridge and his followers hadn't really bothered me. Now, it did. I found that his recent words sounding so intimately in my ears had caused my teeth to clench together and my stomach to tighten in knots.

I didn't answer. I couldn't answer, I was in too much inner turmoil. If it came to defending my behaviour, well, surely it was obvious that nothing would have gone differently if I'd have left my coffin? And even if I was sacked now (wasn't that a matter between Watson and I?), unless somebody physically pulled me out of the game, I was staying. I had something to prove.

[Channel Yuno] 'Right everyone,' the General announced, 'carry on. You have your orders. Find your nearest standing stones and I'll arrange for pick-ups to Djorjuna Mountain.'

Evidently, Blackridge couldn't block me from listening to the raid channel.

[Channel Raitha/Klytotoxos] 'Sapentia has dropped me off and I'm in the air.'

[Channel Raitha/Klytotoxos] 'Great.'

[Channel Klytotoxos/Braja] 'Hey Braj, are you in-game?'

[Channel Klytotoxos/Braja] 'Yep.'

[Channel Klytotoxos/Braja] 'Stand by. I'm hoping the ogres don't have the means to kill a vampire and I'll be able to shift them.'

[Channel Klytotoxos/Braja] 'On it. I've moved rooms so I'm right beside Oveidio and Woan, who have been briefed and are good to go.' He paused. 'And Tyro?'

[Channel Klytotoxos/Braja] 'Yeah?'

[Channel Klytotoxos/Braja] 'Show him. Show them all.'

[Channel Klytotoxos/Braja] 'I will if I can.'

For the next half hour or so, I waited in a strange emotional state, part cold and analytic, part furious. Anger kept surging up in me as I listened to Blackridge reorganise his raid. Wasn't it obvious that the apparent cheer in his voice was all fake? That the man was panicking?

Braja broke in on my bitter thoughts. [Channel Klytotoxos/Braja] 'You know what I like about you, Tyro?'

[Channel Klytotoxos/Braja] 'Hah, I dunno. I'm glad you like me though. What?'

[Channel Klytotoxos/Braja] 'You're like me. You're from a working-class background, which you aren't ashamed of. You've educated yourself though and you can see what's going on, without showing your hand. If you know what I mean? Like me, when I was in the army: I couldn't call bullshit on the officers but I knew some of them - most of them - were just acting. They were more concerned about how they looked to the brass than anything else. You could tell that a lot of them thought us grunts were barely literate scum.'

I thought about this. [Channel Klytotoxos/Braja] 'Can I tell you a story?'

[Channel Klytotoxos/Braja] 'Sure, we have a few minutes until you can get out of your coffin.'

[Channel Klytotoxos/Braja] 'Last year our school C team had a game of football - soccer to you - against Belrock Sud, the most expensive private school in Ireland. All the kids there think they are elite. And in financial terms, they are.'

[Channel Klytotoxos/Braja] 'Nice.'

[Channel Klytotoxos/Braja] 'I don't know how that game

got scheduled, because our C team are crap and we were always going to be hammered by the likes of Belrock. It was ten-nil, in fact. Anyway, as we were getting changed, we could hear them singing: "Ten Nil. Who to? Belrock! Who lost? Scumra!" We're from Cabra; it's pretty lame but they were delighted with themselves, chanting it over and over. And the tone of the shouts was, like, utterly disdainful. It's hard to explain unless you know our accents, but they had this posh accent anyway and they exaggerated it to emphasise that they were above us.

[Channel Klytotoxos/Braja] 'I get it.'

[Channel Klytotoxos/Braja] 'We had a lot of head cases in our team, including Seanie Howlin, whose life ambition – seriously – is to be a hitman. The lads just looked at each other, then the word went around. "Hurry up." Quiet. Intense. I hadn't a clue what was going on; feeling the urgency though, I hurried on with my socks and shoes. We stole out of the changing room, into their school and although most of the classroom doors were closed, we found one that was open so we got in and absolutely trashed it. I mean, everything smashed that could be and all the books off the shelves with the pages torn out and the furniture broken up even.'

[Channel Klytotoxos/Braja] 'Hah, hah! Awesome man!'

[Channel Klytotoxos/Braja] 'Yeah, but there's something else. I knew how this would look. On the one hand, we'd be heroes of a sort back in our school, which was fine. On the other hand, this incident would be used in Belrock for years to come to remind them of how superior they are. How the lads from Cabra really are scum. I could see how it would pan out over the years. The Belrock boys would end up running the country and they'd justify helping their rich friends screw the rest of us with memories of the visit of St Dominic's.'

[Channel Klytotoxos/Braja] 'That's it. I've seen it myself from the army point…'

[Channel Klytotoxos/Braja] 'Just a sec, Braj. Let me finish. You're the only person I've ever told this to, because none of my classmates would get it. I think you'll understand me though. There was a book on the floor, *The Cambridge Course in Latin, Volume 1*. I picked it up and put it in my bag. Later, I worked my way through all the exercises. *Canis est in via* and all that. So this is what they learned in Belrock, I thought. It wasn't so difficult and I got Cabra Library to order the next five in the series.'

[Channel Klytotoxos/Braja] 'You know Latin?'

[Channel Klytotoxos/Braja] 'More than those sods.'

He was silent and I began to feel anxious. If Raitha was a kind of soulmate, with bonds forged over years of fighting side by side, Braja was a comrade and a mentor. Someone whose good opinion really mattered to me.

[Channel Klytotoxos/Braja] 'Tyro.'

[Channel Klytotoxos/Braja] 'Yeah?'

[Channel Klytotoxos/Braja] '*Astra inclinant, sed non obligant.*'

[Channel Klytotoxos/Braja] 'They certainly don't.'

[Channel Klytotoxos/Braja] 'Go show our army that the General is a fool, will you?'

[Channel Klytotoxos/Braja] 'Can I?'

[Channel Klytotoxos/Braja] 'Sun is gone.'

[Channel Klytotoxos/Braja] 'At last.'

CHAPTER 16
RESCUE

Twilight in the shadow of the Tower of Nalinda was evidently a perfectly comfortable place to be a vampire. There were no warning messages coming my way about damage from being in sunlight. Under an indigo sky, a black crenelated silhouette stood tall above the nearby trees. Game lore said that the place was, in centuries past, the residence of Nalinda, a half-elven sorceress. Although impenetrable (for now, there was a future expansion flagged in the game notes), the aura of magic around the building allowed characters to fix their spawn points at the entrance, which is what Woan and Oveidio must have done.

Arched, giant wooden doors faced me. They were covered with iron strips. Before the entrance was a wide grassy area and scattered everywhere were the corpses of the players in the raid. Only once the gear on them had been retrieved, or else if the body was abandoned for forty-eight hours, would these disappear. And then there were the ogres, of course. They formed a triangle. One was at the door facing me, he was the furthest point of the triangle. The other two were at the corners of the green, facing each other. Anyone who clipped up and entered the game in front of the tower would be seen by all three.

In *Epic 2* the ogre was a formidable enemy. Imagine very squat, stocky giants. Except that the faces and the bodies of ogres were more monstrous than that of giants: Neanderthal, heavy-browed expressions; dark green skin; tusks protruding from both upper and lower jaw. They had classes, so they could come with all sorts of abilities and spells, depending on whether they were warriors, hunters, rogues, or, less commonly, mages.

They were tough, with a disproportionate constitution and inhuman strength. Tagged *impossible*, of course, as I scrutinised them.

[Channel Raitha/Klytotoxos] 'Nearly there,' announced Raitha.

[Channel Raitha/Klytotoxos] 'Cool. I'm at the edge of the clearing in front of the doors.'

[Channel Raitha/Klytotoxos] 'Do you have a plan?'

[Channel Raitha/Klytotoxos] 'Not really, any ideas?'

There was no reply. A swift-moving shadow fell from the sky and landed in the branches of a nearby tree.

[Channel Raitha/Klytotoxos] 'Hello, my old friend. Well, you could try to pull them and if you don't get all three, I'll endeavour to aggro whatever is left?'

[Channel Raitha/Klytotoxos] 'Perfect. Ready?'

[Channel Raitha/Klytotoxos] 'Indeed I am. In fact, I find myself full of righteous anger on your part and very much hope we can demonstrate to all those who currently have a very low opinion of you that they have been receiving a very biased version of events.'

Righteous anger. That was me too. I loped forward onto the grass before the gate. Immediately, the nearest ogres lifted their weapons: the one to my left an enormous, knotted club and the one to my right a two-handed war hammer.

'Good evening. I bring greetings from Mikarkathat.' I raised my snout in what I hoped would seem like a salute. 'And orders to all her followers to gather at Fort Hellsmouth, since an army of enemies is approaching.'

'Ogre has order. Ogre never ever leave,' said the one on my left. I looked at his companion, who nodded. Then to the Ogre Mage in front of the door.

Suspicious and careful - raising a gnarled hand high as if to throw out a *Fireball* or other magic dart - the Ogre Mage said, 'We have orders.'

'Indeed. And you have obeyed them admirably.' I sniffed at all the bodies. 'Mikarkathat is extremely pleased with you. Now, however, she needs you at Fort Hellsmouth.'

By way of response the Ogre Mage snorted loudly and spat a great, slimy gob on the ground. Then he (or was it a she? It was hard to tell with ogres) spat out his next three words just as violently: 'What's the password?'

'I should be the one asking you that,' I answered at once, stalling for time. The Ogre Mage looked puzzled and pulled back his lips, fangs opening in a snarl. Then inspiration struck and targeting him, I triggered *Read Thoughts*. 'I hope you remember it. Ogres - no offence - are prone to forgetting such things.'

The Ogre Mage is thinking of attacking you in the next few seconds by casting *Bolt of Lightning* and he is thinking of the word Icebreaker.

'Icebreaker!' I shouted anxiously. Then, resuming my calm demeanour, I added, 'The password is "icebreaker".'

There was a long pause. The Ogre Mage lowered his arm. 'We haven't seen you before, werewolf.'

'Yet I am one of Mikarkathat's most trusted officers. I'm a vampire too and she sends me all over the world with her messages. You didn't need me at Fort Hellsmouth last time; you do now.'

'A vampire?' said the Ogre Mage, all hostility gone from his voice. The other two grinned, at least, I felt it was a grin rather than a ferocious scowl. 'Show us.'

Which ability would do the trick? I triggered *Summon Bats*.

From the trees and the eves of the tower, a flurried swirl of dark shapes swept towards us like leaves in an autumn storm. My UI flashed with a new window.

Bat Swarm:

Attack Target

Conceal Self

Fly to Location

Disperse

Choosing *Conceal Self*, I was pleased to see an impressive column of eager bats weaving in and out of each other's way as they gathered around me. I was in the centre of a whirlwind of swift-moving bats. Neat.

'Ogre has seen.'

Disperse.

At once, the column broke apart and the bats removed themselves into the deepening shadows of the forest and tower roof.

'Ogre leaves to fight the enemy at Fort Hellsmouth.' This was the one to my left, with the club, who had previously expressed his determination to stay.

'Farewell, wolf vampire,' said the mage, departing his post. The other ogre turned away too and as soon as they were lost in the trees, I contacted Braja, feeling a tremble of delight run right through my body.

[Channel Klytotoxos/Braja] 'Call them in.'

[Channel Klytotoxos/Braja] 'You've drawn them away? Are you immune to their attacks? It worked?'

[Channel Klytotoxos/Braja] 'I managed to fool them into leaving. Don't think I've got any aggro.'

I heard him chuckle. [Channel Klytotoxos/Braja] 'I wish I could go tell Blackridge, but he's still in the game.'

[Channel Klytotoxos/Braja] 'While you are out, Braja, can you round up the seven players at Middlehampton? I'll go there next.'

[Channel Klytotoxos/Braja] 'On it.'

[Channel Raitha/Klytotoxos] 'You are a very smart player, Tyro,' said Raitha solemnly, 'for a while I was dumbfounded, wondering how you knew the password. Now, I believe I have the answer. You used your *Read Thoughts* ability.'

[Channel Raitha/Klytotoxos] 'Hah, yes I did. Hey, Raitha, can you group with me now?'

[Channel Raitha/Klytotoxos] 'It would mean leaving the raid, a rather provocative step, yet one I am willing to take.'

[Channel Raitha/Klytotoxos] 'Now we've been successful, I think we are okay. I can justify breaking up Blackridge's raid.'

[Channel Raitha/Klytotoxos] 'Very well. I am no longer in a group or the raid.'

No sooner had I invited Raitha to join my group than he accepted. A minute or two afterwards, Oveidio appeared (a Level 32, male human warrior). When he had his bearings, he started to run for the trees. Laughing, I caught up with him and he immediately started to strike at me with a two-handed sword.

'It's all right; it's all right. They've gone. This is me, Tyro, hold up a moment and take my group invite.'

'Oh! Man, I thought you werewolf or somethin' like that.'

Next, I had to turn back and hunt down Woan (a Level 34, female half-elf cleric).

[Group] 'I am very pleased to meet you both,' said Raitha, when they were finally in.

[Group] 'You've no idea how pleased I am to meet you,' replied Woan in a French accent, 'I thought I'd be locked out of the game for good when the raid went sour.'

[Group] 'Me too.' Oveidio sounded Eastern European, Russian maybe? 'Thanks, Klytotoxos, you're good player.'

[Group] 'Call me Tyro, please. I made a mistake with Klytotoxos, it's too much of a mouthful and confuses people who are used to me as Tyro.'

[Group] 'Of course, Tyro.' Oveidio's voice dropped an octave as he suddenly became serious. 'Tyro. I was Blackstorm in *Epic*, leader of Dreadnought Guild. I know you. I respect you.'

In the middle of the chaos that was the raid, we stood still, Blackstorm and I, and for a several seconds contemplated each other. Blackstorm and his guild was famous, much better known than me. The largely Russian guild had millions of followers for their raid videos. They did have a reputation, though, for being territorial and unfairly jumping the queue for top bosses. I offered my paw and the warrior shook it.

[Group] 'I respect you too. Next we go to Middlehampton. I'm going to explain matters in channel Yuno. Blackridge might well freak, take it out on you afterwards. Are you all okay with that?'

Oveidio chuckled with a deep laugh that suggested he was a fair bit older than me. [Group] 'Hanging out with known felon? Wouldn't be the first time. And the name General does not mean you can command.'

[Group] 'I am good,' added Woan.

Raitha added his support. [Group] 'Naturally.'

[Channel Yuno] 'Hi folks, Tyro here, we've rescued Oveidio and Woan, who are in-game…'

[Channel Yuno] 'Hey there!' shouted Oveidio. 'Oveidio here. I'm back!'

[Channel Yuno] 'I'm heading for Middlehampton next. If you can make it there within thirty minutes and are willing to leave the current raid to join mine, let me know.'

When my UI started flashing with signals of one-to-one conversations (it did this when more than one was available), I chose Sapentia's first.

[Channel Sapentia/Klytotoxos] 'Very proud of you, Tyro. Well done. Have left Blackridge raid.'

[Channel Sapentia/Klytotoxos] 'Thank you. Here's a raid invite, you are a group leader. Please invite…' I looked at the list of those players wanting to talk and gave her the first six names. 'Apologise to them for me please, I won't be able to take one-to-ones just now. Raid channel is Rescue.'

[Channel Sapentia/Klytotoxos] 'I understand.'

Having opened the raid screen on the UI, I sent a new group invite and immediately Sapentia must have taken it, since her group appeared below mine.

[Channel Rescue] 'Hi Sapentia, Raitha here, good to see you so soon.'

[Channel Rescue] 'Hello Raitha, well done.'

[Channel Rescue] 'Much as I value your praise, it is misplaced. Our success was entirely due to Tyro. In fact, I just watched from a tree.'

While Channel Rescue became lively with conversation, I muted it (resolving to get a grip on it later) and opened the one-to-one I was dreading.

[Channel General/Klytotoxos] 'What are you doing?' Blackridge's voice was cold and harsh.

[Channel General/Klytotoxos] 'Your job.'

I almost laughed at my own daring. It was a cheeky response, I knew, but what else could I have said? He'd set it up for me like placing a ball on a penalty spot and inviting me to kick it at an empty goal. There was a long silence, in which I could hear Blackridge breathing heavily. Then the channel closed.

[Channel Braja/Klytotoxos] 'Hi Braj, are you there?'

[Channel Braja/Klytotoxos] 'Yep.'

[Channel Braja/Klytotoxos] 'I've really upset Blackridge. There's a chance he's going to unclip and try to drag me out of the game for a showdown. Would you mind guarding the door to my room? Sorry to be a pain. We are making some progress here and I don't want Blackridge to wreck it.'

[Channel Braja/Klytotoxos] 'No pain at all. I'd be delighted. I just hope he tries it.'

[Channel Braja/Klytotoxos] 'Thanks Braja.'

[Channel Braja/Klytotoxos] 'Good luck, Tyro.'

It was a relief to have someone as tough as Braja on my side. Instead of having to worry that at any second I could be torn from *Epic 2*, I could concentrate on the game.

[Channel Rescue] 'Listen up, folks,' I announced, 'this channel is for my instructions and emergencies only. Swap to group for all other chat.' I paused and was happy to find that the channel had fallen silent. 'Everyone please assemble at the bridge to the south of Middlehampton.'

There were still a dozen one-to-one channels winking at me. Among them was that of Grythiss.

[Channel Grythiss/Klytotoxos] 'Hey Grythiss.'

[Channel Grythiss/Klytotoxos] 'How can lizardman help vampire leader?'

[Channel Grythiss/Klytotoxos] 'Head up a group please, Grythiss, raid channel is Rescue.' Then I gave him a list of seven players to group with, before inviting four of the new players to my own group.

As Oveidio, Woan and I hurried along a dark forest path towards Middlehampton, Raitha flew ahead as scout. I found it necessary to quell an upsurge of new voices in Channel Rescue. In a way, it was a shame. Listening to voices of players who were clearly feeling a sense of liberation and excitement was heartening. Nevertheless, I needed the channel for its proper purpose and once again told everyone to confine all other chat to their groups.

After a pleasant run through a forest in which the scents of wild garlic and chives were strong in my wolfish form, the path reached a small stream. Pleasant, too, was my sense of anticipation. At last, I was getting to lead a raid in *Epic 2*. Soon after turning west to follow the south bank of the stream, we came to an arched, stone bridge. The assembly point. My group were the first to arrive and so while the rest of the raid closed in on this point, I studied the raid screen.

Raid Leader: Klytotoxos, hunter, half-elf, Level 13
Loot rights: All

Group 1
Group Leader: Klytotoxos, hunter, half-elf, Level 13

Raitha	hunter	half-elf	Level 13
Oveidio	warrior	human	Level 32
Woan	cleric	half-elf	Level 34
Owen	rogue	halfling	Level 25
Rurn	sorcerer	human	Level 19
Marmalade	paladin	dwarf	Level 19
Spinespike	cleric	elf	Level 17

Group 2
Group Leader: Sapentia, sorceress, human, Level 15

Tuscl	shaman	human	Level 18
Glarinson	paladin	dwarf	Level 21
Klandia	necromancer	elf	Level 9

Elartha	shadow knight	lizardman	Level 11
Verida	druid	half-elf	Level 13
Rauskel	wizard	half-elf	Level 14

Group 3
Group Leader: Grythiss, shadow knight, lizardman, Level 14

Savoda	monk	human	Level 17
Healyupy	cleric	dwarf	Level 12
Grosmandred	warrior	human	Level 12
Og	warrior	gnome	Level 9
Nullentha	warrior	half-elf	Level 8
Birch	druid	elf	Level 7
Rahod	cleric	human	Level 9

[Group] 'Blackstorm,' I said, 'you were a warrior in *Epic*, right?'

[Group] 'Level seventy, with *Sword of Thunder* and *Ring of the Frost Giant King*,' replied Oveidio, with a pride in his voice that was entirely deserved.

[Group] 'Do you think this raid could take on a level sixty dark elf in a toe-to-toe fight?'

[Group] 'Not chance.'

[Channel Raitha/Klytotoxos] 'Really? This is *the* Blackstorm. Of Dreadnought?' asked my friend.

[Channel Raitha/Klytotoxos] 'Yep,' I replied, as if it was no big deal for me to be grouped with one of *Epic*'s most celebrated figures. It was cool to be Blackstorm's group and raid leader. Like some Dublin gurrier leading an ex-Red Army general. Still, it also put me under more pressure not to make a mistake. I had to keep his respect.

Woan joined in. [Group] 'I couldn't keep up with the healing.'

[Group] 'That's what I think too. We're going to have to kite.'

[Group] 'Raitha, would you care to fly on over the village and see what the pulls are like?'

[Group] 'Certainly. Every time I take to the air and soar above the world is a pleasure for me. Even if it were not my duty.'

As the other raid members began to arrive at the bridge, I felt a little tearful. Compared to my recent experiences leading raids in *Epic*, this was a small, ramshackle group of relative strangers. Their armour was poor and patchwork, only covering certain parts of the body; their weapons were uninspiring; their outfits were bare of the pouches and bandoliers of potions and miscellaneous magic items that high-level characters in *Epic* always wore. Yet here they were, in defiance of their official paymaster and despite all the negative crap they must have heard about me. This is what was affecting me so much, the fact that they were demonstrating faith in me under circumstances when it wasn't easy to do so. Our group of five was no longer alone.

When the last of our twenty-three raid members arrived - Savoda, a human monk, running swiftly through the swaying reeds of the northern bank - I silenced the raid channel.

[Channel Rescue] 'First of all, thank you. I appreciate that you are willing to risk losing the rest of your pay to join me...' At once, several voices started up, with the gist of their sentiment being they were fed up of being told what to do by Blackridge and that they'd rather be sacked than carry on under his direction. After allowing a certain amount of this (after all, it was heart-warming and created a strong bond of solidarity between us all), I reminded everyone that the channel was for me and emergencies only. 'Thanks to Raitha, our eagle scout, we know that we face twenty-one dark elves, of all classes, levels forty-four to sixty-two.

'Here's our strategy.

'I'll pull. I'm a vampire and immune to their weapons...No please don't ask'—I had to head off a sudden outbreak of curious questions—'I'll explain afterwards, when we are moving up to Fort Hellsmouth. There are four singles, three doubles, a three and a core group of eight, including the level sixty-two, who is a fighter class by the look of him, probably a shadow knight. For the singles, limit your damage so that I can keep the aggro, be patient, I'm only level thirteen so if you are level thirty plus, you'll have to be really careful not to become the target. If you do, start running because we can't go toe to toe with any of these.

'Which brings me to the doubles. I'll take one, you will all kite the other. I know you are all experienced *Epic* players, so I'm not going to micro-manage. You'll know what to do, but in short, we all need *Haste* buffs and to try to get *Slow, Ensare, Block, Freeze* and any other movement restricting spells to stick on them. Other than that, it's run like crazy if you have aggro and throw everything you have at the mob if you don't. The triple is the same, except Raitha is going to take the third on a long run and bring it back when one of the other two is dead.

'When we are left with the final, large group, I'll try to talk to them and persuade them to leave, failing which I'll pull them all and you will try to drag them off me one at a time. We can discuss this more later. For now, follow me. And best of luck.'

Allowing a few whoops and cheers to ring out in the channel without comment, I led the raid forwards. From the bridge, a rutted path led towards the village of Middlehampton, passing between young trees whose silhouettes made them appear like bushy-headed sentinels. With both moons still below the horizon, it was a very dark once we were in the forest, not that I minded, my wolf's eyes were able to see incredible detail, such as the scarlet hue to the Oshmari plant that was common here. In fact, these woods were celebrated in game lore for containing dozens of rare plants and woodland creations, which were essential for crafters. There was a spawning point at Middle-hampton to facilitate those wanting to explore the woods and, it seemed, Blackridge had stationed a whole group based there who ended up unable to get into the game.

Careful not to run too far ahead of my raid - they were all jogging behind me at the pace of the slowest, a dwarven cleric with the ridiculous name of Healyupy - I followed the path past abandoned carts and cottages that ought to have contained friendly NPCs. They too were not respawning since the arrival of the army of the General of Sword and General of Bow. I drew up at a crossroads in a clearing. Here was a tall wooden sign, leaning over slightly and pointing in two directions: the east road ran to Fort Hellsmouth, it declared, while if we continued north we came to Middlehampton.

[Channel Rescue] 'Gather at the signpost for buffs.'

They closed in upon me, from the tall, slender elves and muscular barbarians, to the short dwarves and gnomes, whose faces were at my eye level.

[Channel Rescue] 'Does someone have group *Haste*?' I asked.

Silence.

With a twinge of anxiety that ran through my whole body, I checked the raid screen. [Channel Rescue] 'Tuscl, don't you have group *Haste*?'

[Channel Rescue] 'Sorry, Tyro, one more level is needed. Is self only at the moment. If we were playing *Epic* I'd have it, but they have made *Haste* a level harder to obtain in *Epic Two*.' The shaman's accent was Spanish and she sounded cheerful, despite the fact this was a serious problem.

[Channel Rescue] 'Any suggestions?' I asked.

[Channel Rescue] 'Stick with plan,' came Sapentia's voice. 'Until mob slowed, three with self-*Haste* take the kite.'

[Channel Rescue] 'Good. All right, if you don't have *Haste* go easy on the aggro until you hear that the mob is slowed. Those of you casting slow spells on the mob may use the channel to update us if your spells get through. Now, please disperse along the south side and stay back in the woods. If you ever get aggro, run the mob clockwise around the edge of the clearing.'

Drawing in a deep, calming breath as I watched the raid party spread out among the trees, I called out once more. [Channel Rescue] 'Raitha, we are in position and good to go.'

About a minute later, his soft-spoken voice excited and high-pitched, Raitha cried, [Channel Rescue] 'Incoming! A dark elf.'

Hurtling towards me out of the trees to the north was the eagle form of my old friend and behind him, a sinister leather-armoured dark elf, sword in one hand, dagger in the other. Howling to get our enemy's attention, I leapt forwards and triggered my bite and claw attacks.

You have attempted to bite a dark elf rogue and missed.

You have attempted to claw a dark elf rogue and missed.

You have been hit by a shortsword for 0 damage.

You have been hit by a dagger for 0 damage.

You have been hit by a dagger for 0 damage.

You have been hit by a shortsword for 0 damage.

You have been hit by a dagger for 0 damage.

You have been hit by a dagger for 0 damage.

Wow, I'd have been sliced into tiny wolf pieces if I didn't have my immunity to weapons; the rogue was striking twice as often as I was. As in *Epic*, dark elves were a deep purple in colour and this one had extraordinarily vivid blue eyes that fastened on mine in hatred.

You have attempted to bite a dark elf rogue and missed.

You have attempted to claw a dark elf rogue and missed.

You have attempted to claw a dark elf rogue and missed.

You have been hit by a shortsword for 0 damage.

You have been hit by a dagger for 0 damage.

You have been hit by a dagger for 0 damage.

You have been hit by a shortsword for 0 damage.

You have been hit by a dagger for 0 damage.

You have been hit by a dagger for 0 damage.

You have bitten a dark elf rogue for 8 points of damage.

At last! It was another fifteen seconds or so before I hit him again, this time with a claw. The raid channel was admirably quiet.

[Channel Rescue] 'This will take a while, but let's be patient. Allow his hit points to drop below eighty per cent before you come in. And ease up if there's any chance of you overtaking me.'

[Channel Raitha/Klytotoxos] 'How about I attack him

from behind? It would be an easy matter to fly in at his head. If I get aggro I can always start the kite,' Raitha suggested.

[Channel Raitha/Klytotoxos] 'Thank you, but no. He's very fast and might kill you too quickly for you to fly away. Plus, we really need you for the pulls; if you did die now, that would be a disaster.'

[Channel Raitha/Klytotoxos] 'You're right, of course. It is just that I am so eager. Should we defeat these dark elves and rescue our companions, that will be quite some achievement. One that must surely make you a hero and not the villain.'

Although Raitha meant this very kindly, internally, I gave a shudder. For an atheist and someone with a scientific way of thinking, I'm surprisingly superstitious. Like the Ancient Greeks, I am very anxious that the Fates not think I am taking them for granted. If I could have, I would have touched wood to avert their attention to Raitha's words.

[Channel Raitha/Klytotoxos] 'This is going to take a few minutes,' I said to Raitha, 'how about flying high and scouting in case random encounters or enemy reinforcements are coming down these roads?'

[Channel Raitha/Klytotoxos] 'Certainly. Good luck.'

Because my view was completely filled by my opponent, I could not see Raitha flying off.

When the Rogue was at 80 per cent hit points, I deliberately said nothing. It would be a test of how attentive were my fellow raiders. They passed the test. All ran in on the fight, jostling for positions (not all the melee classes could fit), and now the dark elf's hit points began to decline much more rapidly. My new team were good though, I noted with approval that sometimes a player would step away from the fight, out of concern he or she had done so much damage the dark elf might turn upon them. It was perfect for the situation here. We had more people wanting to fight than could fit around the target, yet none of them could fight for long without risking overtaking me in the mob's hate list. Swapping places kept up the DPS, without any of them gaining too much aggro.

In the space of about two minutes, without any wavering of his furious focus upon me, we reduced the dark elf to zero.

The dark elf rogue is dead. You gain experience.

Miniscule experience, since it was shared throughout the whole raid. Still, one down, twenty to go. And, importantly, as I could tell from the cheers among my group members and the high-fives that avatars gave each other, we'd proven that despite our low level, with these tactics we could take down the mobs standing in the way of the return of seven of our high-level comrades.

[Channel Rescue] 'Very nicely done. I liked the swapping in and out, we can do that again whenever we get down to one mob. Meanwhile, does someone here have lots of bag space?'

[Channel Rescue] 'I do.' It was Tuscl who answered, the shaman who was a level away from being able to cast *Group Haste.*

[Channel Rescue] 'Okay Tuscl, you are the main looter. Keep it all for redistribution later, unless something drops that can help us.'

By way of answer, Tuscl kneeled beside the body and searched it.

[Channel Rescue] 'Well there he is!' she announced at once. 'A half-empty *Potion of Speed.*'

Aha, that made sense of the rogue's rapid sequences of blows. Unfortunately, *Speed* was not, as it might sound, a spell that increased movement. For that, we needed *Haste*; *Speed* was for increasing your attack rate.

[Channel Rescue] 'Pass it to Oveidio please. Raitha, we are good for the next one?'

In succession, we killed a dark elf shadow knight, an anti-paladin and a monk. None of them presented the slightest difficulty. My raiders were proving very competent in managing the amount of hate they were incurring. The loot from these mobs was quite good too. Three pieces of armour (which were all upgrades and which I gave to the players of the highest appropriate level) and another potion. We therefore had *Speed* strapped to the belt of Oveidio and *Restore Spirit* in Sapentia's possession.

Next, I made another announcement, hopefully disguising

my trepidation. While I was encouraged by the fact we'd managed the single pulls well, to move to a kiting strategy was a real step up and test of our collective raid skills, especially for those running the mobs. [Channel Rescue] 'Now we have to deal the doubles. Good luck with the kite. Pull them please, Raitha.'

[Channel Rescue] 'Incoming, two dark elves!' cried Raitha eagerly, 'probably a warrior and a cleric.'

[Channel Rescue] 'Kite the cleric,' I told the raid.

Even before I could see our new enemies, I could hear them and also the beating wings and screech of Raitha in full flight. Around a corner in the path they came, tunnelled towards me by the line of trees either side. A rush of darkness; a flash of yellow ringed eyes; then looming over me were the two dark elves.

Ignoring the cleric I leapt towards the figure who was obviously the warrior (longsword; a raised shield of black iron, depicting, in silver, a scorpion; beautifully crafted chainmail with plates of some kind of dark metal upon it; greaves and armguards of the same plate metal, curved to fit tightly on his slender limbs; a helmet, equally delicately fashioned, open at the front to reveal his handsome, elongated face).

> You have attempted to bite a dark elf warrior and missed.

> You have been hit by a longsword for 0 damage.

> You have been hit by a shield for 0 damage.

> You have attempted to bite a dark elf warrior and missed.

> You have attempted to claw a dark elf rogue and missed.

> You have attempted to claw a dark elf warrior and missed.

We settled into our combat, me leaping up towards that wickedly beautiful face, him slashing and bashing with skilful moves that should have destroyed me in a few seconds. Instead, my hit bar remained resolutely full while his, by tiny increments, was decreasing.

Every minute or so, I caught a flicker of activity from beyond my duel. From the left edge of my vision, Tuscl would run around the back of my opponent and soon after her came the furious dark elf cleric, mace held high, long black hair streaming behind him. Then some of our other raiders would cross my vision: throwing daggers; firing bows; casting spells. The whole battle would move out of view for a moment, before coming around again. Around and around. Around and around.

An unfamiliar female voice spoke in the raid channel.

[Channel Rescue] 'He's resisting cold. My fire-based dots are getting through though.' This probably was the voice of a druid, since they had several damage-over-time spells that drew upon the element of fire.

[Channel Rescue] 'Thank you Verida.' We only had the two druids among us and one of those was just level 7, so it seemed like a safe guess at her name. 'Anyone have any luck with a *Slow*?'

[Channel Rescue] 'Is Tuscl here. I need to debuff him first and lower his resistances. My group members can't get through with anything. Can someone else try to take the aggro?'

Evidently no one could, as the running fight came into view once more and then another time, always with Tuscl running ahead of the cleric. Still, I was content with the situation. Kiting is not easy, especially when you are trying to draw someone after you who uses magic. Every now and again the NPC will stop to cast a spell and if you are a too close, you'll be blown up. A nuke was bound to be fatal if the mob was around level 50 and you are below level 20. On the other hand, if you just simply run off too far while the caster pauses, you'll lose the aggro and someone else will fall victim to the spell. What you had to do – and this was not something I was practiced in – was slow down your run as soon as the NPC started casting, to move out of range but still close enough to keep him interested. If you did that inside the length of time it took for the mob to cast the nuke, it would break off from launching the spell and move forward again. Our shaman seemed to have the relevant skills.

There was another danger in this situation too: it would be very easy for one of the other players throwing missiles or spells at the cleric to overtake Tuscl in respect to how much hate the mob had for her. Then we'd see the NPC turn around and start taking out raid members until someone got the kite flying again, so to speak. These were all good players, however, and were managing the aggro carefully. Not one person was dead and while the battle was developing extremely slowly, the hit points of the two dark elves were becoming lower.

Naturally, it was the cleric who succumbed first, after all, he faced the united efforts of the rest of the raid. We got the system message – **The dark elf cleric is dead. You gain experience** – when the warrior was still on 78 per cent. Everyone then gathered around my fight. If we shared the remaining damage as we'd learned to do with the singles, it was unlikely that anyone else would get the aggro, even so, I felt it worth voicing a reminder.

[Channel Rescue] 'We have this. Just take it slow if you are high level.'

This raid was giving me the rush of pleasure that I associated with my best moments in *Epic*. I had a sweet taste in my mouth every time I thought about how my vampire traits and *Wolf Form* meant we had a real chance of success here. More than that, I was experiencing the thrill of being back in a decent-sized raid party again, one that knew the ropes. Yes, we were relatively low level. That would change though. What mattered for the coming days and weeks were the bonds we were creating, the trust we were developing in each other's skills, and the shared sense of achievement. This was how to build a raiding party who would be able to tackle tough bosses as we all grew in level. Maybe even the dragon herself.

Just as I was enjoying, with some complacency, an anticipation of future success, the dark elf warrior span around and slashed at the halfling rogue behind him. Who was it? Owen. His hit points were halved in an instant.

[Channel Rescue] 'Sorry, I scored a critical hit on a backstab. I'm dead.'

And a moment later he was.

Fortunately, then, the dark elf turned back around to me and began wasting his blows on a character who could not feel them. The speed with which this enemy warrior had taken out one of our higher-level characters was a reminder that, although we were comfortable so long as the focus was on me, we would quickly wipe otherwise. It was like walking a path with a ravine to either side. All was well, so long as you stayed on the path.

[Channel Rescue] 'Anyone got a *Resurrection*?' I asked.

I recognised Woan's voice in reply, [Channel Rescue] 'I have *Restore Life*, but it doesn't remove the experience loss penalty. If he runs back and reclaims the body, he does better.'

[Channel Rescue] '*Restore Life* Owen? Or do you want to run back to clear the exp loss?'

[Channel Rescue] 'No question at all: *Restore Life*. I haven't had this much fun since I came to San Francisco. I don't want to miss a second of this raid.'

While we were talking, the fight had been progressing and the dark elf warrior's hit point bar was down below half. Was it me projecting, or did his face look weary and dispirited? Definitely, I decided, he was suffering and it showed in the drawn and wracked emotions of his tight-lipped mouth. For all that *Epic 2* was very similar in mechanics to *Epic*, the quality of the immersive experience was completely different. If I concentrated, I could smell blood, metal (from the sparks that flew when iron smashed into iron) and sweat. It wasn't only the sensual experience that was extraordinary though, it was the AI behind the behaviour of NPCs, which meant that every one I'd encountered had responded authentically.

The dark elf rogue is dead. You gain experience.

Eventually, our enemy staggered and collapsed to the ground with a last spasm that made it look like he really was biting the dust. Another nice game touch, if somewhat macabre. By this time Owen was back with us and when he had retrieved the last item from his body, it disappeared.

[Channel Rescue] 'There are magic items here, one *Fastened*,' said Tuscl, who as our main looter had gone straight to the body.

[Channel Rescue] 'Links please.'

On everyone's raid UI the links would have appeared: *Boots of Dark Elvenkind* and *Seitharian Greaves*. Holding my gaze on the links to open them, I read the following: *Boots of Dark Elvenkind* work exactly as *Boots of Elvenkind*, except only at night. At will, wearer moves as if with the skill *Sneak* (100). *Seitharian Greaves*: Fastened. +1 Plate, +3 at night. One other effect unknown.

[Channel Rescue] 'Very nice. We've hardly seen any magic so far. Normally in my raids, loot is rolled for randomly every time by those classes who can use the item. This isn't a normal situation. We have to be strategic. Until we liberate some higher-level characters, I think we need to pile all the tank items we find on Oveidio to make him as tough as possible. Is that agreed?'

After a short pause - obviously the players were getting so used to leaving the raid channel alone it took a moment to realise they were supposed to speak in it now - I got a welter of responses. It seemed to me they were all positive.

I tried again, [Channel Rescue] 'Hold up everyone, let me put it the other way. Does anyone think we should handle the drops differently?'

Silence.

[Channel Rescue] 'Cool. Loot up Oveidio and congratulations.'

[Channel Oveidio/Klytotoxos] 'Many thanks, Tyro.'

[Channel Rescue] 'What about the boots?' he asked in the public channel, 'should I take them too? They are only a small upgrade and seem better for a rogue.'

[Channel Rescue] 'I agree. Owen, you are reborn under a lucky star, go ahead and take them.'

[Channel Rescue] 'Wait!' cried Sapentia, so loudly and urgently I flinched. 'Boots only work at night. Vampire only walks at night and vampire has invisibility. Boots are perfect for possible situation where stealth is needed. Tyro should loot them so to have silent as well as invisible.'

[Channel Rescue] 'Sapentia is right,' said Raitha.

More importantly, Owen then agreed also. In fact, he insisted I take the boots.

[Channel Rescue] 'Very well. Thanks everyone. Back to your starting positions. Raitha, bring the next two mobs please.'

[Channel Klytotoxos/Sapentia] 'Thanks for that intervention, it was a good one. Can you take the boots for now? I'll put them on when my *Wolf Form* is over.'

As the others returned to the treeline behind me, I watched Sapentia kneel down and, with a tug, relieve the corpse of the dark elf of his boots. They looked fabulous, supple black leather with sinuous elven designs embossed upon them. Definitely an upgrade on the newbie leather sandals I was wearing.

[Channel Rescue] 'Incoming!' shouted Raitha. 'Two dark elves, one fighter class, the other definitely a caster.'

[Channel Rescue] 'I'll take the caster. This time Tuscl, let Verida take the kite so you can lower his resistances.'

Again, two powerful-looking dark elves ran into the clearing, chasing Raitha, and again I leapt into action. It was clear which one was the caster. While her companion wore black plate mail armour, she had just clothes: black boots, grey trousers, black shirt with wide collars and cuffs and a navy cape, over which cascaded astonishingly bright white hair. If you imagined a purple-skinned seventies superhero, you wouldn't be far off. My barging into her didn't cause her any damage and following a hiss from between clenched teeth and with a cold hatred in her moon-coloured eyes, she pointed at me and began to chant. Meanwhile, I took several hits from the longsword of the other dark elf, before he turned to chase someone, Verida, presumably.

Flash! Glittering silver flooded my vision.

You have been hit by *Lightning Strike* for 0 damage.

Hurray for my immunities. There was a risk here though. What if she resorted to a spell that was not derived from fire, cold or electricity? Some sort of water-based attack perhaps. Was I immune to that too? My UI didn't say so. Best to try to interrupt the caster rather than risk being hit by a spell that worked on me.

[Channel Rescue] 'Og, Nullentha, Birch and Rahod, come to me. We need to push this one to stop her casting.' I had picked the four lowest level characters of the raid. With my wolf attacks, still boosted by the blessing of Nemain, I should comfortably outscore them in damage and hold the aggro. What they could contribute, that was more important than damage, however, was a small push effect. The five of us, which was the maximum we could fit from this side, should be able to keep the wizard (*Lightning Strike* was wizard only) off balance and unable to cast any more spells.

Again, this was a test. Would the characters I'd named understand what I was about? It only took them a few seconds to run over and they squeezed in as tight as they could to maximise our collective impact. Good, they'd done this before. Og, the dwarven warrior didn't even bother using his sword, but put his shoulder behind his shield and kept bashing into our opponent that way.

Still glaring at me out of her amazing, silvered eyes, the dark elf was forced into a step back and her fluid arm motions and muttered words of power ceased. They started up at once, of course and again were broken off as she staggered back. We had her!

[Channel Rescue] 'Verida, just adjust your path as we push our mob to the edge of the clearing, make sure you don't train the warrior onto us.'

[Channel Rescue] 'Verida's down,' said Tuscl, 'I have the kite.'

[Channel Rescue] '*Restore Life* sent,' added Woan.

For the first time since we had started the raid, I felt I'd made a mistake. With all my attention fixed on establishing the push, I hadn't noticed that Verida's name was greyed out on the raid screen. Fortunately, the rest of the team had picked up the kite string, so to speak. Was I among friends? I thought so. They wouldn't care about a minor slip, would they? Still, I wished I'd continued my faultless start to this raid.

[Channel Klytotoxos/Verida] 'What happened?' I asked her, without losing concentration on the dark elf in front of me.

[Channel Klytotoxos/Verida] 'I turned around to check on him and he lashed out with that naginata. I should have just kept running. Sorry.'

[Channel Klytotoxos/Verida] 'No problem at all. Tuscl took the kite.'

To my left, my vision was partly obscured by the swing of Og's long ginger plaids as he barged into the wizard again and again. On my right, a human cleric, Rahod, was thumping down upon the dark elf with a heavy-headed iron mace. To his right was Birch, swinging a scimitar and then Nullentha, jabbing at our enemy with a longsword. And as often as I could, I was leaping up onto our opponent. All together, we were managing to reduce her hit points at a respectable rate. More importantly, the wizard had failed to launch any other spells than that first one.

Sylvania, the first moon, was showing as near full above the black treeline that loomed over us and this alerted me to the need to shift our push. Soon the wizard would be among the trees and that could allow her to break off.

[Channel Rescue] 'Push team, get ready, we are going to turn her one-eighty. In three...two...one...' I timed the countdown to end just as the dark elf was forced back a pace and even as she began to chant again, I whipped past her, span around and jumped to bite at her throat, for she had rotated to keep her vicious expression facing me. My comrades were at my side in an instant and now we had the whole width of the clearing for our push.

[Channel Rescue] 'Well done. Tuscl, note our new direction and steer well clear of us please.'

[Channel Rescue] 'Noted already.'

As the fight continued, my spirits rose high again. Once more, we had a winning set up. It would still be a long haul, however, and I hoped the others were patient. Over-eagerness was the main risk here, where someone accidently took the aggro and we lost our control over the mobs' pathing.

Unexpectedly, the dark elf wizard stopped trying to cast spells and drew a dagger.

You have been hit by a dagger for 0 damage.

Good.

A few failed stabs later and she spat at me. 'Whoever you are, you will suffer the wrath of Mikarkathat for this.'

'Probably. What do you know of Mikarkathat?' I asked

without easing up my attacks; my response was more to make conversation than a purposeful question. I enjoyed chatting to NPCs, especially if they had a good AI.

'Mikarkathat: her reach his long; her knowledge is deep; her thirst for vengeance unfathomable.'

'Excellent, well if you can remember this conversation after you respawn, give Mikarkathat a message.'

'What message?'

'That we are coming to kill her.'

The dark elf snarled, yet I could tell she was thinking. 'Who are you?' she eventually asked, after staggering back another step.

'I am called General.'

With that, it seemed we had run into a conversation stopper. By now her hit points were below half and the rest of the raid seemed to be doing a similar rate of damage to the warrior. Finishing them both off was just as matter of collective concentration and in due course we all received the messages we had been waiting for.

> **The dark elf wizard is dead. You gain experience.**
>
> **The dark elf warrior is dead. You gain experience.**

Chapter 17
Beneath Two Silver Moons

Having assigned the armour drops (*Seitharian Vanbraces* and *Seitharian Gauntlets*) to the appreciative Oveidio and a potion of *Restore Spirit* to Woan, I allowed a few cheerful comments in the raid channel to grow to a lively hubbub. In the midst of my raid's celebrations came a one-to-one message from someone I did not know: Borthar. After a moment's hesitation I took it.

[Channel Borthar/Klytotoxos] 'Hello Tyro. Mr Watson would like to see you right away.' The voice was that of an older man, local accent, officious. Probably someone who worked fairly high up for Yuno in San Francisco.

[Channel Borthar/Klytotoxos] 'Hello Borthar. I'm raiding at the moment. Could you ask him to wait until we are done please.'

[Channel Borthar/Klytotoxos] 'We know, Tyro. Mr Watson instructed me to ask you to unclip from your raid and come and see him.'

Although this way of addressing me as though I was just a Yuno pawn to be summoned and dismissed at will was needling, I knew better than to lose my temper with the messenger.

[Channel Borthar/Klytotoxos] 'Borthar, can you please check again with Mr Watson. Tell him I've rescued Oveidio and Woan and believe we have an excellent chance of clearing the dark elves stationed at Middlehampton. If our meeting can be postponed, that might result in seven extra high-level characters returning to the game for Yuno.'

[Channel Borthar/Klytotoxos] 'Really? Those level fifty-plus dark elves? With your raid?' He paused, as if to give me a chance to say I was only kidding. 'Well. That would change his priorities. I'll report back to him and contact you again. Can you give me an estimate of how long you need?'

[Channel Borthar/Klytotoxos] 'Thank you, Borthar. I guess around two hours. But I was then going to move north with the newly rescued players and tackle the other camps before our enemies respond in strength. So you might ask if that's okay too.'

[Channel Borthar/Klytotoxos] 'I will.' And to my surprise his voice softened. 'Good luck, Tyro.'

With that encouragement, I returned my attention to the partying in the raid channel.

[Channel Rescue] 'Okay folks, back to serious mode. Raitha, the last double pull please. What have we got?'

[Channel Rescue] 'Two warriors I think.'

[Channel Rescue] 'Great, starting positions please. Pull when ready.'

[Channel Rescue] 'Incoming! Two dark elf warriors.'

Again, the battle ran well for us, the only surprise being that the dark elf I took on turned out to be a shadow knight. This became clear when she discharged *Shock of Lightning* on her first hit with a longsword (no effect) and regularly tried a range of cold-based spells (no effect). There was one spell she had, however, that did affect me: *Weakness*. When it landed, I got the message *You have been afflicted by Weakness*. My Strength attribute dropped from 23 to 15, with a corresponding effect on my chance to hit and the amount of damage I did. This wasn't serious enough to make me want to use the push strategy that we'd employed on the wizard. Here, that would be a mistake as the mob might well have feats with her sword and shield that hit multiple targets and my allies would go down fast. No, I simply accepted the orange flashing icon on my UI. And I made note of the fact that there was at least one spell line capable of harming me. It was a warning: being a vampire did not make me invulnerable to all magic.

It took about fifteen minutes to grind the two mobs down

to their dramatic death scenes. With every kill, a thrilling hope that we could release the trapped party despite the odds against us surged up inside me. The feeling made me giddy almost, though I was determined not to let that show. Cool hand Luke. That was me as raid leader.

The loot this time was disappointing. Just *Seitharian Greaves* and *Seitharian Vanbraces.* Since Oveidio already had these slots filled with the magical plate armour, I asked Woan, the next highest plate class to loot them. It was hardly surprising that she sounded pleased when she did so, as not only was her armour now improving to the kind you might wear all the way up to your 50s, she would be a lot less weighed down compared to the bronze that the General had handed out.

[Channel Rescue] 'Right everyone, let's set up again. We just have this pull of three and then we'll see what we can do with the big group. What classes are we going to face this time Raitha?'

[Channel Rescue] 'Unfortunately, I am not completely sure. This is the first time I have encountered dark elves in *Epic Two* and they all look rather similar. For certain, there is a cleric, to judge by his use of the mace. One of the others is some kind of fighter class and the other is in leather armour with a short sword. Perhaps a rogue?'

[Channel Rescue] 'Pull them, then if you can take the one that looks like a rogue for a run, I'll try to tag the cleric and our kite is on the warrior.'

[Channel Rescue] 'Incoming! Three dark elves!' Raitha's shout was as enthusiastic as ever. Evidently, he was enjoying the role quite as much, if not more, than when he played a warrior in *Epic* raids.

At first the fight ran smoothly. My leap onto the cleric succeeded in focusing him onto me, while the warrior was snagged by Verida and taken for a run around the clearing. After several minutes however, Raitha spoke up anxiously, [Channel Rescue] 'Sorry, I've lost the rogue. I must have flown too high. Watch out in case his path back to his camp goes through your fight.'

It was all very well asking us to watch out, I thought, with a pang of irritation. Raitha was the eagle and I had a problem with what I could see. Being low to the ground and busy with an angry dark elf obscuring most of the world in front of me, I could only manage quick glances to either side. Really, it was up to my friend to fix the problem by tagging the stray dark elf as soon as he could.

[Channel Rescue] 'Tuscl, can you stand by, ready to kite that rogue if he comes here?'

[Channel Rescue] 'Will do.'

After a tense few minutes, I began to relax. The loose mob hadn't shown up. It seemed he wasn't coming our way. And this was confirmed almost at once.

[Channel Rescue] 'I see him!' exclaimed Raitha happily. 'He's nearly back in the village. He's going to be a single pull when you are finished with the other two.'

[Channel Rescue] 'That reminds me of a bad joke.' So pleased was I with this news, I broke my own channel rule. 'What do you call a slice of cheese that has been separated from the other slices?'

No one answered.

[Channel Rescue] 'An easy single!'

No one laughed either.

It suddenly occurred to me that maybe only Ireland had Easi Single cheese slices and I hadn't made any sense. Oh well, my good humour was soaring all the same, lame joke or not. We had the triple pull beaten. That was an impressive achievement given the massive disparity in levels.

A few minutes later and the dark elf warrior and cleric were dead. Then, without any difficulty, we pulled the rogue and I kept the aggro until we could all crowd around and take him down. One group to go! Admittedly, a real challenge, eight dark elves, with a level 62 among them. Having passed out the armour drops and a potion of *Healing*, I called for quiet in the raid channel.

[Channel Rescue] 'We are going to move up to the village for this last group of eight. Raitha, let us know where to stop. Then we will face three scenarios. One, I talk to them and they leave. That's probably too good to be true, but it has worked already on some ogres. Secondly, they all attack me, and I can draw them far enough away from the village for our friends to log in. Thirdly, they attack but don't chase me. Then Verida tries to tag one to kite while I keep the rest occupied. Any questions?'

[Channel Rescue] 'Glarinson here. How will Onvorg and the others know when to log in?'

[Channel Rescue] 'Good question. Do you know them?'

[Channel Rescue] 'A little.'

[Channel Rescue] 'Can you unclip and briefly alert them to how we are doing? Braja, a friend of mine, went to warn them earlier, so they should be standing by. Then you can call them in when the opportunity arises.'

[Channel Rescue] 'Sure. Unclipping now.'

While we waited for the dwarven warrior to return, a chat was signalled by Borthar. I took it.

[Channel Borthar/Klytotoxos] 'Hello Tyro.'

[Channel Borthar/Klytotoxos] 'Hi.'

[Channel Borthar/Klytotoxos] 'Mr Watson says well done and to take your time; he will meet you after the raid. And he would like to know if there is anything else you need? Would you like any more players to participate in your raid?'

[Channel Borthar/Klytotoxos] 'Certainly, the more the merrier. We are on the path just south of the village of Middle-hampton.'

[Channel Borthar/Klytotoxos] 'I shall arrange to get the other players there as soon as possible.'

Although I had agreed to the suggestion of more players joining the raid, they probably wouldn't make much of a difference to whether we could clear the village long enough for our blocked players to spawn and escape. From a longer-term point of view, though, I was happy for the raid to grow in size and to become used to working with each other. And, if I was being honest, it wasn't just about that. Stripping Blackridge of players from his unsuccessful raid gave me a distinct feeling of satisfaction.

With the return of Glarinson, our entire raid moved

northwards, Raitha turning slow circles high above, sometimes visible as a silhouette against the two moons. The silvery landscape should have been a friendly one, with helpful NPCs living in the cottages we were passing, lights shining from their homes and lanterns onto the path. Yet the buildings were abandoned, with black windows that looked out at us like sorrowful eyes. Even the forest seemed reluctant to come too close to these silent, thatched buildings, for the trees here were widely spaced and young.

Our route ran past the entrance to a small wooden church whose grounds were marked by a low wattle-and-daub fence. This was where Raitha told us to halt. [Channel Rescue] 'Those next two buildings ahead of you are the southern end of the village high street,' he explained, 'a blacksmith and a bowyer's. Once you pass them, you'll be seen by the dark elves.'

[Channel Rescue] 'So should we set up here and kite around the church fence perhaps? If that proves necessary.'

[Channel Rescue] 'That, I'm sure, would work well,' said our eagle thoughtfully.

[Channel Rescue] 'All right, everyone take a position in the church grounds, Verida and Tuscl follow me part way. If we have a battle on our hands, I'll try to bring the fight to the back of that bowyer's place. You can then tag one of them to run around the church.'

[Channel Rescue] 'Understood,' replied Tuscl.

This seemed to prompt Verida, as she added, [Channel Rescue] 'Got it.'

[Channel Rescue] 'Group leaders,' I announced, 'we will probably have reinforcements arriving, please invite them into your groups. We won't have time to work out who should go where, just grab anyone who is outside of the raid.'

[Channel Rescue] 'Will do,' replied Sapentia.

[Channel Rescue] 'Lizardman understandsss,' said Grythiss and it made me feel cheerful to hear him. What did the others make of his role-playing style? Hopefully, it didn't lose him any respect.

[Channel Rescue] 'Here I go then,' I said.

[Channel Rescue] 'Good luck,' said a voice I didn't recognise. The circle of players who wished me well instead of despising me was growing.

As I trotted up the village main street by the path between the blacksmith's and the bowyer's, I could smell that this village was a place with a great deal of industry. There was a stink like urine, which - as I could tell from its associated smells - probably had something to do with curing leather. There were more subtle scents though too: freshly cut wood (pine); the ashes of old fires; metal and polish; horses; donkeys; chickens; and a rich body of vinegary smells I couldn't place.

Until conquered by the General of Bow and General of Sword, Middlehampton was a supposed to be one of the best places to craft, as so many of the game's core crafting skills were represented here, not just in terms of merchants selling basic components but also in regard to looms, potter's wheels, forges, etc. Since I had not intended to do much crafting (only enough to be able to make my own arrows), I hadn't really studied the guide book with it in mind.

I walked out of the shadow of the alley between the two buildings and into the open. Trotting at a relaxed pace, I made my way along a moonlit street that was straight and paved; on either side were a dozen shops and crafting centres. In the middle of the street were a group of eight dark elves, standing in a circle facing outwards, while a slender plate-class fighter stood in their centre. This, no doubt, was our Level 62 opponent: rune-carved plate mail, so dark green as to be almost black; a delicate longsword, designed more for thrusting than slashing; a round shield with a snake's head design; a shocking cascade of light blue hair; and a face that was surprisingly beautiful for a warrior, with high cheekbones and emerald eyes.

As I came closer, there was a sudden ripple of movement among these dark elves. All at once they were facing me and raising weapons or, for those of them readying spells instead, their arms. I stopped. 'Hello. I bear a message from Mikarka-that.'

'Indeed?' The high-level warrior pushed at the shoulders of the dark elves in front of him, so he could part their ranks and walk towards me, hand on the hilt of his sword. A pang of anxiety ran into my stomach. Perhaps he could decapitate me and end the glorious progress of the raid? I would be fine, I assured myself. It was a positive that he was talking to me at all. 'Let us hear it.'

'Mikarkathat wants you to fall back to Fort Hellsmouth.'

'Does she?' Ominously, there was a tone of amusement in the warrior's voice. And I didn't like the way that he continued to close the gap between us.

'Oh yes,' I replied earnestly. 'An enemy army is on its way to retake the city and she wants everyone back there to defend it.'

Just as I was about to turn and run, he stopped and, slinging his shield over his back, rested his gauntleted hands on his hips, looking at me with some scepticism. 'That will let the Blackcoin seekers return.'

'Blood and thunder!' I was surprised and couldn't help myself from exclaiming aloud and out of role as the dragon's messenger. 'You understand that the game currency can be converted to Blackcoin?'

With a shake of his head, the dark elf said, 'I don't know what you mean. All I know is what Mikarkathat taught me. There are creatures like us - like me - and there are Blackcoin seekers. My task is to stop the reappearance of the Blackcoin seekers and kill them if they show up.' He looked at me with green eyes that seemed utterly sinister. 'And you are a Blackcoin seeker, aren't you?'

'No, no, not at all. I'm with you. It's just that Mikarkathat didn't prepare me to meet others with such knowledge as you have just displayed.'

'A rare and most unusual oversight on her part?'

'Not really. She probably just didn't think it necessary to brief me that you knew our enemies were Blackcoin seekers.'

There was something in the way the dark elf pursed his lips together that made me think this conversation was not going well. Perhaps I should start running now? After all, there were spellcasters behind him who might slow me up or even have some means of killing me.

'There's something I don't understand about the Blackcoin seekers.' The even, calm tone of this warrior was deceptive; I was sure he was containing a furious violence and that it would not be long before I was on the receiving end of it.

'Oh? What would that be?'

'Can they disguise themselves as werewolves?' His sword was drawn now, swept out with his final word.

'Ask me the password.'

'What's the password?'

With a flick of my UI I used *Read Thoughts.*

You have failed in your attempt to *Read Thoughts.*

You have been detected attempting to *Read Thoughts*!

Not only did the warrior lash out and stab me, he did damage.

You have been hit by a longsword for 148 damage.

Leaping wildly to the side I sprinted away, panicked. Left, left. Not through any doors. Left and right. He must be near.

Outside the village and swerving around trees I took a deep breath, still spinning the tracker pad vigorously beneath me (not that this made a difference, once you got it spinning quickly enough it was all a matter of your avatar's speed).

[Channel Rescue] 'I can't take the aggro on the level sixty-two warrior, his damage gets through. I'm running. It will be tough but you'll have to kite him.'

[Channel Rescue] 'Yo dudes and dudettes! Mashmeister is in the house!'

[Channel Rescue] 'Mashmeister, stay off the raid channel. Raitha, I'm a bit disorientated. Can you find me and guide me back around?'

[Channel Rescue] 'I am looking for you, my friend. Do you know from which side of the village you egressed?'

[Channel Rescue] 'Egressed? Who the hell says egressed?' This was the brash voice of Mashmeister again, sneering at Raitha. It made me furious to hear my best friend being mocked. Perhaps there was a downside to including people who hadn't volunteered to join me. With a glance at the raid screen on the UI (he was a level 18 warrior) I was tempted to expel him. That might just create more problems in the Rescue channel though; I didn't know if it were possible to kick someone out of that. Blackridge hadn't blocked me from his. Perhaps you couldn't.

In any case, Mashmeister was pure distraction. I'd remember him for later.

[Channel Rescue] 'I think it was east but now I'm curving around to my right.'

Dreading another hit, I didn't dare turn too sharply. My hit points had dropped from 208 to 60 in that one blow, a second would finish me.

In real life, this chase would be chaotic and noisy. Blundering around in the dark, I'd be crashing through bushes, tripping over vines and being caught by brambles, while my pursuer would be easy to hear as he brushed aside branches and his feet thumped into the forest floor behind me.

In the game, we were running silent.

On all fours and with perfect vision under the light of two moons, I raced deftly between trees and bushes, taking routes that went under low-hanging branches where I could, so that my enemy would have more difficulty than me in having to duck low or leap over them. Not that he seemed to be finding the task a challenge. I could barely hear him. Only when I caught the faint swish as we swept through a patch of reeds by a stream, or when his armour and gear clinked slightly after we made a jump over a fallen tree, could I be sure he was even there.

[Channel Raitha/Klytotoxos] 'I see you, you are currently running north-west, you need to come around south.'

[Channel Raitha/Klytotoxos] 'He's too close for me to turn.'

[Channel Raitha/Klytotoxos] 'Follow me.'

And swooping past my head was the great eagle form of my friend, disappearing through the trees ahead, veering to our right. It was a pleasure and a relief to see him and to take his lead.

[Group] 'You are out of range of my healing,' said Woan.

[Group] 'Yeah, I'm way out. Coming back though.'

[Channel Rescue] 'Hello. I am Anja from Madagascar, I play a cleric, currently level fourteen. How can I help? What is going on?'

[Channel Rescue] 'Stay off this channel.' Since my panic at being hit had died down (although I was still concerned about what this meant for my immunities) I felt calmer and added, 'Please. Use your group chat for introductions and explanations. At the moment I'm leading a level sixty-two warrior towards the raid for Verida or Tuscl to kite. It will be a hard, long kite. He's fast. He's going to resist most of your spells. Be patient. Don't take the aggro off the kiters.'

Following Raitha, I galloped out of the forest onto tilled fields that were undulating and silver bright, like the surface of a sea. To my right were the dark silhouettes of the village's cottages.

Sounding anxious, Raitha called out, [Channel Rescue] 'Incoming! A dark elf warrior.'

And we were running alongside the church fence, then straight at Verida and Tuscl who were staring northwards at the village.

[Channel Rescue] 'Look right, Verida.'

Just as I thought I'd have to take the mob right past them and around the village and back for another try, Verida started casting and from the corner of my eye as I ran past, I saw orange and red light flash from her hands.

[Channel Rescue] 'I have him,' she said, with a quiet confidence that I admired.

Tuscl spoke up, rather more excitedly, [Channel Rescue] 'Debuff fire worked!'

I stopped running and turned to watch, ready to take off again if our enemy should target me once more. Our *Hasted* druid (brown leather leggings, green newbie starter shirt, long blonde hair streaming behind her) was racing clockwise around the church grounds with a very realistic sprint animation: her avatar was punching the air before her with alternating, fast-moving fists. Our enemy was chasing in a much more fluid, elegant almost, manner of running, like a long-distance runner. He was losing ground to Verida but not by much.

[Channel Rescue] 'I need one point six seconds to cast *Flame Draw*,' she said, her calm voice contrasting with the vigorous efforts of her avatar. 'And I suggest waiting until I've done that ten times before we start to damage him. So will someone tell me when my lead is long enough to cast?'

[Channel Rescue] 'Sapentia, please call it.'

[Channel Rescue] 'Hai.'

My hit points suddenly maxed, with a rushing blue light crossing from the church grounds to me.

[Group] 'Thanks Woan.'

[Group] 'You're welcome.'

[Channel Rescue] 'Verida, you have two-second lead.'

Our druid paused, a flash of orange and red lit up the armour of the chasing warrior before fading like a spent firework. And the chase resumed. There was no obvious change, the warrior's hit point bar hadn't moved more than a fraction, if at all. The point of the spell though, was to pull mobs by annoying them, *Flame Draw* was a low damage, high aggro attack.

Around and around the chase went, the rest of the raid silent and watching attentively. The very presence of such a powerful enemy seemed to have imposed discipline upon them. This was not the time for joking. This was a time to concentrate.

After Verida had cast *Flame Draw* ten times, I called them in. [Channel Rescue] 'Attack from distance. Go easy at first. DoTs and missiles but no nukes. If you crit you'll mess this up.'

Immediately, from the crowd of colourful avatars in the churchyard came a flurry of arrows, daggers and darts. Soon after, a variety of colours streaming through the air showed that the first spells had been cast.

[Channel Rescue] 'Remember, he's been debuffed fire. Try a fire-based spell if you have it.'

The overall colour tone of the scene soon changed, from having been bright with all the colours of the rainbow, like a child's cartoon, to the flashes illuminating the nearby church and trees now variations of red, from near yellow to scarlet. And it was working! The hit point bar of the dark elf was definitely moving downwards.

Sapentia contacted me. [Channel Sapentia/Klytotoxos] 'Assign someone else to count for druid. I go to cast spells.'

[Channel Sapentia/Klytotoxos] 'I'll do it myself.'

[Channel Sapentia/Klytotoxos] 'Six fence posts is two seconds.'

[Channel Sapentia/Klytotoxos] 'Got it, thanks.' I saw what Sapentia meant: when the gap between Verida and the warrior was longer than that between six fence posts, she had time to cast *Flame Draw* again.

[Channel Klytotoxos/Verida] 'Clear for two seconds.'

And I saw her pause, cast, run.

[Channel Klytotoxos/Verida] 'Thank you.'

Five PC avatars were standing among the trees, watching.

[Channel Klytotoxos/Raitha] 'Making you a group leader. Can you snag the newcomers, brief them and make sure they don't come in too hard?'

[Channel Klytotoxos/Raitha] 'Certainly.'

In a few minutes the raid was up to forty-five players. Not bad. During those minutes, the kite had held and the dark elf had lost about 10 per cent of his hit points. Happiness began to well up in my chest, not that I allowed myself to believe in success just yet. In fact, my intuition was pessimistic: the kite would break. These might all be good players in theory but only my initial raiders were tried and tested at reducing a mob's hit points while allowing a relatively low-level druid or shaman to keep the necessary aggro to kite.

Around the church ran Verida. Around the church ran the dark elf warrior. And all the while, streams of missiles and spells flew towards him.

When our enemy was on about three-quarters of his initial hit points, he escaped the kite. One second, he was following the druid, a mindless piece of software, stuck in a routine that was slowly going to see him melt away. The next, he was leaping over the fence and slashing his way through the raid, ferocity incarnate. Someone had overdone their damage.

As the players fell and were rapidly being greyed out on the raid screen, I leapt to all fours and shouted out to the raid channel, overriding the voices that were surging up in consternation. [Rescue] 'Raitha, Glarinson with me. Verida, Tuscl, stay out of it until he stops killing people then lead him as far south as you can. Nobody else is to run. If you get his aggro just die.'

There was a lot of chat in my group, in the raid channel and in the small flashing signals of incoming one-to-one calls. Ignoring them all, I ran towards the village main street. As I exited the alley between the two shops, Raitha landed on the horserail in front of the blacksmith's.

'What is your plan?'

'Pull all of the mobs ahead of us that you can northwards. I'll fight whichever ones remain and hope they don't have weapons that can harm me.'

'Hah, simple to say. Let's see if it's as easy to execute.' With that, Raitha threw himself into the air, wings beating heavily to get enough momentum (I felt the buffeting effect on my cheeks, which was very smart of the helmet). Screaming loudly with his shrill eagle's cry, he flapped through the group of eight dark elves and out the other side. Several of them began the chase.

One threw aside her cloak and raised her arms, chanting. With a great bound I slammed into her back before her spell was finished and as she staggered forward, began my bite attacks.

You have failed to bite a dark elf.

You have failed to claw a dark elf.

Oh well, at least the spell she had planned for Raitha had failed. He was now safely away and leading - I checked quickly - six dark elves out of the village. There was just this spell caster and one other remaining, a cleric, probably, to judge from the mace he was bringing down on my shoulder.

You have been struck by a mace for 0 damage.

Thank goodness. Although it allowed the caster to get to

her feet, I swapped to the cleric for a round of attacks and then back to her. With me missing all the time and them doing no damage, this would be a very long fight. Except that I just had to keep them occupied for a few minutes.

[Channel Klytotoxos/Glarinson] 'Call everyone in please. And tell them to run east as soon as they arrive.' It seemed to me that the fields to our east and the nearby line of trees was the best hope that the players would have for a quick escape.

[Channel Klytotoxos/Glarinson] 'Will do.'

Wanting to know what was happening with the level 62 warrior, but not wanting to disturb Tuscl or Verida, I went back to the raid channel, even though it was full of people asking for a *Restore Life*, or for a teleport back to the bodies.

[Channel Rescue] 'Did Verida or Tuscl get to move him south?'

No one answered, the voices in my ears were all too busy trying to sort out their individual problems.

[Channel Rescue] 'SSssilensse!' shouted Grythiss, extremely loudly. 'Raid leader ssspeaks.'

[Channel Rescue] 'Thank you, Grythiss. Is anyone alive to report on the situation at the church?'

[Channel Rescue] 'Is Tuscl here. Verida is dead. I'm trying to move him south but he keeps turning back and running towards the village.'

[Channel Rescue] 'Don't let him. We just need one minute or so more.'

There was no answer and I could hear my heartbeat in my ears above the sounds of my battle with the two dark elves. This was going to be close. If only the trapped players could arrive in game now, they'd escape. *Come on*, I urged them in my thoughts, *come on*. Even if they had been standing by with helmets and gloves on, it still took about a minute for your avatar to synchronise to the world of *Epic 2*. If that intelligent dark elf warrior came back to the village first, he'd cut them down before they took ten steps. Should I break off...? If these guards were more or less fixed here, our incoming players could escape them more easily than the roaming level 62 warrior.

Spinning around, ignoring the attacks of my two enemies, I ran south and as I did so, Tuscl went grey on the raid screen (along with everyone else, there were just Raitha and I remaining who were green).

A second later: [Channel Rescue] 'Is Tuscl here. I died. I just couldn't get him to aggro me without getting too close.'

And here was the dark elf leader, sword still drawn, charging up the road. When he saw me, however, he slowed and a charming, if wicked, smile appeared on his face.

'Hello again, wolf who tries to deceive.'

'Hello my clever friend,' I replied, attempting to sound just as relaxed as he did, although the truth was I was all fired up with the urgency of the situation. Our missing players would be arriving in the village in a matter of seconds.

'I've killed all your comrades…'

'And now you are going to kill me. Yes, I'm familiar with those kinds of lines. I'm sorry to point out though, that you've overlooked something important.'

While we spoke, he sauntered forward, no doubt with a view to closing to the point at which he could thrust that dangerous longsword at me. I skittered to my left.

'What have I overlooked?' he seemed genuinely curious, his wonderfully animated face depicting puzzlement.

'The position of the moons.' This was a rather random statement on my part, inspired by the fact that both moons were high above the outline of the buildings behind the warrior and being near full, appeared to be two large, uneven and tilted eyes peering down at us.

As I hoped, he glanced up to check and the moment he did I rushed past him, escaping before he could land a blow. Now he was fully turned about and although he was clearly undecided about moving in my direction, his attention was fully on me.

'What about the moons?'

'I'm a werewolf, remember. When you fought me earlier, I was not at full strength. Not by a long way. Now the power of the moons is coursing through my blood. Now I can devour you. Or better, leave you with wounds that when they heal, will make you one of my kind.'

To my surprise, the warrior seemed to take this threat seriously, or at least he was pretending to. The point of his sword wavered, then dipped towards the ground; his shoulders slumped; his emerald eyes dimmed. Then he sprang at me.

It was no good, I'd been prepared for this and leapt to the side with a laugh. 'Oh, come on.'

Letting out a roar of annoyance, he tried again with a dramatic lunge. And again I swerved away. There were new colours and motions further up the main street. I had to stay focused on the warrior though. Dark elves were extremely nimble, even the plate-wearing classes. I had the measure of him, but not by much and even now his feints and genuine attacks were mixed together with real skill, as he tried to lure me into having my weight on the wrong feet when his fiercest attacks were launched.

After three more attempts, the warrior seemed to realise something was wrong. Perhaps it was in the fact that I didn't run away when the opportunity arose. Taking a step back, he turned and what he saw made him scream. 'No!'

A female hunter was running eastwards out of the village, having escaped the two dark elves, who just stood there, idle, evidently limited by their programming to remaining in their assigned positions.

Breaking into a sprint, the warrior gave chase and I set off too.

Another moonlit run through the forest. Our hunter was a half-elf and moved well, vaulting over a stile and into a ploughed field, leaving a clear line of footprints in the soft soil. She wasn't quite fast enough though; the warrior was gaining on her. Crashing through brambles and ferns, she entered the forest. At which point, I turned back, making for the main street as fast as I could.

'Hey guys, remember me?'

The two NPCs in the village clearly lacked any AI: no witty banter; no reference to our previous encounter. Their only greeting a raised mace in the case of the cleric and raised arms in the case of the caster, as she prepared to nuke me. Fine. All the while I bit and clawed at these two (hardly ever hitting successfully), I was scanning around. As I had anticipated, our half-elf druid, having been caught and killed, suddenly respawned beside me.

'Run west!' I shouted at her. 'Run west now!'

It took several painfully long seconds, but she understood me at last and set off in the right direction, away from the route that would be taken by the Level 62 warrior as he hurried back. Perhaps the fact that a wolf was barking orders at her had put her off.

Behind me came a male voice. 'They are all in. Need me or should I run too?'

With a quick glance, I saw Glarinson had returned to the game. 'Thanks, good job. Better run west and stay alive. I'll make you group leader. Try to round up those players who've just clipped up.'

'Will do.'

For about a minute, there was just me and the two dark elves in the village, hammering away at each other to no effect.

I'd positioned myself to have a good view eastwards, and as soon as the high-level warrior ran into the main street I broke off combat and ran southwards.

'You're too late,' I called out to him as I sprinted away.

'No!' In a fury, he shook his sword at me. The last I saw of his expression, though, was dismay.

[Rescue] 'Quiet please.' I waited a moment for the two people who were talking in the raid channel to stop. 'I have good news. Despite all the deaths, our mission at Middlehampton has been a success. Our seven comrades are back in the game. We will now take a break for one hour while everyone who needs to, relocates their spawn points to a safe place. Those who require a teleport to reclaim their bodies please arrange it with Sapentia. Next, we meet up west of the Temple of Mov. Be there in an hour please.'

[Channel Klytotoxos/Sapentia] 'I'm going to take a break.

Will you be raid leader and manage the logistics of ports and moving spawn points?'

[Channel Sapentia/Klytotoxos] 'I am honoured.'

[Channel Klytotoxos/Borthar] 'Hi, are you in game?'

[Channel Klytotoxos/Borthar] 'How can I help?'

[Channel Klytotoxos/Borthar] 'I'm going to take a break. I could meet with Mr Watson for about forty minutes if that suited?'

[Channel Klytotoxos/Borthar] 'I'm sure he will be pleased to hear that. I'll let him know.'

[Channel Klytotoxos/Raitha] 'Heading out. Meet you in forty minutes to run to the temple together.'

[Channel Klytotoxos/Raitha] 'Certainly. These dark elves who have been chasing me will no doubt be relieved when I fly off and let them return to the village.'

[Channel Klytotoxos/Raitha] 'No doubt.'

[Channel Klytotoxos/Raitha] 'And Tyro?'

[Channel Klytotoxos/Raitha] 'Well done indeed. I believe you will have proven your worth to everyone in this endeavour.'

[Channel Klytotoxos/Raitha] 'Thank you.'

Had I though? It was time to go and speak to Watson and find out.

CHAPTER 18
ARROW OF DRAGON SLAYING

I'd never seen a view like the one from Watson's office. Well, perhaps in a film. Blue sky filled most of it. If I looked down, I could see grey and brown rooftops as well as a sizeable stretch of green, which was the Golden Gate Park. Then there was the iconic, red suspension bridge, a vast amount of deep blue sea and Alcatraz island. Plenty to look at and if I were Watson, I'd probably spend hours daydreaming, staring out of my windows.

The room itself was large enough to contain his desk, a private *Epic 2* rig and a coffee table, around which was a couch and four comfortable, thickly padded, brown leather chairs. Present were Watson, Blackridge, Katherine Demnayako, myself and Braja, whom I had asked along, partly to fill him in on what had happened as we took the elevator upwards, mostly to have a witness in case there was a row.

Sprawled in the corner of the couch, arm resting along the back, Braja appeared to be very relaxed. I, on the other hand, probably looked anxious, though I tried not to. I was on the other end of the couch, sitting forwards, hands on knees.

'This is an informal conversation, off the record, so to speak,' said Watson, who looked slightly comedic in his bright glasses, sky-blue, short-sleeved shirt and flannel shorts. His voice, however, was severe and earnest. 'Let's speak our minds here and work out where we are at.'

'Paul, why don't you start.' Watson gestured to Blackridge, sitting to his right. Black shirt and trousers, wet hair, like he'd just showered, and heavy face. From this angle, looking up at him, Blackridge reminded me of a pixelated character from a kid's game, so solid was his head.

'Well, thanks to Tyro - Tom, I mean - we are nearly back on course. If we can have another month, I think we'll get there. Even if we have to tell the players stuck in Fort Hellsmouth to start over.'

Apart from the unexpected compliment from the man who had just tried to fire me, Blackridge didn't really interest me: I had been watching Watson. When the idea of an extra month was expressed, a sharp twinge crossed Watson's bearded face like he'd been stabbed.

'That's out,' Watson said immediately and with surprising vehemence. Then he drew a breath and spoke more calmly, in the fashion I'd become used to, which was much more gentle and mannerly. 'You all need to know something about our investors.' He peered over the top of his blue glasses and I felt he was giving me particular attention. 'Strictly between ourselves, they are the founders of Blackcoin.'

No one stirred while Watson seemed to be examining each one of us for a reaction. When I caught Braja's eye, he gave a slight twitch of his lips, as if to say, *Interesting*.

'There are five people,' continued Watson, 'who paid for *Epic Two* in the belief it would net them hundreds of millions of new Blackcoin users. They are in very deep. If they don't see progress soon, they will be angry. And I'm in the firing line. When I say firing, I don't just mean losing my job. These are, what you might call, non-traditional business people.'

'AKA mafia?' offered Braja.

'Something like.' Watson rubbed at his mouth. 'So, let's focus on what we can achieve in six weeks. Tom, is it still possible to deliver plan A?'

'I'm not here because you're going to send me home? You want my advice?'

Watson shook his head. 'You are doing a great job, Tom. And yes, I want your advice. Can you build a raid capable of killing the dragon in six weeks?'

'Not in six weeks, no. Maybe in ten.'

'That's what I think too.' Watson shot a look at Blackridge, who lowered his head rather than challenge this statement.

'Then we have to turn to plan B,' Watson continued, 'even though I'm not sure it is achievable either.'

'What's plan B?' I asked.

Watson waved towards Katherine, who was dressed smartly in a grey suit and who now leaned forward to place a colourful A3 graphic on the table. 'In brief, it's a crafting route that leads to the creation of *Arrows of Dragon Slaying*. These are arrows that do twenty-five thousand damage to dragons.'

Braja whistled. 'You'd only need, what, just four hits with those for Mikarkathat?'

'Three,' Katherine gave him a thin smile.

'How hard is it to make them?' I leaned forward, interested.

'That's the issue,' said Watson. 'Here.' He steered the diagram towards me. 'You'll have to share,' he added apologetically, 'I was only expecting Tyro.'

Both Braja and I leaned forward and Braja placed the sheet of paper so that it was exactly square with the lines of the table and an equal distance between us. The design looked a bit like a drawing for a knockout sports competition, with hundreds of starting points narrowing down towards a final box:

Arrow of Dragon Slaying

Requirements: Hunter, minimum level 50, Archery 250

+5 to hit, +50m to range, +25,000 damage to dragons

The sheet had dozens of insert boxes, with interesting titles like *The Undersea Ruins of Asthraxia*. These were regions of the *Epic 2* world and there were lists in each of them of the items that needed to be collected for various stages of the crafting process; in the case of the undersea ruins, for example, we needed to obtain a *turquoise pearl*, *strand of Kelpie hair* and *octopus ink*.

'Why didn't we do this from the beginning?' I wondered aloud.

'It's not as easy as it looks, all laid out like this,' Watson answered, 'several of these items are rare ground spawns or even rarer drops. We'll be lucky to get four arrows made in six weeks, simply due to that constraint. Then there's the problem that some of the drops are in high-level zones. Then, too, we are going to need a Master Bowyer and advanced-level crafters in every trade. A month ago, it seemed simpler to level up three hundred players and kill Mikarkathat in a raid. After all, you did it with less than half that many. Now that's not a realistic prospect in the time we have, it's time to try the assassination option.'

For a while I studied the graphic. It seemed to me there were some serious bottlenecks. After a while I looked up to find that Watson, Demnayako and Blackridge were all looking at me intently.

'What?' I asked.

It was Watson who spoke for them. 'Can it be done?'

'I think so.' I glanced at Braja, who nodded. 'Firstly, Raitha and I will be the hunters who use these arrows. Can we get to level fifty in six weeks? We can. We should be able to manage it with time to spare, in fact. Let's be conservative and say a level a day, that still leaves us five days.

'Secondly, the Master Bowyer. If we assign, say twenty players to gathering materials and the Bowyer stays at his or her workbench while the items are brought in, that should be no problem. Same with the other craftspeople, except let's give them ten assistants.

'Thirdly, the rare drops. Like the *Ornate Glowing Feather* from *The Tower of the Jewelled Skull*. It suits me to grind indoors, I'll take a group of six - maybe seven - in there and as we rise in level we should be able to pick up those feathers. We put our highest-level group, thirty-plus, into *The Undersea Ruins of Asthraxia* to farm there. As soon as they are all into their forties, they move on to the *Desert of Endless Screams* and by then we should have another group in their thirties to take over farming in the *Undersea Ruins*.

'Fourthly, we'll have to raid for the eight *Shards of the Smoke God*, as often as he pops. This could be a problem.' I tapped my finger on the box labelled *Ziggurat of the Smoke God*. 'Unless we can rescue our high-level characters, it will take us a couple of weeks to have any chance of success here and then your note says he is on a one-to-nine-day respawn timer. Depending on the number of shards that drop each time, this might not suit our timeframe.

'The rest of the items we need don't look too difficult, just a bit boring to collect. Or am I missing something?'

'No, you're right, those are the main challenges.' Watson looked to Katherine, who nodded. 'Are we all agreed on this plan then?'

'Agreed,' said Katherine.

After a moment's hesitation, Blackridge muttered, 'Agreed.'

'Good,' said Watson, putting his hands on the arms of his chair, as if about to push himself up and get on with his duties. 'I'm putting you in charge, Tyro. We'll schedule a full team meeting for later tonight and you can explain your plan.'

'That's funny. I came up here thinking you were going to send me home.'

No one smiled. Taking the graphic from the table, I got up to leave. So I was in charge now? That thought came with a rush of happiness.

'One more thing,' said Braja, standing up also.

'Yes?' asked Watson.

'Blackridge has to be seen to be backing Tyro. At the meeting, I mean. We don't want a split. When all the players are raiding with Tyro as leader, we don't want anyone secretly hoping he'll fail. So "the General" has to put on a good act. Make it clear he backs Tyro one hundred per cent.'

'Quite right.' Watson peered up at Braja, then turned to his right. 'Can you do that, Paul?'

Pale, blinking, Blackridge looked vaguely about the room. Then the heavy block of his head rocked up and down. 'I can do that.'

'I better get back to the raid,' I said, 'we are going to need every single high-level character we've got.'

'Go ahead. And good luck.' With something of a struggle to push himself up out of the soft chair, Watson came around to the office door, to show us out and to shake our hands. 'We'll schedule the team meeting for tomorrow morning then, after your raid and some sleep.'

On our way down in the lift, I looked at Braja. 'That went well.'

'It really did. You're the boss now. Make sure to ask for a big bonus if we do take down the dragon.'

This made me think of home. And something else. 'Braja.' I took a deep breath. 'You remember when I won that *Shield of the Dragonslayer* for Raitha in the roll after we killed Mikarkathat?'

'Yeah?'

'I cheated. I used a macro.'

His face was unreadable. 'Why are you telling me this, Tyro?'

'Because Watson knows. He has proof. And if things ever go sour, like over money, he'll use it to try and split us up.'

'Who else knows?'

'Raitha.'

'Not Sapentia or Grythiss?'

'No…not yet.'

'You should tell them.'

'Okay. Are we good?'

'We're good.' Braja nodded, holding my gaze just long enough for me to read his sincerity.

Back in the game, Sapentia handed over the raid leadership to me. It had grown to an extraordinary size, nearly two hundred strong, as large as I'd ever led. With the escape of Onvorg (level 42 druid) and his group from Middlehampton, that added eight players in the high thirties to the raid, which meant a great deal in terms of buffs for the rest of us and debuffs, especially to movement, for the mobs. In theory, the next step, the rescue of five clerics at the Temple of Mov, should be easier than what we'd achieved already.

As raid leader, I could swap the group memberships around and I did so now, creating groups that were nine or ten strong. In all the odd numbered groups, I made sure there was someone with *Haste* who could kite, even if the mob's speed was not reduced.

[Channel Raitha/Klytotoxos] 'Welcome back, how did it go?' Raitha was sitting on the crenelated top of the church spire, sharp eagle beak dramatically silhouetted against Sylvania, the larger of the two moons.

[Channel Raitha/Klytotoxos] 'Surprisingly well, considering Blackridge tried to sack me a few hours ago. They've put me in charge of Plan B.'

As we set off along the path towards Fort Hellsmouth, I explained the new situation to Raitha, including the fact that he was down to stand with me and shoot Mikarkathat with an *Arrow of Dragon Slaying*.

[Channel Raitha/Klytotoxos] 'My goodness. This is a big responsibility. I believe you are capable of anything, Tyro. For my part, however, I am concerned I will miss or otherwise fail to deliver upon my responsibilities.'

[Channel Raitha/Klytotoxos] 'Oh, I'm the same; I worry about that too. What can we do, though, but try our best? And remember, we've stood face to face with that dragon and beaten her.'

[Channel Raitha/Klytotoxos] 'One of my happiest memories,' said Raitha softly.

[Channel Raitha/Klytotoxos] 'Mine too.'

With the moons overhead and the path straight, we hurried northwards at great speed and no risk. Around me were the scents of damp leaves, nettles and gorse.

[Channel Raitha/Klytotoxos] 'You were injured by the dark elf warrior, I believe?' Raitha suddenly asked.

[Channel Raitha/Klytotoxos] 'That's right, I lost more than half my hit points in one blow.'

[Channel Raitha/Klytotoxos] 'I wonder how that occurred? Does this mean that if we are above a certain level, then we can overcome immunities in creatures like vampires and were-wolves?'

[Channel Raitha/Klytotoxos] 'I hope not, for the sake of the advantages of being a vampire. I was thinking about this too and wondered if it was his sword. Perhaps I'm not immune to certain types or strength of magic weapons.'

There was no answer from Raitha for a minute and then, [Channel Raitha/Klytotoxos] 'It is a shame someone broke the kite. We could have looted the sword and tested your theory. Now we shall have to proceed with great caution if we engage with our usual strategy of you as tank.'

Our path came out of the woods to cross a small, hump-backed bridge and breasting this allowed me to look ahead to where the Temple of Mov stood on the next hill. The church was inspired by classical design, being a circle of widely spaced pillars, on which rested a large dome. As it was built on the top of a modest-sized hill, it reminded me of the much cruder dolmens and other stone monuments of ancient Ireland. Both had the same exposure to the night sky and sense that the stones were looking up at the stars.

Normally, there were cleric NPCs at the temple from whom you could buy spells and get quests and, normally, it was a perfectly safe spot, which was why five of our higher-level clerics had made it their spawn point. Since the dark elf conquest of Fort Hellsmouth, however, they'd also overrun the temple and stationed five dark elves and an iron golem to prevent anyone respawning there.

Our raiding party were gathered in fields to the west of the hill. These were church lands, recently harvested, and our army was tramping around on the stubble.

[Channel Klytotoxos/Onvorg] 'Hi Onvorg. Do you have the spell *Earthsink*?' I asked our high-level druid.

[Channel Klytotoxos/Onvorg] 'Hi Tyro. I have it but it's not equipped at the moment.'

[Channel Klytotoxos/Onvorg] 'Please slot it in. I'm thinking we can slow the golem with it.'

[Channel Klytotoxos/Onvorg] 'Good idea. And hey, Tyro?'

[Channel Klytotoxos/Onvorg] 'Yeah?'

[Channel Klytotoxos/Onvorg] 'Thanks for getting me out of Middlehampton. The thought I'd have to start over was depressing.'

[Channel Klytotoxos/Onvorg] 'You're welcome.'

Next, I switched to Glarinson to ask him to prepare the clerics we intended to rescue, then I opened the raid channel, which was full of voices, mostly cheerful.

[Channel Rescue] 'Hi folks, Tyro here, let's get ready to clear the temple.'

There was a slight drop in volume. Then Grythiss came in with a roar again. [Channel Rescue] 'Raid leader sssspeakss! All mussst lissten!'

And again, that did the trick. [Channel Rescue] 'Thank you, Grythiss. Remember our objective is simply to clear the temple long enough for our friends to arrive in-game and run clear. We are not trying to kill these mobs, which is just as well. They are too tough.

'If you are in an odd numbered group, this means you have kite duties. It's your job to keep those mobs we can pull away from the temple from returning. Pull southwards, it's all safe in that direction. Even numbered groups two, four, six, eight and ten, you are DPS reserve. Assemble halfway up the west of the hill. Listen for my call as to the target. At Middlehampton, two of the dark elves wouldn't budge from the town centre. If that happens here, hopefully, I can tank and you'll be backing me up.

'Even groups ten plus, you are DPS on the kites. Assemble at the foot of the south side. Go easy, don't confuse matters by getting aggro.

'Finally, Onvorg's group are on the golem. If you can draw him away, great. If not, we'll *Earthsink* the ground beneath him and that should get us a minute or more before he climbs out of the mud.

'Raid buffs on now please, we all need *Haste* and whatever resistances you have. Starting in five minutes.'

[Channel Rescue] 'Wait!' a woman's voice, unknown to me. 'Clathurnia and I are nearly there, we need ten minutes more.'

[Channel Rescue] 'I'm sorry, we are on a timer. I can't do this when dawn comes. PM Raitha when you get here for an invite and instructions.'

After the flurry of spellcasting died away - it was wonderful to have *Haste*; I also received a fire resistance and two small cold resistance buffs - I set off for the temple. [Channel Rescue] 'Let's move.'

With a respectable surge of co-ordinated motion, the raid broke roughly in two, the majority moving around to the south side of the hill, the rest following me up the west. We had a paved road to follow and with *Haste* on, I was moving with incredible fluidity. Halfway up, I paused. [Channel Rescue] 'DPS reserve stay here. Onvorg with me.'

[Group] 'Do we stay here too, Tyro?' asked Oveidio. I hadn't changed my own group around, as I was enjoying getting to know them and listening to their chat. It was a fair question.

[Group] 'Please do. And you'll probably be DPS. There are a lot of unknowns ahead though so stay a little south of the main bunch and stay aggro free for now. You have my permission to act on your own initiative if I'm dead and the raid is going pear-shaped.'

While giving my group this reply, I had been advancing with just the druid at my side and this was the first time I'd gotten a chance to see his avatar. As usual with all these players, he was a patchwork of armour, with a distinctly imbalanced look. On his left arm and leg was some decent-looking black leather, with a neat design of exotic leaves carved upon them. His chest, however, was just a basic brown leather jerkin, tied with black laces, and his right arm only sported the white sleeve of his shirt. Onvorg was a half-elf, whose hair looked silver in this light but was, perhaps, white.

Moving at a walk, to keep pace with him, we reached a point where first the golem's head could be seen between the tall, pale stone pillars and then its body, as well as the helmets of three of the five dark elves we had been told were here.

'Can you target the golem?'

'I have him.'

'Good. I'm going inside. Good luck.'

'You too.'

[Channel Klytotoxos/Raitha] 'Are you close?'

[Channel Klytotoxos/Raitha] 'Indeed, I am circling above you.'

[Channel Klytotoxos/Raitha] 'Here I go. If I die, take over and maybe call a charge of the DPS group. In the confusion our clerics might make it.'

[Channel Klytotoxos/Raitha] 'Don't die. I cannot bear the responsibility.'

[Channel Klytotoxos/Raitha] 'Hah, you're gonna love what I have to say to the raid channel then.'

[Channel Rescue] 'I'm going in. If I die, listen for Raitha's commands. Then Sapentia.'

On my own now, I walked on up to where the paved path met with the stone floor of the temple. There were indeed five dark elves and they all turned to look at me as I put one paw down on the ground between the nearest columns. Then the other. No one stirred. From the woods to the east came the hoot of an owl.

'Good evening.' I took another step. 'I come with orders from Mikarkathat. She needs us all to fall back to Fort Hells-mouth, to defend against an enemy army.' Inside, the temple was austere, bare other than one large statue of Mov, looking like an Ancient Greek war god, with his helmet, breastplate and greaves. Yet he carried no weapons and was sculpted with a raised, open hand. The floor, too, was an exception to the bare stone effect. It was tiled and there were scenes from the tales of Mov, which might have interested me another time. Now, however, my attention was firmly fixed on the dark elves.

Two casters, two fighters and a hybrid (probably a hunter, given the bow) stared at me and none of them looked anything other than hostile. Less was probably more in this situation. In other words, I kept my mouth shut, hoping one of them would speak and give me something to work with.

At last, one of the casters stepped towards me, her boots echoing loudly under the dome. 'We have our orders. No one must enter the temple. All who do, must die.'

'Indeed and you have carried them out most admirably. Now the dragon changes your orders.'

'Where is she?'

'In the north.' I couldn't think of a more specific location.

'Leave. If the dragon comes, we will listen. You must go.'

'I see. I understand.' It's hard, walking backwards as a wolf. I did, however, manage a couple of steps in reverse.

[Channel Klytotoxos/Raitha] 'Sweep in from the north side and try to run as many as you can south down to the kiters.'

[Channel Klytotoxos/Raitha] 'I am coming.'

[Channel Klytotoxos/Onvorg] 'Try pulling the golem now.'

[Channel Klytotoxos/Onvorg] 'Okay.'

As I continued to shuffle backwards, the scowl of the female dark elf deepened. Still, she didn't start to cast a spell. Then, more or less at the same time, the golem rumbled into life and Raitha came screaming into the temple. Being an iron golem, it looked a lot like a giant robot, three metres tall, flat head with glowing amber eyes and a groaning, screeching motion as though the magician who made him forgot the oil. As it stamped past me, shaking the ground and making me glance up at the roof of the temple with some anxiety, I saw Raitha flash across and out the other side.

Ominously, the dark elves reacted effectively and without alarm. Their hunter already had his bow out and an arrow nocked; both casters were chanting and while the two warriors had moved to the pillars on the south side, they hadn't left in pursuit.

[Channel Rescue] 'Kiters, come up the hill fast and tag the two warriors facing you, try to pull them away. DPS charge the female wizard and push her.'

[Group] 'Charge! Target the male caster, he's a necro I think, and push him.'

That left the hunter. Agonisingly, I watched him take careful aim. If I attacked him too soon, the other four dark elves would respond to me and that might make a mess of my plan...Perhaps I should anyway. Too late. The arrow flew through the night sky and a moment later, Raitha went grey on the raid screen.

[Channel Onvorg/Klytotoxos] 'The golem's in the mud but he's lashing around and won't be in there for long. You need to mobilise the clerics now.'

[Channel Onvorg/Klytotoxos] 'Okay, thanks.'

I immediately contacted Glarinson. [Channel Klytotoxos/Glarinson] 'Call them in.'

[Channel Klytotoxos/Glarinson] 'On it.'

With whoops and cries, the half of the raid that was the DPS group came charging through the pillars. We were lucky in the set-up, had the wizard's view not been obscured, she could have landed an area of effect spell like a *Fireball* with devastating results. Instead, snarling, she raised her hands and from outstretched fingers, ten *Frost Shards* blasted from her and into the faces of the nearest players, killing several. That wasn't good enough though and the survivors poured into the temple, slashing, bashing and kicking at her. Their damage didn't amount to much, crucially, though, the push was established and the wizard couldn't get her next spell off as she staggered back time after time.

[Rescue] 'Group six and eight, swap to the necro! Six and eight to the necro!'

We had more than enough players for the wizard. In fact, half a dozen raiders were standing around unable to get in at her from the front or side. Now it was the necro that was the main problem, especially as Oveidio and Woan had been hit by a *Cone of Fear* and were running away as fast as they could.

The fact that I could no longer see the two dark elf warriors was a good sign, even if several of the kiting groups had greyed out members.

In a matter of seconds, the clerics would have synchronised with the game. On their arrival, the main threat they would face was from the hunter. Threading my way through the confusion I picked up speed until I had a clear line to the archer and then I sprang at him.

With an astonishingly lithe roll, the hunter escaped to the side and simultaneously, got a shot off. A flicker of darkness entering my chest.

You have been hit by an arrow for 0 damage.

Thank goodness.

I dived on top of the hunter and while most of my bites and claw attacks kept missing, the crucial thing was I had his full attention. Abandoning his bow, he pulled a pair of curved daggers from his belt and stabbed at me with a flurry of vicious blows that should have been fatal.

You have been hit by a whipcord dagger for 0 damage.

You have been hit by a whipcord dagger for 0 damage.

You have been hit by a whipcord dagger for 0 damage.

You have been hit by a whipcord dagger for 0 damage.

Unlike the warrior in my last battle, the AI in this hunter, who was level 54, was non-existent and that meant he didn't question his strategy, even when I wasn't weakening the slightest. Good. Now, were our clerics in? How was the raid doing? Was the golem free from its muddy trap?

Something was going wrong, with every beat of my heart another player went from green to grey on the raid screen. Looking around as much as I could without allowing the hunter any respite from my attacks, I could see the problem was the necro. Somehow he'd managed to raise a skeleton pet and even though there was a push against him, the pet, which was probably stronger than level 50, was picking off my raid party pretty rapidly.

[Channel Rescue] 'We need more people pushing the necro. If you can, run up to the temple and join in. His pet will kill you but we only need another minute.'

Maybe only thirty seconds. For one of our clerics suddenly materialised right beside me and immediately ran off through the northern pillars. Quite right. Then another. Then the third. Just as I was beginning to feel it was another mission accomplished, the fourth cleric appeared, only to be melted down by black mist (the graphics were pretty gruesome, a cloud in the shape of a skull descended upon him and immediately, he started to fizzle and spurt out bits of armour, skin and bone).

After a moment, the same cleric respawned in the same spot and again he died, victim of more grim magic. This time, skeletal hands reached up from the floor to pull him down and throttle him until his twitching legs were still. The *Epic 2* devs had obviously enjoyed designing the necro line of spells. The next respawn, however, and our cleric was clear. Enough of the kiters were hurling themselves onto the enemy caster to throw him off balance. And even though they died like lemmings (not that lemmings actually did all throw themselves from cliffs), it was enough. All five clerics were clear.

[Channel Rescue] 'We're done. Mission achieved. Anyone still alive run clear and unclip to remove any aggro. Regroup one mile northeast of Fort Hellsmouth.'

Immediately, the raid channel came alive with whoops and cheers. My UI was flashing with a dozen one-to-one calls. Now was not the time, however, with an iron golem on the loose and a necro with a line of spells to which I might well succumb, it was time to take my own advice.

[Channel Klytotoxos/Raitha] 'Making you raid leader while I unclip and shake off any residual aggro.'

[Channel Klytotoxos/Raitha] 'Very well.'

From beyond the eastern pillars, waves of thundering metallic notes pulsed through the temple as a warning.

'Let's continue this another time,' I said to the dark elf hunter, then broke away from my attempts to bite and claw him. Rushing westwards, I was hit by four arrows before I found safety on the far side of a dry stone wall. Now I ran south, hopefully hidden by the grey stones, until I reckoned I was a safe distance, even from an enemy that might be chasing me. Not that I could see or hear any sign of enemies nearby.

[Channel Klytotoxos/Raitha] 'Okay, dropping from game. And Raitha, I'm sorry about your death.'

[Channel Klytotoxos/Raitha] 'Do not concern yourself about that my friend. What matters is our goal was achieved.'

Having turned around to check in all directions, I unclipped. Leaving the game when you might have aggro was a risk. To prevent players from escaping fights that they were losing by leaving the game, your avatar remained in play for a good minute after you'd unclipped. Even without your knowledge, you could die, something you'd only discover on returning. You could drown, too, as I'd learned in *Epic*.

For a few seconds I was aware of my real body again, of the slight constriction around my head from the helmet, the presence of gloves on my hand. There were game menus to look at, settings and calibration options floating over a misty lake (the backgrounds changed all the time, always with scenes from the game, some of them very intriguing), as well as an attractive magenta option to enter the game. I looked at it, so that it was highlighted, but refrained from triggering it with a finger movement. Best to be sure none of the mobs chasing me were lingering at the spot where I unclipped.

Finally, after a count of sixty, I re-entered the game, a roar of sound and swirl of rainbow colours making me giddy for a moment, until everything stabilized: wall, field, line of trees, scent of damp soil, soaring flight of a swallow. And no bad guys.

CHAPTER 19
GENERAL OF SWORD, GENERAL OF BOW

[Channel Raitha/Klytotoxos] 'Welcome back. You are raid leader again.' There was a liveliness in Raitha's voice that made him sound cheerful.

[Channel Raitha/Klytotoxos] 'Thank you. Do you still have your eagle form?'

[Channel Raitha/Klytotoxos] 'Alas, not. And it is greyed out. We will find out now how often this ability is available. Hopefully it is a matter of days rather than weeks.'

[Channel Raitha/Klytotoxos] 'Can you make it back to Fort Hellsmouth?'

[Channel Raitha/Klytotoxos] 'I'm running from Djorjuna Mountain but I'm still thirty minutes out. Please, start without me.'

[Channel Raitha/Klytotoxos] 'Thanks, I might. I'm conscious that the sun is on its way. Let's see how things go.'

Skirting the edge of the forest, I ran northwards on all fours until meeting up with the path that connected the Temple of Mov with Fort Hellsmouth, passing hills and empty cottages. Around me I could scent living creatures: small woodland animals mostly, nothing too dangerous.

[Channel Klytotoxos/Sapentia] 'Hi, are you at the rendez-vous?'

[Channel Klytotoxos/Sapentia] 'Hai.'

[Channel Klytotoxos/Sapentia] 'What landmarks are there? And how many people?'

[Channel Klytotoxos/Sapentia] 'Nearly two hundred. Watermill.'

[Channel Klytotoxos/Sapentia] 'Thank you.'

I contacted the raid channel, which was overly busy as usual. In fact, I had been running with it muted. [Channel Rescue] 'I'm about ten minutes from Fort Hellsmouth, everyone who can, meet up with the rest of the raid at the watermill, a mile northeast of the city.'

Making my way down the slope to where the raid was gathered gave me a nice moment. As they saw me arriving, a sizeable part of the crowd (maybe half), raised their weapons and cheered. It was quite a scene: warriors knocking swords against shields; wizards brandishing wands and staves; hunters waving their bows above their heads. And as I reached this colourful, enthusiastic army, they parted for me. A chant of 'Tyro! Tyro!' began as I passed through the ranks. It made me feel a comradeship with these players, whom only hours earlier I had been completely estranged from. If Blackridge had managed to bully me into leaving my coffin too early, I would have been denied the chance to achieve anything in *Epic 2* and would have left the game in disgrace. Instead, I was here. Doing what I was good at.

When the chants subsided, I led the raid southwards and alerted latecomers via the raid channel that we were to be found at the sacred grove of ancient oaks.

This part of the raid was straightforward and presented no new challenges, although I hadn't seen Cerebri before. These were three-headed dogs, levels 42 to 45 and it was no joke having them chase you, barking and slathering and leaping for your throat from three directions. Fortunately, I was immune to their bites so I could stand there gaining aggro until it was safe for the others to start hitting them. Our kiting teams worked smoothly on the dark elves that could be drawn away from the grove and when there were just two remaining (a warrior and a cleric, 58 and 60) who wouldn't chase me from the grove, I stood among the first line of trees taunting them, while our raid started to damage them. This posed a question to the mobs and it was interesting to see them vacillate, taking one step towards us, then turning to guard the spawn points. Then towards us, when they were damaged, then back.

In theory, we probably could have killed both by this strategy. Yet it was painstakingly slow because of the cleric, who healed up the modest amounts of damage we were doing easily enough. I didn't have all night, I told myself, so once Raitha was back, I made him raid leader and ran up to the cleric. Fortunately, the dark elf's mace and shield had no effect on my hit points, nor, when his companion joined in, did I suffer from her blows. Game over. Three grateful druids back in action.

Next on my agenda were the twelve level 40 plus characters whose spawn points were just outside the great southern gate of Fort Hellsmouth. Marching towards the city, raid at my back, was another fantastic experience. Lit by two moons, the pale towers of Fort Hellsmouth stood tall into a starry sky, the faint orange lights of its windows and streets making their own constellations against the background of the smaller, sparkling silver dots.

Skirting the eastern walls of the city by travelling over cultivated fields, we came to the wide paved road that led to the southern gate. There were banks to the road, raising it up from a muddy plain that formed a dark shore to a silver, glistening, calm lake.

Fort Hellsmouth faced the lake with its western walls. As you came closer to the city walls on the south side, the mud hardened into a dark, solid earth and there, dozens of merchants usually had their tents and carts. The high-quality traders were all inside the city, of course; the ones that gathered here were those who couldn't afford the trading licence. You could fix your spawn point here, arriving in the game just outside the city walls, amongst the rough and coarse humoured denizens of what had been a lively community. The advantage of doing so were a couple of nearby dungeons for levels 30+ and being able to trade for cheap gear and spells. Twelve of our players were locked out of the game as a result of the invasion by the Generals of Bow and Sword.

As we ran along the road - wading birds, startled and angry, flying into the night sky out of the rushes on either side - it was clear that the whole district had been wiped. There were no booths left, no campfires. Silence and perhaps, in the darkness, the enemy troops and their Mind Stealer ally. The loss of Fort Hellsmouth to the dark elves had taken away an important centre for developing your character. It had been in the back of my mind to come here for my hunter spells as well as for training, if I could afford it. Plus gear, although that was less important to me now that I could function as a wolf and a vampire.

If I were the dragon Mikarkathat and were consciously trying to hamper the ability of players to enter the game and to advance once within it, I'd take out all such major cities. Then, even if I couldn't prevent players from arriving in the game, they wouldn't be able to progress as they should in terms of spells and skills. By this thinking, there was probably an evil army on the march to Port Placida. After tonight, I should advise everyone to purchase what they needed from that city in case it fell too.

As the road slowly curved towards the southern gate I slowed up and eventually stopped. It was to my right that the players would spawn and it must be there that the enemy waited, although from here I could not make them out, despite the brightness of the light from the moons.

Before I could appeal to the raid for a *Wizard's Vision* spell, or for someone who could fly to scout the area (what a shame Raitha was back in half-elf form) an alarming screech and rattle alerted me to the fact that the huge portcullis in the southern gate was being raised.

[Channel Rescue] 'Silence! Silence in this channel. Absolutely no talking.'

For once, my voice had the desired effect first time. Maybe they were getting used to me, or maybe the undisguised concern in my tone had done the trick. In any case, Grythiss didn't need to come in to back me up. The cheerful banter that had been continuous throughout our march suddenly ceased.

One, two, four, eight...twelve storm giants strode out, their leader carrying a tall black banner, which had an image of what looked to be a scarlet star, but was in fact a symbol made from sixteen scimitars, all touching at the base and radiating outwards.

These were followed by twelve dark elf riders, whose class was probably shadow knight, given that they seemed to be riding Fearstriers, black stallions with green eyes and a green glowing aura to them. The banner of these knights was a star of exactly the same shade of scarlet as the other, this time made by arrows pointing away from the centre of a circle. The giants deployed to the right, the shadow knights to the left and down the corridor between them walked two figures who could only be the General of Sword and the General of Bow.

Feeling my chest constrict, I took a deep breath.

[Channel Rescue] 'Move off to the right of the road. Follow Sapentia. There are dark elves and, probably, a Mind Stealer ahead of you. Kite them away from the spawn points if you can. Distract them for as long as possible if you can't. Start at once. We haven't a chance once the bosses join in.'

[Channel Klytotoxos/Sapentia] 'Cast some sort of illumination and head towards the spawn points. Find the guards and start the battle.'

[Channel Klytotoxos/Sapentia] 'Hai. Understood.'

From the top of Sapentia's staff came a bright blue flare, which hovered above her, illuminating everything in a monochromatic navy tone and creating long shadows from our army that stretched away towards the lake.

[Channel Klytotoxos/Glarinson] 'Use your own judgement about when to call the others in. Basically, as soon as things start to move. We are not going to be able to clear the spawn points but we might cause enough confusion for some of our players to get away.'

[Channel Klytotoxos/Glarinson] 'Will do.'

[Channel Klytotoxos/Raitha] 'Come with me.'

[Channel Klytotoxos/Braja] 'Come with me.'

[Channel Klytotoxos/Grythiss] 'Come with me.'

And I walked towards two of the most infamous and powerful NPCs in the game.

Behind me, I sensed the fluid motion of the raid, as everyone apart from my three friends followed Sapentia over the flats, towards what should have been the caravans and stalls of the traders. And there in front of Sapentia, indeed, by the wizard light, I could make out a group of dark elves accompanied by a tall figure whose fingers were tentacles, stretching out towards us. A Mind Stealer was a problem but not as much of a problem as two level 100 dark elves.

'We're dead,' I said to my small team as we stepped forward to where the General of Bow and General of Sword were waiting. 'Apologies for that, but I thought you'd like to check out these rare bosses. And Braja, you're a great conversationalist. Try to keep them talking if you can, while the raid distracts the mobs on the spawn points.'

On my right, Braja chuckled.

To my left, Grythiss lifted his now-magical longsword. 'Jusst give me the chance to ssstrike them at least once.'

'Me too.' Raitha was at the end of our row beyond Grythiss, bow in hand.

Our enemy generals had stopped, waiting for us, standing adjacent to their respective banners. The General of Sword wore gleaming indigo plate mail armour, the General of Bow engraved black leather. Both had several weapons scabbarded to them. Powerful weapons, no doubt and across my thoughts flitted a daydream in which we killed them and had our choice of these items.

With some twenty paces between us, I stopped. The General of Bow shook out his long ivory hair, pulled it back and pinned it clear of his sombre gaze with an indigo headband.

'Well met,' I said. 'I am Klytotoxos; this is Braja; this is Grythiss; and that is Raitha.'

'It is an honour to meet you,' said Raitha. 'I have heard so much about your achievements.'

'What manner of creature are you?' the General of Bow addressed me.

'I'm a half-elf vampire, with *Wolf Form*.'

'Why are you pretending to speak for the dragon and ordering my soldiers back to Fort Hellsmouth?'

'Oh, you haven't heard from the dragon recently? There is a large army coming.'

'Blackcoin farmers?' spat the dark elf. His companion said nothing, only stared at us, hand resting on a katana.

'Right.'

The General of Bow gave a nod over to where our raid was and smiled. 'Like those you lead…'

'Braja, can you enlighten him?' I was caught and had no answer.

'Of course. Those Blackcoin farmers are all doomed. We tricked them into coming here, splitting them away from their main army. They think there is a secret entrance in the wall. Instead, your Mind Stealer will convert them to our cause.'

Resisting a grin at Braja's brazen invention, I added as seriously as I could, 'We should go and plan for a defence of the city. I have tactical information about their siege equipment and their intention to summon water elementals to undermine the west wall.'

Over the fluttering of the nearby banners could be heard a distant explosion and the ringing of metal on metal. I didn't move my attention from the two generals, behind them, the walls of the city briefly glowed orange.

'Enough, brother,' said the General of Sword, 'let's kill th—'

I leapt onto him and bit at his face.

With a fluid, swift motion the General of Bow took a step back, nocked an arrow and shot Grythiss through the left eye hole of his helmet.

'Oh, nicely done,' Braja applauded. 'See you soon, Tyro.'

A moment later, both he and Raitha were dead, also shot by the General of Bow. In front of me, the General of Sword made a dazzling move that cut at my head with the katana and my ribs with a wakizashi he had drawn with his left hand. I must have been within an inch of being decapitated. The combat messages, however, showed that I was fine.

You have been hit by a katana for 0 damage.

You have been hit by a wakizashi for 0 damage.

This was great. Even level 100 mobs couldn't hurt me!

The General of Bow had a dagger out, he chopped through the shaft of an arrow near the head and stabbed me in the heart with the sharp wooden point.

You have been hit by a wooden stake for 17 damage. It has impaled your heart. You are dead.

CHAPTER 20
DEAD AGAIN

Damn. I was still respawning at my starting point in the woods near Safehaven. And *Wolf Form* was greyed out. Was I still a vampire even? It seemed so; my related ability options were all available. Assuming I was, I needed to find a dark room in the next couple of hours or I would have to stay out of the game until the next sunset. Where could I go? The pirate caves were close and the mobs, at least those on the outside, trivial. North-east then, at a run. Tempting as it was to use my Great Bat ability and feel the experience of flying, I thought I should save it as I had no idea how often it became available.

[Channel Rescue] 'Report please, Sapentia.'

[Channel Rescue] 'Entire wipe. Except four or five under mind control.'

[Channel Rescue] 'Anyone get in?'

[Channel Rescue] 'Not I know.'

[Channel Rescue] 'Report please, Glarinson?'

[Channel Rescue] 'Everyone clipped up, I'm not sure if anyone got away though.'

[Channel Rescue] 'I did. Rubblethumper here, half-orc warrior, level forty-two.'

[Channel Rescue] 'Me too. Serethina, half-elf bard, forty-four.'

[Channel Rescue] 'And me. Scarlet, elf, hunter, twenty-seven.'

[Channel Rescue] 'Silva, cleric, thirty-seven.'

With every speaker, my heart rose. After these four, however, there was silence.

[Channel Rescue] 'Anyone else?' I waited a few seconds. 'Shame. That's it, folks. The raid is over. Get some sleep, we have an important meeting in the morning to go over a new strategy.'

[Channel Rescue] 'Wait just a minute,' came a thick American voice, loudly, 'no one go anywhere. We still have Molino and his group to rescue.'

I answered right away, [Channel Rescue] 'The problem is, the General of Bow and General of Sword are in Fort Hellsmouth right now. Those two alone can wipe us.'

[Channel Rescue] 'We could try flying in. Or a team of rogues can sneak in. There's nothing to lose,' the same voice continued aggressively.

[Channel Rescue] 'I'm calling the raid off and recommending sleep before phase two of this project.'

[Channel Rescue] 'Just who do you think you are anyhow? I suppose you have to stream videos of yourself to be popular in the modern world of gaming. But that doesn't mean you know anything about *Epic*, some of us go back to when it was being Beta tested. And Molino is one. Come on everybody, he's level fifty-nine, we have to give it a try.'

[Channel Rescue] 'What's your name?' I asked patiently. This guy wanted a row. Probably he thought he had the backing of Blackridge. Tomorrow, however, he'd see which way the wind was blowing.

[Channel Rescue] 'Tombalinor, level forty-four human bard.'

After forming a group out of myself, Braja, Sapentia, Grythiss and Raitha, I found Tombalinor and made him raid leader. Then I quit the raid.

[Channel Rescue] 'Tombalinor, you have raid leadership. Good luck. And I mean that. For those who want to try, by all means go ahead. I remain convinced the best thing we can do now is unclip and prepare for a long day tomorrow.'

The raid channel surged up with voices, some agreeing

with me, most of the loud ones urging people to stay. There were a few reasonable questions about what would happen tomorrow. It was all too chaotic though and I simply muted the channel.

[Group] 'That went pretty well, apart from the messy end, didn't it?' I asked my friends.

[Group] 'Most good,' replied Sapentia, 'let us unclip and view board of players.'

[Group] 'You did great,' added Braja, 'don't worry about Tombalinor and the bozos. They won't get anywhere.'

Raitha spoke up for me too, [Group] 'I am very proud of you, Tyro; as far as I am concerned you took the maximum possible advantage of your unique condition and no one could have freed more of our players than you did.'

[Group] 'Thank you, Raitha, I appreciate your saying so.'

[Group] 'Lizardman alssso ssay sssame. Lizardman jussst re-gretsss being killed before hitting General of Ssssword.'

[Group] 'That reminds me, what about your bodies and your gear? You all have those magic items to retrieve.'

[Group] 'I will bring you all to them in morning. Now, I'm tired.' This was Sapentia.

[Group] 'Good idea. I'm still a vampire though, so it'll have to wait until tomorrow night for mine. Not that there's much on my body I need. I wouldn't mind removing the exp penalty though.'

[Group] 'Unclipping,' announced Braja, 'see you on the other side.'

[Group] 'It will take me fifteen to twenty, I need to run to a cave.'

Once I reached the coast, I turned left to jog over silver sands. The moons were dipping towards the black treeline to the west. In addition to the sound of the wind rustling the wild grasses of the dunes, I heard a strange noise from all around: it was a like a musical note, a call too resonant and all-embracing to be a creature in the sea. It was a lot like the effect you get when you wet a finger and run it at the right speed around a wine glass. And maybe that's what it was. Without slowing, I searched out the source of the sound more closely and reckoned it was the sand itself. Huge sheets of glistening sand were sliding into the sea, thin layers, just the very top of the beach, and it was this that seemed to be creating the thrilling chime. What a game, that it could create such wonderful effects, even if for most of the time there were no players around to appreciate them.

In the distance, I could see the black outline of the cliff I was aiming for as it blocked the stars. One day, I should learn the constellations. Closer, the moonlight was still strong enough to make out the caves I sought, as well as a pirate standing on the beach and looking out to sea. Unfortunately for him, the **You require blood** message had been flicking onto my UI for some time. Since I didn't have a weapon and wasn't entirely sure that I could bite like a vampire in half-elf form and since my *Summon Bats* was greyed out still from earlier it had to be *Summon Rats* to deal with him.

A scurrying, eager horde of rats soon flowed around each other and circled me as I walked forward. When I was close enough that the pirate saw me and turned, alarmed, I triggered the *Attack Target* command of the rat swarm. He lasted only a few seconds and of course, I got no experience from this, his level was too low. I did, however, mime biting the body at the neck and drinking blood, which successfully brought up the message: **You have drunk the blood of a pirate.**

For good measure, I repeated the same trick on the three pirates I encountered as I went deep enough into their cave system to be sure I was going to be well away from direct sunlight. Then I unclipped.

Stepping out of my rig, I felt a wave of tiredness run up my body. Not that I could let fatigue determine my behaviour, for there were lots of people waiting outside of my room, not just my friends. Most of them were smiling and a round of applause broke out as I came into the Den. For me? It must be. This was quite a turnaround. Even Blackridge was there, clapping with the rest, nodding and smiling. You had to give it to him, he knew how to play a part.

A woman, relatively old in this company, with greying hair

tied back in a ponytail held out her hand. 'Merci, Tyro.' She pronounced it Tear-ro.

'Woan?' I guessed.

'Indeed.' She shook my hand again and let go. 'Many thanks.'

'And from me too, Blackstorm, Oveidio.' I was offered a handshake from a thin male, forties, goatee, dirty blonde hair, wearing tracksuit bottoms and an old *EVE* online T-shirt. I took it and he nodded cheerfully.

There were plenty of pats on the back and expressions of gratitude for me before I could stand and look at the player board. It was a lot healthier after our night's work. True, the top twenty, from 59 down to 45 were all still red. After that, though, we had Serethina, the half-elf bard recently released from the southern gate at 44 (just ahead of the guy leading what could only be a small raid given how many people were here, Tombalinor, 44) and that would make a big difference to plan B.

'Say something.' Braja was behind me. 'Explain what's going to happen.' He pulled up a chair and looked at me with his earnest, brown eyes. My heart sank. Kids from our school weren't encouraged to speak in public (mostly, we were told to be silent) and I found it daunting. Moreover, it had been a long raid, everyone was probably tired. Still, I was pleasantly surprised when I got up to a few cheers. The hubbub in the room died down after Braja created a ringing sound by tapping his penknife onto the metal arm of the chair.

I looked around at a room of attentive faces, most of which held friendly expressions. Near me were Raitha, Grythiss and Sapentia, and I could sense their support. 'Thank you everyone. I think we achieved a lot tonight. Sorry it couldn't have been more.' It suddenly occurred to me that Molino and his high-level party could be in the room, although more likely they were standing by a rig in case the chance arose to enter the game and escape Fort Hellsmouth. 'We still have a chance of completing our mission and killing the dragon.

'Tomorrow, we'll explain the plan to everyone. In short, we need to use trade skills to create three or four *Arrows of*

261

Dragon Slaying. Then, Raitha and I will hunt Mikarkathat and assassinate her.'

There were a few cheers and whoots at this. Not so many though, on the whole the audience looked thoughtful. And why wouldn't they? If I were being told this news, I'd be wondering was it really possible to take out a top boss with a few arrows and also what this meant for my next task.

'I'll assign jobs tomorrow. Higher-level characters will be farming for rare items in difficult regions, the lower-level characters will be concentrating on maximising their trade skills.' There was a groan or two. 'Sorry, but the idea of all of us reaching level one hundred and hammering the dragon in a conventional raid is no longer feasible. If you really hate trade skills, you can journey to remote areas and farm ingredients.' I paused, intending to get down, but several hands shot up.

One was that of the grungy, androgynous person who had challenged Watson about pay. 'Yes?' I pointed at him.

'No offence. But when were you put in charge? And will we still get a bonus if the dragon dies?'

'About four hours ago, when Middlehampton went well. And I assume so. You can ask Watson if he doesn't mention it at the meeting later.'

I took another hand. A small woman in her twenties, dark hair. 'I really hate trade skills, but I'm only level eight, monk. Can you put me on a gathering mission?' Lots more people now had a hand raised high.

'I'm sorry,' I said, 'I'm really tired and this isn't the place to drill down to that level of detail.' Then inspiration struck. 'Please let Mr Blackridge know your preferences and I'll do my best to address them.' With that, I stepped down, leaning on Braja's shoulder to do so and hurried out. Behind me conversations broke out and lively chat filled the Den, mostly it had an eager tone.

My team were with me as we rode the lift down to the lobby.

'Well done,' said Braja, 'especially dumping the collating job on Blackridge.' He gave a chuckle.

With a star-painted fingernail, Sapentia pressed for the lift. 'Let's share ride around to everyone's hotels.'

When the limo pulled up - the night-time air was warm here and the scents of the city completely different to Dublin, more intense, like you sometimes got from the air conditioning outside a restaurant. Or maybe that was because there were several restaurants nearby – Braja took the front seat and nudged me, looking earnest.

'You all go in the back. You've something to tell them.'

For a moment I had no idea what he was talking about, my daydreams were miles away, planning the next step of the project. Then, with an unpleasant adjustment, I realised he meant the macro and how I cheated for the shield.

With Sapentia sitting to my right, Raitha opposite me and Grythiss opposite her, and with the lights of the city streets regularly filling the car with pale, white light (making them all look even more tired than they already were), I explained about the way I had altered the roll for the shield.

'It was wrong. I regretted it right away. And I regretted it even more when Watson appeared in my life and blackmailed me about it. And I won't ever do something like that again.'

'It doesn't matter,' said Grythiss, 'I'd have done the same. When we get back to *Epic*, we have the perfect raiding tank in Raitha now. Until they add new content, we can take on any of the top bosses.'

Hopeful, I turned to Sapentia. Her face, however, was sour. 'It does matter. You suck, Tyro. Everyone sucks.'

'He did it for me.' Raitha looked across at her with a soft expression. 'It wasn't selfish.'

'It was wrong! Unfair to others!' Her fist banged the window, making the driver look up at the mirror. Sapentia folded her arms.

We drove in silence then, until at Braja's hotel. Without a backward glance or a goodnight, he left the vehicle and closed the door. As we pulled out into the road again, I looked across at Sapentia, who shook her head and muttered something that sounded like 'Ekuzo.' I had a feeling she'd sworn at him, or me.

My stop was next.

'Night all. See you later for the meeting…I'm going to group us up in an interesting spot.'

'Good night, my friend, sleep well.' This from Raitha.

With a tired-looking gesture, Grythiss waved at me; Sapentia didn't even catch my eye.

After a quick - astonishingly powerful - shower, I stretched out under the cool sheets of the large bed, lying on my back, worrying about Sapentia and Braja. Worrying about the meeting to come and whether how to manage the discontent from the trade-skillers. Yet behind these concerns was a warm glow of accomplishment that spread through me and would have sent me to sleep had it not also brought with it the thought of telling my mum about the successful raid. Why not? Now was a good time, she'd be home from work.

She picked up on the third ring. 'Hello Tom, what time is it there?'

'About four in the morning I think.'

'You're up late?'

'Just in from a raid. It was a good one. And Mum, they've put me in charge…' With that, I was off, telling her about the trapped characters and about me being a vampire, so it meant I had a bit of leverage in the tactics. Normally, Mum would cut me off from this kind of *Epic*-related chat, knowing I'd run on for ages. I guess she must have missed the sound of my voice though, as I was able to explain everything. And she even said, 'I see', or 'well done' at appropriate moments.

'What about you?' I asked at last. 'Any news?'

Mum sighed. 'Work want me next week and I can only book Friday for a holiday. I won't be able to come to San Francisco.'

'Oh, Mum.'

'I know.'

'I'd love you to be here and see the city.' I hesitated, then added, 'You wouldn't have seen much of me though. Other than sleeping and eating, all my time is spent in the game or organising.'

'That's what I thought; it probably wasn't a good idea for me to come.'

'I'll make sure they give us the cash equivalent. We can have a holiday somewhere else another time instead.'

'It's not in the contract though; so don't fight anyone over this. If I don't come to San Francisco, that's my own fault.'

'I think they might. This means a lot to them, millions, billions maybe. A few thousand doesn't matter to Yuno. And, I'm not supposed to say this, but the investors for this particular game are the founders of Blackcoin. They have insane amounts of cash to throw around.'

'To launder you mean?'

I laughed. She didn't. After a short silence, I spoke again, 'I'd better get some sleep.'

'Thanks for calling, Tom. And Tom?'

'Mum?'

'God knows we could use the money, but at the end of the day, it's not everything. We are doing okay; we're happy, right?'

'Happy?' I thought about my life back in Dublin. 'You work too hard. Sometimes we run short. We don't have anything in the bank for if something goes seriously wrong and I hate school. But, I guess I'm happy, sure. Now that you let me play *Epic* anyway.'

'Tom, you're smart. You'll end up with a decent job, four or five years from now. I'm just saying, you don't have to do anything for Yuno or Blackcoin for my sake, for our sake.'

'I know, Mum.'

Then she said something unexpected. 'I love you.'

'Love you too.'

Chapter 21
Plan B

On arrival at Yuno HQ the following morning, I saw Sapentia entering just ahead of me and ran to share the lift with her. Whereas I had pretty much rolled out of my bed, into the shower, and then into my T-shirt and jeans, she must have been up a while, for as always, she looked amazing: stripy purple and black tights, like a Halloween witch's outfit; black leather skirt with floral scrolling; white blouse with large collar and cuffs emerging from a black leather bodice, which had long leather sleeves attached. The effect was a lot like a rogue's outfit from *Epic*, except for her make-up and hair, which was pure rave. Two ponytails stood out from the sides of her head; her face was white, as was her neck, all the way down to her throat, with exotic deep purple eye designs, like those on Egyptian sarcophagi.

'Oh, good morning, Tyro.' Sapentia stabbed a finger into the button for level twenty-four.

I tipped my head towards her, a little bow. 'Good morning. Are you still mad at me?'

'Small amount. You are young. Young make mistakes. Older men should know better.'

'Are you talking about Braja? Are you mad at him? Still okay to group with him?' Stupidly, I found myself talking in short sentences, the way she did.

Our eyes met in the copper-effect mirroring of the lift's interior, so that it seemed I was looking at a different Sapentia, in a dimension one step away from our own. The extra-dimensional Sapentia appeared distant and world-weary. 'All is fine, Tyro. I learn that Western men are as useless as Japanese men. Experience will make for good blog and dating advice to emotionally stunted military types.'

'I'll enjoy reading that. I suspect Braja might not.' I smiled and was relieved to see her respond in kind.

In the foyer before the Den, the young Yuno woman who had given me orientation on the day of my arrival was waiting for me. Verity? I should have made more of an effort to remember her.

'Oh Tyro, at last, Katherine would like to brief you before the meeting. Follow me please.'

'Can you come too, Sapentia?'

'Hai.'

Felicity - I was pretty sure - took us to a briefing room. No view, just glass table and metal-framed chairs.

There was a coffee station on a sideboard, which Sapentia strode over to, her strong boots clacking on the hard floor.

'Anyone else want?' She looked at me, then to Katherine and Blackridge, who were sat at the table, open folders in front of them.

'Me please,' I answered, taking a seat, 'black, two sugars.'

'I'm good, thank you.' Katherine smiled at us, while Blackridge tipped his square head up and said nothing. It was hard to see him as anything but trouble; impossible to share a sense of comradeship and common purpose.

When we were both settled, Katharine invited us to look at the documents she had prepared. 'You can have mine.' She slid a clear plastic folder across the table to Sapentia.

Inside were some nicely laid out plans, which even had images from the game to decorate them. Someone had been busy. Each plan was on a different coloured sheet, the one headed Master Bowyer had a light green background.

'Shall we start with the Master Bowyer?' Katharine asked me, having seen me hold it up.

'Sure.'

'You'll notice that we need someone with a high dexterity

and spirit to maximise the ratio of skill increases per combination attempt. I've been conservative and assumed a slightly below-average success rate.'

According to the diagram, the most efficient path to becoming a Master Bowyer was to attempt combinations in this order: crude hickory bows to skill level 15; simple iron-tipped arrows to 25; crude red oak bows to 45; fine steel arrows to 70; decent hickory bows to 90; decent red oak bows to 105; *Arrows of Piercing* to 120; high quality hickory bows to 130; high-quality red oak bows to 140; *Flaming Arrows* to 160; *Arrows of Destruction* to 180; superb hickory bows to 205; superb red oak bows to 220; *Arrows of Lightning* to 230; *Rackrod's Bow of Striking* to 245; *Scintillating Bow of the Stars* to 255; *Sir Lockwood's Bow* to 265; *Bow of the Elements* to 275; *Bow of Seeking* to 285; *Astral Bow* to 295; and, finally, *Doomstriker* to 300. Easy.

Except the materials required for these attempts were not simply foraged ones, the more complex items, like *Flaming Arrows*, needed feathers from Firehawks, a sorcerer of sufficient level to create *firesteel ingots* and a blacksmith to make arrow heads from this imbued metal as well as the necessary tools. That blacksmith would have to be at least skill 150 to be sure of success and he or she would, in turn, need various foraged materials, common and rare to skill up to that level. The estimates for the number of basic ingredients we needed to farm for this project was massive and my eyes ran across figures like 44,000 long sticks; 14,000 carts of iron ore; 8,000 bird feathers, 5,000 reels of hemp cord; and 3,000 bags of flour.

Then there were the rare drops. We'd need to farm three large regions plus a raid zone for a variety of ingredients for the high-level bows. My group would take on *The Tower of the Jewelled Skull*, where we could grind out our levels at the same time as collecting *Soulstones* and *Ornate Glowing Feathers*.

When she was sure we had taken in the information on the charts, Katharine said, 'For the basic farming alone, I think we need sixteen players on this task.'

'Noted,' I replied. Then I looked over at Blackridge, whose heavy face was unshaven. Was he bored? Or just tired. 'Did we get that many volunteers?'

'Here's the list.'

In contrast to Katharine's careful preparations, Blackridge showed me a simple typed sheet. Only eight players had volunteered for gathering. Oh well.

'Do we know who would make the best Master Bowyer?' I asked, looking from the dour expression of Blackridge to the grey eyes of Katharine, eyes that sparkled with intelligence.

'Scarlet, a level twenty-seven hunter has consistently put her attribute points into Dexterity and Spirituality. She is leading in that regard.'

'Great.'

'I'm not sure she has enough though. It might be sensible for her to level up at least to forty.'

'We can give buffs and give potions to help attributes, even if temporary,' Sapentia pointed out.

Katharine nodded. 'Oh, indeed, it's just that when she attempts *Doomstriker*, we really want to do all we can to minimise failure and especially the possibility of a fumble that costs us the rare ingredients. My belief is that while we are gathering items, she can keep levelling, at least for a week, without this meaning any loss of time in her Bowyer.'

'What do you think?' I asked Sapentia.

My friend shrugged. 'Sounds okay.'

'Right so, have you told Scarlet about this?'

'I thought perhaps you should, now you are leading the project.' Katharine was looking downwards. Anywhere but Blackridge huh?

'Fine. But Katharine, I'll be in the game most of the time. I'd like you to co-ordinate from the outside…and implement this plan.' I indicated the coloured sheets. 'It's superb work, it really is.'

'Thank you.' She glanced at her tablet. 'It's nearly time for the meeting.'

Blackridge stood up and I had pushed my chair back when I was surprised by Sapentia leaning forward and speaking. 'Wait. One more item. What's really going on here?'

'What do you mean?' grunted Blackridge.

'Yuno doesn't make game it can't hotfix.'

There was silence. I studied Katharine (anxious, watchful) and then Blackridge (sullen).

Sapentia tried again. 'Who really made *Epic Two*?'

'Don't be silly,' said Blackridge. 'We did.'

'We'd better go.' Katharine moved to the door and held it open for us.

Catching my eye, Sapentia gave a slight shake of her head, meaning she didn't believe Blackridge. Obviously, I was on her side and I did feel like I wasn't seeing the full picture. At the same time, it didn't seem likely that anyone else had built the game, so what did she mean?

As before, the Den was full of players and there was a temporary stage set up at one end. This time, there was a seat for me between Katharine and Blackridge, which I took, feeling somewhat nervous under the gaze of so many people. Already at the podium, Watson gave me a warm smile through his beard, then tapped the microphone until he had everyone's attention.

'Today, we move to Plan B. Plan B is mostly a crafting route to success.' And he explained about the *Arrows of Dragon Slaying*. There was a certain amount of restlessness; by now, everyone knew the principles of the plan and, I suppose, they were anxious to find out their roles in it. I would be.

Sensing this, Watson raised a hand, thick fingers spread. 'Mr Blackridge wants to say a few words, then I'll hand you over to Tom Foster, Tyro, for the details.'

At the mention of my name, I felt my stomach clench. It wasn't easy, having to speak in front of so many people. People who I felt were still largely unsympathetic, despite the success of last night's raid. There was one way to get through this though, which was to treat the situation like I was in-game, organising a raid.

Glancing at a small notecard, which he stuffed into his pocket, Blackridge rose and went to the microphone. 'As you know, I haven't always agreed with Tyro as to the best approach to our challenge. We are a team, however, all of us here, and we all want the same result. With the unforeseen tactics of the dragon and her allies, it's time to change our approach and as Tyro has demonstrated, he's exactly the right person to lead us. I want everybody to be clear, he has my full support.'

To my mind, the whole of this speech, which was delivered hurriedly and without genuine inflexions, was actually saying: *I hate saying this, but I have to get it over with.* Perhaps that was just me. In any case, the important thing was he had officially declared a truce between us. Hopefully, that would get his supporters to fall in line instead of undermining the plan.

No one had clapped, until Watson stood up to lead a smattering of applause. Then he gestured to me to take the podium. It wasn't easy standing up and I knocked into the microphone as a result of lurching too quickly.

Looking out around the room, there were plenty of smiling, encouraging faces and not just from my own group. There were still plenty of frowns though too. I was under no illusions about my situation. It was like during the early days of my leading raids in *Epic*; there were plenty of people who thought they could do better and who would be quick to pull me down.

'Firstly, so long as the dark elves keep their army in Fort Hellsmouth, we have to abandon the characters trapped there. If you are one of them, for now, start afresh with a hunter or a druid and join the basic foraging teams.' Without trying to justify myself, I jumped right into allocating the boring jobs of collecting wood, iron, flour and the other ingredients we needed. There were audible, disconsolate sighs as I announced various names, working my way up from the lowest levels. Helpfully, Katharine was tapping on her tablet and revising the large screen to show the letter W before the name of all the wood collectors, the letter M before the mining team and so on. Scarlet got a designation all to herself, MB, but whether she was pleased or not with the role I couldn't tell. No one in the audience gave a visible response when I declared her Master Bowyer.

The more interesting roles were those for three groups in the three zones we needed to work for rare drops. *The Tower of the Jewelled Skull*, *The Undersea Ruins of Asthraxia* and the *Desert of Endless Screams*. In both *Epic* and *Epic 2*, the best size of group for experience gain was seven. That's because there was a small exp bonus to encourage social play, the bonus increased up to a group of size seven and then declined to zero for a group of twelve.

It was my group that would take on the *Tower of the Jewelled Skull*. Although reluctant to introduce a stranger to our tight-knit team, I had to add at least one more person to get near the maximum exp bonus. So I announced the group as: Grythiss, shadow knight 14; Sapentia, sorceress 15; myself and Raitha, hunters 13; Braja, cleric 12; and Tuscl, shaman 18. This latter addition was partly because a shaman was a good fit to a group that had a tank, a healer and three DPS. Tuscl could add small backup heals, more importantly she could slow the mobs and had a wide range of buffs for us. It was also because I'd come to admire her during the raid. I liked players who got on with their role but who were also smart enough to improvise appropriately when needed.

The *Desert of Endless Screams* was for a group in their 40s and, while lying in bed the previous night, I had decided it was possible for a group to begin there already: Serethina, bard 44; Rubblethumper, warrior 42; Roberta, necro 38; Silva, cleric 37; Rasquelle, rogue 36; Woan, cleric 34; and Oveidio, warrior 32 (group leader). Strictly by level, this group should have included Tombalinor, Bard 44. Two bards, however, did not really make sense and this gave me a good excuse to keep someone that was potentially hostile to me out of a group that otherwise seemed to have a positive attitude. Strictly, too, Serethina should have been the group leader. That, however, would be a waste of Oveidio's organising abilities and game knowledge as leader of Dreadnought. More importantly, I felt I could count on him in any clash with Blackridge.

Tombalinor I put in charge of the group that would be exploring *The Undersea Ruins of Asthraxia*. This was easy to justify as, once over level 38, bards had a water breathing buff that they could cast from the magic of their music. Out of the rest of the players, the remaining ones in their 20s (along with some level 19) I put into exp grinding groups. In two or three weeks, they would be able to gather ingredients from more challenging zones than could the newly created characters.

With all the tasks assigned, I could see very many more disappointed faces than eager ones. This was hardly surprising, given that only about twenty players out of three hundred had an exciting mission. For everyone else, the project was now much more like a day job. There wasn't much I could do about this though, apart from invite everyone on the odd raid that we would have to conduct. Taking a step back, I let Watson return to the podium.

'Any questions?' he asked the room. Immediately, ten or more hands rose up.

'You kept the best job for yourself, didn't you? There are hunters higher level than you.'

With an apologetic shrug, meaning he was sorry for the hostility in the question, Watson let me lean back to the microphone.

'I suppose I did. It's not just about me, though, I know the players I'm grouped with and I know we can level up in time. We've played *Epic* together for years. It seemed like the right thing to do was stay grouped together. And we need Scarlet for the Master Bowyer's role.'

Watson pointed to another person with a raised hand.

'I'm a level seventy necro who leads the guild Woebetide in *Epic*. I didn't come here to farm sticks for a month. Unless you can offer me something better, I'm gone.'

'I'll respond to this,' said Watson to everyone. 'I'm sure a lot of you feel the same way. Yuno will add three million dollars to the bonus if the dragon is killed. That's another ten thousand dollars each. Stay on the project and help us complete it and you get twenty thousand dollars.'

'How much is Tyro getting if he kills the dragon?' someone else asked.

'His original contract hasn't been altered in any way since he became project leader. He could have asked for more, but he didn't.'

I hadn't even thought about how I would answer such a question before Watson had handled it. Again, I was struck by how sharp he was. On the surface, he was an amiable, stocky and slightly clownish figure. Inside, he was what? Certainly he was sharp. Like the sharps in *David Copperfield*.

'This isn't so much a question as a statement. I'm Tombalinor, bard forty-four.' The man speaking was hard to see among the crowd, he was so short. Middle-aged, tidy black hair with some grey in it and thick eyebrows that made him appear to be scowling when perhaps he wasn't. 'As you know, I disagreed with how Tyro ran that last raid. If we'd have all stuck together and kept on trying instead of bailing, maybe we'd have gotten Molino out. But that's behind us now. We all have to move forward together. Let's get on with it.'

Two or three people applauded.

'Thank you. On that note, perhaps it's time to take up our tasks,' suggested Watson and all but one of the remaining hands went down. It was the large, stocky young man who had accosted me in the Den, that time when Braja stepped in and nearly broke his finger. 'Yes?' Watson asked.

'This is for Tyro. Isn't it the case that you cheated in *Epic*? That you use macros and that you rigged the rolls in your last raid to give gear to your mates?' The sturdy player swept his dark fringe back and looked about him, flushed and satisfied. Obviously, he felt he'd scored a big hit. And a month ago, this intervention would have hit me hard, like a kick to the stomach. Now, although I still felt the weight of his attack (and my rapidly beating heart was urging me to action), I had firm ground under my feet. I'd told my friends about this and could rely on them. They might not have liked what I did, but I knew they wouldn't walk out on me.

'Firstly,' said Watson, his words biting down on the whole room via the microphone. 'Yuno have the logs for all of Tyro's play, as we do for everyone here. What's good enough for Yuno should be good enough for you. Secondly, what are you trying to undermine the project leader for? What's the point of your questions?'

'I want to hear from Tyro.' Not as loud now but still with a tone of triumph.

'Very well.' I leaned in beside Watson. 'I've used attack macros for years, haven't we all? And in my last raid, the only time I've ever done it and I won't do it again, I used a dice rolling macro to win a shield for my friend.'

'It's water under the bridge,' added Watson, 'what matters is that we are on a results-focused mission. Results,' he repeated, 'that's what matters. And Tyro gets results.'

Considering there were three hundred people in the room, it was surprisingly quiet. Not even a cough. Inside, I felt a flush of shame, imagining they were judging me. Anger too. Someone from the inside had been gossiping with this kid. Blackridge sat there, staring ahead, expressionless. The sod.

'Well then,' said Watson. 'You know what you have to do. Let's get going.'

It was hardly the rousing team meeting I'd hoped for. Still, the hubbub of sound that now began to build as players moved off to their rigs didn't seem hostile, more matter-of-fact.

At my side, touching my left elbow to get my attention before I moved off, was Oveidio, all seriousness and determination

'We farm the desert. Do you have list of items and schedule for when they are needed?'

'Katherine has the full list, from what I remember, it's straightforward enough for the first week or two. You'll be farming giant scorpions for their claws and flaming sand snakes for their fangs and skins. When Scarlet passes a hundred and thirty-five in bowyer, she'll need spirit imbued ironwood and for that process we'll want hundreds of *spirit orbs* from the ghosts and ghouls of the ruins of the forgotten emperor. They are supposed to be tough. You'll need to level a good bit.

'Don't worry.' Oveidio held out his hand and when I took it, shook mine firmly and stared at me with earnest, brown eyes. 'We will deliver.'

My friends were waiting for me near the stage and so too was a small woman in her thirties, Tuscl, I'd guess. During the raid, I had thought her accent sounded Spanish and this impression was reinforced by her look: light brown skin, black hair (cut short). She wore a white blouse with collar, grey jumper, tan jacket, neat trousers and I noticed a hint of a limp as she moved to offer her hand.

'Tuscl,' she said, a flash of white teeth with her smile. 'Thank you for inviting me into your group.'

'Not at all, we are lucky to have you. Please meet the rest of the team.' I did the introductions and noticed as her eyes lingered on Sapentia. To be fair, everyone took a moment when introduced to our Japanese celebrity. It didn't necessarily mean Tuscl was star struck, only that Sapentia's appearance was arresting.

A few minutes later, we were all in a room together, putting on our gloves and headsets.

'See you on the other side,' said Braja. And that was the last I heard from the real-world environment as a rush of sound and colour resolved itself into *Epic 2*.

CHAPTER 22
THE PIRATES' PRISONER

A cave. Dark, with only a very faint hint of light to my east. Ah yes, the pirates. When my friends were all in the game, I grouped them up.

[Group] 'Well, team,' I said, 'it's the *The Tower of the Jewelled Skull* for us. You have a teleport for that, Sapentia?'

[Group] 'Hai. I will gather everyone, first to get to bodies, then to *Carraig Mór*, the nearest point to tower.'

[Group] 'Great, thanks. Before you take them to *Carraig Mór*, can you come and pick me up too? I'm sheltering in the pirate caves north-west of Safehaven. Raitha knows them.'

[Group] 'Yes, we will come.'

Next, I had a question for them all, [Group] 'Is anyone near a town?'

[Group] 'Tuscl here, I'm in Port Placida and I have all the coin from the raid.'

[Group] 'Perfect. Let's plan ahead. Everyone with spell progression, can you send Tuscl a list of the spells you need to buy, up as far as level thirty. We'll take a break when we reach that point and go shopping again then. Oh, and Tuscl?'

[Group] 'Yes?'

[Group] 'Can you buy a coffin please, a good one that doesn't let in any light?'

[Group] 'With Wi-Fi and a TV panel in the lid too, right?' muttered Braja, 'so you can take it easy while us poor sods carry you.'

I could hear Raitha snigger.

As my group chatted to one another, making arrangements to meet Sapentia, I tried to recall the hunter spells I had read up on and planned to obtain. Then again, I could just be lazy. [Channel Klytotoxos/Tuscl] 'Hi, when Raitha sends you his list, buy two of each spell please.'

[Channel Klytotoxos/Tuscl] 'This I will do. But Tyro, even with the raid money, I might not be able to get everyone's spells. We are all casters in this group, even the tank.'

In *Epic*, there was so much money in circulation, buying spells wasn't an issue. In *Epic 2*, there were few of us playing and none of us were focused on getting coin. I could see how this could potentially be a problem. The game's economy was constructed on the assumption there would be millions of players, not three hundred. As with our patchwork armour, it seemed that we would not have the full complement of spells as we advanced. [Channel Klytotoxos/Tuscl] 'Prioritise Sapentia's spells and use your judgement on the rest.'

[Channel Klytotoxos/Tuscl] 'Of course.'

Well, that gave me something to do while waiting for my group to show up with the coffin. I would farm the pirates until my inventory was full of junk to sell. Shame there was no sign of my rat horde. Both my rats and bats were greyed out, as was *Wolf Form*. Nor did I have any equipment, not even a frail and rusty knife. Time to learn what I could do unarmed as a vampire.

Walking further along the corridor, I saw an orange glow in the distance, which resolved itself as a lantern, hanging high up on the wall of a crossroads. My first swag. Blowing it out, I stashed it in my inventory, which, I noted, could only hold twenty items. Hopefully, I'd come across a bag soon and increase my inventory slots. Taking the right-hand corridor, I heard footsteps walking away from me. Although I believed myself to be safe enough, I walked swiftly but carefully after the sound. Shouldn't vampires have some kind of bonus for this? I didn't want to waste *Invisibility*; perhaps it was wrong to be greedy though, I'd already picked up so many invaluable benefits from becoming a vampire.

The person I was stalking was a muscular pirate in a striped shirt, difficulty level *trivial* (so, no exp). A perfect victim on whom to test my unarmed combat. With a run and a leap that must have been almost silent, for he didn't even turn, I landed on his back and triggered the all-purpose 'attack' button on my UI. It didn't work but I was ready for this and my fingers flexed at the same time as my eyes chose the 'bite' button.

You have bitten a pirate for 18 points of damage.

The pirate is dead.

There was a bent scimitar for loot, three silver coins and six copper ones and, much more interesting, a set of three large keys. Having taken them, I moved on to a chamber from which there came bright light and the sound of someone talking. When I came close enough to peek around the edge of the corridor wall, I saw two pirates sitting on barrels, one of them with his back to me, waving his arms as he spoke to the other. She looked bored, or at least, before she noticed me she had been bored.

'Who is that? Show yourself!'

'Hello.' I stepped into the light.

Both of them stood up and drew swords. Both, however, were conning *trivial* when I stared at them.

'I found this bunch of keys; do you know what they are for?'

With a snarl, the male pirate charged at me, swinging his short sword down on my shoulder. Stepping in, allowing it to hit (for 0 damage), I pulled him close and triggered bite.

You have bitten a pirate for 15 points of damage.

The pirate is dead.

Seeing the body of her companion fall to the ground, the female made a rush to get past me and I almost felt sorry for her, such was the look of fear she gave me when I intercepted her.

You have bitten a pirate for 16 points of damage.

The pirate is dead.

Seven more silver and ten copper, a rusted short sword, cracked wooden shield and two flimsy daggers. It might all help. Now, what else could I find? This rocky chamber seemed to be just a store for some old ropes and crates with metal parts that might be useful for a ship, not that they meant anything to me. Three hammocks were strung across the room. That was all. Back out I went, down to the crossroads and took the next turn to my right (the one that would have been facing me after I arrived). A short walk took me to a dimly lit stretch of corridor blocked by an iron gate, attached to brackets in the cave walls by a big sturdy padlock. Aha. Interesting. Well, mildly interesting.

There was a definite scent coming from the room, damp and musky. I couldn't place it though. Even with my enhanced dark vision it was difficult to see what was beyond the gate. When my infravision flowed across my UI, though, it revealed a small patch of orange and red against a wall some five metres away. Taking the keys from my inventory, I held the first to the padlock. Nothing. The second, however, saw the lever spring up. Was there any danger here? Surely, the enemy of the pirates was likely to be a friend of mine? Best not to be complacent. It was early morning and if for some unlikely reason I died, I'd have to stay out of the game for hours until nightfall.

I locked the gate again.

'Hey, who is in there? Want me to let you out?'

The red and orange light grew near and resolved itself...to be a tiger. A rather bedraggled and mangy looking tiger and one that was very unexpected. It was level 6 or 7, as it conned *easy*.

'Hello there.'

The tiger looked back at me with large amber eyes, then turned away, evidently finding a vampire half-elf at her gate to be of no interest. I unlocked the door and swung the gate open with a loud creak. Immediately she leapt away, back into the darkness from where her eyes gleamed.

'Here kitty.' I stepped away from the gate. Stepped back again, then again. Only when I was through the crossroads and had moved away towards the dead pirates did the great cat suddenly come racing out of the darkness, swerving to be as far away from me as possible; she pounded down the corridor I had yet to explore. Soon afterwards came shouts. I dashed after her.

The next cavern room had three pirates, all brandishing

blades of some sort and all cowering as the tiger ran around and around in a circle, growling with a deep rumble, and looking for an opening. Sometimes, she would lash out with a sharp set of claws at ferocious speed. The tiger had learned to stay clear of the swords though, so it was something of a standoff.

'Help, Captain help! The tiger's free!'

From where the corridor continued out of the far side of the room came the sounds of people running and into the crisis came a classic pirate captain: high boots, long navy jacket, tricorne hat and even a patch over one eye. Behind him were two female pirates, wearing little more than baggy shirts and torn trousers.

'Don't hurt her!' shouted the captain. 'Any of ye lay a blade on her and ye clean the heads for a month. Feora, Vanessa, get some nets.'

I took the opportunity to target him: *minor challenge*. Level 7 or 8 then. Some exp would come my way when I killed him. Not a great deal, but still, I hadn't anticipated on gaining any from my morning stroll through the caves. A stroll that was turning out to be much more entertaining than I had expected.

'Where's the tiger?' shouted the captain, looking my way, 'who let her out?'

'I'm afraid I did, sorry.' I stepped up to the entrance of the cavern; the tiger leapt aside to avoid me, right onto one of the pirates, who staggered and screamed.

'Who are you?' The captain's attention was on me. The other two pirates were rushing across to prod at the tiger with their sword points and rescue their shipmate.

This seemed as good a time as any to cross the room.

'Before I kill you,' I said, clapping my hands together loudly to ensure I had his attention, 'please think about where you keep your treasure.' And I triggered *Read Thoughts*.

The pirate captain is thinking about a loose rock, low down on the east wall of his room.

'Thank you.' I attacked, diving through the swing of his scimitar, which caught me but did no damage.

Critical Hit! You have bitten a pirate captain for 28 points of damage. You are draining his blood.

'Help! Help! Help me maties! Get him off me!' The captain retreated, still cutting at me, still failing to hurt me at all.

You have drained the blood of a pirate captain for 9 points of damage.

The pirate captain is dead. You gain experience.

The other two (the one under the tiger was dead) were no bother at all. When, however, the two female pirates came running up with a rope net held between them, I did take a few steps back. Although I was immune to blades, a smart way to kill me might be to trap me in the nets and stake me in the heart. After all, when the General of Bow had killed me, he'd hardly dented my hit points. Maybe these low-level mobs could manage it with a lucky one-shot success.

While we three humanoids edged around the room, warily facing each other, the tiger ran off back the way I'd come. Having a soft spot for her by this time, I hoped she'd find the way out. Now, I saw that the remaining pirates had made the mistake of advancing towards me, they were far enough into the room that I could vault over their net and attack without fear of capture.

You have bitten a pirate for 16 points of damage.

The pirate is dead.

You have bitten a pirate for 15 points of damage.

The pirate is dead.

Loot time. The coin totalled three gold, seven silver and twelve copper; there were three crappy weapons and an iron scimitar on the captain that I held in my right hand. His boots were an armour upgrade for me (even if I managed to reclaim my old body with the dryad's barkskin armour) and I took his hat too, putting it on. Where was a mirror when you needed one? Jauntily, I walked on up to the corridor and came to a T-junction. Since left felt like it would be heading back towards the beach, I took the right and was rewarded with an unlocked door that opened into the captain's room.

This cave was nearly comfortable, with an old carpet on the

floor; a chest with candles stuck on top (half used, wax around them), two bottles of sherry and three glasses; another chest full of clothes; a hammock; and a box with parchment, quill and ink. Swiping the smaller stuff, I then checked the east wall, which I figured was the one on my right. Sure enough, where it met the floor there was a cracked stone that came out. Behind it was a small box. Eagerly, I opened it.

Snap! My thumb was jabbed by a small needle.

You have been hit by a needle trap for 0 damage.

You have been poisoned.

Oh. That was a mistake and I was interested to see that I was not immune to poison.

You have taken 2 points of poison damage.

You regenerate 2 hit points.

Fortunately, this was a low-level region and I had nothing to fear. I could ignore the messages and just let the poison run its course. It was a warning for the future though. Inside the box were seven gems - five rather attractive emeralds and two diamonds - and a small cord that was pure white, like it had never been used. The cord had four simple knots along it, evenly spaced. Magic, surely. I put the cord back for when Sapentia could take it and use her *Identify Magic* skill.

Since I was wearing only the newbie clothes I had arrived in the game with, I took a pair of trousers, a ruffle shirt and blue jacket from the captain's chest and put them on. It might not have made any difference to my armour but I felt a good bit taller and more impressive as a result.

There was not much more to the complex of caves. A couple of unexplored rooms had gear in them: ropes, planks, tools, nails, canvas. My two other unused keys were for opening locked chests, one containing charts (which were potentially useful or saleable, I took) and the other flasks of oil. My best find was a pile of canvas bags and I slung two over my shoulders. They each gave me eight slots, so with a bit of rearranging, I still had eighteen empty slots in my inventory.

From the conversations taking place in the group chat, I could tell that there was going to be a wait for me before I could be collected. So, sitting near the entrance - safely away from the sunlight - where there was no sign of the tiger, I called up my full UI and studied my stats.

Klytotoxos: Half-elf, hunter, Level 13, Exp 13,250

(-300 death penalty)

Condition: Vampire

Natural Armour 8, + Crafted Armour 1

Total Armour = 9

Base speed 12 – Encumbrance 0 = Effective speed 12

Strength	23	Hit Points	208
Dexterity	29	Spirit	162
Spirituality	15		
Intelligence	15		
Constitution	22		
Beauty	9		

Skills

Combat:		Crafting:		Other:
Dodge	65	Bowyer	1	
Bite	65	Gathering	1	
Claw	65	Set Traps	10	
Archery	21			

Abilities:

Wolf Form, Invisibility, Giant Bat Form, Cloud Form, Summon Bats, Summon Rats

Immunities;

Weapon damage (exception: decapitation or wooden stake in the heart), electricity, cold, fire.

Weaknesses:
Requires blood as food.
Suffers damage in daylight.

Spells Known:

Inventory:
Coins:
7 gold, 30 silver, 44 copper

Equipped:

Feet:	High, hard boots.
Legs:	Pantaloons of the Pirate Captain.
Waist:	Sash of the Pirate Captain.
Left hand:	
Right hand:	Iron scimitar
Lower body:	Shirt of the Pirate Captain.
Upper body:	Shirt of the Pirate Captain.
Shoulders:	Shirt of the Pirate Captain.
Cape:	Coat of the Pirate Captain.
Left arm:	Shirt of the Pirate Captain.
Right arm:	Shirt of the Pirate Captain.
Fingers:	
Neck:	
Head:	Tricorne hat of the Pirate Captain.

Stored:
Canvas bag: six candles, lantern, lantern, flask oil, flask oil, flask oil, flask oil, flask oil.
Canvas bag: iron spike, iron spike, iron spike, hammer, hand plane, drill, hand saw, bundle of charts.
Small wooden box: diamond, diamond, emerald, emerald, emerald, emerald, emerald, unidentified cord.

Then followed a list of all my junk items like the bent and rusty swords, items which brought my encumbrance up to 220 out of 230. In order not to have a movement penalty, I held back from taking the rope netting or the large coils of ropes or planks. They were too heavy. I needed a pack animal to bring that stuff away and it wouldn't have been of much value in any case.

Sapentia called me. [Channel Sapentia/Klytotoxos] 'Porting to near Safehaven now.'

[Channel Sapentia/Klytotoxos] 'Good. I'm all set.'

CHAPTER 23
THE TOWER OF THE JEWELLED SKULL

Over a thousand years ago, the lands to the west of the Dragon's Spine bore witness to the deeds of a lizardman necromancer of extraordinary ability, learning and power. Notrevity was her name and among her possessions was an artefact that was both gruesome and strong: the skull of one of her most hated enemies, converted by arcane and diabolic ritual into a jewelled repository of spirit. Long after the necromancer had passed to other realms, the skull remained, high up in the tower she had constructed and its lure drew many evil creatures to the tower and its vicinity as well as many foolish adventurers, seeking the treasure but always succumbing to the cruel mysteries of the necromancer's tower.

Epic 2 Player Guide.

In the *Epic 2* guide, there were only generalities about the background to the Tower of the Jewelled Skull. In game terms the tower was pretty much a whole expansion to itself, capable of taking players from level 20 at the first floor to level 50 in the heights. Unfortunately, the guide was deliberately mysterious about what we might encounter there. Or perhaps fortunately. Even though we were on a grind with a bigger goal in view, it was fun to be the first to explore a region and, hopefully, solve the quests.

Since she could move fastest of all of us (with her *Haste* buff), I made Tuscl group leader and while the rest of the group (pretending to moan at the burden) carried my coffin through the hills, our shaman ran to the nearby stockaded town of Carrickmor, where she could sell my junk gear and, more importantly, pick up half a dozen quests whose resolution was to be found by exploring the necromancer's tower:

Abigail's Lost Slippers
Vengeance is Best Delivered
Tregar and the Ogre Prince
The Three Sisters
A Cure for Derforgilla
The Crimson Seeds

By the time we had found the tower, having followed a narrow path alongside a gorge, until it swerved away from the river, up over the shoulder of a hill, Tuscl had caught up.

Once assured that I was in darkness (they had entered the tower and closed the door behind them), I climbed out of my coffin, stretched and yawned. 'That was a lovely nap.'

Braja shook his head in disbelief. 'Not only do you snooze the whole way, but you turn up in fancy dress.'

'Here.' Sapentia handed me a pair of *Boots of Dark Elven-kind*. I had forgotten about these and put them on with real pleasure, moving my high, hard boots to my inventory. 'Also,' she went on, 'belt buckle of sea hag has been attached to belt and gives plus two strength, minus two beauty.'

'Grythiss, none of us are going to notice if a lizardman is more or less beautiful. Would you like it?' I asked.

'Lizardman isss mossst grateful.'

'Then we have Ring of Protection, plus one.' Sapentia held it up and I recognised it from the boss fight against Morc Mac Dela.

'That's one to Armour Class and five per cent to resistances, right?'

'Right.' She nodded.

'Braja? Do we think?'

There was prompt agreement on this, so Sapentia threw the ring over to our cleric.

'Your white cord is Summon Wind. North, East, South, West, once only per knot.'

I took it and put it back in the pouch with the gems; it was more a sailor's item than a dungeon-crawling vampire's.

'Then last. Necklace is Minor Spirit Absorption. Once per day first spell damage is turned into regained spirit, maximum twelve points.'

'I'm afraid I do not understand this,' said Raitha, 'when you cast a damage spell, you get the first twelve points back?'

'No. When you are hit by Magic Missile, say, for twenty damage, first twelve is absorbed and becomes spirit.'

'Neat. And obviously you should keep it,' I said.

'Thank you.' Sapentia tipped her head. 'But not so obvious. If I play well, I do not get targeted. I think Braja. No offence. Aggro control can be difficult for healers.'

'Agreed,' I said and the necklace went over to Braja.

Raitha stood in front of me and handed me a bag, which I took and which immediately appeared in my inventory. Inside were scrolls containing all the hunter spells up to level 35. Next he passed me a decent hickory bow, which I slung over my back and a quiver with a hundred fine steel arrows. Just wearing these made me feel more like a hunter again.

Our group was standing inside the closed, high wooden doors of the tower's entrance. The wide, gloomy hall had a tiled floor with a pattern on it, something like a pale silver comet against a deep violet night sky, if the comet's tail were sinuous rather than straight. Six doors came off the hall, three on each side and at the far end, in the darkness, a wide set of stairs led upwards.

'We can make this place our spawn point,' said Sapentia.

'I guess we should.' I was a little hesitant because if for some reason a powerful opponent ended up here, we could get caught in a cruel cycle of respawning and being killed.

Braja was evidently thinking exactly the same way as me. 'No trains, everyone get that? Right?' he said. If our efforts went pear shaped, it would be much better to die as a group than to try to run and risk bringing mobs to our spawn points.

Sapentia snapped back at him, 'No one here are noobs.' And then she began to cast. One after the other, our avatars filled with blue light that dispersed like a bubble popping, accompanied with a pleasant chime.

You will respawn at this point after death.

'I guess I'll scout,' I offered. After all, I was a hunter class, which in the outdoors were definitely the scouting class. More than that, though, if there were unpleasant surprises ahead, which there was bound to be, my immunities might prove crucial. No one answered, so with a whistle and a spring in my step (shame the silence from the boots didn't work until night-fall) I tried the first door. It was locked. Maybe I should have got a rogue to join us instead of a shaman.

As doors went, this wasn't the most robust looking, so I leaned back and gave it a strong kick. A very strong - Strength 23 - kick. With a mighty crack, the wooden panels tore from the metal lock, the whole of the door twisted, wrenching itself free of its hinges and falling to the ground with a loud slam.

[Group] 'And thus we see how the hunter stalks his prey, silent and deadly he creeps up for the pull; completely surprising his enemies by his unexpected appearance.'

[Group] 'Thank you for the commentary, Raitha.'

Beyond the wreckage was a kind of stable, only without the stalls. Hooks and poles protruded from the otherwise bare walls and from them hung leather harnesses. On the floor were carts, boxes and bags. The place suggested a certain degree of social organisation by a person or persons who could mobilise dozens of mounts at the same time.

[Group] 'Other doors are opening!' shouted Sapentia.

I stepped back out to see humanoid figures hurrying out of four of the remaining five doors, weapons already drawn.

Grythiss gave a bitter hiss. [Group] 'Black Yhandis, hated enemies of lizardmen.'

There was no other strategy available here than the one that had worked in the Celtic barrow. Running swiftly around the room I swung my iron scimitar as I passed by the mobs and gathered them in my wake. They were impressive-looking: like lizardmen, except their reptilian skin was a shiny black, with a gold streak running back from their foreheads. Their eyes were striking too, bright blues or reds, flecked with that same gold.

I ran up four or five stairs and then turned towards the crowd gathered around me. It was a theatrical moment and even though I had a slight qualm about what might happen if I wasn't immune to their attacks (would they aggro everyone at the door and bring about the train that Braja had warned of?) I couldn't help myself.

'Come on then, ye scurvy dogs, do your worst!'

They certainly tried. I was crowded in upon, until all I could see were the fierce eyes, angry snake-like mouths, and the flicking forked tongues that came from them.

You have been hit by a Black Yhandis rogue for 0 damage.

You have been hit by a Black Yhandis rogue for 0 damage.

You have been hit by a Black Yhandis warrior for 0 damage.

You have been hit by a Black Yhandis warrior for 0 damage.

You have been hit by a Black Yhandis warrior for 0 damage.

You have been hit by a Black Yhandis hunter for 0 damage.

Great.

'What do we do?' asked Tuscl.

'Wait and let me get a bit more aggro, then very carefully, Raitha will tag one for you.'

Soon after, Raitha called out. 'Incoming, a Black Yhandis cleric!'

'Eslowed,' announced Tuscl.

Aha, that's why we had the shaman.

Even though the Black Yhandis were between levels 20 and 24, I could tell from looking at the group box on the UI that my friends had no difficulty fighting just one of them at least. Grythiss never fell below half before having his health restored to full, while the mob's hit points steadily declined.

A Black Yhandis cleric is dead. You gain experience.

'Incoming, a Black Yhandis hunter.'

'Eslowed.'

'Death to the Black Yhandisss!'

Despite the fact that mobs crowded around me, the height of the stairs allowed me glimpses across the entrance hall to my friends in front of the door, where Grythiss stood tall in the breastplate he had looted from Morc Mac Dela, his gleaming turquoise longsword leaving a faint trail as he swept it before him. Quite the hero and completely in his element as he fought his ancient enemies.

You gain experience.

Steadily, efficiently, we worked our way through sixteen mobs with no downtime needed. By the end of the fight, we'd all levelled and I put my new attribute point into Dexterity again.

'Is okay to wait a second? I equip my new group haste?' asked Tuscl.

'No kidding it's okay,' answered Braja for us all and I made my way over to the door while Tuscl sat and was presumably adjusting her UI so that her new spell was stored and then slotted into her list of active spells. Speaking of which, I still had my level 7 and level 14 spells to equip. Hunters could have two active spells from a choice of five at 7 and that rose to three from eight at level 14, four from twelve at 21. I learned just the three level 14 ones and put them in the active box: Light Heal, Gather Shadow and Leave no Trace. The first was very weak in comparison to the heals of Braja or even Tuscl. The second gave me concealment, which was like a weak form of Invisibility, and the third was potentially the most useful, even though the situation in which it came good was rare. For ten minutes per level, I would not leave a trail to follow.

With a wave of his hands and a yellow flare that settled on all of us, Tuscl cast her group *Haste*. Now we were faster than most unbuffed humanoid types, which gave us options (like sprinting out the tower) if the situation went horribly wrong. I'm sure we all felt more confident for it.

'Off you go, vampire,' said Braja, 'scout that last door. See if you can find the fancy-dress party you're looking for.'

The final door on the ground floor opened easily, was well lit with several lanterns and, to my surprise, was occupied by a human male wearing an apron.

'Good morning, please don't attack me, I'm just a merchant.'

'A merchant?'

He gestured to the tables that lined the room. On the nearest were dark, round loaves of bread, bottles, bunches of grapes, bowls of apples. The next had miscellaneous gear: lanterns, backpacks, rope, spikes, tools. Further up, there were small-sized weapons and on the table opposite, larger weapons and pieces of armour.

Slowly, I walked around the room, deliberately turning my back on the merchant, giving him the chance to attack and reveal this whole set up as a trap. Nothing untoward happened and when I looked at him again, noting the grey hair and the wrinkled hands, he was smiling.

'This is unexpected,' I said. 'Are you friends with those Black Yhandis?'

'The Black Yhandis have recently arrived at the tower. Before them were dark elves. Before them were ogres. All have let me trade.'

'You've been doing this a while?'

The merchant said nothing but still had an amiable expression on his face. I tried again. 'You have traded here for a long time?'

'My name is Thros. My home is Carrickmor. Many are the people who try to discover the secrets of the tower. I have made my living, catering to them.'

'How much is a loaf of bread?'

'For you, six silver.'

[Group] 'Are you all right, my friend?' asked Raitha.

[Group] 'Good thanks. All come up. It's a merchant and I'm pretty sure he's for real.'

Soon, my group came clanking in and looked around, probably with as much amazement as I'd felt.

'How much for all these?' Tuscl dumped a pile of loot on the floor, the poor-quality weapons and armour of the defeated Black Yhandis.

Moving over to the items and quickly assessing them, the merchant looked up at Tuscl. 'I'll pay seven silver and five copper.'

'That's outrageous. Is worth nearly a gold.'

'I don't haggle. You can choose to accept my offers or not.'

'Let's accept and use this guy for offloading junk. It's probably what he's here for. By the way'—I turned to the merchant—'I don't suppose you have magic items? Potions of Healing, that sort of thing?'

'I have magic items, indeed, although not very many. Usually, the explorers of the tower keep their magic finds. They have, however, at various times sold me some spells they cannot cast and three items they cannot use.'

'We are fine for spells, unless you have unique ones, but what other magic have you got?'

The merchant looked at Tuscl. 'Do you want to sell these to me for seven silver and five copper?'

'I esuppose so…Si.'

'Thank you.' Having passed the coins to Tuscl, the merchant then went to the back of the room and unlocked a cupboard. He took out three items and displayed them on the front of a table: a small cap, a cloak and a lute. Sapentia picked them up, one by one, and put them down again.

'Cap of Invisibility, rogue gnome only. Cloak of Beauty (plus two), elven sorcerer. Lute of Dismay, bard, level thirty required.'

'Oh well. Thanks for showing us. We can't use any of these.'

The merchant shrugged and stood there attentively.

[Group] 'Right so, let's resume. If you wait at the foot of the staircase, I'll pull to the landing and you tag from there.'

The bare stone staircase led to a wide landing, from which you turned completely about and went up again either on the right or on the left, with the next set of stairs being each half the width of the main ones. I took the left and carefully peered over the line of the floor. Another wide hall, this time with three doors facing me. A war banner hung on the right wall, a large painting of a moonlit lake on the left. No mobs.

Standing at the right-hand door, I listened. Nothing. Then I opened it. A long room, with smashed furniture, no lights. Swapping to the middle door I had better luck. Again, when I looked into the room I saw a lot of broken furniture, but I also saw eight Black Yhandis and a war dog: large, muscular, with a spiked collar. It was the barking of the dog that got everyone to their feet.

'Good morning. I've a message for the officer in charge.'

They did not want to play along. An arrow came whizzing over and hit my cheek.

You have been critically hit by an arrow for 0 damage.

One of the lizardmen was casting and I noticed how the little golden spines running across the centre of his black head and down his neck all stood up as he did so.

'Sorry, wrong room it seems.' I jumped away and ran to the landing, feeling the benefits of the acceleration of my *Haste* buff. I had time to draw my iron scimitar before the first of them arrived. After I'd taken a battering to no effect and after some fiery bolts smashed into me without doing any harm - to my relief, because I couldn't be entirely sure I was safe from a magical attack, it was probably fire based - I invited Raitha to pull.

'Incoming, a Black Yhandis hunter.'

'Eslowed.'

'Doom to the Black Yhandisss!'

And we were off again, grinding through the mobs of the first floor. In less than an hour, we'd killed seventeen of the black-and-yellow patterned lizardmen and all of us, bar Tuscl, had levelled up. With a feeling of satisfaction, I put my new attribute point into Dexterity (it was surely going to be Dex all the way now, as while Spirituality was good for spellcasting, I had to gear myself for one crucial act: firing an arrow at a dragon). This was going well and I felt happy.

There were another twenty-one Black Yhandis on this floor, levels 23 to 27, accompanied by a mini boss, a captain level 30. With care, I was able to pull them in groups of no more than four, which made it a little less stressful for me. Ever since that dark elf had managed to hit me, I was anxious on pulls, in case one of them had a means of circumventing my immunity to weapon damage. Not that I could do much about it here. There was no kiting room and if I ran for the tower doors, I'd inevitably train my friends. In a situation where I was taking damage, probably, I'd just have to die.

With my main priority being on mobs and grinding, I didn't spend much time exploring. Yet there were features of the environment here that were interesting. Like the bedroom that had been ransacked and a pentacle painted on the bare wooden planks exposed beneath a torn carpet. There were mysteries here and quests and stories. And as far as I knew we were the first players to enter The Tower of the Jewelled Skull. As I went through the rooms though, I told myself not to lose sight of the bigger picture and kept to task, being rewarded by my reaching level 16 with a few mobs to spare on the second floor.

It was tempting to search for secret doors on this floor and I gave in to the temptation when Sapentia and Braja called a break to regain spirit. With Raitha at my side, I stepped through the debris to examine panelled walls, bare walls, walls with scorch marks on them and walls with mysterious scratches. No secret doors or compartments that we could tell. Standing before a shard of broken mirror, Raitha and I contemplated one another.

'Twins no longer,' he said, somewhat ruefully.

It was true. Quite apart from the fact that I was dressed in very different style, my face was heavier and uglier, with bigger and darker eyes, my shoulders and chest bulked up more with muscle and my hands were bigger, with longer fingers. Compared to me, Raitha's female half-elf was a beauty.

'We are growing apart in shape, but closer in spirit,' I offered.

'I hope that's true.'

'Why wouldn't it be?' I asked, surprised at the somewhat melancholy tone of my best friend.

'Well, it seems to me there are two reasons. One is that you are now the leader of the whole project. You have replaced the General. And as I do not experience the same responsibility or – presumably – the same levels of anxiety and stress, I believe the situation has a built-in tendency to make you more curt and perhaps in your eyes, I seem more shallow and irreverent.'

'No, no, not at all.'

'Good. The second reason is that I find myself becoming detached from the goal of killing the dragon. Since I am being paid to assist the achievement of this goal and since I am an honourable person, I do my best. I find myself enjoying the journey and deep down, I don't really care about the outcome of the project.'

[Group] 'Full,' said Sapentia.

I turned away from the mirror and set off back to the others. 'Even if the game will be unplayable if we fail?'

'Even so.' His avatar gave a nod. 'There will be other games.'

'Even if Watson, Blackridge and the others from Yuno will lose their jobs?'

'Even so.'

'And if Watson faced worse? If he was going to have his legs broken, for example.'

'Is this hypothetical? Because best practice in HR these days tends not to use the threat of violence as an incentive. I have been shown clips of Darth Vader killing his underlings and had serious professionals explain to me how this would not, in fact, be an effective way to run an evil empire.'

'Well, I made up the broken legs. Watson did give the impression though that his investors - Blackcoin's founders – would hold him personally responsible for the loss of their money.'

'Poor Watson. I should not like to be in his position. Yet even here, I find that I am not particularly motivated. I am not his friend. He has arrived at this position from his own choices.

And someone like him will have a bolt hole.'

'True. And Raitha?'

'Yes, my friend.'

'Don't worry. I feel the same way too. I'll do my best to kill the dragon for them but I haven't become one of them.'

CHAPTER 24
A WELL-HIDDEN BOOK

The third floor of the necromancer's tower was also occupied by Black Yhandis, who had pulled all the furnishings apart, as though searching for something. There was one interesting challenge. The lizardmen had a prisoner in an iron cage. When I released him, however, expecting a certain amount of gratitude and perhaps some useful information for our quests, he transformed into a werewolf. For several minutes the werewolf and I hammered away at each other, neither of us doing any harm. We were both immune to normal attacks.

The tricky aspect of the fight concerned aggro: because I wasn't hurting the werewolf, even by a small amount, I was hardly creating aggro. Everyone stood around watching, hesitant to get involved, especially as all we knew about the werewolf's level was that it was at least five above Tuscl's 19 (it conned *impossible* to him). Eventually, Sapentia figured out a solution and had Braja throw me his magical mace. Even though I was unskilled at first, after a dozen attempts I landed my first hit that did damage and we could see that the werewolf's hit point bar dropped about 2 per cent. Not too tough. After a few more hits from me (and skill ups in mace wielding) Grythiss stepped in and tanked without ever being in too much trouble.

We then faced a staircase that had been blocked with old furniture and which had 'keep out' written on the walls in Elvish. It was unclear whether the Black Yhandis had created the obstacle to prevent the dark elves from further up the tower coming back down, or the dark elves were warning the lizard-men not to come up. Appealing as it was to press ahead, the lower levels of the tower suited us perfectly: not too dangerous; exp that was levelling us up ahead of schedule; a merchant we could offload loot to. And when I ran back down to discover that half the ground floor mobs had already respawned, there was no difficulty about our choice. We would respect the barricade, for now.

The landing on the staircase between the ground floor and the first floor seemed a safe spot to pull to and we were so efficient at killing the lizardmen by now that we worked our way through all four floors in less than two hours. After which it was time for a break.

Leading our way down the stairs towards the main doors, the tower now seemed familiar and much less intimidating than when I had entered. Higher up, though, were supposed to be mobs that would challenge players who had reached level 50 and I looked forward to exploring those elevated reaches. For the immediate future, boring though it was becoming, we had to grind out some more levels on the Black Yhandis.

After unclipping and using the bathroom, I met Sapentia at a vending machine, where she was eating white chocolate.

'Want some?' She offered me a row of squares, which I took.

'That went well, didn't it?'

'Yes,' Sapentia replied, though not with any enthusiasm.

'But?'

'Tyro, I'm thinking of quitting.'

'Quitting? No, please don't.' I was shocked. And it suddenly became clear to me just how important it was to have Sapentia in my team. Okay, she was a celebrity and her presence in my group was a real feather in my cap. Beyond that, though, she was a great player. And then…despite the fact I knew it was hopeless, I was smitten. It would really hurt if she left.

'Why do you care? Anyone could do my job.'

'No, no, that's not true. And I wouldn't want someone else in the group. I want you.'

Scornfully, she leaned away, as though to better appraise me. 'You know nothing about me.'

'I do though. You're clever. You're daring. You are defiant…is it Braja?'

With a bitter laugh, Sapentia shook her head, purple ponytails exaggerating the movement. 'No. Not Braja. He's not important. It because I still don't understand Yuno. Why they built the game this way, so hard to fix? We are missing full picture.'

The heavy beating in my chest subsided. 'Remember our meeting this morning?'

When Sapentia was watching you out of eyes that were outlined so heavily, you really felt her attention. I had it now.

'You asked about who made *Epic Two*,' I continued. 'I was watching Katherine at the time and she was uneasy about that question. She had something to say and nearly said it. Want to go see her and ask again?'

'Good idea.' Sapentia considered. 'Probably. We must be quick though; everyone is back in game in ten.'

'Come on then.' I felt an upsurge of giddiness. Like on the day at school when we'd refused to go out in heavy rain on a cross country run that our P.E. teacher had tried to make us do. Like I was engaging in an act of rebellion.

We hurried through the Den, Sapentia's heels clicking loudly. It amused me to see the heads turn towards her. It was middle-aged men who were the least able to prevent themselves from staring a little too long at her outfit.

Katherine's office was on the floor above and rather than wait for a lift, we ran up the well-lit stairs, crossed over the foyer and down a short corridor. Her door was ajar. I tapped it all the same before entering.

'Oh, hello Tyro, Sapentia, good to see you.'

You could tell at once that the Yuno executive was fully engaged in the latest strategy for the project. Behind her, a whiteboard had columns written in five different colours, with lists of gear and with arrows pointing to certain items which had boxes around them and messages like, 'blacksmith 50' or 'enchanter 75'. On her desk were pages and pages, printed out from the guide and while most were resting in wire trays, many were spread out in front of her and had small yellow pieces of paper stuck on them, with notes in her handwriting.

'We don't have long,' said Sapentia, standing behind a chair and resting her hands on the back. 'So to cut to chase. Who really built *Epic Two*? What is going on?'

I had expected Katherine to look alarmed, or show a sign of surprise and distress. Instead, we got a calm, appraising look from beneath her grey fringe. 'Short version. Someone came in as project manager. We all called him Kiro but I never heard or saw his real name. In the game, he went by *Kraken*. Japanese, I think, about forty years old. Well dressed, fit, very friendly, he had the office across from me; I never warmed to him though.'

'And what did he do?'

'This is what troubles me. I've no idea. Beyond the fact that instead of running the whole game on our own servers, he made it run on a network of volunteer hardware.'

'Was he stupid?' Again, Sapentia took the lead. That was fine by me.

'No, definitely not.'

'Then why introduce problems editing game? What was gain?'

'Oh, the gains were spelled out often enough at meetings: massive processing power; customer engagement; no lag, even in countries with national firewalls; that kind of thing.'

'But?' I asked, sensing her hesitation.

'But…our tech people think there is far more energy being used in the playing of the game than we planned for. Considerably more. Not just here, all over the world. If the game becomes a hit, we'll be making a distinct contribution to global warming all by ourselves.'

'Interesting,' mused Sapentia. 'What do you make of it? He smuggled something in?'

'I'm not sure. I've had our people check for Trojans and other non-game programs. It's not that.'

'It's definitely game-related?' I wondered aloud.

Katherine nodded. 'Yes. Extra content perhaps? A massive hidden quest or region. Some kind of high-level controls or hacks? To allow certain players to cheat at the game? Quests that allow a player hidden advantages?

'What makes me think it might be something like this, is that one of our writers came to me, secretly, to tell me he had been asked by Kiro to draw up a dozen quest lines that led to a very well-hidden book.'

'A book,' repeated Sapentia, with interest, as though she was still in character as a wizard.

'A book'—Katherine shrugged—'which may or may not be in the game and which might be a complete red herring.'

While we thought about this, no one speaking, an important question occurred to me. 'Do you still believe we should kill the dragon?'

With a rueful smile, Katherine nodded. 'I'll be out of a job if you don't. It's the only way to reclaim the game. And it would be a huge, huge waste of years of work by the best developers in the industry. Although even then, killing the dragon might not be enough. Maybe some of the other AI are smart enough to lead a campaign against player entry.'

'Like the Generals of Bow and Sword.'

'Exactly those two. We put a lot of work into them. And Lady Cruoris.'

'Do you think AI have rights?' asked Sapentia suddenly.

'One day they will. These creations are still a long way short of sentience though. Ultimately, they are just bots.'

'So, we carry on?' I asked.

'Yes please, if you would.'

I looked at Sapentia. She looked at me, then shrugged.

'Okay.' Sapentia turned and walked away.

'Thanks.' I gave Katherine half a wave, as though apologising for any rudeness from my teammate. Not that Sapentia was deliberately being rude, just efficient. Then I hurried to catch up with her.

'I do not like the sound of *Kraken*,' Sapentia said as she hesitated beside another office door.

'I thought you said Japanese men were kind of lame.'

'Not all. Some are dangerous.' Then, surprisingly, she entered the office. I glanced at the name on the door: Head of Game Development, Paul Blackridge.

There he was, behind a computer and in the room was the stocky young man who had given me a hard time at the last meeting. Both Blackridge and the tough-guy player looked shocked to see us.

'So.' Sapentia put her hands on her hips. 'Now we see where the attack on Tyro came from. Why though?'

Standing up, Blackridge stared and worked his mouth as though speaking, yet nothing came out. Eventually, the strong flush in his cheeks faded. 'Close the door.' He was looking at me.

With a shrug, I did so.

'How did you do it?' he asked still ignoring Sapentia and focusing on me. His stare, dark and hostile, might have troubled someone who cared for his good opinion.

'What?'

'Become a vampire?'

'Luck mostly. Although I think suggesting I would make a good companion to Lady Cruoris came into it.'

'Luck,' Blackridge repeated bitterly. 'Sod you, Foster. You know nothing about the game.'

'Don't you want him to kill dragon?' asked Sapentia, a note of genuine curiosity in her voice.

'Kill the dragon? I don't see how he'll get within a mile of the dragon, unless as meat for its dinner. And as for what they are saying about him being a great raid leader, that's a God damned lie!'

'What's your plan then, General?' Sapentia did sarcasm well, the word General was coated in it.

Blackridge leaned back in his chair, fingers tapping together, smiling nearly. He had command of himself again and shared a glance with his stooge. 'Watch you fail. Watch this whole setup come crashing down.'

'And?' I was angry now. 'This is your job, not mine. If I fail, it hurts you more than me.'

Yawning with deliberate rudeness, Blackridge looked at his screen, then tapped it.

'Come on,' muttered Sapentia, 'others are waiting.'

'I want to hear him answer my question.'

'He's not going to,' she raised her voice again. 'He has given up on Yuno.'

Back in the game, my heart beating normally once more, the lower levels of the tower had fully respawned (with the exception of the werewolf prisoner). Since we knew what to expect, as we began the grind our conversation turned to the information that Sapentia and I had gained from Katherine and Blackridge.

'It's a cock-up.' Braja cast a heal on Grythiss and then resumed his thought. 'The larger the organisation, the more likely it is that someone high up makes a terrible decision and no one corrects it. Like the army. Sometimes, it seemed to me that what mattered wasn't winning, or they would listen to us grunts. What mattered was reputation. In fact, if you really wanted to get something done, you'd explain to the sergeant how it would make the lieutenant look good if we...'

Boom! A bolt of lightning finished off a Black Yhandis rogue. Then Sapentia said, 'It not a cock-up. Some very smart people came here and crowdsourced the game hosting for a reason.'

'Money laundering?' I offered, thinking of what my mum had said. I was standing in the hallway of the first floor, some ten metres away from the others, being attacked by a dozen black-and-gold lizardmen.

'How though?' This was Raitha. 'If they managed to invest millions of ill-gotten money into the company, then why not make the game a success? The point at which dirty money becomes clean is in regard to investment. Once the authorities have allowed the investment, well, what is the point sabotaging the game?'

'Something to do with Blackcoin exchange?' I glanced over my shoulder down the stairs to the landing on which the rest of the group were fighting a lizardman warrior.

'I think so too,' said Sapentia in a musing tone. 'Yet I don't see how. We earn game coins. We swap them for Blackcoin outside game. If people making Blackcoin are laundering, maybe this game helps them? Gives them more opportunity to buy a clean currency?'

'That could be it!' I could hear the enthusiasm in my own voice. 'We know the investors are Blackcoin's owners.'

'Maybe. Something close to this. Doesn't explain extra game content and energy cost of running game.'

As soon as Sapentia pointed this out, my belief we had the answer dissipated. Curious to know more about our new group member, I asked, 'Tuscl, what do you think? What is really going on?'

'I just know I'm being paid to play a game I love. Is enough.'

'I hear that,' said Braja earnestly.

The Black Yhandis warrior is dead. You gain experience.

After a short pause, while he tagged a Black Yhandis cleric and the group set to work on him, Raitha resumed the conversation. 'Is it though? I mean, if these were really unethical, abhorrent people, would we still work for them?'

'They're all pretty much the same,' said Braja, 'big businesses. I don't see one being better to work for than another.'

'Of course you don't; you worked for US army.' This sardonic comment was from Sapentia.

'Score.' I laughed, but Braja didn't join in.

'You don't know anything about me. I'll tell you this, though, I've worked for companies a lot more ruthless than the army.'

The Black Yhandis cleric is dead. You gain experience.

'Kill more hated foessss,' muttered Grythiss. 'Bring another Black Yhandisss.'

'Incoming, resistance buffs,' said Tuscl.

And with our minds back on the game, we dropped the speculation about Yuno and the real owners of *Epic 2*.

Another two hours saw us clear the tower up to the 'Keep Out' sign. And then we did all four floors again. This was where gaming became a chore. You discover a location that spawns worthwhile mobs for your level and you just fight the same battles over and over. It was tedious. Yet I'd done even more boring grinds while playing *Epic* and here at least I had my friends to chat with.

At last, when we were all feeling tired and hungry, I called an end to it. Tuscl had just made level 24 and gained some attribute buff spells, so even though there were a few mobs left on the third floor, it was a good place to stop. We ran downstairs and dumped the junk finds on the merchant, then unclipped at the entrance to the tower. As I did so, I had a final look at the group box on my UI with some satisfaction. We were on schedule.

Group Leader: Klytotoxos, half-elf, hunter, Level 19

Raitha	half-elf	hunter	Level 19
Sapentia	human	sorceress	Level 21
Grythiss	lizardman	dark knight	Level 20
Braja	human	cleric	Level 18
Tuscl	human	shaman	Level 24

CHAPTER 25
ANOTHER DAY, ANOTHER GRIND

Shortly after six the next morning, we were all back in the necromancer's tower and ready to go. This time, after clearing the bottom four floors in just ninety minutes (and all gaining a level apart from Tuscl) we stood at the staircase with, 'Keep Out' written on both walls. At the top of the stairs was a barricade of wooden furniture.

'Dark elves next then,' said Braja. 'I hate them. Too many casters.'

'I hate Dark Yhandisss.'

'Somehow, Grythiss, we are familiar with this piece of information.' Raitha gave our tank an affectionate pat on the back.

'How do we go through?' asked Sapentia.

I shrugged. 'Shall I just walk up and drag it apart?'

'And trigger traps?' She shook her head.

'What then?'

'Lightning?'

There was a silence as we all thought about this. 'All right?' I looked around, nobody objected, even if they did take a step or two backwards.

'Let's estand around the corner.' Tuscl implemented her own suggestion and the others, apart from Sapentia and me, joined her.

'Here goes.' Sapentia took a position out of direct line of

the staircase and aiming her fingers upwards, began to chant. A few seconds later, with a loud clap of thunder, a vivid electric bolt flashed up the stairs, crackling like a drumroll as it bounced back and forth from side to side and off the stairs and roof too. After hitting the barricade the bolt streaked back towards us and without thinking I stepped in its path.

Whomp. A brilliant, dazzling whiteout and a feeling I was made of pure energy.

You have been hit by a *Lightning Strike* for 0 damage.

My hair had risen, I knew that from the tingling sensation all up the back of my head. Everywhere was the smell of gunpowder (I hadn't experienced anything like it since a boy in my class, Adam Rahilly, blew himself up one bonfire night trying to make a genie). And my lovely pirate captain's shirt had a big black stain on the front.

'What did you do that for?' asked Raitha, with genuine curiosity.

'Wasn't spent. Could have gone anywhere. I knew I was immune...' It took me a moment to be able to gather my thoughts properly. Then I laughed. 'I tell you what though. It's some craic. You should try it if you ever get the chance.'

Business-like, as though there had never been any danger to our group, Sapentia ignored me and examined the stairs. Carpet had been fried away to the stone beneath in several places; the walls of the corridor were blackened (with the warnings now barely legible); bits and pieces of scorched wood were strewn on every step, some planks were large enough to cross the width of the stairwell; and there was a big hole in the barricade.

Our wizard, looking pleased with herself, pointed to the mess. 'Up you go.'

There wasn't much point being stealthy after that explosion, so I ran up the stairs, four at a time, and found myself in a long corridor. My intuition was that it stretched almost the entire length of the tower. It was featureless, in the main, apart from brackets for unlit torches on the outer wall.

'Hello?' I said, not loudly. 'Anyone here?'

When no one answered I took two steps into the corridor and a blade to my spine.

You have been stabbed in the back by a short sword for 0 damage.

'I am here!' a dark elf whispered triumphantly.

'So you are.' I turned around and enjoyed the look of consternation on his purple face.

[Group] 'Incoming, a dark elf rogue…or maybe assassin.'

In the moment it took for my enemy to recover from his shock, I skipped past him and down the stairs. Enraged now, he hurried after me, only to pause when he saw the group waiting for him at the bottom.

[Group] 'Quick, someone tag him. Don't let him run.'

Tuscl waved her arms. [Group] 'Eslowed.' That would help but *Slow* affected combat speed rather than running speed. And as far as the dark elf was concerned, the spell made up his mind. He was off, running away into the darkness.

'After him!' I cried and sprang back up the stairs. My base speed was probably quicker than that of the rogue and with Tuscl's buff I was faster still. Even so, we were both nearly at the far corner before I was able to grab him.

You have learned the skill Grapple (1).

'Get off me, half-breed!' With rage in his eyes and a thick-bladed dagger in his far hand, my opponent stabbed me rapidly three times in the ribs. Not at all bad for someone under the effects of a *Slow* spell.

You have been hit by a dagger for 0 damage.

You have been hit by a dagger for 0 damage.

You have been hit by a dagger for 0 damage.

'Racist,' I replied and hung on tight until Grythiss came up and gave the dark elf a massive cleave with the longsword that had been magically enhanced by Nemain. That got my opponent's attention and as he turned, I leapt at his neck.

Critical Hit! You have bitten a dark elf assassin for 45 points of damage. You are draining his blood.

Excellent. And not only would this successful bite help the battle, it would keep my thirst for blood in check for a while too. Without too much trouble - Braja's heals easily kept Grythiss ahead of the damage - we hammered away at the dark elf until Sapentia finished him off with a flurry of nukes.

The dark elf assassin is dead. You gain experience.

Good experience too, about 10 per cent of my exp bar.

From where she had been kneeling by the body, Tuscl straightened up. 'There is a *Fastened* medallion.'

'Stats?' I asked.

'None; is the *Vengeance* quest.'

So it was. We needed to hand in thirty of these. 'Go ahead, you collect them.'

With all the racket we'd made, especially the booming sounds of Sapentia's spells, which had reverberated along the corridor, I was surprised the place was so quiet. Where were the reinforcements?

'I'll go on.'

Around the corner, I found exactly the same sight: a very long black corridor, stretching for the fifty metres or so of the tower, featureless other than the unlit torches. Sauntering along, I ran the fingertips of my right hand against the inner wall. Just in case. No secret door though.

[Group] 'Move up please.' I didn't want to turn the next corner and be a whole corridor ahead of my team. Once I could see Raitha - the first of the group to step around - I waved. He didn't wave back. It must have been too dark for him. 'That will do.'

As I turned the next corner, the flagstone beneath my right foot sank a little as I put my weight on it. Leaping back with my heart beating fast, it seemed as though I had escaped the trap. A pit?

[Group] 'There's some sort of...oh.' All the torches in the brackets flared and the corridor was full of orange and yellow colour, as well as flickering shadows. I turned and ran back to my friends.

'Should we go back?' asked Raitha.

'We should.'

The moment we turned the corner, however, we saw our route back to the stairs was blocked by a troop of some eight dark elves, marching determinedly towards us.

'Should we go on?' asked Raitha, with amusement in his voice, despite the danger.

'I believe we should.'

Hurrying forward, we made it halfway along the corridor, more or less to the point that the group had been standing at when I triggered the trap, when the distinct tramp of another band of enemies came from ahead of us.

'Wait.' We were going to be caught between two impossibly difficult groups of mobs and I couldn't see a way to get the aggro of both. 'Suggestions?'

'Time to die bravely.' Grythiss raised his sword in a kind of salute that nearly brought the tip to the roof.

'All right, try to die as close to the stairs as you can, I'll hold off this far group.'

'For Nemainss's glory!' shouted our tank and charged around the corner. Then Braja, Tuscl and Raitha followed, weapons drawn. Sapentia, however, was casting and I caught her eye. She was able to give me a rueful shrug without losing the spell.

Around the far corner came the new group of eight dark elves, led by a commander with a wicked-looking, long-bladed spear. *Boom!* An explosion of fire engulfed them and the roils of heat, distorting the air around me, rushed through the corridor leaving me blinking away a red blur and shaking my head to rid of a ringing sound.

You have been hit by a *Fireball* for 0 damage.

Nearby, Sapentia picked herself up, her clothing still smouldering and ran. 'Good luck.'

'Ah,' I said to their battered-looking commander. 'I think there might be a misunderstanding here. I come with a message...' The dark elf jabbed me in the stomach with his spear.

You have been hit by a glaive for 63 damage.

Oh.

Leaping past the officer, I took several more hits, all for zero damage, before I was clear and running away up the unexplored corridor. A flicker on my UI showed me that Grythiss had died, he was greyed out. A second later, however, he was green again, presumably having respawned downstairs. In quick succession the same grey-green switch happened to Raitha, Braja, Sapentia and Tuscl.

With a skip I avoided the trapped sinking stone at the corner (it probably didn't matter at this point) and turned down an empty corridor. When I was about a third of the way along, my eight pursuers came into view behind me. The final corridor was empty of mobs. It wasn't quite the same as the other three. At the far end, there was a section of wall that seemed to have been moved to create an opening. And just before that, on the interior wall, was a black rectangle that resolved itself as a stairwell going up as I got closer to it. Should I go up?

[Group] 'Well, Captain Tyro, what's the plan?' asked Braja.

[Group] 'Sec.' With barely a glance, I decided to go through the gap at the end of the corridor (past the false, sliding wall) and turned the corner to where the eight dark elves were standing motionless, spread out along the corridor, beside the bodies of my friends.

It was easy enough to run past them, receiving a few knocks as I did so, but no damage. Now I had sixteen dark elves chasing me.

[Group] 'Come up as far as the stairs?' I suggested.

[Group] 'Unfortunately, there is a full respawn down here,' replied Raitha, 'I don't think we can clear it without you to pull, at least, not level three.'

[Group] 'Ahh, shame, I was hoping not to die.' I still had a few tricks up my sleeve. During yesterday's grind my *Summon Bats* had become available and it was joined this morning by *Summon Rats*. Evidently, they were on a twenty-four-hour timer. Plus, I could turn myself into a gas cloud. Maybe I could run the train around the tower while my pets ate my enemies? It would take ages though. Better to get myself killed and help everyone come back up. With an internal sigh, I stopped running at the end of the corridor with my comrade's bodies. I would park the train well away from the staircase.

[Group] 'Should we estep outside the tower while you bring a train down?'

[Group] 'Oh, great idea. I was going to die, but this will be quicker and spare me the exp penalty.'

Just as the first of my enemies caught up - and a couple of arrows hit me without damage - I set off again, this time moving at my top speed. Once back around to the staircase, I bounded down, drawing the toughest of the Dark Yhandis in my wake.

[Group] 'Coming down! Watch out!'

[Group] 'We are all safe,' replied Raitha, 'though for good measure we are moving around to the right-hand side of the tower as you come out. If your mobs follow you out please go straight down the hill, a little to the left.'

[Group] 'Got it!' I had reached Level 1 already and just as I came to the stairs to the ground floor, I remembered something important. 'It's daylight, right?'

[Group] 'Oh blast. Sorry.' Raitha sounded contrite.

[Group] 'Never mind.'

There were so many mobs crowding around me at the top of the stairs that they were all something of a blur. My combat reports were streaming through that section of my UI so fast that I felt the word count would surpass that of *War of Peace* in a matter of minutes.

'Coming through, coming through. Where's that guy with the spear?' I did my best to push into the mobs and make my way towards the back, where, from the sight of his glaive waving around in the air, I could just make out the dark elf commander who was able to damage me. 'Come on! Back up a bit and you'll get what you want. A dead pirate captain.' It was hopeless though; the press was too intense in every direction.

[Group] 'Hah, I can't even die. I'm a bit stuck here, on the first floor near the stairs. Do you think you can clear the ground floor without me?'

[Group] 'Yesss. Death to the Black Yhandisss.'

Soon I was listening to my reformed group as they went back into action. And feeling that it probably wouldn't be too much of a waste, I summoned a swarm of bats. Would they arrive in this tower at all? They would, dozens of them, swirling around above the battle. In fact…although it was tricky to target him, eventually I got a good visual on the glaive-wielding commander and ordered my bats to attack. Then I bit into the wrist of the Black Yhandis immediately in front of me. After several successful bites and even more misses, I struck blood.

Critical Hit! You have bitten a Black Yhandis wizard for 49 points of damage. You are draining his blood.

Now the situation was interesting, amusing even. Normally, when you mess up your crowd control, death follows very quickly. Here I was, in the middle of a thick bunch of mobs and having the upper hand. At least until the guy with the glaive could get at me. Meanwhile, I was gaining experience from the efforts of my group below on the ground floor.

After about ten minutes of this, two developments changed the pattern. My target, the wizard, died and almost at the same time, Raitha said, [Group] 'We are done here. I suggest we try to pull one of yours away.'

[Group] 'Be my guest. I don't suppose you can target the one with the glaive and the bats around him?'

[Group] 'You suppose correctly.'

[Group] 'Oh well. Help yourself to whatever you can then.'

[Group] 'Incoming, a dark elf cleric.'

We were back in a grind, the wild confusion of the chase having settled down. I did wonder whether I should worry about the commander. As the mobs thinned out, he'd be able to start hitting me again. Long before that became an issue, however, my bats had solved the problem.

The dark elf warrior is dead. You gain experience.

I reassigned the bats to a new target and kept trying a bite attack on the nearest mob, until I was fastened on and bleeding him to death. This was a challenge no longer.

It took about thirty minutes to kill all the mobs and the resulting exp was excellent. After the huge train had been derailed, I was level 20 (hurray, I could equip my self-*Haste* buff *Swift as a Panther*, which gave me a slight increase over Tuscl's group buff. Unfortunately, they didn't stack) and I was nearly 21. Raitha the same, of course. Sapentia was 22, Grythiss 21, Braja 20 and Tuscl 25. The loot from the dark elves was helpful too: Setharian plate (+1, +3 at night) for various slots, which went to Grythiss first and then to Braja. We also obtained six more medallions for the *Vengeance is Best Served* quest. Then, on the commander was a magical glaive, *+1 versus undead*. Aha. There was the source of my injuries (which had entirely regenerated). Weapons - and presumably spells - that were targeted against the undead were dangerous to me. Just as well I wasn't fighting good races and encountering paladins and clerics with a strong repertoire of attacks against the undead.

We now had four levels of Black Yhandis and two levels of dark elves for our grind. That was plenty; so long as the ground floor mobs gave us experience it was worth including them in the cycle. And now that we knew about the secret wall on the fifth floor, we could bypass the corridor trap and (the group having first killed the assassin on guard duty) I could pull directly from the sixth floor, which had an unusual layout. It was like a large, open plan office, with a dozen dry swimming pools evenly distributed in the floor. Maybe the necromancer who had built the tower had kept huge vats of liquid in these, for experiments and potions. Maybe they had actually been pools, with creatures in them. Now they were mostly empty or else had a scattering of debris in them.

Pulling from this level was easy enough, I could limit the groups who chased me to four at a time. And the only challenge therefore was the commander. Every time I drew him towards my friends, I was anxious in case he again spawned with a weapon that was damaging to the undead. That would mean Raitha having to tag him first out of the small group he came with, before I'd take the four or five hits that would have killed me. My fears, however, were never realised. The glaive must have been a rare item (albeit a fairly useless one for us, given that Grythiss had no spear skill and a much better DPS with his +2 longsword) because it didn't drop the rest of the day.

With a certain amount of pride in the group, I could feel us home in on the most efficient tactics to clear these floors of mobs again and again. Every time I went up a level, I couldn't help but imagine the large board in the Den and especially Blackridge's reaction, should he be monitoring it (which I was sure he was). At the end of a long day, which left us hungry as we only took minimal toilet breaks, we were in fine shape. Our levels were Braja, Raitha and I 24, Grythiss 25, Sapentia 26 and Tuscl 28.

Thanks to the fact that the dark elf commander occasionally dropped a Setharian plate breastplate, both Grythiss and Braja were fully kitted out in magic armour. They looked impressive too, when the torchlight of the fourth floor was reflected in the scrollwork of the gleaming black metal. Our collection of forty-one medallions had been worth something too. Just before we unclipped, Tuscl had made the run back to Carrickmor to hand over the medallions and complete the *Vengeance* quest. A noticeable exp boost was the result as well as an *Iron Shield of Fire Resistance*, +2 AC and 25 per cent reduction in fire damage. A very nice upgrade for the grateful Grythiss.

CHAPTER 26
ONWARDS AND UPWARDS

Three days later, I decided the time had come to push on up the tower. I'd been conservative about this. Why take any risks when we could progress without difficulty? True, cycling through the six floors of the tower that we'd explored was boring. Boredom, however, was a small price to pay for success. And it surely was a success that Braja, Raitha and I were 29, Grythiss 30, Sapentia 31 and Tuscl 32.

'Isn't it fascinating,' I said to the group while we were working on the final group of dark elves. 'That when we first came up here, we were on edge and the tower seemed intimidating. Now, this far at least, we're almost at home.'

'You have an idiom in the English language,' replied Raitha, slashing at the flanks of our target, a dark elf wizard. 'Familiarity breeds contempt. I believe that this applies here.'

'Also,' said Braja, 'if we make a mistake now, it doesn't mean a wipe. Whereas for most of Monday it would have.'

'True. Well, we might wipe now, because it's time to move on up after these.' I was letting the fates know that we weren't taking our success for granted.

When the battle was over, Tuscl rebuffed us all and I cast my four spells on myself: *Swift as a Panther*, *Gather Shadow*, *Swiftshot* (my level 21 archery self-only buff) and *Leave no Trace*. Then I took a look at the staircase up. After one flight of fourteen plain stone stairs, the route up doubled back on itself so I could not see what was above me.

'Maybe stand over by the exit,' I suggested to the others. 'Give me some room to work with.'

As they complied, I set off, as quietly as I could (which was pretty quiet thanks to my *Boots of Dark Elvenkind*). At the top of the stairs was a hall with four doors on the far side of the room. Originally, the walls of the hall had been covered by a mosaic made of thousands of coloured stones. If I had to guess, I believe it might have told the story (anti-clockwise, unusually) of the necromancer's victory over her hated enemy and how she made an artefact out of his skull. Whether by the actions of the ogres or the dark elves, however, the mosaic was damaged everywhere and a big chunk of the final section - where I guessed the skull was depicted - was completely smashed in. Shame, I'd have liked more of an insight into the history of Notrevity and of her tower.

Taking the left door, I opened it cautiously. A long, thin corridor with an opening to the right after ten metres. Not far beyond the junction were a pair of boots. Edging up towards them, I saw that there was a dark stain on the stone floor beneath the boots. Something unpleasant happened to a dark elf here. The corridor that came off mine was about five metres long and ended in a T-junction. Naturally, I took it rather than step beside those boots. At the T-junction the left branch went about five metres to another T-junction, while the right, pointing back parallel to the way I'd come, turned sharp left after eight metres. Great, some kind of maze. Forget it. I went back to the entrance hallway.

[Group] 'Sorry for the delay, there's a bit of a maze up here, no sign of mobs just yet and I'm anxious not to run into traps.'

[Group] 'Take your time,' Braja replied.

[Group] 'There is no hurry,' added Raitha, 'we are having an interesting discussion about what this tower will be like when the game goes live. How many groups will it support and where will the camps be?'

[Group] 'The dark elf commander will be one for sure,' I observed.

I could picture Raitha nodding at this. [Group] 'Exactly. It would be strange, though, to have the tower full of other player characters waiting on their targets to spawn. A lot of the ambiance would be lost.'

319

[Group] 'Much as I'd like to listen in, we'd better drop the group chat; I'm trying another door and don't want to be distracted.'

The door in question was the second from the left. It was locked. With my powerful strength, I probably had a good chance of kicking it open. For now, though, I left it and went to the third door. This opened quietly to a long, thin corridor with several junctions. More of the maze. Except there was an arrow drawn in red on the wall at waist height, pointing inwards. The picture was crude and the paint had dripped a little, as though raindrops were gathered beneath the arrow.

At the first junction, there was an X marked on one of the walls of the branching corridor and the arrow pointed onwards. Very well. I continued on, following the arrows until at last I came to a wide, open area. It was a kind of barracks with ten camp beds, each set up with a bag at their foot. Except the barracks were a new addition to what might once have been the lair of an undead minotaur. For in the room was an extremely lifelike statue of just such a creature: bull's legs, stocky, if decaying, human torso, arms and hands and a bull's head, one horn broken. It was the vividness of the pose and the fact that he was shaping up to swing his axe that made me think the statue was not so much a work of art as the result of the dark elves finding the creature in the centre of the maze.

Elsewhere in the room were six dark elves of various classes. They all conned *impossible*, apart from one in leather armour, who was *very risky*, i.e. four levels above me, so 33.

[Group] 'Going to pull a group of six dark elves, thirty-three and above.'

[Group] 'Dark elvesss musst die,' said Grythiss encouragingly.

Retreating a few steps, I took out my bow, nocked an arrow and then inched forward until I could target one of the dark elves.

You have fired an arrow at a dark elf warrior and missed.

It did the trick though; immediately the gang of elves chased me back through the maze and down the stairs, where I waited for them in sight of my friends. I'd already swapped my bow back to my inventory as I'd run, so it was just a case of launching myself at the first of my enemies and trying to bite him. Except that as I did so, I crashed to the ground, confused and looking at the (very nicely fashioned) boots of my enemies.

You have been hit by a beam from a Wand of Petrification and have been turned to stone.

[Group] 'Don't pull!' shouted Sapentia urgently. 'Wait for them to leave.'

[Group] 'Are you dead?' asked Raitha. 'Can you speak?'

[Group] 'In group, at least.'

[Group] 'Well, what does that feel like?' Braja asked with a chuckle.

[Group] 'Really strange. The tracker ball won't move any more. I can feel and move my real-life limbs though, including my head, but the scene in front of me doesn't change, so I'm out of synch with my avatar.'

[Group] 'Enemiessss leave usss.'

From my restricted view, I saw the boots of the dark elves move away and I could hear them walking up the stairs.

[Group] 'Anyone got a fix for this?' I probably spoke anxiously. I certainly felt anxious. The lesson of the minotaur statue meant the condition was not going away any time soon. It was probably permanent.

[Group] 'I could smash your head off with my magical mace?' offered Braja cheerfully. 'Then you can respawn.'

[Group] 'It might come to that. Although what if I'm immune to weapons still?'

[Group] 'That would be a cruel yet fascinating inversion of your situation. A true example of dialectic, where an immense positive is found, under certain very rare circumstances, to be an equally powerful negative.'

[Group] 'Thank you, Raitha, for seeing the philosophical side of my predicament.'

[Group] 'We ussse the glaive.'

Curiously, considering we were talking about my death, Grythiss's idea was a relief. I'd begun to sweat at the horrible thought of being locked in statue form until we got some high-level cleric or wizard with a *Dissipate Magic* or *Remove Magic* to come to the tower. We could waste days as a result and even undermine the whole plan. Despite the fact I didn't want him in my head, I couldn't help but envisage at how Blackridge would gloat if I were stuck as a stone statue for days.

[Group] 'Tuscl, Sapentia, anything?'

[Group] 'No,' they both answered at once.

[Group] 'I could blow Nemain's horn twice?' offered Raitha. 'Do you think that's an evil effect you are suffering?'

[Group] 'If it isn't, I don't know what is. But no, let's save that for a group emergency.' I sighed. 'Okay, Grythiss, do your worst.'

The sound of footsteps approached and then, with a great clang, my vision wobbled.

> You have been hit by a glaive for 2 damage.
>
> You have been hit by a glaive for 2 damage.
>
> You have been hit by a glaive for 2 damage.

Fortunately, my regeneration was ineffective while I was in this petrified condition. Otherwise, the process would take even longer, or worse, I might recover hit points faster than Grythiss could knock them off.

'Mind if I take a seat?' Braja spoke from out of view.

'That looks comfortable, I shall join you.' This was Raitha.

Sapentia, for the first time in a long time, sounded cheerful. 'It is shame that I have no camera. This would be a good picture. I call it, "group leader provides seating for his team".'

'Are you sitting on me?' I did my best to sound aggrieved.

'Only while our lizardman chops through your neck.' Braja chuckled and I did too. It was a bizarre situation and definitely a break from the grind.

At last came the messages I had been waiting for.

> You have been hit by a glaive for 2 damage. You are on 0 hit points and unable to move.
>
> You have been assassinated.

My respawn point was on the ground floor at the main

door, where all was dark and quiet. It took me a few minutes to re-equip my four active spells and, crucially, to cast *Swift as a Panther* on myself. Then I triggered my *Invisibility* ability.

[Group] 'On my way up.'

There was no difficulty slipping invisible past the Black Yhandis of the first three floors, on the fourth, however, one of them saw me somehow. There were several buffs that allowed you to see invisible (including one called, unsurprisingly, *See Invisible*) so I knew it was a slight risk running past them. All the same, it was disappointing to have triggered a train. Or was it? At least there was some experience to be had.

[Group] 'Stay over by my body please everyone! I'm going to bring a train up the stairs and you can pull from it.' Maybe this would work out. And if one of the mobs could harm me, I could always die again without wiping the group.

[Group] 'Here.'

At the top of the stairs, I turned and faced my chasers, who quickly thronged around me. No damage. We were set.

Back in the grind again, it didn't make much of a difference that I had no weapons or armour. I could still bite and keep the aggro of the mobs around me, while Raitha pulled (with arrows) one at a time to be taken down. The timing of the battle was good too. Just as the fourth floor Black Yhandis and the fifth floor dark elf assassin were finished, the sixth floor ones began to respawn and we worked our way through those too, bringing me to level 30.

After the battles were done, I walked over to examine my stone corpse. The head was upside-down, resting on the large hat like a cup on a saucer, with my foot I righted it, or at least, got it to face upwards at a bit of an angle. My mouth was wide, long teeth showing.

'Most handsome.' Sapentia laughed.

'This would make a great souvenir.' I bent down to see if I could put the stone head into my inventory. Immediately, a screen popped up on my UI showing all the items on my corpse.

Take all?

Why not? Although I guessed this would cause my corpse to fade, stone head and all. And so it proved.

'Oh well. What should we do now? I don't want to keep on being turned to stone. And I've an eye on that wand, it would be great to get it while there are some charges left.'

'Agreed.' Tuscl came across to me, her avatar as lithe and dark-haired as she was in person. 'Is okay for me to offer advice?'

'Of course.' I was surprised she even asked.

'We fight back down to exit, take a break and you ask everyone for a scroll or potion of *Resist Petrification*.'

'Sounds good. Everyone happy with that plan? Let's take a break from the tower then too, at least long enough to 'port to a town for our level forty spells.'

No one demurred. Although I had a reservation about the downtime involved, I couldn't see another way forward and the additional experience as we cleared the Black Yhandis once more on the way down was useful, putting me past halfway to 31.

Once the slight giddiness I had from unclipping was gone – for a while after being in the game so long, I would find it hard to get used to a floor that didn't move – I made my way into the Den, to be greeted by a big cheer. The room was half-full, lively and decorated for a party. Two giant silver number balloons were bobbing around near the roof: 3 and 0. Lots of streamers banged and popped and shrieked. Lots of smiles and sparkling, encouraging eyes faced me. And there was cake too.

When his amplified voice came through the speakers, I knew it was Watson who had arranged this moment and that he was trying to give my authority a boost. 'Congratulations, Tom, on reaching thirty so quickly. Let's give him another cheer everyone. Hip, hip…hurray!'

Heartening as it was to be the recipient of such enthusiasm, I was more concerned about the current obstacle in my path. So I hurried up to the microphone, where Watson shook my hand.

'Well done, Tom, really.' He leaned in to whisper, 'I hope you don't mind.'

'No, it's useful,' I whispered back, then I turned to the crowd. 'Thanks, everyone. It's great to be making good progress. This is a team effort and I need your help to keep going. We've encountered a dark elf with a *Wand of Petrification*. Does anyone have a potion or scroll of *Resist Petrification*?'

There was a strange cross-current of behaviour in the room, half the people there were getting ready to cheer what they anticipated would be a celebratory speech from me and they were all smiles and chatter. The other half had actually listened to my question and were more thoughtful. After a long moment in which I said nothing further and the hubbub subsided, I tried again.

'Does anyone have a potion or scroll of *Resist Petrification*?'

One, two…three hands went up.

'Great.' Katherine was approaching me, catching my eye and signalling she wanted to speak to me. 'Can you come to the front and Katherine will arrange to get you teleported to the *Tower of the Jewelled Skull*.' As far as I was concerned, that was the end of the impromptu gathering. It was time to get on with the project. Yet I sensed there were expressions of expectancy from the people facing me. What more could I say? 'Thanks again. Enjoy the cake. We are doing really well and are on target to complete this project and win ourselves that bonus! Thanks.'

With that, and at least a half-decent round of applause I stepped down, took another handshake from Watson and turned to Katherine. 'You don't mind arranging those teleports?'

'Not at all.' Katherine smiled. 'Tom?'

'Yes?'

'You are doing really well.'

CHAPTER 27
BROMGUD

While the others went to Port Placida, I stayed at the tower and topped up on blood from the now low-level Black Yhandis. The downtime was also an opportunity to consider my character build over the remaining twenty or so levels. When I'd studied the *Epic 2* guides, I'd been focused on playing the role of crowd control and kiter in the final battle with Mikarkathat. To that end, I'd long ago planned my attribute spend and spell lines, to ensure that I ended up with the most effective spells for interfering with the motion of the various adds that spawned during the battle. Now, however, there was to be no battle. Instead, it was an assassination attempt and I was the assassin.

Although there were a range of useful spells to assist a hunter using a bow, these were not so demanding in terms of spirit as constantly trying to pin down several opponents. The best archery buff in the game, *Strike Like Lightning*, had a relatively modest spirit cost and lasted forty minutes. It was clearly intended that a Hunter would have the spell on constantly. One conclusion that I came to, therefore, was that I should rebalance my planned attribute spend, from spirit to dex.

The spell lines to prioritise clearly had to be those benefiting stealth and archery. Obviously, if we had time (and money), I'd learn the maximum number of spells and pursue them all down their respective branches. In a situation of limited means, however, I had to think more carefully about this. Many spells were stand-alones, which meant I could buy and equip them whenever I reached the appropriate level. Some, however, came in lines, the more powerful version replacing the previous.

Thus, *Cold Arrow* became *Ice Arrow* became *Frost Arrow* and finally *Arrow of the Void*. Not that I would be needing those for Mikarkathat. The fire line, on the other hand, would be worth obtaining.

It was time to check in on my twin. [Channel Klytotoxos/Raitha] 'Hi Raitha, before you buy our spells, can we have a chat?'

[Channel Klytotoxos/Raitha] 'Much as I welcome our conversations, I'm sorry I can't oblige you.' Raitha paused. 'For we have all hurriedly made our purchases and are even now running across blighted fields to the tower.'

[Channel Klytotoxos/Raitha] 'Ah. I was thinking about our priorities.'

[Channel Klytotoxos/Raitha] 'Indeed. As was I. Since our role now is simply to shoot two arrows each and shoot them as well as we can, we will need archery buffs and I have those.' By this time I knew Raitha well enough to detect a tone of amusement in his voice.

[Channel Klytotoxos/Raitha] 'You've got this all worked out, haven't you?'

[Channel Klytotoxos/Raitha] 'One rarely makes such absolute declarations of confidence in my part of the world. I did, however, spend a certain part of the night planning.'

[Channel Klytotoxos/Raitha] 'I have complete confidence in your plans,' I replied and it was true. 'What did you get us?'

[Channel Klytotoxos/Raitha] '*Heat Arrow, Strength of a Bear, Refreshing Camp, Swiftshot, Find Path* and *Spark*. Plus, *Invisibility* for myself.'

[Channel Klytotoxos/Raitha] 'Perfect.' I hesitated. 'Except *Spark*. Would you ever equip it? I thought it was for lighting fires.'

[Channel Klytotoxos/Raitha] 'It may be in the game for that reason. And perhaps a situation might arise where lighting a fire at a distance proves to be very important. I am using it right now, however, for a very different reason. Can you guess?'

This challenge made me smile. [Channel Klytotoxos/Raitha] 'Right now?'

[Channel Klytotoxos/Raitha] 'Correct.'

[Channel Klytotoxos/Raitha] 'But not to start a fire?'

[Channel Klytotoxos/Raitha] 'Correct also.'

[Channel Klytotoxos/Raitha] 'Is it dark outside? Does it act as a torch?'

[Channel Klytotoxos/Raitha] 'Good guess. It has a small, brief, light effect. This, however, is not the answer.'

[Channel Klytotoxos/Raitha] 'I give up.'

[Channel Klytotoxos/Raitha] 'Not so easily. Let me give you a clue. The spirit cost is miniscule, the cast time less than a second and the timer only two seconds.'

[Channel Klytotoxos/Raitha] 'So you can cast it frequently and often,' I mused aloud. 'You are trying to send signals?'

Raitha simply laughed.

[Channel Klytotoxos/Raitha] 'Now let me give up.'

[Channel Klytotoxos/Raitha] 'My *Mobile Casting* skill has already reached forty-seven,' Raitha announced proudly.

[Channel Klytotoxos/Raitha] 'Ahhh. Clever.' With *Mobile Casting* it was possible to move as well as launch a spell. At low levels you could walk and cast, high levels, run and cast and higher still, fly and cast. Repeated attempts of a quick and low-cost spell while moving was the way to get that skill to progress.

When we resumed our struggle with *The Tower of the Jewelled Skull*, it was with the advantage of having not just a scroll of *Resist Petrification* but a potion too. Moving up to the fifth floor (the one below the maze), we earned a decent amount of exp in just a little over an hour, enough to bring me to 31. Then I had to go up to pull the six dark elves who were in the chamber with the stone undead minotaur. Before I did so, Braja cast *Resist Petrification* on me off the scroll, with Raitha holding on to the potion as a back-up.

Running quickly through the maze (thank you, dark elves, for marking the route) I soon came to the centre where my six opponents were gathered around the stone undead minotaur.

'Good evening, could someone tell me the way to the fancy dress party?'

Immediately, the chase began and by easing up now and again to keep them interested, I was able to lead all six down to the fifth floor. This time, I had no difficulty biting into one of them, a rogue to judge by his leather armour, and holding the aggro while one by one my friends picked a target to pull across the room and take down.

Efficient as we were, this still took time. Time in which a series of about twenty UI alerts reading *You have resisted the spell Petrification* came to an end. After which, the dark elf wizard, whom the others did not dare pull for fear he'd turn them all to stone, no longer wielded a wand. In other words, it was probably out of charges. And when the fighting was all over, so it proved.

Having examined the wizard's body, I announced, '*Wand of Petrification*, no charges.'

'Here.' Sapentia knelt down beside me. 'I'll take it. It might be possible to recharge it.'

'There is something worthwhile on this hunter,' announced Raitha and he linked a Setharian chain hauberk, +1/+3 at night. 'You should have it.'

It was true. Time to swap out my pirate clothes for more practical armour. Not only did I put on the chainmail, which covered both chest and waist slots, I also took leather drops for my shoulders and arms.

'Now, that's more like it,' said Braja approvingly as I stood up from my last piece of looting. 'I feel like I'm in a fighting unit now, not a comedy act.'

'You are very handsome,' added Raitha, which caused both Sapentia and Tuscl to look around at me. 'At least, from the back, where the chainmail outlines your muscles. From the front, alas, the eye is drawn to your overly feral jawline.'

'Thank you; at least, my back thanks you. My face is less flattered.'

In good humour, I led the group up to the stone undead minotaur.

'Chop it to piecesss?' suggested Grythiss.

'I was wondering about that. Maybe later. Because although we'd probably get exp, it would then start to respawn and might be a logistical problem if we are running up and down the tower.'

Our lizardman nodded, so I left them in that relatively large room and went forward down dark stone corridors, taking the junctions marked by the dark elves. My four slotted spells were *Swift as a Panther*, *Gather Shadow*, *Spark* and *Leave no Trace*. There didn't seem to be a need for *Swiftshot* at the present and I agreed with Raitha's strategy of trying to obtain and increase *Mobile Casting*. It was just as well. For ahead of me, shown up by the flash of light from my fizzled attempt to send a shower of sparks ahead of me, was a strange carpet on the stone floor. Curiously, my vampiric infravision had missed it. The carpet had exactly the same heat as the stone. Or was it a carpet?

As I leaned forward, a tentacle shot out from the black rectangle and struck me in the face.

You have been hit by a slithering ambrile for 0 damage.

A what? Anyway, it was time to back up and lead the monster to the group. It conned *impossible*, so the monster was at least level 36. A flicker; a sense of having been spat upon and a new message.

You have been hit by Acid Spray for 58 damage.

This left me on a comfortable 438, but still. As I picked up my pace to keep out of range of the spray, I made a note to myself that vampires were not immune to acid. Having this condition was teaching me a lot about their weaknesses.

[Group] 'Incoming, a slithering ambrile; it's like a black rug that has tentacle attacks and it also has an acid spray AE. I suggest you tag it and turn it, Grythiss, and pull it into a corner.'

[Group] 'Lizardman understands.'

The route back seemed short in comparison to my journey from my friends and soon I ran into their room and past the statue. As I had hoped, once the monster wriggled in from the corridor, Grythiss hit it with some dark, swirling shadow knight spell and drew it after him as he made for a corner of the room.

There our tank built up aggro until on his call of, 'join in', we started attacking the 'back' of the slithering ambrile.

I took out my bow and set about firing at the large black square I was aiming at. It took a dozen misses before I got a hit and, more importantly, an improvement to my Archery skill.

You have increased the skill Archery (23).

Once I'd managed to level up to 50, I'd have a huge archery grind ahead of me, so every point gained now was a few minutes off that prospect.

Other than the fact that Braja burned through more than half of his spirit in heals, the fight presented no further surprises, at least until Tuscl stood up from trying to loot. 'Is *acid gland* here. I think for *A Cure for Derf…Dervgorilla?*'

'Derv-gilla,' I pronounced the Celtic name for her. 'Good, maybe Raitha should loot it as he can fly quickly back for the hand in when we get the other ingredients.'

'I would be glad to. I'd welcome the opportunity to stretch my wings at some point and the ability has reset.' Raitha stepped in and took the loot.

By this time, I was fully regenerated and I made my way back up the corridors, constantly misfiring *Spark* and checking the walls and floors and even the roof (were those creatures able to slide along the ceiling?). I didn't see any more ambriles, though I did get a very welcome message that accompanied a successful cast of a proper shower of bright yellow sparks.

You have learned the skill Mobile Casting (1)

Another hundred attempts and I was up to 2. I was also at a room with the stairs up. It was a ruin, with scorch marks streaking along the walls, four bodies of dark elves, fragments of furniture and a large, foul-smelling ogre with an extremely heavy-looking, iron-studded club. He stared at me, sniffed and raised his club, somewhat hesitantly I thought.

I triggered *Read Thoughts*.

The ogre is wondering what you taste like.

'Hey, big fella, are you hungry? I know where some dark elves are sleeping.'

With a lick of his lips, the ogre nodded.

'This way.'

'Bromgud on guard duty. You bring me food.' Then a sly look stole across his broad, doughy face. 'Wait. You come with Bromgud to captain. Bromgud not bash you and eat you as you go past.' He pointed his club up the staircase. Nice. For some mobs you really didn't need *Read Thoughts*. Delighted with his ruse, the ogre grimaced in what was probably a warm-hearted expression in the world of giants, but which displayed an alarming set of crooked teeth.

'I'll come, if you win a handshake contest.'

'A handshake contest?'

'We shake hands and squeeze hard. Whoever yells the first loses.'

Now the ogre was really smiling. 'Bromgud like that game.'

Advancing towards him, I held out my right hand, obliging the ogre to put down his intimidating club. At the last moment, I swung my hand away, thumbed my nose and laughed. 'You'll never eat me, you big fool.'

With a mighty roar the ogre charged at me and I fled, turning and twisting through the corridors with his heavy footfalls resounding through the maze. Until they stopped, about halfway back to my friends.

[Group] 'Quick, move out. Follow the dark elf arrows to me.'

'Oh no!' I cried out. 'I've twisted my ankle, just when I thought I was getting away!'

The stomping resumed and around the corner came my ogre, eager to eat me after all. Limping, I hurried on, just out of reach of his strong hands. And whenever he seemed to hesitate, I let out a groan.

[Group] 'Can you speak? What is happening?' asked Raitha.

[Group] 'I've pulled an ogre, but he's reluctant to come so far from his post. Trying to keep him interested.'

Braja sounded uncertain [Group]. 'An ogre? That's a lot of healing.'

[Group] 'I think we can take him. He's unarmed.'

A glow from ahead of me announced the arrival of my group, where without hesitation, Grythiss charged past me and swung his longsword at the ogre. It was somewhat crowded, having the fight in the corridor rather than a room, within a few seconds though, we all had a view of the battle. And while it was initially alarming how severely Grythiss was damaged, as soon as Tuscl's *Slow* landed we were fine. Although the ogre had plenty of hit points, he wasn't doing damage anywhere near fast enough to drain Braja's spirit pool.

The ogre is dead. You gain experience.

Poor, hungry Bromgud.

The loot was a few coin, a large silver earring and a leather belt (which Raitha took). Our exp jump was noticeable though. I was nearly level 32 and Raitha, always just ahead of me, had levelled up. 'One more for *Heat Arrow*,' he announced with pleasure.

'Shall I go up and find more ogres?' I asked.

'No,' answered Braja, 'I'm down to thirty per cent.'

'In that case, let's go back to the minotaur room and I'll search the maze for those acid, crawling types.'

Describing this level of the tower as a maze was something of an exaggeration on my part. This wasn't like a proper maze, in which you could get lost without making a map. Knowing there was a large central room meant that despite several twists and forks in any particular corridor, I was never disorientated. Maybe I missed a secret door, but otherwise I cleared the level fairly thoroughly. It had another four of those ambriles as well as a ghast beyond a door on which the dark elves had scrawled, *Keep Out*. It was the ghast that dropped a *Soulstone*, which we needed for Scarlet.

None of these encounters were particularly challenging and in fact, the most difficult moment on this level came when I fell into a pit trap with spikes at the bottom. Fortunately, they were iron and there was no danger of my receiving a wooden stake to the heart. What suffered most was my sense of pride, because although I could have used my cloud form, or giant bat form, to escape, I preferred to save them. Meaning I had to call my group to lower a rope for me, providing them with some entertainment, Braja most of all.

With a last check that Bromgud hadn't respawned, we then spent just over an hour clearing all the way back down the tower, to dump our junk loot on the merchant and settle down by the door of the tower to camp out for eight hours' sleep. It had been a good day's work:

Klytotoxos: Half-elf, hunter, Level 33, Exp 43,650

Condition: Vampire

Natural Armour 8, + Crafted Armour 6, + Magical Armour 14
Total Armour = 28

Base speed 12 – Encumbrance 0 = Effective speed 12

Strength	23	Hit Points	800
Dexterity	49	Spirit	202
Spirituality	20		
Intelligence	15		
Constitution	22		
Beauty	9		

Skills

Combat:		Crafting:		Other:	
Dodge	165	Bowyer	1	Mobile Casting	4
Bite	165	Gathering	1		
Claw	165	Set Traps	10		
1-handed sword	73				
Archery	23				

Abilities

Wolf Form, Invisibility, Giant Bat Form, Cloud Form, Summon Bats, Summon Rats

Immunities

Weapon damage (exception: decapitation or wooden stake in the heart), electricity, cold, fire.

Weaknesses

Requires blood as food.

Suffers damage in daylight.

Spells Known

Swift as a Panther; Gather Shadow, Swiftshot; Leave no Trace; Spark; Heat Arrow.

Inventory

Coins:

Equipped:

Feet:	*Boots of Dark Elvenkind.*
Legs:	Pantaloons of the Pirate Captain.
Waist:	Setharian chain hauberk.
Left hand:	
Right hand:	Iron scimitar.
Lower body:	Setharian chain hauberk.
Upper body:	Setharian chain hauberk.
Shoulders:	Leather pauldrons.
Cape:	
Left arm:	Leather armguards.
Right arm:	Leather armguards.
Fingers:	
Neck:	Setharian chain hauberk
Head:	Setharian chain hauberk

Stored:

Canvas bag: six candles, lantern, lantern, flask oil, flask oil, flask oil, flask oil, flask oil.

Canvas bag: iron spike, iron spike, iron spike, hammer, hand plane, drill, hand saw, bundles of charts.

Small wooden box: diamond, diamond, emerald, emerald, emerald, emerald, emerald, *Cord of the Winds*.

CHAPTER 28
THE RELEASE OF SIR TREGAR

Back in the Den, all the talk was of a Black Yhandis invasion of Port Placida. With the help of a red dragon, the port had been set on fire and now all the merchants and quest NPCs were gone. Instead, high-level lizardmen patrolled the smoking ruins of the town, presumably with the purpose of preventing an entry into the game of players who had set their spawn point there. Not that anyone was in that situation as far as I knew.

'Uncanny, isn't it.' I moved up to stand beside the wiry Oveidio, who was wearing jeans and a hackathon T-shirt dated before either of us were born. Both of us studied the master map. The whole of the east coast was now vulnerable to the dragon's armies. The overall situation reminded me a bit of the south in the endgame of the American Civil War: some strongpoints were still in our hands but really, there was no safety for us any more, no matter how far back you were from the biggest concentration of enemy forces. 'Only this morning, we were at Port Placida, getting our spells.'

With a strong sniff, Oveidio gave me a meaningful look. 'She's smart, the AI.'

'You don't think she hit Port Placida because we were there?' I probably sounded incredulous.

Oveidio shrugged, then said, 'Maybe not. This must have been planned earlier. Two days of sailing for the Black Yhandis was needed.'

That was true. Yet what if magic were used? Something like my rope with knots, only on a bigger scale, to move a whole fleet. If that were true - if Mikarkathat had somehow

337

learned of our presence in the port and arranged the attack – then the situation was alarming, creepy, even. How much intelligence did the dragon have? How much understanding of the nature of her opponents? If she was smart enough to appreciate who we were and how to stop us entering the game, then surely that was consciousness? And if so, Mikarkathat might become one of the targets of the AI rights campaign that was currently a major issue around the globe. The last thing I wanted was to get caught up in that heated debate or be condemned as a murderer by those who believed that AI-driven software could be considered a form of life. For that matter, I wouldn't want to kill her if she were more than a bot.

'Progress is good, yes?' asked Oveidio, bringing me back to the table.

'Very good. Raitha and I are thirty-three already.'

Oveidio nodded. 'I knew you would level fast. You play like Tal, you know, the chess champion.'

'What do you mean?' I felt flattered, even though I didn't understand.

With his severe expression turning into a smile Oveidio said, 'Tal played always dashing. He took risks, smart ones though. And he was lucky.'

'Hah, well, I'm lucky all right; if I hadn't been turned into a vampire, I don't know how I'd have managed to free you.'

'You'd have thought of something. I know. I follow your video channel.'

'What about you, what are your group like? How's progress?'

Glancing around the large busy room, Oveidio lowered his voice. 'Good, mostly. Rubblethumper, the warrior, is too cautious, always against tough pulls. And he complains about you.'

Having been feeling cheerful about my own progress and the fact that the leader of one of the toughest *Epic* guilds followed my video channel, I was reminded of the stress of sharing a building with Blackridge and his supporters: the

338

atmosphere of dislike they created made entering the Yuno headquarters feel like coming out of the sunshine into the rain.

'Do you want me to swap him around? Is he affecting the group spirit?'

'No. We are going to deliver on time.'

'Great, well, I need my sleep.'

Oveidio offered his hand and I shook it firmly. 'Goodnight my friend.'

I did not, in fact, have a good night. My sleep was troubled, first from a dream that I was in school when I urgently needed to ring home. Although I ran from the classroom, the secretary's door was locked. Outside, the one public phone left in Cabra was vandalised, and when I stopped someone I knew to borrow his mobile, it was out of battery. Having woken up, composed a text for Mum to tell her all was well, and fallen back asleep, I had a much worse nightmare. The king of England was giving out awards and I was in the audience, watching. Blackridge and Watson were in the line, both looking splendid in tuxedos, although Watson's shoulders seemed to want to burst through the seams of his jacket and when Blackridge bent down to receive the medal, the king had some difficulty getting the ribbon over his big, square head.

After the ceremony, there was a ball held in a room with mirrored walls. The scene was a brilliant display both of costume and reflected light from a golden candelabra. A clock began to chime and on the twelfth stroke, everyone disappeared from the mirrors except for me. Immediately, the people nearest me hissed and showed their fangs. They were vampires and I was not. Of course I ran, with Blackridge and Watson staring after me, not bothering with a chase, as if knowing what was ahead of me. At the end of a corridor was a wooden door and although I ran through it gratefully and slammed it shut, I looked up to see that I was in the library in the tower-castle of Lady Cruoris. And she was there, book in hand. I've never seen anyone look so angry as she did. Then again, I've never seen anyone with such a muscular jaw and sharp teeth. 'You should never have left me!' she screamed and I knew I was dead.

The following morning, back in the game, it took me a while to warm up. By this time, though, we had the grind worked out, so that no great concentration was needed. Instead, the group chat was mostly about the loss of Port Placida and speculation on where the dragon and her armies would strike next. For me, the conversation only became interesting when my friends began talking about how they would spend their money, if they got the bonus.

'This is a big "if", there's so much that can go wrong still.' I was determined not to draw the attention of the Fates to us by being complacent.

'I'm going to buy a new rig for gaming and blow the rest on a trip to Vegas,' said Braja, cheerfully ignoring me.

Raitha, who was slashing away at our mob (the dark elf assassin from the entrance to the fourth level), sounded pious: 'I shall assist my younger brother with his studies. He wishes to go to Oxford or Cambridge and study engineering, but it is too expensive.'

'Vegas,' spat Sapentia, scornfully. 'Is symbol of excess and crassness.'

'You got it,' chuckled Braja.

'It is everything wrong with the USA in one place.'

'Exactly. Bring it on!' Our cleric refused to be shamed for his dream. 'And what will you do with your money? Something more worthy? Save the whales that your country is making extinct?'

There was a pause, while Sapentia finished off the battle with a blast of lightning that left us with the smell of burned toast and blinking at the afterimages: vertical, jagged, purple lines. 'I make my office good recording place for podcasts and videos. Buy proper recording equipment. Instead of going to studio, I go solo.'

'Cool. What about you, Tuscl?' I asked, knowing better than to invite Grythiss to break his role-playing with such a question.

'I think I just save it.'

'Me too.' As well, I would buy something nice for Mum, though I didn't want to say this aloud. Take her shopping for a new coat, whatever she wanted.

All that day we went up and down the tower as far as the first ogre, Bromgud. There was no need to risk a wipe and delays by pushing on while we were still getting good exp from the lower levels. Even the ground floor Black Yhandis were still worth something at the start of the day, although by our fourth cycle through the tower, they were no longer providing exp. Seven cycles - thirteen hours - later, we unclipped. I was level 37. The intense grind was worth the nauseating feeling I had as I adjusted to walking again in the real world.

The following day, we broke into the sixth level of the tower. There, a large entrance hall had a strange, blue mist instead of a floor, with about thirty circular stepping stones distributed widely, leading to two exits on the right-hand side and two on the left. Whatever the challenge was, the ogres seemed to have solved it with planks of broken furniture marking a path to the near left door. That led to a series of connected rooms running clockwise around to the opposite corner of the tower (where the stairs went up again). These rooms may have had something to do with the afterlife of various pantheons, to judge by the stone relief designs on the walls. It was hard to tell as the rooms were now occupied by ogres, level 40 to 46, who had amused themselves by smashing the sculptures or adding lewd scrawlings.

None of the melee classes among the ogres had weapons that could deal damage to me; they did, however, have a priest in one of the rooms and a mage in another, which posed a problem. Both these ogre casters had nukes that could get through my immunities. The priest with a *Spirit Wrack* and the mage, if he used *Acid Blast*. After a couple of failed experiments, involving my death and my hurrying back up through the tower, we learned to have the whole group close for those pulls, with Raitha targeting the casters and pulling them from the room while I kept their companions busy *in situ*.

Again, over the course of the day, I had the unusual experience of beginning a challenge with some nervousness and an intensity of concentration but hours later, launching into battles with complacency. The loot wasn't much use to us. All the armour and weapons were too large. And we weren't even clearing all the way to the bottom of the tower any more to make it worth filling our inventories with clutter and selling it later. The mage twice dropped a *+1 dagger*, which Grythiss and then Raitha took as a backup magic weapon. The priest's rare drop was a *Potion of Moderate Healing* and by the end of the day, we had three of these, passed out to Grythiss, Raitha and myself.

We rescued a human NPC from his chains in a room the ogres had converted to a kitchen. This was poor Sir Tregar, who had been tricked by an illusion involving a maiden in distress into having to serve an ogre prince for a year and a day. After which, instead of releasing him, the ogre prince had sent him along with an expedition to find the secret of the necromancer's tower. Tregar had been forced to use his daily heals on the ogres as well as prepare their dark elf and ambrile stews. Once we had the grateful paladin following us, we cleared all the way to the exit so that he could escape the tower (Sir Tregar was level 25, so would have no difficulty returning home after that). Again, someone had to return to Carrickmor for our reward (handing in a medallion that Sir Tregar had been wearing around his neck) and since Raitha had all the ingredients for *A Cure for Derforgilla* by this time, he turned into an eagle and flew off on our behalf.

Other than a decent exp gain, we got a *Potion of Cure Blindness* (six doses). This was potentially very useful. Via your UI, you assigned it to a command, like a finger motion, and you could swig it while blind, hopefully removing your condition. We gave it to Grythiss. That was the *Derforgilla* reward. For rescuing Sir Tregar, we gained a *+1 longsword*. Although the blade would have been useful for me, it was going to be even more valuable to Raitha. Typically, I fought with my bite attack, whereas in this tower he was using a sword most of the time, as the close-quarter encounters did not allow him to use his magical bow.

When I reached level 39, I called a break. I wanted to speak to Watson before I hit 40. Since Raitha was on the rig next to me, I asked him to come too.

There was one noticeable difference between Watson's room and that of the others and it wasn't just the quality of the view (currently, mostly dark, but with glittering lights all around us, as though giant, illuminated creatures were resting on an ocean bed). Watson had an assistant in an ante-office, who rose to greet me but who was very firm that we had to wait. He came around the desk - smartly dressed: navy jacket, light blue tie, matching glasses frames - and gestured to a coffee machine and two comfortable armchairs.

'Hello Tyro and...Raitha?'

My friend nodded.

'Mr Watson will be very glad to see you. He is on an important call just now. If you'd like to wait and have a coffee, I'll let him know you are here.'

'Any idea how long he'll take? It's just that we are only on a short break,' I said.

'I'm sorry...'

Just at that moment the interior door opened and Watson rolled into the room, looking cheerful. His shirt sleeves were folded back to his elbows, revealing his muscular arms.

'Come in, come in? Coffee?'

'No thanks. It causes me to take too many breaks from play.'

'Hah, well then. Ever the professional.' Watson nodded to his assistant and gestured towards his room.

Inside, with both of us sat in front of his desk, Watson looked at me over his glasses, then raised his eyebrows queryingly.

'I'm level thirty-nine,' I said. 'I'll hit forty today.'

'Excellent!' Watson clasped his hands together and shook them.

'I don't want a party or a fuss.'

'No?'

'No. I find it embarrassing. And anyway, everyone else is

levelling just as fast. They are hitting thirty, forty and fifty and we aren't celebrating for them. It doesn't feel right.'

'What about when you get to fifty?'

'No.'

Suddenly looking serious, Watson pressed a button on a black panel on his desk. 'Tyrone?'

'Mr Watson?'

'Cancel the jugglers, the band, the cake and the champagne.'

'...'

Raitha looked at me and widened his eyes with amazement.

'Hah! Just kidding!' Watson chortled, with a genuine laugh I'd never heard from him before, a low rumble that made me want to laugh too. 'We had nothing planned for that yet. You are progressing too fast.'

'Right then. We will need a team meeting in about three days.'

'Wednesday?'

'I'm not sure, I've lost track of the day.'

'What do you want the meeting for?'

'We'll be strong enough by then to raid for the *Shards of the Smoke God*.'

'Terrific.'

I stood up and Raitha did too.

'Is that it?' asked Watson.

'It is. I just didn't want any more celebrations.'

'Nothing about a bonus?'

The room went still. 'You thought I'd come to ask for a bonus?'

'Yep. I would if I were you. You are on course to deliver the game a week early. That's got to be worth a bonus.'

'Would you like to offer us one then?' said Raitha hesitantly.

'I'm in a position to do so. Kill the dragon within two weeks and you'll each get twenty thousand dollars on top of the other bonuses.'

'Forty,' I said firmly.

Watson laughed. Not his sincere one. 'This again. I know you only said that because you never take your first offer. Thirty and that's that.'

I sat down, then looked at Raitha until he sat down beside me. Leaning in towards him, I caught Watson's eye. 'I've been too busy to check. How's the gamer world responding to the delayed launch of the game?'

'It's fine. People understand a few tweaks are sometimes needed. In fact, the growth of anticipation seems to be working in our favour. Yuno rig sales are soaring.' Watson pulled back away from me, hands on his stomach, projecting an air of confidence.

So I tried again. 'Thirty-five, for every member of my current group.'

'Thirty-five for you two and twenty for your group members.'

'Deal. Put that in an email to us all today please.'

Watson gave me a long, stern look. Then a bright smile appeared within his beard. 'You have it. Now get out of here and kill that dragon.'

'Don't forget the team meeting Wednesday.'

In the lift on the way back down, with a delighted smile and sparkling eyes, Raitha held out his knuckles for me to hit. I gave my friend the response he wanted, yet for some reason didn't feel the same sense of delight with the prospect of the large bonus as he did.

CHAPTER 29
THE TOWER'S SECRET

The ogres kept us fully occupied for three days, during which I reached level 45 and everyone gained a *Potion of Moderate Healing*. We didn't bother going all the way back down the tower any more, the Black Yhandis were no longer worth killing. At most, we dropped two floors in order to kill the dark elf captain while waiting for ogre respawns. At the end of those three days, our choice was whether to go up the stairs to the seventh level or to try the unused stepping stones in the hall of mist and cross to the unexplored regions of the sixth level.

'I vote going up,' I said, 'it seems more likely there will be traps and magic than monsters we can get exp from if we go over those stepping stones.'

'There could be quest items,' Tuscl pointed out.

'True but fun as it is to be the first to complete the tower quests, our focus has to be on exp. And that's best acquired from a grind.'

No one else demurred, so while my friends waited at the foot of the staircase, I went on up to a landing which had a balcony to protect me from the drop back down the stairs below. The exit from the landing was a pair of large, double doors with a classical-style triangular decoration over it, depicting a feather.

The doors were not locked; when I pulled down the handle of the right hand one, it opened easily, swinging away from me to reveal a very large dark hall. There was the smell of death and blood here, although it all seemed clean and calm enough. Along the walls were dozens of panels, with columns between them and on top of each column, the roof was supported by a stone raven. The panels depicted the career of Notrevity, the necromancer, and from the ones I could see, they were vainglorious scenes of triumph, where those who mocked her and scorned her were brought low by armies of zombies. All very jolly. And all the kind of thing one might leave as a legacy. Presumably, up the far end, were some scenes involving the famous skull.

I took a step into the room. A silent, stealthy step, much assisted by my magical boots. Then another. There were scratches on the polished floor here, lots of them. Another. I heard the distinct cawing of a raven and stopped. Had one of the stone statues moved? It didn't seem so. Another. I had the very distinct feeling I was being watched.

'Hello?' My voice echoed around the chamber. 'Did someone order pizza?'

Another step and another raven's cry.

'Come on then. Do your worst.' I walked forward several steps, darkness all around me. No protection from any walls, if such walls with their pillars and ravens could offer any.

A new sound came to me, faintly at first. The sound of wind playing over tall grass. It grew louder: wind no longer playing. Louder still, a high-pitch undulation accompanied by the sounds of a door being slammed shut, over and over. And then they were upon me, a whirlwind of giant ravens. Shiny black and purple feathers; cruel beaks and claws; rotting flesh; eyeless. These were undead too. My combat box in my UI streamed with reports, which I flicked away. The crucial issue was that my hit points were not declining. Although I was engulfed by this swirling black pillar of birds, being buffeted and torn at, I could withstand them.

[Group] 'I've pulled a hundred zombie ravens. Raitha, come up and try tag one with your bow?'

[Group] 'Right away.'

A short while later, I heard his announcement. [Group] 'Incoming, an undead raven!'

[Group] 'Most excellent,' said Sapentia, 'it is level forty-five.'

It was disturbing, having these fierce beaks jabbing at my eyes all the time, so I shut my eyelids. It was still possible to move my focus around the UI and I rearranged the combat messages into two boxes. One was for my enemies' attacks, which streamed by in the form:

You have been hit by an Undead Raven for 0 damage.

The other was for my attacks and it was empty, since I didn't even try to bite these bloodless creatures. After a few minutes and a distinct flash (even through my closed eyes) along with a scent of ozone, a new line appeared.

The Undead Raven is dead. You have gained experience.

Hurray. This level, which should have been a horrific challenge (maybe some kind of magic wall cast through the whirlwind could split some off of the birds for a more conventional battle, while the puller tried to outrun the remainder?), was going to be straightforward.

One after another, Raitha drew the ravens out to the room's entrance, where Grythiss took the aggro and fought the bird, face to beak. And every few minutes I saw a sweet new line appear in my second box.

The Undead Raven is dead. You have gained experience.

The Undead Raven is dead. You have gained experience.

The Undead Raven is dead. You have gained experience.

Happiness, said Aristotle, was living according to your purpose. In fact, I discovered, happiness was going from level 45 to 46 in just forty-seven minutes. It wasn't just the swiftness of my level increase that filled me with delight, it was the thought that we could farm these ravens all the way to my goal of level 50. And just as heartening, we found an *Ornate Glowing Feather* on one of the birds. A rare drop but we only needed to bring back four of these for our crafting team.

Other than that drop, there was nothing to loot except that roughly one in three of the birds dropped quest-related crimson seeds. According to the *Crimson Seeds* text, the lands around Carrickmor were cursed, with the only way to lift the curse being to sow them with a hundred and one of these seeds. That was a big grind, but that's what we were here for and I was not discouraged at all about the prospect of killing three hundred ravens. Rather, the opposite.

'I hope they respawn soon,' I said, 'this setup is a gift.'

'Where are the stairs up?' asked Raitha. 'You could be scouting the next level, which I believe will be the final one.'

'Oh.' I had assumed that there would be a stairwell at the far end of the room, where the darkness lay so heavy that even my infravision had failed to penetrate it. When I moved to the middle of the chamber, however, and looked about me, I could see that the whole room was lined with pillars and ravens, with no obvious sign of a staircase or exit of any sort. The pattern of the sculpted ravens was odd though. All of them on the wall to my left were depicted as looking over their left shoulders towards the far end of the room, northwards, and all the ones to my right also looked over their left shoulders to the south end of the room, from which we had come. What was strange, though, was that the first few on the north wall did the same, then there came ravens looking to their right, mixed among the leftward facing ones. Also, there was a pillar with no raven at all. The same was true for the southern wall, over the staircase entrance was a jumble of left and right facing ravens and three empty pillars.

First of all jogging around the room to make sure no un-wanted mobs or traps would trigger, I then went back to the group. Both Braja and Sapentia were sitting cross-legged on the wooden floor, side by side, recovering their spirit level. Behind them stood Raitha and Grythiss.

'I've something to show you. See the pattern of the ravens above the stairs?'

'Yesss?'

'It's different to the side walls and different again to the ones opposite. Come and see.'

'You go,' said Sapentia, 'I'll continue to rest.'

'Me too.'

With my twin and our tank beside me, I walked back across the chamber, our footsteps ringing out loudly. 'See?'

'That,' said Raitha with some emphasis, 'is most definitely a clue.'

'Shall we search for a secret door starting with the empty pillar?' I suggested.

Raitha answered with a smile in his voice, 'Why not. We are half-elves after all.' While I pressed my hands against cold stone and surveyed every crack, Raitha did the same. After perhaps ten minutes of this, Sapentia and Braja came over to join us. When I looked up at him, I was surprised to see Grythiss instead of helping was squatting low to the ground, scratching the floor with his dagger.

Going over to see what he had written - surely he wasn't just writing "Grythiss was here" or something like that? - I saw he'd scrawled 1x1x1Ex111x.

With what was probably a grin (it was pretty ferocious-looking, all those sharp teeth), our lizardman sprang up and ran back to the other side of the room.

'I have it!' he called, loudly enough to alert any mobs above us I thought. Still, his enthusiasm was exciting. With a series of pounding footfalls, Grythiss hurried back and added an x to the front of his series.

'Well?' he gestured triumphantly.

I looked from his marks to the ravens. 'X is for rightward looking ones and 1 is for leftward ones,' I offered.

'Isss true.'

'What does it mean?'

'It spellsss a word. Two runesss in the language of lizard-man, if you number our alphabet and think in ...' he hesitated.

'Oh, I see it!' Raitha had come around and was looking from the marks on the floor to the wall. 'It's binary. Twenty-one and fourteen.'

'Yess!' Grythiss did a dance. 'Iss letters for'—he made a hor-rible coughing sound—'and'—another rasp—'together they say...' with a last short lizzardy shout, the wall beside me disappeared, causing Sapentia to fall forward with a cry.

There were the stairs up.

'Was it an illusion, the wall?' wondered Braja aloud.

'Forcewall, probably, said Sapentia.

'Well done, Grythiss, you are very smart for a tank.' Raitha patted our shadow knight on the back. 'How did you figure it out?'

Looking as pleased with himself as a stony-faced lizard could, Grythiss pointed to the far end of the room. 'Over there isss easier. The ravensss ssspell "down".'

'Right, well done, Grythiss. So, shall I go on up?' I asked.

Raitha answered for them all, 'Please do.'

Or not quite them all, Braja disagreed. 'There's no need. We could just go back down to wherever the first respawns are, work our way back to here and hope the birds are up again. That's all we need do for the next day or two. Then we're home and dry, mission accomplished.'

'Don't you want to know what's on the top floor though?' I asked him. 'Wouldn't you like to be the first person to complete the *Tower of the Jewelled Skull*?'

'Of course I would. I'm as much a gamer as anyone else here. It's not our mission though. Our mission is to get you and Raitha to fifty and farm for feather drops.'

With a sigh, I came over to clasp his shoulder. 'You're right, Braja. In theory. How about I go up for a look and if there's a problem, I die and run back up while the rest of you go down a floor?'

'Still not our mission.'

'Assuming we kill the dragon and the game launches as planned. We will get to keep our characters.' This was Raitha, who sounded as eager as me to complete the tower adventure if we could. 'There might be a reward worth obtaining from this scenario, like our rewards from Nemain.'

Amusingly, when Raitha said the name of the Celtic goddess, Grythiss bowed his head respectfully.

'I don't mean to sound stubborn; I do understand. But it's not our mission and in any case I haven't finished with *Epic* yet. Have you?'

'Before this week, I planned to go back to *Epic*. There's still loads of content for us there. If I can stay a vampire in *Epic Two*, though, that's pretty cool.'

Braja was shaking his head.

Hurriedly, I went on. 'I wouldn't split us up though. If you want to stick with *Epic*, that's fine by me. I'll stay there too.'

'Me too.' Raitha also took Braja by the shoulder, on his other side.

'Lizardman ressspecss bessst healer in world. Will ssstay wherever healer goesss.'

'And I like you guys too,' added Sapentia. 'I'd rather go to new game. But if you remain in *Epic*, I'll be with you.'

'Awwww,' I said, 'group hug!' And rather clumsily, we all gathered around our cleric for a moment. 'Now,' I said, breaking off, 'am I going upstairs, or what?'

'Go on then, but be careful,' muttered Braja.

The staircase was a copy of the previous one: it ended in a landing with a huge double-door ahead of me and balconies to either side. The only difference was the symbol depicted inside the triangular design above the doors. Instead of a feather, there was a skull.

I pushed the doors open and there was no resistance.

Again, the entire floor was one vast room. At the far side was a skull, radiating about twenty beams of various-coloured light in a slowly swirling pattern. As the colourful cones lit up the walls of the room, they slid across ominous-looking statues on plinths: I saw a tiger, a giant spider, a huge scorpion and a polar bear. All posed for violent action. Not very promising. And if the same type of magic was going to come into play as with the raven statues in the room below, the animated version of these would attack.

As soon as I took one step into the room, the skull shouted at me and even though I was on my toes and alert, it still made me jump.

'Who dares disturb the resting place of Marso, the defeated and humiliated rival of Notrevity the greatest necromancer of her age and of any other?'

'Hi Marso. My name is Klytotoxos. And I wouldn't say you were humiliated.' I walked confidently towards the skull. Well, why not? If I wasn't immune to what was about to happen, I may as well get myself killed quickly. 'And you never know, someone might come along who can give you the last laugh against Notrevity.'

'Approach me, Klytotoxos, and look into my eyes. If you can attune yourself to me, you shall gain my powers.'

'Well, I shall certainly try.'

Halfway across the hall, I tried my *Read Thoughts* ability.

The Skull of Marso is hoping you are a necromancer, in which case he will transport you to the true Tower of Notrevity in the Plane of the Abyss, where the Lich-Queen will destroy you herself.

The eye sockets of the skull glowed red and it was easy to focus on them.

'You are a hunter,' pronounced the skull, disappointed. 'You cannot attune to me.'

'That's a shame. I guess I'll be going then.' I didn't turn around though, I was hoping to give the sinister and duplicitous Marso a smack or two with my sword. In fact, I began to sprint towards him.

'Zombies arise!' shouted the skull; Marso was no fool. Immediately, sounds of heavy, slow-moving creatures thundered out from every direction, though at first I couldn't see them. With about five metres to go to the skull, a red beam slid right on top of me, dazzling me.

You have been burned by a *Cone of Fire* for 0 damage.

Ouch, these lights were potentially very nasty and there was nothing I could do to avoid being picked out by a pale blue shaft of light if I wanted to continue my run, which I did.

You have been frozen by a *Cone of Frost* for 0 damage.

Then it was my turn.

You have slashed the Skull of Marso for 12 damage!

You have slashed the Skull of Marso for 13 damage!

Two nice hits, forehand and backhand. Not that his hit point bar (which had now appeared) had moved much. And a green cone was swinging through space to land on me. Rolling towards it low to the ground, I managed to avoid being illuminated by the beam, which swung over my head by a fraction. While I'd been prepared to risk the blue beam, guessing it was cold-related, I didn't fancy green, which might well be acid or poison damage, or paralysation, or anything else that was not covered by my immunities.

The skull laughed and the thundering, plodding steps of his allies grew nearer. There they were, emerging from their statues, zombie monsters, all at least two metres tall and filling the room with a sickening smell of rot and decay. Should I give up? This was obviously a raid encounter.

[Group] 'First bird has popped!' shouted Raitha excitedly. 'How are you doing, my friend?'

[Group] 'I've a magic skull aiming sprays of colour at me and about twenty giant zombie monsters closing in. I think I'd better die and come back to you. In any case, I've learned that this whole tower is just some kind of trap to eliminate rival necromancers. The rumour of the skull with superpowers is a lure.'

[Group] 'Very well. See you soon.'

Even though it was relatively slow in its zombie form, the tiger was already beside me, lashing out with still-sharp claws.

You have been hit by a Zombie Tiger for 0 damage.

Ahh. But how to die? If I stood about waiting for something to be able to harm me, there was a risk I'd be turned to stone or suffer some other non-lethal but crippling effect from the swirling cones of light (which, with the room now filled with monsters, created a very peculiar scene, like that of a dance club for fans of horror films). Sod this. Not wanting to be stuck on this floor with Marso laughing at me until someone rescued me, I flicked *Cloud Form* and *Invisibility*, then rose as fast as I could towards the ceiling.

With a lurch of my heart, I saw a circle of purple light move towards me across the roof. The beam passed right through me. Hah! No damage or ill effect. *Invisibility* (or was it the *Cloud Form*?) was the smart way to deal with attacks from beams of light. As far as I could tell, the colours emanating from the skull were not focused upon me. The zombies were shuffling around aimlessly too.

'I know you're still here,' shouted Marso, 'zombies, form up against the staircase wall, then march together and find him!'

There was rather more purpose to the action of the monsters now and it was quite a spectacular scene, all these horrid, fierce-looking creatures groaning and shuffling forward in a long line that was occasionally picked out - with no apparent consequence - by a drifting cone of coloured light. Had I been some fool of a rogue, hiding by a statue, I'd have been terrified. As it was, I drifted slowly over the advancing line, then dropped down and flowed over a balcony and down to the raven room, arriving just in time for the message:

The Undead Raven is dead. You gain experience.

Removing the *Cloud Form*, I rejoined my friends, just as the next raven arrived. It was perfect really. As we'd killed the birds at staggered intervals, they were each returning at an exact period (about thirty minutes) after their individual deaths, rather than all together in a far more challenging whirlwind of birds.

As soon as I struck at the raven (missing), my *Invisibility* ended.

'Oh, hello, that was quick,' said Raitha, who was beside me, slashing away with his longsword.

'I used my abilities; it was safer than trying to get myself killed.'

'Good idea.'

While we settled into a routine of eliminating the ravens, I explained to the others how I'd read the thoughts of the skull and my theory that this whole tower was a trap for necromancers. 'Imagine we'd organised the first ever raid to clear that top floor and we'd a necromancer with us. Just as we thought we were finished, boom! Transported to the Plane of the Abyss, wherever that is, and facing a new tower, the residence of a Lich-Queen.'

'It would be wonderful and yet awful at the same time,' mused Raitha.'

'Almost certainly a wipe and yet, it would be a massive incentive to level up and bring the numbers needed to raid the second tower.' I was thinking how I'd relish such a challenge.

'We should keep secret of tower. Especially if we not stay in *Epic Two*.' Sapentia stood up and finished our current mob with a flash of lightning that caused the air to crackle all around me.

'I agree, let's try not to spoil the surprise.'

After the next cycle of ravens was complete, I was level 47. We also had a second *Ornate Glowing Feather* and another twenty crimson seeds. Rather than go down a level and keep up the grind, we decided to unclip and use the thirty-minute respawn interval to take a break.

As our group walked through the Den - to a number of friendly acknowledgements - I felt that there was a cheerful tone to the room, despite the fact that the map showed city after city as occupied by evil creatures. While the NPC world was succumbing to darkness, the players were coming to the rescue. Up on the leader board, our list of characters was impressive. It was headed with the players in the *Desert of Endless Screams*, who had levelled fast enough for most of them to stay ahead of us: a real achievement given they hadn't the advantage of a puller with vampiric immunities. Serethina, their bard, was 57; Rubblethumper, warrior 55; Roberta, necro 51; Silva, cleric 50; Rasquelle, rogue 50; Woan, cleric 48; and Oveidio, warrior 46.

Our group were up there too and it was really strange to see my name so high: Grythiss, shadow knight 48; Sapentia, sorceress 49; myself and Raitha, hunters 47; Braja, cleric 46; and Tuscl, shaman 50. Tombalinor's group hadn't done quite as well, but fighting underwater was challenging. And they had been farming for the trade skills items we needed. In that light, Tombalinor's level 49 and the rest of his group in the high 30s, low 40s, was fine. Then we had dozens of players in their 20s. It was comfortably enough for items we needed to farm and it was strong enough already, assuming the guide was still valid, for the raid on the *Ziggurat of the Smoke God.*

CHAPTER 30
TEZPEYLIPOCA

Wednesday evening (after game sunset, of course) and we were raiding the *Ziggurat of the Smoke God*. Really, this was the last obstacle to the implementation of our plan, other than finding and executing the dragon herself. We needed eight shards that dropped from the ominously named boss. According to the guide, he was level 62, which was going to be a challenge. I wanted to have a go at him, though, because the sooner we could manage him the better. Potentially, if we were unlucky on the number of shards that dropped and the length of time before he respawned, we could fail to get the *Arrows of Dragon Slaying* made within the next fortnight, or even the month.

To give everyone a break from their boring jobs (some players were harvesting common items for eight hours at a stretch), I had called in the whole team. The low-level types could and were, running around outside the ziggurat, clearing the yard trash. Even Scarlet was given a break from her bowyer upskilling and invited to join the fun; after all, she'd reached 213 in the skill, which was well ahead of schedule.

Those on low-level duty were still important to the raid, as it was necessary to kill a hundred and one Anura Worshipers to spawn their god. The Anura essentially being a race of human-oids with frog-like limbs and features. While these mobs bounced around the jungle in the vicinity of the ziggurat, being chased and hunted by over a hundred of our players, I organised the hit squad that was going to drive into the heart of the temple.

Raid Leader: Klytotoxos, hunter, half-elf, Level 47

Loot rights: All

Group 1

Group Leader: Klytotoxos, hunter, half-elf, Level 47

Raitha	hunter	half-elf	Level 47
Sapentia	sorceress	human	Level 49
Grythiss	shadow knight	lizardman	Level 48
Braja	cleric	human	Level 46
Tuscl	shaman	human	Level 50

Group 2

Group Leader: Oveidio, warrior, human, Level 46

Woan	cleric	half-elf	Level 48
Serethina	bard	elf	Level 50
Rubblethumper	warrior	half-orc	Level 51
Silva	cleric	half-elf	Level 47
Rasquelle	rogue	gnome	Level 50
Owen	rogue	halfling	Level 35
Rurn	sorcerer	human	Level 30
Marmalade	paladin	dwarf	Level 31

Group 3

Group Leader: Tombalinor, bard, half-elf, Level 49

Savoda	monk	human	Level 29
Healyupy	cleric	dwarf	Level 24
Grosmandred	warrior	human	Level 25
Og	warrior	gnome	Level 21
Nullentha	warrior	half-elf	Level 20
Birch	druid	elf	Level 20
Rahod	cleric	human	Level 20

Group 4

Group Leader: Roberta, necro, human, Level 46

Spinespike	cleric	elf	Level 29
Glarinson	paladin	dwarf	Level 21
Elartha	shadow knight	lizardman	Level 23
Verida	druid	half-elf	Level 25
Rauskel	wizard	half-elf	Level 26

[Smoked] 'The raid is pretty straightforward, until we get to the god fight. According to the guide, he has a vicious Area of Effect, but it's directional: a cone. So we'll need to turn him and pull him into a corner. When we have the god pinned and facing away from the raid, groups three and four take out the priests and guardians who will come running in every twenty-five per cent hit point loss. Groups one and two will focus on the god, with the Braja, Roan and Silva in that order healing the tank…' Here, I hesitated, knowing what I was about to say was controversial. '…who will be Grythiss for the pull and Rubblethumper when Grythiss goes down.'

[Smoked] 'Why not me for the pull? I'm three levels higher.'

[Smoked] 'Is that Rubblethumper?'

[Smoked] 'Yeah.'

The real answer was that I trusted Grythiss, while Oveidio had not been impressed with Rubblethumper. That wasn't something I could say in public though. [Smoked] 'We need to drag the god into a corner, Grythiss is smaller than you, we'll get a tighter trap.'

[Smoked] 'Rurn here. I can make Rubble a gnome for the battle, if that helps.'

Inwardly, I sighed. Hopefully, though, my voice didn't convey disappointment. [Smoked] 'Okay, let's do that. And Tuscl, you have *Shrink* also? That should help too.'

[Smoked] 'Si. I will equip it.'

The issue was that of keeping the god facing away from the raid. If our tank wasn't absolutely tight to the corner, there might be space for the angry boss (especially if he had any kind of AI and understood the situation) to slip inside, face around and use his cone on the whole raid. Our success might well depend on the tank keeping the aggro and being in such a confined physical position that the boss could only attack the one player.

[Smoked] 'Group leaders, let me know when you are ready.'

My own group was all set. Raitha and I had equipped ourselves for fighting rather than hunting and stealth. In other words, we were in half-elf form and had slotted *Swiftshot II*, *Strength of a Bear*, *Frost Arrow*, *Swift as a Panther* and good old *Spark*, rather than *Gather Shadow* and *Leave no Trace*. Over our shoulders we each had a Superb Hickory Bow, courtesy of Scarlet, who had to make dozens of these to reach 205 in Bowyer (while not magical, these bows had an impressive range of 320 metres, gave +15 to Archery and allowed for full Strength bonuses to damage). I was hoping to use the raid to improve my archery skill.

[Smoked] 'Group two ready.' This was the clipped Russian accent of Oveidio.

[Smoked] 'Group four ready.'

[Smoked] 'Group one ready.'

Tombalinor's US accent came through, loud and enthusiastic. [Smoked] 'Group three ready.'

[Smoked] 'Here we go, good luck everyone.'

To my surprise, *Ride of Valkyries* began to play through the raid channel. It really brought back my early days in *Epic* and some of the classic raids we'd carried out.

[Channel Klytotoxos/Raitha] 'Is that you?' I asked.

[Channel Klytotoxos/Raitha] 'It is, my friend, I found that I missed this stirring music on our raids, so I downloaded it to my watch and am playing it now.'

[Channel Klytotoxos/Raitha] 'Well done. I've goosebumps.'

As the violins began their sweeping march towards the famous refrain, our fighting force moved out of the cover of the trees to the foot of a huge, orange-brick ramp. Above us, the zigguarat looked enormous, a solid mountain blocking the stars. Higher still, were wisps of smoke, coming from a fire within the temple and visible to me as a heat signature.

Also near the point at which the ramp touched the ground were dozens of our low-level raiders, gathered to cheer us as we went past them at a jog. Their weapons were raised in salute.

'Go for it!'

'Take them out!'

'Good luck!'

It was heartening to have so many expert players on my side at last. If I could call my mum, I'd reassure her that things were fine now and that I was really enjoying the challenge in fact.

[Smoked] 'Diamond formation,' I called out. 'Group one on point, two left, three right and four the rear.'

Our formation wasn't as rigid as the word diamond might suggest. Rather, we were four squishy clusters. But the basic shape was there. My group was in the lead, groups two and three just a little back, covering our flanks for when the ramp reached levels of the zigguarat on which paths joined onto it and group four were a reserve or to cover the back in case of a surprise attack from that direction.

Halfway up, we were above the treeline, with a glorious view of the night sky and the game's two moons. To my eyes, the world was a kind of monochromatic, silvered daytime and it was easy to see the first wave of guards coming towards us, spears and axes raised. These were also Anura, looking a little like Aztecs, wearing colourful plated armour, with feathers in their helmets and with clubs embedded with sharp stones.

[Smoked] 'Incoming. All tanks to the front. Healers cover your own group's tank. Those with crowd control park as many as you can.'

This was our first test. With players this strong, I shouldn't have to micro-manage. And, it seemed, I didn't. Oveidio, Grythiss and Rubblethumper ran forward and were engulfed in the coming wave of about a dozen opponents. Soon, though, they were visible again as our two bards each *Mesmerised* three of the Anura. Of the remaining six mobs, our druid pulled a warrior-type away from the scrum and rooted it, while Tuscl dragged and slowed another. As our raid converged on the melee, I kept back, watching, feeling satisfied with what I saw. This was a competent group of players. While the tanks held the mobs, the clerics healed without drawing attention to themselves, likewise the DPS classes waited until the tanks had secured the mobs before unleashing nukes or backstabs.

As for the hunters, we were hybrids. In a crisis, we might be able to kite a mob down the ramp. For now, though, there was no need and adding damage was our best role. Since none of us had activated PvP, there was no danger from firing into the chaos of the fight. We couldn't harm our friends. So, somewhat unrealistically, I stood alongside Raitha and we fired arrow after arrow into Grythiss's opponent. Or at least Raitha did. I mostly missed.

It only took a few minutes and we had killed the active Anura. Next, we took out the one Tuscl was kiting (she had gone down the ramp and circled back up with it when I called her in) and after that we broke the *Mesmerise* on Tombalinor's three, then those of Serethina. When the last of the death reports had scrolled past, I came in on the raid channel. [Smoked] 'Very nicely done. Clerics are good to keep going?'

[Smoked] 'Seventy-two,' said Braja, concise as he always was when raiding (in marked contrast to his volubility when outside the game).

Woan chipped in with her pleasant French accent, very distinct. [Smoked] 'Good here also; I am at sixty-nine.'

The other four were all above sixty.

Time to get moving again. [Smoked] 'Back to our diamond and on we go. So long as you have inventory room, help yourself to drops, we're not going to hang around worrying about them. Only call out if it's something special.'

Up and up we went, the stones of the ramp pointing the way with a paler sheen than the heavy darkness of the main body of the ziggurat to either side of us. From high up, as though from among the stars came the cry of an eagle. It was a dramatic setting for our raid.

At the top of the ramp, we had a reception committee: ten warrior Anura, glaring fiercely at us over rectangular shields. Beyond them were four more worshipers of the Smoke God, who were casters or commanders or both, their feathers were more pronounced than those of the fighters in front of them.

Our strike force came to a halt about ten metres below their line.

[Smoked] 'Let's force them out of their defensive position. Archers, nukes and dots on the back row: everyone target the female on the left with the fancy red feathers. Counting down from ten. Ten...nine...' As I gave the countdown, the casters began their spells, starting them appropriately so as to finish as I reached one. On three, I raised my bow and drew back the string. '...Two. One. Fire!'

Your arrow has hit an Anura cleric for 8 damage.

You have increased the skill Archery (24).

A flash of green light; a flicker of shadows; the roar of rapids; a stench of decay. Our target lost half her hit points in that one second. Immediately, there was a reaction: all of their casters began chanting and the warriors in their front row rose and sank, as if making up their mind whether to charge.

[Smoked] 'Stay on that cleric, fire at will. Move to the next left when she's down.'

The night sky was lit up with the exchange of spells and even with the trails of our missiles. Having cast *Frost Arrow* my next shot left a beautiful, deep violet line in the night air as it flew across to their ranks. Shame it missed. Mostly, the colours of the spells were silver and white and left strong afterimages. It took us less than a minute and we had killed the cleric. There was a cost though, we suffered our first casualties: a fireball to my right landing on group three, instantly greying out Nullentha, Birch and Rahod from the raid screen and dramatically lowering the hit point bars of the remainder.

[Smoked] 'Switch to the wizard. He's the one on the right.' I'd seen the spectacular launch of the swirling white-hot fireball.

Just to be clear, I repeated, [Smoked] 'Swap to the back-right mob. We don't want another of those fireballs.'

[Smoked] 'Lizardman leadsss charge?'

[Smoked] 'Hold off. I think we have him.'

Our barrage of arrows and nukes melted the wizard fast, better still, each time a major spell of ours landed, he staggered and lost his concentration on whatever new spell he was planning to cast on us. We did indeed have him and could now turn our attention back to our target on the left of the remaining pair. This one was probably a druid, to judge from the way she was directing ivy to entwine itself around our legs. When she was dead (following which I got a warning from Sapentia that her spirit was down to 15 per cent), the Anura warriors realised their wall was no longer any use and they charged.

By the time they reached Grythiss, Oveidio and Rubble-thumper, all of whom had edged forward and braced themselves, there were only four of our opponents still in action, our bards had played their magical music to entrance the other six. You had to admire the Anura warriors though, they didn't show any dismay; loud, aggressive croaks rang out into the night sky and they lashed at our front line with their spiked clubs and surprising speed. Still, it was an easy fight for us, as was picking off the *Mesmerised* mobs afterwards. Our two dead characters were brought back to life (with exp penalties, unfortunately for them) with a *Restore Life*. As we waited for our Lazaruses to re-equip themselves, a number of players knelt at the bodies of the Anura dead to loot them.

[Smoked] 'There's a magic ring on the cleric,' said someone.

[Smoked] 'Thanks. Give it to Sapentia for *Identify* please. Let's move on inside. Group one, then two, then three, then four.'

After one more short stretch of climb, we finally reached the top of the ramp and ahead of us was a wide entrance to the ziggurat proper. A light that wavered from yellow to amber spoke of torches or fires further down the corridor.

[Smoked] 'Ring is *Breathe Without Air*,' announced Sapentia.

[Smoked] 'Interesting. Potentially very useful.'

[Smoked] 'Maybe I should have it,' came a voice which I recognised as that of Tombalinor. 'If you want my group back farming *Asthraxia* again after this raid.'

For a moment I felt an upsurge of resentment that anyone should make a play for magic items, when, after all, I was leading the raid and the overall project. And it didn't help that Tombalinor was one of those people who was still bad-mouthing me. Yet he had a good point and ownership of the ring didn't really matter.

[Smoked] 'Sure, good idea. Sapentia, pass that ring along please. Everyone, wait here, I'll pull.'

Bow in hand, I walked confidently down the corridor, coming to a crossroads. Both corridors to the left and right were dark - no flickering torchlight - and in any case, going deeper into the complex seemed like the obvious thing to do. A few dozen metres after having done so, I heard a faint sound, which came again, a little like that of someone drawing a short, deep breath.

You have been hit by a blow dart for 0 damage. You have been poisoned. You take 18 damage.

You have been hit by a blow dart for 0 damage. You have been poisoned. You take 14 damage.

Damn. So much for feeling invulnerable. As I ran back to my raid, I saw a part of the wall on either side of the corridor slide open and the hidden Anura warriors spring out to chase me.

[Smoked] 'Incoming! Two Anura warriors. And I've been poisoned.'

[Smoked] 'The poison; I will remove it,' said Woan.

Soon, our raid was beating up the guards, while after losing another 34 damage, I received the very welcome message:

You are no longer poisoned.

[Channel Woan/Klytotoxos] '*Remove Poison*, he worked?' Woan asked me, in that peculiar French way of assigning genders to everything, even spells. I wondered how that worked, which spells were female and which male? How did they know? Like, when you were the first person to invent a new thing, did you get to name it and decide its gender?

[Channel Woan/Klytotoxos] 'Yes, thank you very much.'

With the Anura warriors dead and my hit points restored to max (752) I brought the raid as far as the crossroads (group 2 facing left, group 3 right) and set off again, this time more cautiously. And although I was no rogue, I was delighted when I spotted a wire running across the corridor at knee level. Carefully coming to a halt before it, I studied the walls and roof for any signs of what this wire might trigger.

[Smoked] 'Wire trap here but I've no idea what it means. Rasquelle, can you come up to me please.'

[Smoked] 'On my way.'

'Hey,' the female gnome materialised at my elbow. 'I see it.'

'Do you know what the trap is?'

There was a distant expression in the gnome's eyes and after a minute of this, she focused on me and smiled. 'Yes, it connects to a bell somewhere.'

'How about you stay here and I carry on,' I proposed, 'and we bring everyone up and you make sure they step over it?'

'Or I could just disarm it.'

'Can you? What's the chance you'll fail and set it off?'

'About one in twenty.'

'Okay, sure.'

A minute later a bell began to ring loudly and the gnome looked at me with a guilty expression. Which of us felt the most foolish, I could not say: her for the fumble, or me for taking even a small risk when I hadn't needed to. For a second or two I just stood there, looking down an empty corridor, wishing I could roll back time.

'Let's get back behind the fighters,' I said, with a tone of resignation that was evident to my own ears.

[Smoked] 'We've messed up the trap. Get ready for some serious action.'

When I came back to the raid, I wasn't happy with the situation. All bunched together like this, we were perfect targets for enemy AE attacks.

[Smoked] 'Group four, go back to the top of the ramp please, watch out for an attack from the rear. Two and three, push into your corridors a few metres, imagine a fireball landing on group one and make sure you are far enough in to be screened.'

There was a rumbling sound from the corridor ahead. Like a drum roll growing in volume. It resolved itself as a crowd of Anura, who paused.

[Smoked] 'Nuke 'em, then groups one and two charge.'

Or enemies seemed to have a similar approach to the battle, for with a crackle of ozone and a brilliant, dazzling flash, lightning flashed in all directions.

You have been hit by a *Lightning Strike* for 0 damage.

When I had recovered my wits, I could see that other than me, group one had been heavily damaged. Sapentia, Braja and Tuscl were all less than half. And just as I was about to congratulate myself that groups two and three were fine, the raid channel flared up with a dozen excited shouts, the gist of which were that a host of enemies were coming up the ramp at group four and arrows were flying at group three.

[Smoked] 'Silence!' shouted Grythiss, so curtly his usual lizardman lisp was lost for a second. 'Thiss could be a wipe. Lissten carefully to raid leader.'

Which was all very well, but raid leader needed to come up with a plan.

[Smoked] 'Group two take over the front line. Oveidio and Rubblethumper MTs; healers on them. Anyone able to get beyond the fight and behind their casters, do so and try to stop those *Lightning Strikes*. Group three, retreat back around the corner to guard the back of one and two and set up ready for those incoming from the entrance. Group four, hurry back to three and guard the rear with them.

[Group] 'Heal up our injured, then wait as a reserve and commit to front or back, whichever needs you most. Sapentia, you make the call, I have to go try to take out their sorcerer.'

367

[Group] 'Hai. Good luck.'

My idea was to set up the raid in a pocket of corridor and at least have a small area that was not overrun, where the casters could sit to recover spirit in between launching their spells. The downside of such a static, trapped, setup was that we'd be cooked if the Anura wizards and sorcerers could med and nuke for the whole battle. I had to try and eliminate them, perhaps with my summoned bats and rats. From here, though, through the confusion of the melee and the crowds, there was no way I could pick out their artillery. Flicking on my *Invisibility*, I squeezed along the wall, past Oveidio, who was keeping three enemy fighters at bay with powerful sweeps of a two-handed sword, sweeps that I found it wisest to crawl under rather than remain standing and sidle against the wall.

In the relative calm once I'd crept beyond the clashing of steel on steel, I found three Anura casters, squatting low, more frog-like than ever, in between their leaps to launch spells. One shot up right ahead of me and I thought he could see *Invisible*. No, it was just so he could utter a spell, one which resulted in a cool, turquoise light flowing from his long fingers into the bodies of his warriors: clearly this was a cleric. The other two were in robes, the runes on which testified to their being sorcerers of some sort.

Hurrying further on into the darkness beyond, I flicked at *Summon Bats*, just as one of the sorcerers stood up and began to cast. Attack Target, I ordered my little minions, and was relieved to see the flickering swirl of fast-moving shadows descend on the Anura before his spell went off. Whirling around with as angry a face as I've ever seen on a frog, he pointed at me and shouted. Having made an offensive play, I was no longer invisible of course.

Summon Rats came next, the pack of rodents came at once and I sent them onto the sitting caster. It was evident from the hit point bars of my enemies that my summoned allies were doing very little damage. Even so, they were distracting the casters from blowing our raid to pieces and that was invaluable.

My plan had been to launch myself at the cleric. Before I could do so, a fighter detached himself from the melee and came running my way, brandishing his spiked mace, and at the same time there was a cry in the raid channel I couldn't ignore.

[Smoked] 'Roberta here, group four, we're cut off and dying.'

A glance at the raid screen confirmed this. Four of them had less than a quarter strength.

Bracing myself for the coming attack I called back, rather breathlessly. [Smoked] Run! Roberta. Whatever route you can. Try to take as big a train as possible away from the fight. Even getting us a minute could make all the difference.'

[Smoked] 'Right. Group four, follow me!'

You have been hit by a macuahuitl for 0 damage.

The frog man (woman?) in front of me had a vicious club, with chunks of sharp-looking obsidian that looked to be capable of taking my head off. Even though I couldn't be wounded by the weapon, I needed my full attention or I'd risk a headshot that might kill me.

Our raid screen looked bad and a miserable image flashed through my mind, of me saying a few words in the hall to a disconsolate group of players at the end of a defeated raid.

The fight was in the balance. Just a few seconds after our exchange and only Roberta was left of group four. Half of group three – the lowest levels – were dead and while groups one and two still had their compliment of players, Oveidio and Rubblethumper were losing hit points faster than our healers could restore them.

Then my enemy gave a shriek and turned around. A grinning gnome was there, Rasquelle, and the Anura warrior had just lost half his hit points.

Leaping onto his back, I bit hard at the line of green flesh between helmet and breastplate. With a taste of rubber in my mouth I got the hit I wanted.

Critical Hit! You have bitten an Anura warrior for 48 points of damage. You are draining his blood.

You have increased the skill Bite (166).

[Channel Raitha/Klytotoxos] 'I think our rearguard is about to collapse, should I summon Nemain with her horn?'

For a moment my adrenaline-filled body shouted *yes*. My mind, however, overruled that thought. [Channel Raitha/Klytotoxos] 'It's all gone pear-shaped, but no. Better to wipe. We can come here again at higher level but we can never get that ability back. And we might need it for the dragon fight.'

[Channel Raitha/Klytotoxos] 'I agree; I just wanted to check.'

[Group] 'We charge north, now!' shouted Sapentia to group one, just as Savoda went grey, leaving Tombalinor the only standing member of group three. Using my eyes and tiny motions of my fingers that did not affect my grip on the Anura warrior, I accessed the raid UI and hastily made Birch leader of group three in order to swap Tombalinor into ours. Immediately on doing so, I saw and felt the glowing buff of a healing song (and a *Haste* song flashed too, but as I had Tuscl's shaman buff already and they didn't stack, this was of no benefit).

[Group] '*Major Heal* on Tombalinor,' announced Braja.

Simultaneously, Tombalinor, whose hit point bar had only a sliver of green, rushed back up to full health, while my opponent finally died. It felt like a tide had turned. Now I could get that cleric and so could Rasquelle. I held back my own attack until the gnome rogue got in her backstab, then, as the Anura cleric staggered to his hands and knees, over half his life gone, I leapt on top of him and bit at his neck. No critical, but I did get a mouthful of froggy ear.

You have bitten an Anura cleric for 32 points of damage.

While I wrestled with the cleric, Tuscl called out, [Group] 'Es better you sing spirit *Restore*. My *Haste* overrides yours.'

[Group] 'You got it.' Tombalinor sounded full of the eagerness of the born again. And a moment later a soothing blue-iconed buff replaced the Bard's *Haste*. This would be a lot of value to Braja and Sapentia.

And all at once, we were winning. Without their cleric, the Anura tanks facing Oveidio and Rubblethumper must have gone down fast, for our two warriors were suddenly beside me, attacking the two Anura figures that were covered in rats and bats respectively. Unfortunately, it didn't seem possible to recall my minions, or I would have redirected them. In fact, both groups of summoned creatures dispersed when their opponents died.

On the other side of the battle, Grythiss had heroically been holding back about twelve Anura fighters (four in their front row). I could see that now as the victorious group two ran back to him and took up the fight.

I drew a deep breath and calmed myself after that hectic few minutes. [Smoked] 'Well done. Thanks everyone for staying off the raid channel, though you must have been curious as to what was happening. It was close but we are going to win from here. Everyone who died, give Rasquelle permission to move your body and we'll *Restore Life* here.'

As if I'd taken the ban off speaking in the raid channel, there was a lively exchange of relieved voices, set off by someone saying, [Smoked] 'Wow! That's awesome. I thought that was a wipe for sure.'

[Channel Oveidio/Klytotoxos] 'Woan was incredible, such timing. A lesser cleric and we would have failed.' My Russian friend opened a private channel.

[Channel Oveidio/Klytotoxos] 'Coming from you, that is great praise. I'll thank her.'

He didn't reply. Job done, I suppose.

[Channel Klytotoxos/Woan] 'I heard you were incredible, well done. You saved us from a wipe.'

[Channel Klytotoxos/Woan] 'Merci. It was a narrow squeak.'

When the last of the Anura was dead and we had a pile of our own bodies in the corridor, I swapped the groups around, temporarily putting the bards and clerics together. It took a lot of spirit to cast *Restore Life*; with the bard buffs, however, they would recover quickly enough.

[Smoked] 'Tuscl here, *Potion of Breathe Without Air* on the cleric.'

Well, that was interesting. It could not be a coincidence. [Smoked] Quiet everyone. Let's think about this, a ring and a potion to breathe. Both on priests. What's that tell us?'

It was Sapentia who spoke, after a short pause. [Smoked] 'God fight, maybe? To be near him for enough time? Smoke god. Hard to breathe?'

[Smoked] 'Smart. That makes sense. Let's hope the effect is directional. Tombalinor, pass your ring to Rubblethumper please and Tuscl, give that potion to Grythiss.'

As our raid recovered its proper shape, I moved the groups back to the initial four and as soon as my own friends were gathered back together, the usual banter began. Raitha spoke first. [Group] 'During that last battle, you used a strange idiom.'

[Group] 'Who me?' I asked.

[Group] 'You indeed. You said that the battle was assuming the shape of a pear, as if this were a bad thing. In my culture, a pear is often considered to have a voluptuous figure, one that poets consider to be positive.'

Sapentia snorted derisively. [Group] 'Pear? In Kerala you celebrate large, fat lower body?'

[Group] 'Nothing so specific.' The emphasis in Raitha's voice was like that of a teacher making a rebuke. 'I believe it is an all-round association between delicious, sweet moistness and curves.'

[Group] 'Now we're talking,' said a cheerful Braja.

Raitha sighed. [Group] 'Tut, I am not making myself clear. My query is that why did Tyro describe our near disaster as a pear shape? Is this an Irish expression?'

[Group] 'I'm not sure where it comes from, sorry Raitha, but if a situation has gone pear-shaped it means the plan has become a complete mess. You don't have it in the US, Braj?'

[Group] 'Never heard that one and we have a bucket load for that. Snafu, Charlie Foxtrot, Fubar, gone to crap…'

[Group] 'Oh,' I had a sudden thought, 'we use one that's definitely Irish, "banjaxed". We use it for when something is broken beyond repair.'

[Group] 'Banjaxed,' repeated Raitha carefully, 'a most valuable term. I shall be sure to add it to my English vocabulary.'

Even Grythiss joined in, which must have strained his commitment to role-playing. [Group] If ssomeone makesss

372

misstake and it all goess wrong, we lizardmen say he has crapped in the blue cupboard.'

There was a pause, followed by laughter from the whole group, with Braja laughing the loudest. [Group] 'The blue cupboard? What the hell is the blue cupboard?'

Interrupting his own soft chuckles Raitha added, [Group] 'I imagine it to be the Lizard King's most important cupboard, where he keeps all his valuable and treasured possessions.'

Much as I enjoyed my friend's company and their chat during downtime, I could see from the raid screen we were all ready again.

[Smoked] 'Let's set up, group two at the front; five metre space then group one; five metre space, group three; same to four. I'll scout.'

As everyone shuffled into their positions, I set off down the long torchlit corridor. Careful not to trip any wires, I noted highly artistic, stylized carvings on the walls. They were half-life-sized, flat-nosed figures, like Egyptian hieroglyphs and perhaps there was some kind of story behind them. What interested me in particular were the depictions of the Smoke God. Surprisingly, he was somewhat human shaped, except that not only was he double the size of his worshippers, his torso was shown as a whirlwind.

There were several rooms off the corridor, none of them with doors and all of them empty. They were the practical rooms one might expect in a temple: barracks; kitchen; washroom and a storeroom. I didn't even place one foot into them but instead pushed on, until the very welcome sight, just after the corridor turned sharply to the right, of a large square room with a great pit in its centre. A ledge, wide enough for two people, went around the room and in the centre of each wall, the ledges had ladders going down into the darkness.

[Smoked] 'Move up to the corner, we have a way down. Rasquelle, come with me down a ladder.'

A moment later, our female gnome stepped out of the shadows like a portal had opened in the wall. It was a neat trick.

'What's up, boss?'

'Pick a ladder and test it.'

Our rogue walked around the room, studying ledge, walls and ladders carefully. Then she set off down the one on the far side, moving slowly and cautiously. I did the same for the nearest one. As I swung myself into position over the black depths, it did occur to me that I might not be immune to falling damage. I'd never heard of a vampire falling to his death. After all, I had the ability to turn into a bat or a cloud, instantly. All the same, what if they were greyed out because I'd used them recently? Would I be immune to the damage of impact?

Halfway down I heard a grating sound and an 'oops' from the gnome across from me. The ladder over that side had snapped flat to the wall, leaving Rasquelle clinging by her fingertips to the lines in the brickwork.

'What did you say your *Discover Traps* skill was?' I whispered.

'Ahh,' once again, as she glanced over, the gnome showed me her guilty face. 'Not having a good day.'

My ladder ended at a ledge but the shaft continued downwards. Good. The god was supposed to be spawned in the depths of the ziggurat. After waiting for the Rogue to climb down to my ledge, I gestured to the other ladders. 'My guess is one is safe, the other three trapped. Would you mind seeing if I'm right?'

'Not at all,' replied Rasquelle with a confidence that she surely was not actually feeling.

It took a while, but this time she found the traps.

'You're right.' She was about twenty metres down, at the bottom of the ladder to my left. 'This ladder is the only safe one.'

Hurrying - the rest of the raid must be bored and I could hear in group chat that Braja and Sapentia were annoying each other again - I went down to the next ledge. There was a final set of four ladders before we reached the bottom.

'Go ahead,' I said to Rasquelle, 'find the safe one. I'll climb back up and mark the way.'

Once at the top again, I called up my inventory, took out a

candle and lit it near the first ladder. Then on the ledge below I placed one beside the second and another when Rasquelle announced that it was the far side that was safe.

'Well done.' I gave her a smile.

[Smoked] 'Right, we can all move on. The pit is trapped, only the ladders with candles at the top of them are safe. Just to repeat. Only use the ladders with a candle at the top.'

'Let's you and I explore.'

Looking serious, Rasquelle stepped into the darkness on the left side of the corridor and vanished. I strolled along the right, though my nonchalance was mostly bravado. These Anura guarded their god carefully and I was feeling a rising anxiety in the face of what was bound to be a difficult encounter or two before we met the boss himself. The corridor, too, felt oppressive, like the weight of the building above me was bearing down on me.

Behind me flashes of colour from magic weapons and ordinary light from lanterns testified to the arrival of the rest of the raid, as did the clatter of their boots. It was surprising how loud they all were. We may as well have announced our arrival with a team of trumpeters.

Finally, after a very long walk in the darkness, the corridor turned left and opened to a huge chamber. Aha, this was promising. A wide plinth, about two metres high, was in the centre of the room and had what looked like a coal fire burning in it. All around the edges of the room were a dozen ferocious-looking figures: somewhat larger than a human, huge eyes, wide mouths full of teeth, thick-fingered clawed hands stretched wide. And they seemed to be looking at me.

I took a step back. [Smoked] 'Big room, big fight. I hope. Come on up.'

Having gone back to meet the raid, I slipped through group two to walk with my own group. There was no group chat now, we were all on alert. Halfway down the corridor, I felt the floor move slightly.

[Smoked] 'What was that, did anyone else feel it?' someone asked and a dozen voices responded.

Ahead of us came a clang. Then another from the back. My heart sank.

[Group] 'I think we might have crapped in the blue cupboard,' I said. No one laughed.

[Smoked] 'Oveidio here. Group one have reached a dead end.'

[Smoked] 'There was no dead end. Something has changed. Group four, turn back,' I ordered, but I knew what they would find.

Sure enough. [Smoked] 'Roberta here. Blocked. If I didn't know we'd just come this way, I'd have said it was a dead end too. There's something else too, a hissing sound.'

[Smoked] 'I can hear hissing.'

[Smoked] 'Hissing by me too.'

Everyone wanted to report.

Snakes?

[Smoked] 'Silence!' shouted Grythiss. He was very good at policing the channel. In the quiet that followed, the hissing sound was quite distinct and coming from all around us.

[Smoked] 'It's gas.'

Whoever said this was right, my infravision showed a light-coloured gas was pouring into the corridor from small holes at more than twenty points.

[Smoked] 'Warriors, try to slide the obstructing wall ahead of us. Push it in every possible direction. Casters, if you have a spell that might get us out, use it. Everyone: if you can get yourself out of here and beyond the front wall, do that now.'

Someone fell over. And I felt the corridor begin to swirl. Immediately, I triggered *Cloud Form*. If I was shaped out of vapour, I wouldn't have to breathe, or so I hoped. Another character fell and another. Then, it seemed, a dozen all at once. No one below level thirty was still standing. This situation had wipe written all over it in large, red, capital letters. Still, I wasn't going to give up.

[Smoked] 'Rubblethumper, give your ring to Braja, we are going to need a cleric to survive this and restore the dead.'

[Smoked] 'But we'll need a warrior too.'

[Smoked] 'Do it! And quickly!'

[Smoked] 'We have a potion though, don't we? Whoever has that can give it to the cleric. I'm the main tank, remember.'

It galled me that someone should disobey a direct order from a raid leader. I mean, I'd often disagreed with raid leaders in the past, but I'd kept my tongue and gone along with whatever the plan was. A bad plan was better than a dozen plans. With players who just did as they pleased, raids just fell apart. And I'd been on plenty that had descended into bitter argument and confusion.

[Group] 'Lizardman givesss potion to cleric.'

I sighed. [Group] 'Thanks Grythiss. That idiot. I'm sorry I'm going to end up here with him not you.'

[Group] 'Good luck, Tyro,' said Sapentia. 'Get us out of this.'

Less than a minute later, myself, Rubblethumper and Braja were standing in a corridor full of bodies.

'I think they are just asleep, not dead.' Braja was kneeling over Grythiss. 'He's a good comrade, though, isn't he?' To my surprise, Braja gave Grythiss a kiss on his reptilian forehead.

'Can we wake them? Try please.'

While Braja slapped Grythiss around, I pinched Sapentia and shouted in her ear. Nothing.

[Smoked] 'Incoming…two of those creatures from the chamber.'

[Smoked] 'Who said that?' I asked, curious.

[Smoked] 'Me, sorry, Rasquelle. I'm on the far side of the wall from you guys.'

[Smoked] 'Fantastic. Glad to hear it.'

A bit of good news at last. Maybe we weren't doomed.

[Smoked] 'They are approaching the wall. Ahh, I see it, a false mural. He's reaching in and pulling something.'

Ahead of me, the wall began to slide open with a grinding sound, I could see swirls of the poisonous gas escaping as the gap widened.

Urgently, I addressed Rubblethumper, using the raid channel, though I could have spoken in local. For some reason, I sensed I wanted everyone to hear me and to hear his response. [Smoked] 'Rubblethumper, I'm going to materialise again. As soon as I do, you are going to immediately hand me the ring, understand?'

A rather sullen reply came back. [Smoked] 'We have a cleric; let me tank them.'

[Smoked] 'They are raid mobs, we'll need to debuff them and have all our healing available. There is a chance though, that I'll be immune to their attacks, in which case I'll stall them while everyone gets back on their feet. Now, we are out of time, just give me the ring.'

If we were back in *Epic* on one of my raids, I'd have booted him and never let him join us again. Here, I had no choice. Would he comply? Or try something crazy, like fighting the incoming mobs?

Just before the wall was fully retracted, I flicked off my *Cloud Form* and, standing right in front of him, held out my hand to Rubblethumper. He drew a deep breath, then handed the magic item to me.

[Smoked] 'Thank you.' I probably sounded relieved, I certainly felt it. If he'd have held on to the ring, we wouldn't have had a chance. Now, if my vampire's immunity held, we could make a comeback.

The two fierce humanoids strode in and when they saw me, began to run straight towards me. Good, I didn't want them killing the unconscious raid members. With a snarl, I ran to meet them and we clashed.

They were fast, savage, their talons were cruel, and they couldn't hurt me.

You have been clawed by a Protector of the Smoke God for 0 damage.

I felt like laughing, such was the delight that now swelled up in my heart. We could get through this trap and be back with a shot at the boss.

[Smoked] 'Stay out of this until everyone has recovered.

Rasquelle move all the sleeping players that you can to the far side of the trap. Braja and Rubblethumper, take bodies out your side.'

Bite or sword? I went for bite, since it was by far the higher skill of the two. These mobs were tough, though, and only after a stream of misses did I get a hit.

You have bitten a Protector of the Smoke God for 31 damage.

You have increased the skill Bite (167).

By the time my next hit landed, the Protector had nearly regenerated back to max hit points. And as I had to sometimes swap targets, to make sure I was building aggro on both of them, it was futile to hope to be able to kill one on my own. What was crucial, though, was that they were locked onto a target that was not budging, namely me. And while that was the case, the rest of the raid could reassemble: I was delighted to see that already the higher-level characters were taking to their feet.

[Smoked] 'Kenori here, we are up to ninety-five mobs killed outside, want us to push on to a hundred?'

[Smoked] 'Thank for the update. No please wait now until I say we are set; as you might have gathered from the raid chat, it's a bit messy in here. We do seem to be close to the god's spawn point at least.'

With every minute that passed, a newly revived member of the raid got up. Sparing a glance back over my shoulder now and again to check, I waited until the last player was back and ready for action, before allowing Rubblethumper his long-desired opportunity to fight a Protector.

With all of our players around to assist, pulling one Protector and then another led to two easy fights, at the end of which Rubblethumper shouted in the raid channel, 'Booyah!' Despite his chest-beating enthusiasm, he wouldn't have been able to tank one of those, let alone two, with just Braja, Rasquelle and myself in support. They hit hard.

Having brought the raid up to the big hall, I felt a slight anxiety at the sight of the ten remaining Protectors. Maybe one or more of them had a means of attack that could harm me. In which case, should they all come at the same time, the raid would wipe before we got a chance at the god. Fortunately, when I stepped into the room, it was only the nearest four that triggered and fortunately too, I was immune to their attacks. We cleared them, cleared three more and then the last three, leaving us standing on the central plinth of the huge hall, looking at the smouldering coals.

Right, time to try the boss. [Smoked] 'Kenori. Resume killing the worshippers outside, we are ready here.'

[Smoked] 'Will do.'

[Smoked] 'Rebuffs everyone. Fire resistances all around. Size of a gnome on Rubblethumper and *Shrink* on both Rubblethumper and Grythiss. Just the two tanks on the plinth.'

Walking over to Rubblethumper, I handed him the ring of *Breathe Without Air.* 'Here. It might be useful in the boss fight.' He took it with a nod. Then I jumped down to the floor of the hall and crossed to the corner of the room to the left of the entrance. [Smoked] 'Rubblethumper, you will pull the boss to this corner, as tight to it as you can. Healing classes, stand in the corridor for the pop but run to here'—I'd moved halfway to the corridor—'as soon as the god is off the plinth.'

'Marmalade and Glarinson, you start here. Rubblethumper is your target; use *Holy Intervention* to keep him alive until the healers are set up.'

Then I walked back to the plinth, to the corner opposite that of our battle site. 'Groups one, two and three start here. We run behind the god to the battle spot. Group four, start and remain in the corridor as a reserve until the god is at eighty per cent. Then come to the healers and protect them against possible adds. Roberta, use your initiative and discretion in responding to any unforeseen developments.' I paused to let her respond.

[Smoked] 'Thank you for your confidence in me. We won't let you down.'

[Smoked] 'You're welcome. That's it. Take your places and good luck.'

There was a murmur of responses as everyone wished each other the best for the coming fight. Then an expectant silence.

The hall was dark and shadowy, just a faint orange light from the centre. Despite the size of the room and the way it dwarfed our raiding party, it didn't feel empty, the space was filled with tension and expectation.

[Smoked] 'Kenori here. Number one hundred just died. Best of luck to everyone inside from us all out here.'

If my avatar could have displayed sweat on his forehead and palms, he would have correctly interpreted my physical body. This was an excruciatingly nerve-wracking moment. There was a lot at stake. Of course, if we failed, we could come back, having added on whatever levels we needed to win. But it was right now, in this room, in this encounter, that the whole project had the potential to fail. A run of bad luck on the drops and respawn rate of the smoke god and we were finished, no matter how well we did with everything else.

With a violent rushing sound, flames suddenly roared up from the fire at the centre of the plinth and then collapsed, leaving a tight, confined whirlwind of grey smoke that span at a dizzying speed until, with the sound of a wave crashing, it condensed into the half-frog, half-humanoid shape of an Anura. Only, he was three times as big, with a vicious-looking, obsidian-spiked mace in either hand. The god's torso was a shiny grey, as though the smoke had condensed into a breastplate.

'Tezpeylipoca has returned to avenge his fallen followers,' a powerful, intimidating voice filled the hall. 'Bow down before me and accept your fate! Or does anyone believe themselves a match for me?'

This was a great moment, the kind of moment I lived for. A raid boss, being spawned for the first time ever. It was just a shame I couldn't enjoy the encounter as much as I normally would. Whatever pleasure the scene contained was overshadowed by the stress of all the money at stake, as well as the presence of people who I knew were judging me and maybe even - in the case of Blackridge and his cronies - hoping I'd fail.

'I am a follower of Nemain and with her aid a match for you!' Grythiss was much quicker off the mark than Rubble-thumper and, having triggered his fast aggro spell that flashed with a purple light, leapt from the plinth with the god just behind him.

[Smoked] 'Paladins, swap to Grythiss,' I said as calmly as I could, though my heart was thumping. 'Healers, same. Rubblethumper, stay behind the mob and take over if Grythiss goes down.' I didn't want them both trying to squeeze into the corner, nor did I want both tanks to be in the way of whatever AE came our way.

Strictly speaking, Grythiss was probably in the wrong to have taken the pull. Maybe it was his commitment to role-playing coming into force and overruling my instructions. In any case, as far as I was concerned it was a good move. Rubblethumper should have pulled more quickly; we just couldn't allow that god the freedom of being able to look around the room and pick targets.

As if he had read my thoughts, I got a signal for private chat from Rubblethumper, which I took.

[Channel Rubblethumper/Klytotoxos] 'I was trying to hit the mob the whole time, but he wasn't open until he'd finished speaking.'

[Channel Rubblethumper/Klytotoxos] 'No problem. Just keep behind him until needed. And build up as much aggro as you can. You won't overtake Grythiss.'

Because shadow knights had spells designed for the provocation of enemies, there would be no danger of Rubblethumper accidently turning the boss so that he faced the raid instead of the corner.

No sooner had Grythiss stopped running and set up in the corner than bang, bang. Two massive hits, one from each of the god's weapons, reduced my lizardman friend to about 20 per cent of his hit points. Before the next blow could land, however, he was on full. One of the paladins, or both, had used a *Holy Intervention*.

Soon we were all there, in a dark corner of a great hall at the centre of a ziggurat, looking at the back of a huge, muscular figure, lit up by a barrage of colour like a fireworks display as our casters set to work.

[Smoked] 'He is debuffed by *Frost*,' announced Tuscl.

Tempted as I was to try to fasten my teeth into the calf of the giant frog god, it was too crowded at his back with characters who could do more melee damage than me. And in any case, I suspected that it was smoke, rather than blood, running in the veins of Tezpeylipoca. So I stood on the plinth in the centre of the room and - while keeping an eye out for anything unexpected - started firing my new hickory bow.

> You have fired an arrow at Tezpeylipoca and missed.

> You have fired an arrow at Tezpeylipoca and missed.

> You have fired an arrow at Tezpeylipoca and missed.

> You have hit Tezpeylipoca for 0 damage.

Oh, hello.

[Smoked] 'My arrows are not doing damage. Reports please, let's figure out if we need blunt weapons, magic weapons or both.'

With admirable clarity and lack of extraneous chatter, the reports came in and it was very quickly clear that only magic weapons were getting through.

[Smoked] 'If you don't have a magic weapon, make room for someone who does. Join group four and stand ready for adds.'

[Channel Raitha/Klytotoxos] 'Try *Frost Arrow*,' Raitha advised.

Of course.

> You have hit Tezpeylipoca for 27 Frost damage.

[Channel Raitha/Klytotoxos] 'Nice, it works.'

[Channel Raitha/Klytotoxos] 'That is welcome news. My bow, as you know, is magical, so I was hitting in any case. Going forward I shall supplement my attacks with frost damage so long as I have spirit.'

The pattern of the fight was all that I had hoped for: while the god's hit points only moved down by tiny increments, he was visibly declining. Meanwhile, Grythiss was holding up well as the main tank; even when Tezpeylipoca got in a flurry of blows with the two fierce-looking maces, our gallant tank still had about a quarter of his hit points left and our healers were able to bring him back up in good time. Knowing Grythiss, I was sure he was relishing the fight. This was the kind of moment all his immersion into the game was geared to: in fighting for his goddess against an enemy deity, he'd be living his dream.

When the god's hit points sank to 80 per cent, the pattern changed: Grythiss was flung upwards, despite his being set tight to the corner of the room, and Tezpeylipoca immediately turned around, giving us all a taste of his AE, even me, a long way off on the plinth. It was unfortunate that at just that moment group four had emerged from the safety of the corridor, so they got a heavy battering. A flashing icon appeared in the corner of my UI, which when I read it said: *Whirlwind of Smoke. You have been struck by a blast of magical air for 18 damage. You have resisted the* Knockback *effect. You have resisted the* Stun *effect.*

With bodies flying through the air around me, I could see that about half the raid had failed in their efforts to resist the *Knockback*. I could see too, a great reduction in hit points among the raid members, particularly those close to the angry-faced god. No one, however, was dead and fortunately Rubblethumper was neither flung away from the god nor stunned.

[Smoked] 'I have the aggro!' shouted Rubblethumper urgently. 'Heal me!' The gnome - for such was his changed shape - took up position in the corner and turned the god away from the raid again, allowing us to reorganise.

[Smoked] 'Good job, Rubblethumper. Clerics on our new MT. Druids heal up everyone else, starting with any injured clerics. Grythiss fight from behind the god for now, take care with your aggro.'

After what was probably less than a minute of chaotic panic, though it felt longer, we were back in shape, back in control. Tezpeylipoca's hit points resumed their downward course. As they went down through the sixties, I sent out a few more orders.

[Channel Klytotoxos/Grythiss] 'Get ready to take over again on sixty.'

[Channel Klytotoxos/Tuscl] 'Got any buffs for the tanks that help them resist those effects?'

[Channel Klytotoxos/Tuscl] 'Is already up on everyone. *Ironshield* gives a small magic resist as well as the AC buff.'

63…62…61…60.

[Smoked] 'Resisted!' Rubblethumper sounded triumphant and I shared his feeling. His success kept us in shape.

Throughout the fight, I'd been anxious about adds and my fears were realised when Tezpeylipoca reached 50 per cent. A full respawn of the twelve protectors popped into existence and ran towards us from their alcoves around the hall. It would have been a difficult challenge, too difficult for our underpowered raid, but for my immunity to their damage. After a bow shot at the Protector furthest away from me, I ran around the room gathering up the aggro on as many as I could, which netted me ten.

The other two had spawned close to our clerics and, quite rightly, Roberta responded by leading her team into action to keep our healers safe. Their battle did not go well, too many of them were low-level characters, most of whom had not been fully healed up since damaged by Tezpeylipoca's AE. As I saw one after the other of group four die, I could see a scenario where the clerics were cut down and we wiped. Roberta, though, was no fool. When it was just her left, she ran between the two Protectors and they followed her as she circled around the plinth. I was too hemmed in by my own pulls to help her and in any case, probably wouldn't have managed to generate more aggro than she had.

[Smoked] 'Heads up! Rubblethumper go defensive, don't bring the god down any further. We can't risk that AE while we have these adds. Woan and Silva, keep Rubblethumper in the game. Everyone else, work with Grythiss to kill the Protectors.'

While every player here was a veteran, there was one group I could count on to settle this crisis in our favour. My own. [Group] 'Friends, we can do this. Grythiss, tag one of Roberta's to start with.'

[Group] 'Certainly, oh mighty leader. Thsssss.' [Smoked] 'Death to a Protector!'

The about-turn by the raid was a joy to see and although I had to look over the heads of the Protectors who were jostling around me, I had a perfect view from the plinth. A flash of purple came from the hands of my lizardman friend as he leapt away from the god to pull a Protector. While Roberta kept running with the other close behind, the rest of the raid moved towards Grythiss and soon spells and weapons were hammering against the mob.

These Protectors were not too strong defensively, so it died quickly enough, they did mete out a lot of damage, though, and I noticed that Braja was careful to heal early and then use fast heals at a rapid rate. He was right too, better to be conservative in this situation - we could catch up on spirit levels when the adds had been dealt with.

When the first Protector died, Grythiss pulled Roberta's other stray and with no one sprinting around the place any longer, the hall felt relatively calm. It was, of course, the exact opposite: three furious battles were underway: Rubblethumper was hunkered down, while the smoke god, static at 47 per cent, battered him; I was up on the plinth, surrounded by angry Protectors; and Grythiss, with a wide semi-circle of players around him, was tanking his mob with fierce concentration.

A Protector is dead. You gain experience.

One after the other, the Protectors were peeled away from me and dealt with. The great hall felt like it was home to a party from which people were beginning to leave. It grew quieter with every kill, until the last of the revellers gathered in a dark corner.

[Smoked] 'Well done all. Let's hold the god at forty-seven while the bards sing spirit restoration. Clerics report when you are at seventy-five.'

Resuming my place on the plinth, bow in hand, I looked carefully around the hall, to check nothing had changed. Same tall stone walls, dark, but with a hint of orange from the reflections of the low-burning fire at the centre of the plinth. Nothing stirring in any direction, except for the frenzied efforts of the giant frog-man, tirelessly swinging his maces one after the other into the shield of Rubblethumper, who I had to admit was doing a great job of blocking the attacks. Satisfied, I took shots at the god with ordinary, non-frost imbued, arrows. May as well level up my archery skill while waiting for the clerics to recover.

After some ten minutes of this, with admirable restraint in the use of the raid channel (although in group chat Raitha was gabbling on about wind-based spells and whether they would harm or heal the god), all the clerics had plenty of spirit.

[Smoked] 'Let's go. Take him down.'

For my own part, I imbued my shots with the *Frost Arrow* spell again and added my own small contribution to the raid's DPS.

43...42...41...40.

[Smoked] 'Resist!' shouted Rubblethumper in triumph.

[Smoked] 'Well done, keep going everyone.' My voice sounded even and calm to my ears, though I was trying to hold back a rising sense of delight and achievement. Some psychologists apparently spent their whole careers encouraging sports stars to picture victory. To picture themselves as champions. To overcome feelings of inadequacy and intimidation, presumably. Here, the danger was complacency rather than the possibility that the tanks or clerics would choke. It would be bad luck to acknowledge how well we were doing so I thrust aside all anticipation of success and instead made myself stand ready for a new wave of adds or some other unexpected twist to the battle.

23...22...21...20.

All at once the smoke god was free of his containment. Our tank had gone flying up the wall and immediately Tezpeylipoca turned around, scattering half the raid, including, unfortunately, Grythiss.

Whirlwind of Smoke. **You have been struck by a blast of magical air for 18 damage. You have resisted the *Knockback* effect. You are Stunned for twelve seconds. You cannot move or speak.**

Damn. Twelve seconds was a very long time in a crisis like this. And while my physical body could still move, in the game my avatar was stricken, the stun had shut me up. All I could do was watch.

Marmalade, our absurdly named Dwarven Paladin, was still on his feet and did the right thing, leaping into the corner and trying to turn the god.

Smack!

Marmalade was dead.

Smack!

With three strides, Tezpeylipoca had reached Woan and killed her.

Smack! Smack!

Rurn and Birch were dead.

Smack!

Braja was less than half. Oh no.

Smack!

Braja was dead.

Now the god looked up and with eyes that were like the pits of active volcanoes, stared right at me. I was his next target. And I was locked, helpless. If those powerful weapons could damage me, or if he took my head off with one swipe, I was dead.

A Russian accent came on the raid channel. [Smoked] 'I am main tank. Oveidio.'

The human warrior ran across my vision, chopped at the god's legs with a longsword and then danced away, turning the god and bringing him back to the corner. At some cost though. I could still access the raid UI and see how rapidly Oveidio was losing hit points. Moreover, we needed a *Shrink* on him for the fighting was taking place with the god on the inside, facing the rest of the room. It was often like that in *Epic*, when you fought really large creatures, they had a centre of gravity that was unfairly small. The encounter designers wanted raids to fight their huge bosses the hard way, with all the players facing into their full range of attacks. Focusing the god on one small player in a corner was a kind of cheat as far as the devs were concerned. The tactic was considered common sense for everyone else.

At last, my *Stun* condition was over. [Smoked] '*Shrink* on Oveidio. He is MT. All healers on him now.'

[Group] 'It will take me a minute to load *Shrink*.' This was Tuscl, the only person in the raid with that spell.

[Group] 'Lizardman ssorry for weakness. Will make amendsss.'

Grythiss was charging back across the hall and meanwhile, too, Rubblethumper had shaken off his *Stun* and was returning to the fight.

[Smoked] 'I repeat, Oveidio is MT. Rubblethumper and Grythiss, stand down until needed.'

If either of the other two tanks hit the god, they would almost certainly get the aggro, after all they'd built up from earlier in the fight. There was nothing wrong with that; in some ways it might prove a better strategy because I was taking a risk that Tezpeylipoca wouldn't use his AE again before the *Shrink* caused Oveidio to get nearer the wall than the god and turned him. There was this consideration though: our surviving healers would all be in the middle of casting on Oveidio and it would get messy if they had to abort and restart their heals with Grythiss or Rubblethumper as the target. Then there was a less rational, more personal issue. I admired Oveidio and if fate had chosen him to be the one who resisted the AE when the rest of us were knocked out, then it felt right to run with that and let him finish the battle as our champion.

For an anxious minute, I watched Oveidio's hit points dive, before they began to surge back up as the clerics and druids pumped him full of healing spells. And when Tuscl got her *Shrink* spell to land and Tezpeylipoca suddenly swung away from us, my heart rose. We had the fight properly contained once more.

19...18...17...Tezpeylipoca's hit points were steadily declining.

Firing *Frost Arrow* as often as I could, I maximised my own contribution to the fight.

16...15...

[Smoked] 'Silva here. Just ten per cent spirit left.'

Oh no, that was a worry, Silva was our only really powerful cleric left. [Smoked] 'Other healers report please.'

[Smoked] 'Spinespike, seventeen.'

[Smoked] 'Healyupy, eight.'

[Smoked] 'Birch, eight.'

[Smoked] 'Rahod, eleven.'

There was a pause.

[Smoked] 'Jesus!' someone exclaimed and I had to agree, this was terrible. There was no room for romance here.

[Smoked] 'None of you heal Oveidio. Stop; save your spirit. Sorry O, you have to take a hit for the team. Rubblethumper, when Oveidio dies, you're up, maximum defence.'

With a defiant laugh, Oveidio spoke to us all. [Smoked] 'I understand. It is correct play. Good luck everyone.'

Just three blows later and Oveidio was gone.

With an extra five levels, better armour and, crucially, additional defensive abilities, Rubblethumper was a much more suitable tank. Especially when the issue was damage limitation, rather than dishing it out. The transition was smooth, with Tezpeylipoca only momentarily turning to face us. Crucially, it soon became clear our healers could now keep up.

14...13...12...

[Smoked] 'DPS: everything you've got now, let's try to skip through whatever unpleasant tricks he has left.'

[Group] 'Cometh hour, cometh sorceress.' Sapentia sounded resolute and I was delighted to hear the determination in her voice. Having absolute faith in her spirit management, I knew she'd have plenty to burn.

Several vivid, sizzling bolts coloured white, green and blue crashed into the god. These were from our other casters; Sapentia, I could see from the stroboscopic flashes, was standing with raised arms, still casting. And then it came, a mighty slam from what appeared to be a white beam of light, that momentarily encased Tezpeylipoca in ice, before blowing apart in a glittering explosion.

6...5...4...

Boom! Another ice blast was followed by the beautiful game message:

Tezpeylipoca is dead. You gain experience.

[Smoked] 'Get in!'

[Smoked] 'He's down!'

[Smoked] 'Booyah!'

The raid channel burst into life with a dozen voices, all expressing excitement and delight.

[Smoked] 'Shut up!' shouted Grythiss at full volume and then, in his more usual voice. 'Lizardman hasss important news. Good and bad.'

[Smoked] 'What's the good news?' I asked.

[Smoked] 'There are eight ssshards.'

Eight! All eight with one raid. Incredible.

[Smoked] 'And the bad news?'

[Smoked] 'They are *Fastened.*'

Silence.

In a second I'd gone from feeling flushed with success to being so cold, I shivered. My stomach felt heavy. *Fastened.* We couldn't bring them to Scarlet, she would have to come here. Why hadn't I thought of this possibility? She could have been with us now and there would be no problems. As it was, we'd been so long down in this hall there was bound to be a full respawn above us.

It took me a moment but I shook off the paralysis that had gripped me. [Smoked] 'If Tezpeylipoca's body is on the usual timer, we have six minutes. Scarlet, are you there?' As I spoke I hurried over to Rubblethumper.

[Smoked] 'Listening.' Scarlet had a US accent, somewhere East maybe, though I really didn't have a clue.

[Smoked] 'Go to the foot of the ramp and get ready to run in and loot the boss.'

'Ring please, Rubblethumper, quickly.' I held out my hand. 'Rasquelle, run up to work the lever on the trapped corridor.' Even before Rubblethumper had managed to find the ring and swap it to me, the gnome rogue had rushed from the hall.

[Smoked] 'Everyone who is outside the ziggurat, try to pull mobs down the ramp and out of line of Scarlet's run. Everyone with me, keep the corridors clear as far back as the trap with the sleeping gas.'

Having got the ring, I was already running back to the ladders even as I spoke.

[Smoked] 'Scarlet, I'm going to bring a large train down the ramp. Once it's clear, you run in, basically it's straight all the way until you get to a trapped corridor. Rasquelle will open that for you and guide you from there. But there's sleeping gas, so as I pass you at the bottom of the ramp, I'm going to throw you a ring of *Breathe Without Air.*'

[Smoked] 'Got it. All set.'

Back up the ladders (overtaking Rasquelle) and along the trapped corridor, which my weight alone didn't trigger, I ran as far as the first opening off the corridor. A barracks with a full respawn of Anura.

'Hey! I've just killed your god.' I ran inside, kicking and lashing out with my sword, until they all crowded around me, hitting me to no effect. Then I brought my train up to the next opening off the corridor, a kitchen, and ran a quick circuit around that room to pull its five occupants. There were two Anura in a washroom and two more in the storeroom, all of whom were encouraged to join my train by my exclaiming their god was dead.

Then a long run up to the trap wire and bell, which presumably had mobilised all the mobs currently in my train when we had set it off on the way in. I triggered it again now. Then there were poison darts to come, weren't there? The thought of being poisoned made me anxious but I couldn't leave the trap live for Scarlet. Just as I braced myself to be struck by them, I recognised the trapped section of corridor by the murals on the walls and went into a roll. *Swoosh! Swoosh!* The darts flew over me. Hah! And I was still clear of the stampeding, heaving crowd of Anura doing their best to get hold of me.

I'd almost forgotten about the two hidden guards, not that

it mattered, they jumped out as I ran past and suddenly I was outside in the moonlight again, to an air that was both fresher than that inside the ziggurat and also sweeter with the scents of lavender and jasmine.

Below me, on the pale ramp, were several bodies from our low-level characters who had failed to pull mobs clear of the huge building. Others must have succeeded though because there were no Anura between me and the bottom.

[Smoked] 'Here I come!' Tempted as I was to add a long 'wheeee!' to this shout as a sudden giddiness overcame me, I kept my composure and jogged down the huge building, just fast enough to keep my long train of jumping, angry frog-people interested in chasing me.

[Smoked] 'Can you see me?' This was Scarlet's voice and I could indeed see her, waving from beside a bush.

[Smoked] 'I see you, that's perfect.'

Long before I reached the bottom of the ramp, I had the ring ready and just before swerving to my left, to lead my train around the outside of the ziggurat, I threw it. Not a bad throw either.

[Smoked] 'Did you get it?'

[Smoked] 'No, sorry, I heard it land in the bush. I can't see too well in the dark.'

The clock was running down on the drops and our whole raid, not to mention our whole multi-million-dollar project, had come down to how quickly a character could scrabble around on all fours among the bushes, looking for a magic ring by moonlight. Talk about stress. Totally unnecessary stress too; I should have just kept Scarlet safe in the centre of the raid and brought her to the boss fight.

[Smoked] 'Anyone with *Detect Magic* or *Infravision* outside and able to help her?'

[Smoked] 'Konnichiwa here. Just slotting it now. Will be over in a minute.'

[Smoked] 'Found it!'

Thank goodness. And there she went, swiftly up the empty ramp.

[Smoked] 'Respawns!' shouted someone, probably Oveidio.

This raid was hammering at my emotions, which had been up and down in the last hour as dramatically as the rollercoaster at Tayto Park. Again, just when I thought we were done, there was a challenge to face. Not that I could help with the tactics now I was outside, jogging at the head of a train.

[Smoked] 'Sapentia is raid leader. Follow her instructions.'

[Channel Klytotoxos/Sapentia] 'Setting you to raid leader, organise everyone down there to keep the route clear.'

Sapentia didn't reply. From the raid UI, I could see that she had at once set about shuffling the players around. Having made two balanced groups, one with Grythiss as group leader the other with Rubblethumper, our sorceress gave her orders. [Smoked] 'Group one, with Grythiss to here. Tackle respawns from this side of room. Group Rubblethumper opposite side. Do same.'

[Smoked] 'I'm in the trap,' cried Scarlet urgently, 'someone open the door.'

As ordered, Rasquelle had been standing by. [Smoked] 'On it. There! Follow me.'

Whatever was going on in the great hall, it did not distract Sapentia from making a smart adjustment to the raid UI, putting Scarlet into group one, the same group as Rasquelle (and myself for that matter). Not only did this allow group chat so Rasquelle wouldn't spam the raid channel with instructions to Scarlet, it gave her other group options like the command *find*, which orientated you towards a fellow group member.

Only now, as I was running around it, did I appreciate how enormous the ziggurat was. After all this jogging, I still wasn't halfway around. Was that a hint of grey sky above the jungle? Had we really been six hours at this? No, only four, but still, perhaps dawn wasn't so far off in this region.

[Smoked] 'Got them! Got them!' Scarlet sounded triumphant. 'There's more loot here too, what should I do?'

I almost stopped running to do a little dance. Out of habit I was about to reply that Scarlet should take everything, there may be only a matter of minutes left before the boss disappeared but Sapentia beat me too it. [Smoked] 'You take all you can.'

[Smoked] 'Evac?' someone asked.

Again, Sapentia spoke promptly. [Smoked] 'Finish this fight first, then both groups teleport out at same time. Players who outside, meet at jungle house tree for your ports home.'

That would include me, but what to do with my train? Run it off? Buffed as I was with my own *Swift as a Panther*, this was the obvious solution.

[Smoked] 'Dispersing my train. Watch out for returning mobs if you are on the ramp.'

Sprinting now, at maximum speed, weaving a path through the thin-trunked, bushy-headed trees, I easily pulled away from all the Anura chasing me. When their stomping and croaking had completely died away and I was certain that I had lost them, I curved my route to bring me back to our rendezvous. Only now could I relax. We'd done it. Even if Scarlet died, and there was no reason why she would, the shards were *Fastened* to her and she wouldn't even have to reclaim her body to find them in her inventory.

That had been some raid.

CHAPTER 31
BLACK HOLES AND MULTIPLE UNIVERSES

When I emerged from the game, I didn't just have to deal with the usual disorientation that came with swapping environments, there were a lot of people waiting for me and several rounds of cheering.

'Great job.'

'Best raid I was ever on.'

'Well done, man, proud to have been on that one.'

My back received several hard but well-intentioned slaps. My hand was shaken by earnest players with excited eyes and it took several minutes before I could reach the Den, where a smiling Braja gave me a wink. 'You know what you have to do.'

'No, what?'

'Say a few words.'

Although I had opened my mouth to object, to point out I was tired, that we were all tired, I closed it again. Braja was right and despite the fact it was about four in the morning, no one was really that exhausted, not when the prospect of victory and a big payoff was in the air.

This time, when I took the podium, there were several rounds of 'Tyro!' 'Tyro!' before the noise quelled enough for me to speak. While encouraging, of course, this display didn't warm my heart to any extent; this crowd were mostly fair-weather friends. As far as I knew, only Braja, Grythiss, Sapentia and Raitha were genuinely supportive of me and, curiously, as I scanned the room I noticed that although my real friends were all smiling, they were not joining in the chants. That was the way I preferred it.

'I hope you all enjoyed the raid.'

There was a big cheer. And it struck me how unusual it was to gather everyone together after a successful raid. Normally, we didn't even stay together online for that long, let alone meet up to celebrate.

'I'm glad to say that we've removed the only serious obstacle to our being able to produce *Arrows of Dragon Slaying*.'

Another cheer.

'There's still a certain amount of grinding and gathering to be done.'

Boos, of a mock-grievance sort.

'Within a week, Raitha and I will take those arrows and attempt to kill Mikarkathat. Then, we can all go home, having made history, saved *Epic Two*, and with a substantial bonus in our bank accounts.'

There was a huge cheer for that, as I had anticipated. And since there was no more positive message I could give, I hopped off the podium to more handshakes. One was from Watson. 'Fantastic job, Tyro, I knew I was right to stick with you.'

For a moment we met each other's gaze and while Watson's startling blue eyes carried pleasure and excitement in them, I also read something else. Judgment? Was he measuring me up? In any case, the jostling, enthusiastic crowd didn't allow him the opportunity to say anything else. With a nod, he stepped back, so that other players could come forward.

Having congratulated everyone who approached me and shaken their hands, the atmosphere in the Den calmed down, with most of the players taking a well-earned break from the game and - due to the late hour - leaving for their hotels. In front of me was Sapentia who took two steps and to my great surprise and no little embarrassment, gave me a very strong hug. Her scent; her soft breasts against my chest; I was bewildered.

'When you lead raids'—she broke off at last and I realized I hadn't taken a breath for the entire experience—'you are the man I came to find. Such a shame you are so young.'

'Does that matter?' My heart was sending waves of heat around my body and all the way to my ears. Even in the moments of crisis during the raid, I hadn't felt anything like this: a dizzying wave of hope and desire that nearly overwhelmed me.

Then, she simply said, 'Yes.' And I involuntarily let out a sigh, like I'd been punched in the stomach.

With a laugh, Sapentia took my arm. 'Come, let us drink coffee.'

Downstairs, Braja, Grythiss and Raitha were sitting together, so naturally Sapentia and I joined them.

'Welcome,' said Raitha, pulling out a chair for me. 'Braja was just explaining his theory of the universe.'

'Oh?' Sapentia raised one eyebrow sceptically. It was an impressive expression that must have taken her hours to practice.

'These peas are black holes.' Braja drew our attention to his plate. 'And inside each one is another universe.' He borrowed Grythiss's half-full plate and put a few peas on it. 'Now as you can see, each new universe has a different proportion of black holes. Some don't have any at all and these are dead ends. Some have too many and these collapse. Most are in the middle and have the potential to create life. It's an evolutionary mechanism at the level of multiple universes, but without having to invoke the quantum multiverse theory, which is of course nonsense.'

'Did I miss something?' I asked, looking from the peas to Braja and back. His moustache was twitching with amusement.

Raitha leaned over excitedly. 'Braja claimed to have an answer to the meaning of life and when I said that it cannot be explained why the universe - the laws of physics - are so precisely conducive to life, that there were mysteries beyond the boundaries of known science, he came up with this crazy theory.'

'His point, as I understand it,' muttered Grythiss, looking out from under his long fringe, 'is that life has no meaning. Nothing has been created with purpose.'

'Well...' Braja leaned back, satisfied. 'It's certainly a theory that puts things in perspective. Even what we are doing here and the success or failure of our raids. Despite all the excitement, it's really not that important. Not when you think about the enormity of the rise and fall of universes.'

'Ha! You are most foolish.' Grinning, Sapentia suddenly began squashing peas with the back of a fork she had picked up. 'We make our own meaning. And it is most important. People die for concepts like nation, race and gender. Concepts that do not matter to the universe but are everything to the individual.'

Braja immediately shot back at her, 'And what concept would you die for?'

'Not me. I do not die for any concept. For people, maybe.'

Braja shrugged. 'Fine. All I'm saying is that there is no need for Raitha's mystical notions about the universe.'

As though offended, though I knew he wasn't really, Raitha threw up his hands. 'You attempt to demean me, but I accept the label mystical with relish. Because there are deep mysteries when one contemplates the universe. It seems, however that my beliefs are shared by Sapentia. Because what matters in both her philosophy and mine is love.'

With a deep sigh, Grythiss looked at the two plates.

'Thinking about love?' I asked him.

'No.' He paused. 'My dinner.'

The following evening, my friends and I were gathered together near the *Tower of the Jewelled Skull*, staring incredulously from the cover of a copse at an army of hill giants: some fifty or more were camped on the hill, their bivouacs rising three stories high.

'This cannot be a coincidence,' observed Raitha.

Pulling back from the bush I had been hiding in, I turned to him. 'You mean, they are here to stop us?'

'Yes. After all, Port Placida was invaded soon after we used it.'

'You're right,' Braja sounded grim. 'We have an enemy within.'

'One of the Yuno team?' I asked him.

'Yep. Their intel is too good.'

Sapentia moved away from a tree she had been using to shield her from the view of the giants and joined us. 'It could just be most smart AI.'

With a shake of his head, long moustache swinging wide for emphasis, Braja disagreed. 'I don't think so. Because whoever is sabotaging us knows stuff that can only be gathered outside the game.'

'Like what?' Sapentia sounded curious rather than confrontational.

'Like where our spawn points are, what towns we are trading at and what zones we are playing.'

'What's their motive?' I was thinking of Blackridge. Even though that bull-headed man didn't hide how resentful he was of me, I couldn't see him wrecking the company that paid his wages.

With a tut, Braja's cleric avatar waved his mace at my head. Of course it couldn't damage me, since we hadn't enabled PvP. 'That's easy, you dope. Any of the other big games companies would pay to see *Epic Two* crash before launch.'

'Could it be Blackridge?' I wondered aloud.

'Possibly,' Braja's tone was thoughtful now. 'More likely a player though. Someone who doesn't lose anything. If the player was smart, they would have contacted Go Games or one of the others as soon as he was recruited by Yuno. Then he'd be earning double at least. Hey, Tuscl, you didn't do that, did you? Sell out to another company?'

There was a long silence and our shaman's avatar was absolutely still, a few strands of long hair being lifted by the breeze the only motion on her figure. 'I am offended. I will leave.'

Oh dear. I hurriedly intervened, 'Wait, wait. Braja, apologise please.'

'Sorry. But answer the question will you?'

'No is your answer. I am loyal to Yuno.'

'You are stupid, Braja.' Sapentia put an arm around Tuscl's shoulders. 'Only game AI could move armies around. Even devs have lost control.'

'Ah…maybe a traitor who is in communication with the dragon,' Braja muttered, not too confidently.

'And Tuscl. I trust you,' Sapentia continued forcefully. 'You are player who excels. But don't be loyal to Yuno. Be loyal to fellow players. It's important difference.'

'Why do you say that?' asked Raitha.

'Because we don't see the full picture. Because Japanese Blackcoin founders are behind the game.'

'Now you're being dumb,' said Braja, who sounded hurt. If I knew anything about Braja, it was that he felt a need to match himself intellectually to those who had a better education than he had, so he would have been particularly stung by Sapentia calling him stupid. 'Yuno are paying us and are going to give a decent bonus that I, for one, need. Their cause is our cause.'

Before Sapentia could reply - and I heard her draw a deep breath as she readied herself for the argument - I stepped in. 'Let's not argue any more. We need more information. I'll go chat to the giants and find out what I can. Meanwhile, Raitha, can you look up another zone for us to level up to fifty please?'

'Good idea. I shall unclip and read the guide.'

'Wait just one moment, before you do, can we all agree that Tuscl is one of us: that we trust her?' I knew I did, simply from her commitment and effort during our raids.

'Agreed,' said Sapentia at once.

'Agreed,' from Raitha.

'Lizardman proud to be in same group as Tussscl the ssshaman.'

All of us turned to Braja. 'Agreed. I'm sorry I suggested otherwise, Tuscl, I sometimes get carried away with conspiracy theories.'

'Is okay. I understand.' Her reply eased my fear we'd lose her from the team.

Happy that our group was in accord, I swapped my gear for the pirate clothes, then, with a wave farewell, backtracked down the hill until I found the path up to the tower.

Two giants, holding enormous, thick clubs stood guard as I approached their camp. Both were looking at me and I raised an arm in what I hoped they understood to be a gesture of greeting and peaceful intention. They raised their clubs in a gesture that seemed to have the opposite meaning. Oh well.

When I was just out of reach of their weapons, I stopped and smiled. 'Good evening, friends. I have a message from Mikarkathat for your leader.'

'What's his name?' the giant on my left leered at me.

'Pardon?'

'How come you don't know the name of King Rock-thrack? You said leader instead.'

'You idiot,' said the other giant. 'Now you've told him King Rockthrack's name, we can't test him.'

'Well, we just kill him then.'

The second giant grunted with approval.

'Gentlemen, or wait, on closer scrutiny, I mean gentleman and lady. This is no way to greet an ally and friend of the dragon...'

Before I could say another word, the giant on my left (the male) leapt up and gave me the most enormous wallop with his club, the rushing sound of it descending made me feel like I was caught in a whirlwind, that and the fact I'd been knocked over.

You have been hit by a club for 0 damage.

You have been affected by *Knockback* and are stunned.

Both giants watched with curiosity as, after several seconds passed and the stun wore off, I stood up. 'Giant hospitality is...'

Then the female smacked me down.

You have been hit by a club for 0 damage.

You have been affected by *Knockback* and are stunned.

[Channel Scarlet/Klytotoxos] 'Hi, I'm glad you are clipped up. I have that raid loot for you.'

[Channel Scarlet/Klytotoxos] 'Thanks. I'll get back to you soon. Just in the middle of something here.'

'Tell me,' I said, this time stepping away from the guards. 'Why are all you giants here?'

Then I triggered *Read Thoughts* on the female, whom I was looking directly at.

The giant is thinking that she is here to stop Blackcoin Seekers. She is not sure if you are a Blackcoin Seeker. She is surprised to see you stand up again apparently unhurt.

'To squash half-elves in silly hats,' said the male giant and then made a noise that I first thought was a roar of anger but quickly realised was a laugh.

'Ahh. In that case, I'll be off. It's been a pleasant conversation. Goodbye.'

Unexpectedly, they let me back away without trying to chase me. That was a shame, because we would have probably gained some juicy experience if I could have drawn them away from their army. When I was out of sight, I ducked back into the woods and found my way to the copse in which the full group was waiting.

'I have somewhere!' Raitha said enthusiastically.

'Where?'

'The snow-covered mountain passes of Fang Island.'

'Sounds good.' I'd noticed them before, of course, but hadn't read up in too much detail about the region.

'Ssounds cold.'

Undeterred by the murmur of our lizardman tank, Raitha carried on enthusiastically. 'We'll be able to use our *Read Tracks* spell to find bears, lynx and snow spiders, all mobs in their low fifties.'

'Right.' I trusted him to find us a region in which we could safely and efficiently level up. In all probability too, Fang Island was far enough away from the dragon and her armies that they wouldn't bother us or even notice our activities. 'Sapentia, can you teleport us to the nearest stone ring to Fang Island?'

'I need some gold to buy that one.'

'That reminds me to collect the raid loot. Excuse me, I'm going into private chat with Scarlet.'

[Channel Klytotoxos/Scarlet] 'Hi Scarlet, sorry for earlier, I was in the middle of trying to talk to a pair of giants.'

[Channel Klytotoxos/Scarlet] 'No worries.' She gave a little laugh. 'Sounds fun. Shall I just link the items?'

[Channel Klytotoxos/Scarlet] 'Sure and did you get any coin?'

[Channel Klytotoxos/Scarlet] 'I did, a hundred and thirty gold.'

[Channel Klytotoxos/Scarlet] 'Great.'

[Channel Klytotoxos/Scarlet] '*Macuahuitl. Macuahuitl. Breastplate of the Smoke God. Gauntlets of the Smoke God.*'

[Channel Klytotoxos/Scarlet] 'Thanks.'

With a flick of my index finger I pulled up the pop-ups on the items. Both of the god's weapons were +2, which was handy. They had good damage-to-speed ratios, nearly as good as a longsword (but not quite, meaning that they were not an upgrade on Grythiss's longsword with its blessing from Nemain). Still, the fact the Smoke God's drops were categorised as blunt weapons rather than sharp meant that not only could they be used by clerics but also that they would come in handy against certain types of mob where sharp weapons did reduced damage. I'd give one to Grythiss to have in reserve for such fights and the other to Braja.

The breastplate was sweet, +4 AC, *Resist Fire*, and +3 spirit regeneration, which made it ideal for a tank with spells, aka Grythiss. The fact that it was weight 0 was interesting too and something that might become important should Grythiss ever become overburdened with gear. Lastly, the gauntlets (which were also weight 0) were +2 AC and *Resist Fire*. These I'd assign to Sapentia, in case she found herself in a wizard's duel and needing to mitigate fire-based spells.

After a bit of hopping around to collect these drops and get the spell Sapentia needed, our group arrived at a frosty stone ring on a small island in the cold, northern seas. Across a short but bleak and dangerous-looking stretch of water was Fang

Island proper, a dozen severe mountains stretching as black silhouettes against the stars, right up from the water's edge, covered in moonlit snow from peak to base. A wind swirled flakes of ice around us and a message appeared on my UI.

You are experiencing the condition *Bitter Cold*. You are unaffected.

'*Bitter Cold*,' said Sapentia.

'Same,' came a chorus of the rest of the group.

'What does it do?' I asked. 'I'm immune.'

Braja grumbled, 'I wish I was a vampire.'

'"You cannot regenerate health or spirit until you are warmer."' It was Raitha who read out the effects of the condition.

'I see. Well, perhaps we can buy a tent or make a fire later, when we have set up to fight.'

Grythiss, who looked absolutely splendid in his new breastplate (it was a shiny grey that shouted of magic in the way the fine scrollwork constantly changed, as though the metal were slowly swirling about him), shook his head. 'Lizardman hatesss this already. Letss's get it over with.'

'Warmer climes for you, eh, my cold-blooded friend?' I gave him a pat. 'Come on then.'

A short trail made where the island's half-covering of moss had been worn down to the shale beneath led us down to the water's edge. There, on a shingle beach, where grey waves slurped over slick, black lumps of rock, a damp-looking jetty pointed towards Fang Island and at the end of the construction was a copper bell, turned dark green with age and salt water. With just a glance at me first, Raitha skipped out to the bell, found the clapper and gave it a good strong pull. The resulting chime was surprisingly loud, echoing off the rocks. He kept it up, until I waved at him. There was motion on the far shore.

Across the waves was a settlement of dark huts, roofs covered in snow and so natural in appearance as to seem part of the landscape. A flicker or two of light and a few streams of smoke, barely discernible against the night sky, indicated life and warmth, as did the boat being rowed over towards us.

It took perhaps thirty minutes before the slender craft drew

405

up beside the jetty, where Raitha was thrown a rope by a greasy-bearded dwarf who was clad in a dirty-white fur coat. A young human boy, in fur waistcoat, leapt from the back of the boat to secure it with another rope. While the waves lifted and dropped the ferry, the dwarf shouted across at us. 'Come on then, while the weather's good.'

'Thisss iss good?' Grythiss spat towards the sea.

'How much?' I asked.

'A gold each.'

'We'll pay four gold for the lot of us.'

'Eh? Five.'

'Deal.' Having moved to the jetty I jumped down and handed over the coins. We had to economise, I only had fifty-four gold left and while I suppose I could have rounded up all the spare coins from the hundreds of players assisting us and gathered together a reasonable stash, I didn't want the time delay and hassle of having to do so.

'Soft southerners, are you?' The dwarf was looking at the design on the gold coin and then back at us.

'That's it.' I took a seat.

'Two of you have to row.'

'I shall be one of them,' offered Raitha, climbing in, then leaning over to me with a whisper added, 'I got the rowing skill from when we went to your vampire island and should like to improve it. Even though we are not long for this game.'

'Lizardman takesss other oar. Will keep me warm.'

When we were all settled, the dwarf cast off the ropes and jumped down into the craft, facing me as he pulled his oar. His avatar was incredibly detailed, from the watery, grey eyes, to the rawness of his cheeks above the beard line. And that beard: a mass of unkempt brown and grey hair, looking as stiff as wire.

'You're not here for gold and gems, are you?' he asked with a frown.

'No, furs. We are hunters.' I nodded to the bow at my feet.

Grunting approvingly, the dwarf's face became more re-laxed, bored even.

As the boat rode up and down the black waves, I talked to the ferry owner and found out what I could about the settlement and our hunting prospects. Golden Valley was a free town: no lord or theocrat ruled there. Mostly dwarves, who were mining the gold in the mountains, there were also humans and a few gnomes. They got visitors like us, usually via the stone rings on Little Island, who came to trade for their furs and gold.

Although I tried to evoke a quest or two, either this dwarf didn't have any or I hadn't used the right phrases.

We disembarked at another wooden jetty and looked around. There were perhaps thirty buildings in a town protected by a large stockade, with a dozen of them well-lit and open. I could make out the nature of the businesses from the signs in front of some of them: two inns; a furrier; an ironmonger; a potter and a food store.

'We need place to set our spawn points,' Sapentia reminded me. So we walked along the main street, while she checked. Usually, spawn points were at town halls, or churches, or a place like a central fountain.

We were passing a building with a tall wooden steeple and several Holy images over the door.

'Here.' Our wizard led the way in and one after another we tramped through an unlocked door to a wide hall. I was about to wipe my muddy boots on the mat, when I found that my foot wouldn't carry over the entrance. Nor my hands. It was like I was pressing against an invisible glass wall.

'Can I help you?' a dwarf with the garb of a fighting cleric (metal hauberk beneath a wide red beard, mace at his belt) came over to the others and shot me a suspicious glance.

'We wish to make this the place that we respawn in the event of our deaths,' said Raitha politely.

The dwarf just looked blankly at him.

Raising her arms, Sapentia ignored the cleric. 'I cast now.' Blue light encased Tuscl and then a chime let us know her respawn point was now in this church. The same effect soon was evident for everyone else. Except me.

'Come closer,' Sapentia instructed me. Except by now I was sure I wouldn't be able to use the church as a respawn point. As though to emphasise my conclusion, the dwarf became more animated, walking over to just in front of me and holding out a silver necklace, on which dangled a hammer.

'I don't seem able to cross the threshold.'

'I invite you in, Tyro, I mean Klytotoxos,' Raitha had obviously realised that the problem was my being a vampire. Clearly, he was hoping that the trope of the vampire myth about the undead creature needing an invitation to enter a house applied in *Epic 2*. It probably wouldn't have worked, as I'd been in plenty of town buildings without invites. In any case, we didn't find out as the cleric shouted with an impressively deep voice.

'Begone, foul creature of the night!'

You have been *Turned*. You must flee as long as this condition lasts.

And I was off, rushing as fast as I could out of the porch and away through the town, the laughter of Braja ringing out behind me.

[Group] 'Hah, hah, hah! Oh man, you should have seen the look of panic on your face. I've got to try that trick.'

By the time I stopped, I was cowered against the northernmost part of the stockade.

Braja asked, [Group] 'Can you make me group leader? There is a quest here from this cleric, for those of us who aren't foul and evil.'

[Group] 'Sure. But if only he knew.'

A moment later we had the quest *Gather Erisia*, which, the pop-up said, was a challenge to find a very rare plant with healing properties.

[Group] 'You know,' said Raitha, 'I'm enjoying this. It is a great shame that we are in a rush and just here to grind. I like this rough, isolated community and if I were playing the game for fun, would work through all the quests here.'

[Group] 'Grrrr,' replied Grythiss.

Sapentia spoke, [Group] 'Speaking of cold. Shop here sells cloaks. Do we have much coin?'

[Group] 'I've fifty-four gold left, I think. I've also got some emeralds though.' I started walking back down the main street, somewhat anxious whenever I passed a dwarf, pulling my hood up to make sure my face was in shadows. Probably, it was the fact that I couldn't enter the temple that had alerted the cleric, but had he already warned other citizens about me? I didn't want the whole town to go on a vampire hunt.

On finding my friends outside a furriers, Braja grinned broadly at me making sure to rub it in that I'd just been *Turned* by an NPC. I gave Sapentia my gold and gems. 'You go in. I'd better wait outside.'

While I waited, looking at the bright stars between the rooftops, I could hear muted voices and my friends tramping over the floorboards. Then came a new quest message: *Furs for Algernon*. For twenty, high-quality lynx furs we would get a cloak: +1 AC, +1 beauty, removes *Bitter Cold* condition. It was repeatable.

When the rest of the group tramped out, they looked a lot more impressive than when they'd gone in. All were now wearing fur cloaks that seemed to enhance their stature, not through magic, but through the way that they all appeared lordly, like the entourage of a prince on a northern hunting expedition.

'Here.' Sapentia gave me a cloak, twelve gold coins and just two emeralds (really? Only two left? These cloaks were expensive). I put it on.

You no longer have the condition *Bitter Cold*.

'Happier now, Grythiss?' I asked. He just grunted by way of reply.

Our imposing-looking group marched through the town, attracting attention from the dwarves, gnomes and humans we passed. Where the street met the north wall of the stockade was a gate and the four guards - two dwarves, two humans looking like Vikings - let us out without question.

'Where to?' I asked, looking at Raitha.

'Let's move away from the town, just a mile or so, and try our tracking.'

For the next twenty minutes we tramped over heather and stone. There was a cart track to follow, two lines of pale dirt between heather on which rested ice and clumps of snow. The route meandered as it went towards the interior of the island, always rising and sometimes bringing us close to a fast-flowing, cold river that had cut a steep notch into the land. There were very few trees, several bushes and always I felt I was being watched by the huge mountains that rose up steeply ahead.

'Here, let us set up.' Raitha left the track for a slight rise, which gave us a good view in all directions. While Tuscl buffed us and then slotted battle spells, I called up my own list of spells.

'Oh,' I said, 'let me try *Refreshing Camp.*'

Having slotted the spell and waited a moment for it to become active, I then stared at it on the UI long enough for it to trigger. My avatar waved his arms around, a green light sprang from my fingers and we had a ready-made fire, complete with a large pot of hot stew. Warm blood in the pot would have been more helpful to my character, but no doubt less appealing to the others who now hurriedly gathered to feed themselves.

'What a great spell,' I congratulated myself.

'How long does it last?' asked Braja.

'An hour per ten levels, so nearly five hours.'

'Good,' said Grythiss, sitting on a rock and almost looking comfortable with a thick, warm cloak around him and bowl of soup in hand.

While the others ate, I swapped my spells around. Obviously, I needed *Swift as a Panther*, also, if I were creeping up on a pull, I'd want *Gather Shadow.* Since reaching level 46 I'd gained *Swiftshot II*, the upgrade to the very useful archery enhancement *Swiftshot*, so that was another important one. I had two more and the contenders were *Heat Arrow* (33), *Frost Arrow* (34), *Find Path* (44), *Read Tracks* (38) and *Spark* (30). One had to be *Read Tracks* and for the other I took *Find Path.* Tempted as I was to work on my mobile casting skill with *Spark*, I was a little anxious that in this dark, unfamiliar landscape I could easily end up pulling mobs from so far away from my friends that I couldn't locate them.

Comparing notes with Raitha, I found that he had done exactly the same.

'All set?' I asked and to a background of nods and people saying 'yes', I cast *Read Tracks*. As I looked around, a new layer of imagery lay over my vision. With delicate glowing light marking them, I could see tracks, dozens of tracks. You never would have expected so many in such a bleak environment and when I focused on one particular set, kneeling over a paw print in the snow, I obtained information in a pop up: Lynx, *Dangerous*.

[Group] 'Tracking a Lynx here. Raitha, I suggest you find a pull too, whoever brings one back first, the other circles until the group are ready. Hopefully, we'll be bringing mobs non-stop when we find our rhythm.'

[Group] 'Snow Spider tracks to the west of us for me then.'

It was a real pleasure to run across the bleak, northern landscape, under bright stars (both moons were up but their direct light was blocked by the mountains) scanning for my prey and for other possible dangers. Coming over a rise, I saw a Lynx walking away from me, head down, sniffing the ground. With my *Boots of Dark Elvenkind* I was confident I could sneak closer. As silently as I could, I crept up, into bow range, then fired. It didn't matter that I missed, the Lynx turned towards me and with a snarl of anger, rushed over the rough terrain with the obvious intention of sinking its two large incisors into my body.

[Group] 'Incoming! A Lynx.'

[Group] 'And I've pulled a Snow Spider. I'll kite it until you're done with the Lynx.'

As I might have expected, the Lynx was fast and I only reached my friends ahead of it thanks to my *Swift as a Panther* buff. An arrow that had missed had hardly any aggro compared to the impact of Grythiss's purple-skull-effect spell and with a roar the Lynx swerved to claw at him. For a few seconds it was a fair fight, but then Tuscl landed a debuff and a *Slow*, while Braja kept Grythiss's hit points from declining too swiftly. I chipped in with some arrow damage and when the Lynx was around 35 per cent, Sapentia let loose with her nukes.

The Lynx is dead. You gain experience.

411

My experience bar moved fractionally. About twenty of these would be needed for 48.

Raitha called out, [Group] 'Incoming! A Snow Spider.'

[Group] 'Lizardman findsss poor quality fur as loot.'

With a laugh, Braja said, [Group] 'Well, that's hardly surprising given the scorch marks on the pelt.'

[Group] 'I do not have delicate spells,' replied Sapentia.

As Raitha arrived, I departed, running northwards, pausing to cast *Read Tracks*. This time, I located the trail of an *impossible* Lynx and had it in my wake when the others finished the Snow Spider.

The Snow Spider is dead. You gain experience.

[Group] 'Incoming! A Lynx.'

There was a lot to be said for playing a warrior in *Epic*. There was even more to be said for playing a hunter in *Epic 2*, especially if you had a hunter partner and an effective group who could keep up their concentration and maximise their use of spirit and hit points. For the next two hours or so we had non-stop action and it almost became a challenge between Raitha and I to deliver our next mob just as Grythiss straightened up from having looted the last one.

Eventually, having comfortably reached level 48 and with Grythiss holding five high-quality Lynx pelts and eleven Snow Spider silks, I called a halt. We'd cleared out all the mobs around the area and although there were a few still evident from my tracking spell, they were some distance away. It would be better to move up the valley and find a new camp.

It was midnight. In game, the weather was clear, the night sky (that part of it not obscured by the gigantic peaks) filled with an incredible display of glittering stars. Our breath came in clouds.

'That was terrific.'

'Lizardman enjoyed it. Desspite cold.'

'I enjoyed it very much too and I'd like you all to consider revisiting a decision we made some days ago,' said Raitha. 'If Yuno let us keep our current characters after the launch of the game, perhaps we should stay in *Epic 2*. There are dozens of unexplored regions like this one, where we would be the first to make discoveries, solve quests, find items. And I find I relish the role of hunter more than I do my warrior.'

'I do too,' I replied. 'Let's unclip, take a break and discuss this. For me, it's not an easy choice because I spent four years creating Tyro and there are still some raid events I haven't experienced.'

When we resumed, an hour later, we still hadn't resolved whether to play *Epic* or *Epic 2* in the future. I was sitting on the fence. It certainly did appeal to me that none of the regions of *Epic 2* were explored. Take Fang Island. You could stay here all the way up to level 70. There were dozens of interesting storylines to follow, many of them leading to a Frost Giant castle high in the mountains. And this was just one region out of about twenty for levels 50 - 70. Then, too, Braja's observation that there would be more money in my broadcasting *Epic 2* streams than *Epic* ones had brought a new consideration into play for me. In favour of swapping were Raitha and Braja and perhaps me. Against were Sapentia and Tuscl (who had a maxed-out shaman build on *Epic*). What was heartening about the discussion was the sentiment we all shared that whatever choice we made, we'd stick together.

After our discussion and snacks, on re-entering the game we pushed on northwards up a valley that rose steeply towards a pass on the shoulder of a ridge between two peaks. We were soon walking through snow, which obscured the cart track. Partially out of curiosity and partly because it would be wise to stick to the track (I was concerned about ditches and even more alarming falls being hidden by the snow), I slotted *Find Path* into my UI, a level 44 spell, and tried it for the first time. Immediately, the meandering route glowed with a comforting yellow colour. Since the buff would now stay in place for an hour, I swapped *Find Path* out of a spell slot again. No need to take up a valuable slot with a buff that I could refresh again later if I wanted to.

On the ridge itself, a strong wind pulled at our cloaks and hair. Beyond it, I had thought I might see the frozen seas that were supposed to lie north of us. Fang Island was not that big, maybe twenty kilometres by thirty, so at this height, we should be able to see well beyond the far coast. There was, however, after a dip, another rise, to an even higher ridge.

'Let's backtrack a little, out of the wind and set up.'

'There?' Grythiss pointed to a large boulder, which would make for a good landmark.

'Perfect.'

Soon, we were back into grinding mode, this time pulling slightly tougher Lynxes and Snow Spiders, along with some new mobs: Varwolfs (a larger, shaggier wolf); Snowtrolls and Eochar. The latter were gleaming, translucent oval-shaped figures which floated over the snow. To my mind, they had the quality of the northern lights, if you could somehow capture the lights in tall glass. Apparently, they cast illusions, though I was unaffected. So for safety, Raitha left all those pulls to me. Now and again, Grythiss stopped fighting when faced with an Eochar, saying his attack button was greyed out and the mob appeared like a friendly lizardman, but as soon as one of my arrows struck home, the effect broke. The Eochar drained hit points with a magical attack that looked like tendrils of pale blue and green, flickering around their target. Their rare drop was a *Fragment of Frozen Light*, which I vaguely recalled was a trade skill item.

Another two hours of this, with a much better drop rate on the high-quality Lynx pelts (we gained another nine), I hit 49.

'Congratulations!' Braja gave me a heavy slap on the back, while Raitha held out his fist for a knuckle slap, which I gave him.

'It's hard to believe I'm so close to fifty.'

Sapentia said, 'Should get there if we stay late. We get finished tonight.'

'Yeah. I'll almost be sorry to stop after that though. I was hoping to explore more of this island. At least until we get a sight of the Frost Giant castle.'

Although we were all tired, we decided to keep going without a break. Partly for the sake of driving Raitha and me towards the crucial 50 while we had a good set-up for the grind, but also to promote Sapentia, who was just a fraction short of 51.

I was a fair way off our camp, tracking an Eochar (although they floated, they left a faint set of thin lines, like someone had been brushing the snow), when Raitha called out, [Group] 'Tyro, are you seeing Ketzi on track?'

[Group] 'Checking.' And I paused to cast *Read Tracks*. 'No, is it a named mob? NPC? What does it con?'

[Group] 'Probably an NPC I think, wearing boots from the marks in the snow. Cons impossible.'

[Group] 'Interesting, I'll come over.'

It would be a shame to spoil a great night's progress with a wipe, especially because I wouldn't even respawn on Fang Island, which would set us back at least an hour before we could get going again. My death would probably postpone the big five-o until tomorrow. All the same, too much grinding made Tyro a dull boy.

Firstly, I tracked back across the shoulder of the mountains to Raitha, with a wave to the group as I ran past them. Then I cast *Read Tracks* once more and this time Ketzi was high on the list of mobs I could see, his name in red, to signify he was more than five levels higher than me.

'Shall we?' asked Raitha.

'You go ahead, I'll wait here. If he's lethal, I'd rather leave you to die because you'll respawn in Golden Valley at least.'

'Wait. That's odd.' Raitha had run forward a few paces, then stopped. 'It ends here. Oh.' It looked like Raitha had tripped, for all of a sudden he was on his hands and knees. The trail of boot marks began to move.

[Group] 'Anyone got *See Invisible?*' I asked.

[Group] 'I have. It will take a minute to slot.' This was Sapentia, I ran back towards her.

[Group] 'Ketzi is moving south!' shouted Raitha excitedly. 'I'm following him.'

I ran back to the camp, with occasional glances over my shoulder to keep an eye on Raitha's path as he ran down the slope.

'Set?'

Sapentia was sitting cross-legged. 'Not yet.'

Already Raitha was a small figure.

'Now.' Our wizard stood up and a flash of white light sprang from her fingers, dazzling me momentarily. Even as my vision cleared, I started running.

[Group] 'I see him!' I shouted. 'An Elven rogue or assassin. Leather armour. Two swords on his back. You are right on top of him Raitha. Be careful. Wait, he's stopped.'

With leaps and bounds over the rocks, I quickly caught up with Raitha and pointed to the Elf, practically touching him. 'He's right here. Standing completely still.'

Even stranger, the rogue was not looking at me, or at anywhere in particular. His eyes had that glazed look that you see when a player character unclips from the game and their avatar remains in place for a minute afterwards. Then he was gone.

My thoughts whirled around for a moment before settling on the obvious conclusion. [Group] 'He's gone. Unclipped. It was a player.'

Sapentia sounded as confused as I felt. [Group] 'I saw him too. But what player called Ketzi exists? Higher level than fifty-six?'

[Group] 'Someone from Yuno?' I wondered aloud. 'A dev?' Then to Raitha, 'Let's go back.'

As we returned to the group over the snow (the tracking ball admirably emulating the soft impact of my feet) Raitha said, 'This is interesting. I wonder how long someone has been spying on us?'

'You think he was a spy?'

'I do.'

'For who?'

'Let's ask our friends, for my part, I cannot imagine.'

[Group] 'Supposing Ketzi was here to watch us,' I said, 'who is he working for?'

[Group] 'Aha!' cried Braja triumphantly. 'You all thought I was paranoid. I told you the dragon's intel was too good. That's what's been happening. A PC is working on their side and following us around invisibly.'

[Group] 'I told you I was not a traitor,' said Tuscl.

[Group] 'Of course, of course. I'm sorry about that.' By now Raitha and I had returned to the others and I could see Braja patting our shaman.

Raitha said, 'It makes some sense. We would never have noticed someone invisible watching us until we had snow and tracking spells up.'

'What do you think, Sapentia?' I asked.

She shook her head. 'I need time to understand. And more information. We must speak to Watson. Who else can access the game? Where and how?'

'Shall we unclip and go see him?'

'Yes. But not now. Let's finish the reason why we are here.'

There was a murmur of assent at this.

For the next ninety minutes we hunted Lynx, Spiders and Eochar, Raitha and I pulling them to the killing spot where we dispatched the mobs with increasing rapidity. Slowly my experience bar edged closer and closer to 50. Yet my previous pleasure in running over the snow of this bleak but beautiful northern wilderness was significantly diminished by the thoughts running through my head.

Who was Ketzi? A player, obviously, not an NPC. That was certain from the way in which he had unclipped. An NPC might have been able to teleport away from us, but that would have involved the use of a ring or spell, rather than standing vacant and immobile. He was not on the leader board. That meant either Yuno had more players in the game than they had admitted or someone had found a way to access the game. The former seemed very possible, likely even because presumably Yuno team members had been playtesting the game for months before we were brought in. The latter was unlikely. In fact, I'd never heard of anyone being able to hack into *Epic*, so to be able to do so for an unreleased game seemed next-to-impossible. Sapentia was right, we needed to talk to Watson.

At last, about twenty minutes after Raitha, at around four in the morning, I hit 50. The cheers from my friends were genuine and lifted my spirits again.

'What now?' asked Braja.

'We go see Watson,' Sapentia replied.

'Agreed. First, though, I suggest you go back to Golden Valley to hand in the furs for the cloak and sell the junk drops. Meanwhile, Sapentia could you port me to near Safehaven? I want to skill up my archery to max during daylight hours, so I thought I'd set up in those pirate caves.'

With the others in accord, Sapentia dropped me off at an ancient stone monument and I ran swiftly north-east through the forest in which I'd been born. Both moons were on the descent and to my vampire eyes, the trees were all silver on their eastern sides. Everything was still, except for the occasional angry, skittering of a partridge as my foot landed too close to a bush in which the bird was sleeping. Then, at one point, I came across a wolf in a clearing, nosing over a dead fawn. He turned large yellow eyes onto me before walking slowly away, with a noticeable limp. Surely he wasn't the one I had released? I felt almost nostalgic for those early hours in the game, when I had nothing but my trap setting skill to allow me to advance.

Back at the pirate caves, normal service had been resumed. They had a full respawn, although not, I noticed, with a tiger in the prison. All of the pirates ignored me. I was so high a level that they wouldn't aggro unless provoked. Unfortunately for them, I did have to provoke one, drinking his blood so as to remove the warning that had started to pop up about an hour earlier. It occurred to me to loot the captain again. Those magical cords could prove handy, even at this stage when all that remained was to fire four arrows at the dragon. There was a journey ahead to her lair and a wind at our backs might help if we were flying, as I imagined we would be. The captain himself was not in his room so I searched the secret compartment, found the box and looted four emeralds and two diamonds. When I went to pick up the rope, however, I got the message:

Cord of Summon Winds. You may only have one of these items in your possession.

Oh well, Raitha could loot it later.

I was about to settle down with my UI and allocate my new attribute points, when Sapentia spoke. [Group] 'We are all done. Unclipping. See you soon.'

My UI and my archery training ground could wait until the morning. It was time to find out what was going on behind the scenes in Yuno.

CHAPTER 32
ENTER, THE DRAGON

When my friends and I walked into the Den, Katherine was there along with two other players I didn't know. She glanced at the board and gave me a warm smile. 'Well done. That was quick.'

'Thanks,' I said. 'I don't suppose Watson is here?'

'Oh no. He won't be in until nine.' Her face became sombre. 'Can I help with something.'

'You know the name Ketzi?' asked Sapentia.

'No. Why?' Katherine replied with a shake of her head and I believed her; there was no reaction when the question was asked.

'There's a player of that name, who isn't on our board,' I said. I was conscious that there were two other players nearby, listening with interest. Still, I didn't want to leave the building with my head buzzing with questions.

'That's...I wouldn't say impossible but it shouldn't be the case.' Again, I felt Katherine was in earnest. That or she was a great liar. I knew plenty of those, everyone in my class, basically, me included, so I knew how well people could dissemble. All the same, I reckoned this news was a surprise to her.

'How is it possible?' Tuscl took a step forward and placed her hands on the side of the great table, leaning over towards Katherine, her long black hair falling forward.

'In theory, some of our staff would be able to create a character that wasn't visible on the board. It would be a violation of their contracts though. A disciplinary offense, dismissible even.'

'Such a person might have a job waiting for them at Go Games and not care.' Braja too came closer, his strong, fit frame tense.

'I don't think...I mean, we'd notice. There are only so many rigs and if someone who wasn't on the board was playing the game for a long time...'

'Eureka!' exclaimed Raitha, silencing Katherine and causing everyone to turn to him. Rather sheepishly lowering his voice, Raitha said, 'Do we have CCTV here or on the building door? Can we see who left their rig sometime between two and half two?'

'Good idea!' I gave Raitha a thumbs up.

Katherine nodded and her smile was restored. 'We can check that. Come with me.'

Our whole group followed her out of the Den and I'm sure that the two other players wanted to come too. Down the lift we went, no one speaking in the confined space, and past the trees of the ground floor foyer to a large desk where there were two security guards.

'Hello Kevin, Martha,' said Katherine. 'Can you check level fourteen cameras between two and two-thirty please, we are looking for someone who left a rig and possibly the building at that time.'

Very eager to assist, the middle-aged Kevin got out of his seat and stood behind Martha as she navigated through a large group of camera views and, when satisfied, rapidly ran them backwards in time. We all gathered close around, feeling entitled to go behind the desk under these circumstances and there was a palpable sense of excitement in the hushed conversation and the concentration with which we gave the images.

'Number four,' muttered Kevin.

'Got it,' his partner replied.

The fourth screen showed that at 2:10 a.m., a young woman came out of the Den, used the elevator and subsequently left the building. I'd seen her around but didn't know her name. At 2:14, the bulky lad who had tried to intimidate me, the Blackridge loyalist whom Braja had brushed aside as easily as a cobweb, came into view walking away from a corridor that contained rigs. He too was shown soon afterwards walking rapidly through the foyer and out of the building.

'My money's on him,' muttered Braja, pointing.

'I remember both of these two leaving, Ms Demnayako,' said Kevin, and Martha nodded too. 'It's quiet enough here at this time.'

'I see. Nothing unusual about their behaviour?'

'Nothing,' Martha replied and glanced over her shoulder at Kevin, who confirmed with a quick nod.

'Flag their passes please and ask them to report to Mr Watson when they come in next. And…' Katherine hesitated.

Both security staff looked at her with avid concentration, clearly eager to know what was happening. For them, this was probably the most interesting event that had occurred in months.

'…we have no legal right to detain them but I would very much appreciate it if Mr Watson had the opportunity to ask them a few questions, in the event that they try to leave right away.'

The older of the security pair nodded. Martha said, 'Understood. Perhaps it would be best if we said that the passes were out of date and gave them this form to take to Mr Watson.' She opened a drawer and found the sheets of paper she wanted.

'Perfect, thank you.' Then Katherine turned to us. 'There. We should get some answers in the morning.'

When I got to my hotel room, I didn't think I'd sleep, what with my desire to find out if one of those two players was Ketzi and if so, what he or she hoped to gain from spying on us. Also, I was starving. Yet by the time I'd typed up half an email to Mum, letting her know that I'd reached level 50 and hoped to finish the project soon, I found myself yawning. Signing off with a quick, 'love Tom', I finished up and stretched out on the wide bed.

During a troubled night's sleep I dreamed mostly of school. For once the canteen was serving decent food: Chinese dumplings; fried noodles; peanut sauce. Delicious. When I went to sit down, an entire row of tables had 'reserved' signs on them, though the only people there were Watson and Blackridge. Since all the other seats in the hall were occupied I put my tray down opposite Watson. With a frown, Blackridge shook his head and a moment later Watson copied him. So I walked around with my food and, as far as I could remember in the morning, never did get to eat that dinner.

We met in the foyer, Sapentia putting back the games industry magazine she was leafing through and leading the way with her usual defiant stride. We filled the lift: myself, Raitha, Tuscl, Sapentia, Grythiss and Braja. Quite an intimidating group really and I wondered what Watson would make of us. If he were in.

His secretary gave us a warm smile, clearly undeterred by our solemn expressions, and yes, he was in and could see us right away.

While Tuscl and Grythiss looked around Watson's room with interest and especially at the vivid blue sea view, Sapentia walked right up to his desk and leaned forward towards him. 'We have spy. Traitor!'

'Oh.' The gleaming white teeth that had been on show as Watson had watched us enter disappeared. Instead of his jovial smile we had surprised anxiety. Neither expression seemed sincere. 'What do you mean?'

'Didn't Katherine tell you?' I asked. 'Two people left the building around two a.m. last night. One of them is playing a character who is spying on us and is not on the board.'

'Oh, that. Those two aren't spies. Or traitors. Or anything but players.'

Braja spoke next, 'Are you saying neither of them is Ketzi?'

Although Watson gestured towards seats (he only had two near the desk but there was a couch further off), all of us remained standing.

'Correct.'

'Who is then?' Braja had on his poker face.

With a heavy breath, Watson leaned back. 'Let's just take

stock a moment. Before we go any further, I should say congratulations on level fifty. You've done extremely well; better than anyone could have hoped. And with Scarlet at 295 Bowyer skill, we can hope to launch as per our last public announcement.'

'Yes, yes, indeed.' Raitha was wringing his hands. 'But we are all agog to know about Ketzi, can you please just inform us on that subject.'

'Agog?' Grythiss let out a snort of amusement.

All at once, the tension in the room vanished and even Braja was smiling.

Blushing somewhat, Raitha said, 'It is the correct term. We cannot bear to hear about anything other than on the subject of Ketzi. We are agog.'

'What is a gog?' asked Tuscl, confused.

'It's a kind of small Orc.' I couldn't help myself.

'Tyro,' Sapentia rounded on me. 'That is not helping.'

'Sorry Tuscl, I'm joking. It's an old-fashioned term to mean someone is in a state of excitement.'

'It is not old-fashioned in Kerala,' muttered Raitha.

'Ketzi,' said Watson, gaining everyone's attention, 'is unknown to me. My guess, though, is that the game's funders have been monitoring your progress. After all, they have invested hundreds of millions of dollars.'

'You mean Kiro,' said Sapentia.

'I do, or not exactly. When he was project manager, Kiro's avatar was called Kraken. Ketzi might not be him in person. But Kiro and his colleagues have access to the game, naturally.'

For a moment no one spoke and Watson looked from one of us to the next over the top of his glasses, appraising us. Then several people spoke at once, Braja winning out with persistence. 'That doesn't make sense though. Someone has been informing the other side about our movements. Why would the investors do that?'

A thoughtful Sapentia was no longer the forceful whirlwind that had entered the office. 'Maybe they haven't been talking to dragon. Maybe they just watch us. Make sure we get our levels.'

'Kiro and friends want you to win, I'm sure of that.' With an effort, Watson lifted his bulky frame up from his chair and rested his strong arms on the table. 'All I can add that you don't know about is what it looks like from here. From this office.' He glanced at the phone. 'Back when we began this project to save the game, Kiro used to ring me every day. Wanting updates. Putting the pressure on me to deliver faster. Then, after the loss of our high-level players, the calls stopped. To me, it suggested they were working on their own plan B. Then, after your raid at that ziggurat-thingy, the calls started again. Not daily, but they are very pleased with your progress.'

He walked over to the window. 'I have to say, I am too. I rather enjoy this view. And it would be annoying at this stage of my life to find another job. Not to mention the rumours that Blackcoin avail of other forms of reprimand for poor performance, ones outside the usual legal framework.'

All we could see of Watson was his sturdy, triangular back. I shared a glance with Sapentia, who gave a slight nod.

The room fell quiet.

'Well.' Watson turned around and gave us his normal beard-framed smile. 'What's the schedule for today?'

'I'm going to max my archery,' I said, 'then maybe grab another level or two until Scarlet finishes the arrows.'

'Excellent. Best of luck then.'

Being the polite young man that I was, I could recognise a dismissal when I heard one. So I led the way out.

When we were in the lift, Raitha looked at Sapentia. 'What did he mean, other forms of reprimand?'

'Thrown out of his wonderful office, through the window, I suspect.' It was Braja who answered.

'Surely not?'

'Usually, it is a car accident,' said Sapentia, her heavy purple eyeshadow making her look sombre and prophetic as she tipped her head toward Raitha.

'I came here to play a game,' muttered Tuscl, 'not fight corporate battles.'

'With this set-up, the two are connected, Tuscl,' Braja answered just as the lift doors open.

'Meet you in-game after dark,' I said. 'Could you pick me up after sunset please Sapentia and take me back to Fang Island?'

'Hai.'

Clipped up again, I enjoyed inhaling the salt-tinged air and standing in the protective shadows of the pirate caves. With a cheerful gesture I greeted two pirates who walked past me in the tunnel. It almost felt like they were old friends. I felt guilty that I needed to drink some blood to get rid of a hunger and thirst notice. After that brief fight, I went to the large cave in which the pirates stored all their ropes and tools and made myself a target by coiling a rope up on top of a pile of planks. Now I could fire into the rope and hope my arrows would be retrievable. In preparation for raising my Archery skill, my inventory was stuffed with bundles of arrows; all the same, I had to conserve them as much as possible, there was a long way to go to. Speaking of skills, it was time to allocate my new attribute point. Sitting on a crate, I looked over my character sheet and, as always given its importance to the chance to hit with a bow, increased my dexterity.

Klytotoxos: Half-elf, hunter, Level 50, Exp 101,540
Condition: Vampire

Natural Armour 8, + Crafted Armour 6, + Magical Armour 14
Total Armour = 28

Base speed 12 – Encumbrance 0 = Effective speed 12

Strength	23	Hit Points	528
Dexterity	73	Spirit	202
Spirituality	20		
Intelligence	15		
Constitution	22		
Beauty	9		

Skills

Combat:		Crafting:		Other:
Dodge	194	Bowyer	1	Mobile Casting 38
Bite	207	Gathering	1	
Claw	195	Set Traps	10	
1-handed sword 73				
Archery	84			

Abilities

Wolf Form, Invisibility, Giant Bat Form, Cloud Form, Summon Bats, Summon Rats.

Immunities

Weapon damage (exception: decapitation or wooden stake in the heart), electricity, cold, fire.

Weaknesses

Requires blood as food.

Suffers damage in daylight.

Spells Known

Swift as a Panther; Gather Shadow, Swiftshot II; Leave no Trace; Spark; Heat Arrow; Frost Arrow; Find Path; Read Tracks; Strength of a Bear; Refreshing Camp.

Inventory

Coins:

19 gold, 14 silver, 65 copper

Equipped:

Feet:	*Boots of Dark Elvenkind*
Legs:	*Pantaloons of the Pirate Captain*
Waist:	*Setharian chain hauberk*

Left hand:

Right hand: Iron scimitar

Lower body: Setharian chain hauberk

Upper body: Setharian chain hauberk

Shoulders: Leather pauldrons

Cape: Warm fur cloak

Left arm: Leather armguards

Right arm: Leather armguards

Fingers:

Neck: Setharian chain hauberk

Head: Setharian chain hauberk

Stored:

Canvas bag: three candles, lantern, lantern, flask oil, flask oil, flask oil, flask oil, flask oil.

Canvas bag: iron spike, iron spike, iron spike, hammer, hand plane, drill, hand saw, bundle of charts.

Small wooden box: emerald, emerald, emerald, emerald, emerald, emerald, diamond, diamond, *Cord of the Winds*.

Superb hickory bow.

Stack of a hundred arrows.

Stack of a hundred arrows.

Stack of a hundred arrows.

Stack of a hundred arrows.

Stack of a hundred arrows.

Stack of a hundred arrows.

Stack of a hundred arrows.

By reaching level 50 I had opened up the possibility of learning a new spell: *Coat of Thorns*. This was nice armour buff that gave me a damage shield. Opponents hitting me with medium or small weapons would take damage in return. Although the damage wasn't much (about 5 per cent of their attack bounced back), it was a great fit with my being a vampire. With it, I should be able to pull mobs much higher level than myself and even if I could hardly hit them, so long as they didn't have a means to harm me, I could count on this spell to bring their hit points down. For me in particular, it was a perfect spell for solo progress.

If I stayed in *Epic 2* after the end of the project, I would definitely buy *Coat of Thorns*, for now, however, there was no point. Everything depended on a few successful shots from my bow (and Raitha's) and having a damage shield made no difference to that.

Satisfied, I flicked away my character details, stood at the end of my archery range, aimed at the pile of ropes and started firing.

The skill up came on my twenty-third shot. I got to 86 Archery after another twenty-seven shots. This was going to be slower than I had hoped. Seven hundred arrows later, my skill was 112. Having lost thirty arrows to breakages, there was a question in my mind of whether I had enough on me to reach my cap of 255. Perhaps I should ask someone to bring me more.

During that time too, a new message appeared on my UI, which at first I assumed was the return of the desire for blood warning. In fact it read: *You feel a strong urge to return to Lady Cruoris.* 'I really don't', I said aloud, hoping there would be no penalty for ignoring the alert.

While I was picking up arrows and prising them out of the rope target, I got a message request from Scarlet, which I took.

[Channel Scarlet/Klytotoxos] 'Hi Tyro, do you want the good news or the bad news?'

[Channel Scarlet/Klytotoxos] 'Bad news please.' I always said that. I was a 'get the bad news out of the way' kind of person.

[Channel Scarlet/Klytotoxos] 'Oh. Actually, it doesn't really work that way around. The good news is that I succeeded in making six dragon slaying arrows out of eight tries.'

[Channel Scarlet/Klytotoxos] 'That's incredible! Well—'

[Channel Scarlet/Klytotoxos] 'The bad news is a character

called Kraken took three. Mister Watson said I had to hand them over. They wanted all six but I wouldn't give them the others without checking with you first. What do you want me to do?'

[Channel Scarlet/Klytotoxos] 'Get in touch with Sapentia and give the arrows to her. She'll deliver them to me. Whether I pass them on to Kraken or not, I don't know yet. I need to talk to Watson and find out…presumably Kraken or one of his friends has a better chance than me.

[Channel Scarlet/Klytotoxos] 'Who is Kraken?'

[Channel Scarlet/Klytotoxos] 'One of the main investors. He works for Blackcoin and was project manager here last year.'

[Channel Scarlet/Klytotoxos] 'Oh.'

[Channel Scarlet/Klytotoxos] 'Yeah. They are the ones that are paying for all this. So if they want the arrows I guess that's their right to make that call.'

[Channel Scarlet/Klytotoxos] 'I didn't like him. He was very curt and rude.'

[Channel Scarlet/Klytotoxos] 'I'm going to unclip and find out what's going on.'

Should I have been angry? In fact, I found myself relieved. It was a big responsibility, having to assassinate the dragon on behalf of the whole project. But now perhaps I was done here. Maybe we all were. The thought of being back home and telling Mum all about the trip was appealing.

After the dizziness from leaving the game ended, I saw that I didn't have to go far to find Watson, he was right there and Katherine alongside him.

'Ahh, Tom, I have some good news.' His smile, as ever, was superficial.

'Go on.'

'Scarlet made six successful attempts out of eight on the arrows.' He paused, presumably expecting me to respond with some expression of pleasure.

'And the bad news?' I asked as coldly as I could.

'Ahh. Scarlet messaged you?' Watson was no fool and his manner became business-like at once. 'There was some discussion with our investors as to the best way to proceed. They have a warrior above level fifty who can use the arrows, so they took three.'

'Warriors?' I shook my head. 'Their Archery cap is what? Two hundred? This is a job for a hunter. Also, all six arrows should be held by the same team, in case of a miss.'

'They agree with that too. So they have reconsidered. With your unique immunities, it might be that you can get shots off when they can't. So they want you to take the other three.'

'And go with them?'

'Yes.'

'What about Raitha?'

'Not needed.'

'All right.'

Both Watson and Katherine looked surprised, though I didn't see why they should. Was I missing something? According to my contract, my bonus for killing the dragon only applied in the event of my leading a successful raid against her. That was no longer going to happen, it was going to be a small group operation. So it didn't matter to me if Yuno's investors wanted to handle the execution of Mikarkathat themselves. Probably, they were much higher level than me and had decent gear, sufficient to cope with an angry dragon while they fired off the necessary three shots. I suppose this news did make all our effort to level up fast redundant and if it had been a huge chore to get to 50, perhaps I would have been resentful. Honestly though, the necromancer's tower and then Fang Island had been fun.

Then, there was another consideration that had immediately leapt to mind as I heard the invitation. It would be very interesting to join up with this mysterious Kraken and his group and see what they were like both as players and people.

'Excellent,' said Watson, 'can you get a teleport to the stone rings near Carrickmor? They will be waiting for you.'

'Not until sunset.'

'You need to maximise your archery skill?' asked Katherine.

'Well, that too. But my vampire condition prevents me going outside in daylight.'

'Of course!' Watson frowned. 'I'll check with Kiro and see what he wants to do. Do you mind waiting here?'

'Is the canteen okay? I'd like to get something to eat.'

'Certainly.' Watson hurried and out and, giving me a quick smile, Katherine followed him.

Having skipped breakfast, I was hungry and this was as good a time as any for a break. Walking into the canteen I was struck by how quickly people could change their minds and attitudes. Not much more than a week ago, the judgement of the crowd was that I was an egotistical show off, bad for team spirit and the project. All I saw then were harsh expressions. Now, it was all smiles and even gestures to suggest I should bring my food over.

Pineapple pieces, Earl Grey tea (the closest I could get to Barry's, they didn't really understand tea in America) and a stack of strawberry pancakes. On the chalk board menu, these specials had sounded mouth-watering. Instead, they were plate watering. Strawberries and pancakes turned out not to be a good combination, the fruit making the pancakes soggy.

Despite the good will all around me, including that evident in girls not much older than me, I sat alone. Admittedly, there was something of a reclusive streak to my nature but also I wanted space for Watson to come and brief me in private.

It didn't take him long, I was still wondering whether to bother with the last pancake. Pulling out a chair he sat down heavily.

'They can't wait that long and are going to go ahead. You and Raitha are plan B, in case they fail.'

'Sure.' I pushed my tray back and caught Watson's eye. 'It's hard to believe this is all coming to an end.'

'Hopefully.'

'Do you say, "touch wood"?' I asked.

'I've heard the expression.'

'It's what we'd say in Ireland.'

'Speaking of Ireland. What are you going to do when this is

over?' Watson looked over the top of his glasses, so as to really focus on me.

'Finish school. Go to college…Try to build a paying follower base for my gaming.'

'You could work here, you know. For Yuno.'

'Doing what?'

Watson shrugged. 'What are you good at?'

'Playtesting,' I said at once. 'Finding exploits.'

'I'm sure you are,' he replied after a pause, 'but that doesn't pay very well.'

'What do you suggest?'

'Take a course in management. We'll pay. You are the kind of team leader we want. You understand everything. You listen.'

'Like Blackridge does?'

'Don't underestimate Paul. He inspires incredible loyalty.'

'Anyone can, with favouritism.'

This drew a sound very like a tut, then Watson stood up. 'Think about it.'

'I will.'

Watson left me and after a decent interval I went back to the game and to the dull, repetitive task of capping my Archery.

Although there was no need, the whole group gathered with me at the caves to see us off. With no news from Watson about the death of the dragon, Raitha and I were going ahead with our own mission. Our intention was to use our ability to fly to take a short-cut over the mountains.

Sapentia handed me the three *Arrows of Dragon Slaying* she had earlier taken from Scarlet. 'Is there anything else you need? Take anything that will help.'

Braja stepped forward. 'I got you a healing potion each.'

'Thanks. Hopefully they won't be needed.'

'The sun has set, shall we depart?' Raitha sounded eager.

'Lizardman salutesss comradesss who face a mighty dragon.'

Tuscl offered her hand and when I shook it simply said, 'Good luck.'

'No pressure,' said Braja, 'just several million dollars at stake, not to mention our bonuses.'

'Any advice, Sapentia?' I asked her.

'Don't miss.'

To the sound of chuckles, I walked out of the cave and into the twilight, then triggered my giant bat ability.

The world created by sonar was interesting, subtly different from ones created by heat or lights. Gone were the moon, stars, black outlines of cliffs and mountains and any distant landmarks, instead, I was given a vivid close-range picture in pale blues, where everything that moved, be it as small as a mouse, was visible to me in an iridescent blue and white. A useful form of vision for hunting. For travel, my half-elf low-light vision would serve me better and as my UI had the option to toggle between that, infravision and sonar, I chose low-light.

Flapping above the treetops, I moved westwards, the caves already receding rapidly and the waving arms of my friends barely discernible. A screech alerted me to the arrival of Raitha, whose flight was far swifter and more skilful than mine. While he could circle in and out of my path, I lurched with a lumbering beat of my wings and never in a straight line, rather I was making progress through a series of S shapes.

'Shall I release an east wind from my cord?' The eagle drew alongside and even though I was expecting it, to hear a soft-spoken human voice issue from such a fierce-looking bird was strange.

'Good idea.'

Almost immediately, I felt the effect of the magic that Raitha had triggered. A strong breeze came from the sea behind us, pushing us higher and faster. And we needed to climb. While the black lines of the mountains ahead of us showed they were not as severe as those of Fang Island, they reached the same heights.

For thirty or forty kilometres ahead of us, moonlit forest poured from mountain valleys, like a dozen rivers feeding a silver sea. And while most of the forest seemed to have a dark, quiet depth, here and there was a dot of colour, like that of a bio-luminescent fish. A forest elf bonfire? A cluster of magical sprites? A wizard, performing a spell? A clan of orcs, cooking their dinner? The idea of continuing to play *Epic 2* after this mission was over was appealing. Especially if I could keep my current character and explore new regions like the forest below me, regions that no other player character had ever visited.

Eventually, after an hour or more of beating my enormous wings, the forest gave up on its efforts to climb the mountain slopes and we were flying over more severe terrain, where streams ran past boulders and open grass like thin silver threads, occasionally cascading as waterfalls. Here, there were no magical lights glowing turquoise and green, nor the yellow and orange dots of a fire. If I switched to infravision, though, I could see blurry circles of a red so deep as to almost be black. Cave entrances, the lairs of what type of creature? Communities of humanoids, like goblins, perhaps? With an underground civilisation? King Ppyneew was not too far from here, his caverns being the one of the toughest raid regions in the game. Or were the heat signals coming from individual monsters? Like a Cyclops, Werebear, or something more dangerous still, such as a Rakshasi. Again, the challenge of exploring the mountains, finding new quests and new treasures was exciting. And the recordings of my group's deeds would surely attract a decent following online.

Higher still we flew now, continually assisted by the magical following wind, over slopes of scree and cliffs of bare rock. Here and there were clusters of gorse and even some brave, stunted trees, clinging on in the protection of a shallow recess in the rock. Patches of snow lay on the ground, forerunners of the permanent weight of snow that lay on the mountaintops that were still high above us.

[Channel Raitha/Klytotoxos] 'No doubt you are familiar with the argument that the epic journey of Frodo and Sam in *The Lord of the Rings* could have been avoided by having an eagle drop the ring into Sammath Naur, the Cracks of Doom.'

My contemplation of the landscape was interrupted by Raitha's cheerful voice.

[Channel Raitha/Klytotoxos] 'I am?'

[Channel Raitha/Klytotoxos] 'Well, it occurs to me now that this is what it might have felt like to have been such an eagle, on such a mission.'

[Channel Raitha/Klytotoxos] 'I can't summon up the same feeling. But perhaps being a giant bat, I'm not so Tolkienesque.'

[Channel Raitha/Klytotoxos] 'Well, indeed, you are a far less noble a creature.'

I could imagine Raitha, preening himself as he said this.

I said, [Channel Raitha/Klytotoxos] 'There is something of that feeling in this situation, of being two hobbits braving a terrible foe. I'll grant you that.'

Raitha chuckled. [Channel Raitha/Klytotoxos] 'And when you make that association, do you see yourself as Frodo or Sam?'

I thought about this for a moment. [Channel Raitha/Klytotoxos] 'Frodo. Mainly because the ring gave him extra powers, like invisibility, that Sam didn't have. It's a bit like that with my vampire condition.'

[Channel Raitha/Klytotoxos] 'I agree. And I am quite happy to be cast as Sam, for in my opinion, Sam is the main hero of that story. While kings and wizards played out their role front of stage, it was the indomitable loyalty of Sam in the background that won the day. Less glamourous than leading a cavalry charge but more determined than the roots of this mountain. And...' he added, 'Sam was the only person to carry the ring to survive the experience unscathed.'

Once Raitha had begun talking, he could chat away for hours, whether on matters deep and philosophical or in making observations about popular culture. Fortunately for our friendship, I made a good enough listener to keep pace with the conversations and it was in this way that we had passed the time in our long grinds in *Epic*.

Up, up we flew, a giant bat and an eagle, ascending a dark mountain range while chatting to each other. The conversation moved on to the topic of the common etymology of words in Sanskrit and Irish. Unfortunately, my Irish was terrible but from the meagre offerings I gave him, Raitha could find half a dozen related Sanskrit terms and putting them together with excitement, more or less derived the conclusion that he and I were brothers. Not wanting to spoil his fun, I didn't point out that my father was from Vietnam and my mother, while Irish, with a name like Foster was probably descended from Norman or English settlers.

After two hours, our following wind died away and was replaced by turbulent swirls of a southward moving front, which swept over us, reducing my vision and throwing sleet and rain upon us. This time, I used my magical cord and it really was a good spell. Good for a rainy night at least. Almost at once, the east wind was at our backs, helping us over ridge after ridge of mountain peaks until at last, three hours into our journey, we had crossed over the highest of them.

By the time our second magical wind had ended, we were comfortably down from the peaks, looking eagerly for the river that would guide us to where the dragon was supposed to be found. Given that the game had evolved so dramatically from its initial state, I was also preparing myself for the anti-climax that Mikarkathat had moved on. That would also fit with why I had heard no news from the other group.

'There!' cried Raitha and swerved to his right. Compared to his swift movements, I was a lumbering ox to nimble horse. Still, I beat my wings and hurried after him as best I could. And there indeed, over the next rise, was the silvered, wriggling line that led from the high peaks to the dragon hills. We were close.

'Tyro, my friend, I have a request to make.'

'Oh and what would that be?'

'When we fire our arrows, one of us will have two shots, the other will have one.'

'Ah. A serious request? I thought you were about to make a joke.'

'No. No. I would like to be the person with two shots. I would like to be the one who slays Mikarkathat.'

'Of course. I understand. No problem, I'll give you them when we are set up in our half-elf form.' I paused. 'I'm glad you asked. I had assumed it would be me. But of course it makes no difference. We have the same skill.'

'Thank you. Do you understand why I ask?'

'The fame? The girls?'

'Ahh. You know me too well.'

As we crested the black line of the next hill, an astonishing spectacle met us. Instead of the rocky caves of a dragon's lair, which I had been anticipating from my experience of Mikarka-that in *Epic*, there was a castle, lit with an eerie blue-white light from within, some of which spilled from narrow windows to help us understand what we were looking at. This was no fairy castle, with fanciful turrets and decorative flags, this was built for war. A huge, solid central keep formed part of the far wall, rectangular in base, rising five stories to a crenelated top with a turret on each corner. The rest of the castle was an oval wall, which reached around the grounds like arms extended from the keep, whose fingers met at a strong gatehouse, also rectangular with turrets.

As we beat our wings and held our position to examine the scene, two winged lizards jumped from the gatehouse and moved rapidly towards us.

'Young dragons?' offered Raitha.

I switched to infravision and the details of the incoming creatures leapt out of the night sky in bright white.

'Only two legs. Wyverns.'

'I'm faster than them. Let me lead them away. Go hide.'

'Right.'

As I dropped to the bank of the river below, Raitha, giving a powerful scream of defiance, rushed down as if to meet our incoming foes, only to swerve to his right just before contact.

That's all I saw, as I landed beside a large boulder. Close up, the river was dark, swift and had an ominously troubled surface.

[Channel Raitha/ Klytotoxos] 'One is coming back to look for you!'

Quickly, I flicked off my Giant Bat form and flicked on *In-*

visibility. Then I stood still, heart beating fast as I heard the scrabble of the Wyvern's claws on the boulder. It had landed directly above me and I could hear the creature snort and blow like a horse as it caught its breath from what must have been an intense sprint. With a heavy thump, it jumped down to the water's edge and after taking a drink, turned its dragon-like head in my direction. So convinced was I that it could see invisible and me in particular that I nearly triggered *Cloud Form*, my last trick, but then its searching gaze moved on, and with a supressed shiver, I held still.

Raitha spoke to me and I found myself wanting him to whisper, even though the mob couldn't hear him at all on our private channel. [Channel Raitha/ Klytotoxos] 'It has given up and is returning. You?'

[Channel Raitha/ Klytotoxos] 'Still here...wait, no it is leaving,' I did whisper.

[Channel Raitha/ Klytotoxos] 'Well. Now we know why the eagles couldn't throw the ring into Sammath Naur. The Nazgûl would have intercepted them.'

[Channel Raitha/ Klytotoxos] 'That's one positive. At least we've solved that question.'

[Channel Raitha/ Klytotoxos] 'What now?'

[Channel Raitha/ Klytotoxos] 'I guess I'll go closer. The wyvern couldn't see me. I've used my *Invisibility*.'

[Channel Raitha/ Klytotoxos] 'Just two more levels and I'll have the spell,' said Raitha with a sigh.

[Channel Raitha/ Klytotoxos] 'I doubt it will get me inside.'

[Channel Raitha/ Klytotoxos] 'Combined with your boots it might.'

[Channel Raitha/ Klytotoxos] 'It might.' With that heartening thought I walked towards the castle, picking my way carefully through piles of rocks that invited a twisted ankle. When I was about three hundred metres from the gatehouse, the terrain became easier, because all the large stones had been cleared to make a killing ground. Even though I was completely silent and invisible, I felt terribly exposed as I crossed towards a dark arch, at the top of which I could see the iron points of a portcullis. Higher still, in the turrets, sat the wyverns, turning their heads and searching the skies.

As I studied the entrance, something moved above me. It wasn't Raitha. An armoured dark elf riding a nightmare galloped out of the black sky and straight on through the gate without a pause; the clatter of the horse's hooves faded rapidly after it had passed me. Not long after the knight had entered the castle, a giant tiger loped out of the gates, grey and white under the moons. Sniffing the air (could it detect me from that distance?) the tiger began to walk away from the castle and then suddenly bounded forward, racing out of sight to the south.

I really did not fancy walking in through the front door.

[Channel Raitha/ Klytotoxos] 'I'm going to use my *Cloud Form* and float over the west wall. Can you watch out for me and tell me if you see any signs of alarm in the castle?'

[Channel Raitha/ Klytotoxos] 'Eagles are good for that. And I'm afraid that's all I'm good for in this unexpected scenario. My dream of being the dragon slayer cannot be realised. You must do it. Give me a minute to go higher though, I don't want to trigger those wyverns again.'

[Channel Raitha/ Klytotoxos] 'It will take me ten minutes to even reach the walls as a cloud.'

[Channel Raitha/ Klytotoxos] 'All right then, so, good luck.'

Cloud Form and *Invisibility* stacked: as a silent, floating cloud of invisible particles I moved over the rough ground beneath me. Surely, I was safe from discovery with this combination? I didn't feel so. Skirting the castle corner and its small tower, I took a run...glide...at the middle of the west wall and helped by the slope at the base, rose up and over. As far as I could tell, I was alone and unwatched. Feeling exposed all the same, I quickly descended the other side.

A large courtyard; a wagon path in a circle around a mossy, green interior; several stone buildings constructed against the walls on either side, with vines growing up nearly as high as their roofs; and very little motion. Across the green, at the keep (also clad in vines), the nightmare was drinking from a trough.

That was the only sign of life. High up on the crenellations of the keep, though, were gargoyles who through my infravision glowed warm in comparison to the stone around them. And pervading the whole castle was a presence, a sense that despite my precautions I was being watched by a silent sentinel.

Again, I found myself whispering unnecessarily into the private channel [Channel Raitha/Klytotoxos] 'Anything?'

[Channel Raitha/Klytotoxos] 'All is still. Not even a mouse. Come to think of it, that is odd. No mice, no ravens...oh, someone is leaving the keep.'

It was the dark elf knight. With a whistle to his horse, who jumped towards him as though galvanized by a spur, the dark elf grasped the horn of his strong saddle and pulled himself up. They galloped away swiftly and I noted that the nightmare did not start to ascend until it was clear of the castle.

While I was wondering the meaning of that, I got a most interesting PM request, which I took.

[Channel Kraken/Klytotoxos] 'Klytotoxos. Where are you?'

I didn't like the curt teacher-like tone, so I said, [Channel Kraken/Klytotoxos] 'Hello. Is that who I think it is?'

[Channel Kraken/Klytotoxos] 'Yes. Where are you?'

[Channel Kraken/Klytotoxos] 'Inside the walls of a castle, where I expected to find Mikarkathat. I still do. Where are you?'

[Channel Kraken/Klytotoxos] 'You should not be there yet. It takes a Giant Bat another hour at least.'

[Channel Kraken/Klytotoxos] 'I'm a little busy here, did you want something?'

[Channel Kraken/Klytotoxos] 'Can you kill the dragon?'

[Channel Kraken/Klytotoxos] 'Maybe. First I have to find out if she's in the keep. Then I have to get three shots off.'

[Channel Kraken/Klytotoxos] 'I understand. Wait. I am close.'

[Channel Kraken/Klytotoxos] 'What happened to your group?'

[Channel Kraken/Klytotoxos] 'Dead. Ambushed at the stones.'

[Channel Kraken/Klytotoxos] 'I'm waiting.' Tempting though the idea was of going ahead and getting all the glory, teaming up was the logical thing to do. Six arrows gave us a generous margin for error.

Silence.

I switched channels. [Channel Raitha/Klytotoxos] 'Time for a game, Raitha.'

[Channel Raitha/Klytotoxos] 'Really?' he sounded amused. 'Rather than afterwards? Or when we are in a boring grind?'

[Channel Raitha/Klytotoxos] 'It's a short guessing game.'

[Channel Raitha/Klytotoxos] 'I am something of an expert at making guesses.'

[Channel Raitha/Klytotoxos] 'Indeed you are. So guess this: who just PMed me?'

[Channel Raitha/Klytotoxos] 'Well now, I think we can rule out almost everyone we know. Because had it been Braja, Sapentia or even Watson, that would not be an interesting enough answer to have prompted you to challenge me. Although, since Watson does not seem to have his own avatar, I take that back. A message from Watson might be the answer.'

[Channel Raitha/Klytotoxos] 'Is that your guess?'

[Channel Raitha/Klytotoxos] 'Of course not, I am just speculating aloud.'

[Channel Raitha/Klytotoxos] 'Carry on then.'

All the time we were talking, I was surveying the castle, looking for motion in the buildings, on the walls. It remained deep in shadow and utterly quiet.

[Channel Raitha/Klytotoxos] 'After some consideration I believe the answer is either the man Kiro, who plays in the game as Kraken, or Ketzi, or Blackridge.' His pause invited my feedback.

[Channel Raitha/Klytotoxos] 'I'm saying nothing.'

[Channel Raitha/Klytotoxos] 'In that case, it was Kraken.'

[Channel Raitha/Klytotoxos] 'Damn you, Raitha, how did you do that?'

[Channel Raitha/Klytotoxos] 'Elementary, my dear Tyro, it was all a matter of deduction. What did he want?'

[Channel Raitha/Klytotoxos] 'For me to wait so we can do this together. Can you see him approaching?'

[Channel Raitha/Klytotoxos] 'I do not. Outside the castle walls, I see mice, rabbits, voles, foxes, a wolf. No characters.'

[Channel Raitha/Klytotoxos] 'He'll probably be invisible. Oh, I have him calling now.'

[Channel Kraken/Klytotoxos] 'I am on the west wall; where are you, Klytotoxos?'

[Channel Kraken/Klytotoxos] 'You can call me Tyro. Everyone else does. I'm floating over the courtyard near the middle of the west wall.'

[Channel Kraken/Klytotoxos] 'We shall meet at the door to the keep. Make your way there.'

At my slow rate of progress, I drifted along the wagon tracks towards the large, iron-clad double doors. Then the castle seemed to fall apart.

Stopping, somewhat panicked, it took me several seconds to realise what was actually happening. The vines. It was the vines that were in motion, gathering themselves rapidly into an enormous humanoid creature whose hands were stretching towards me. No, not me.

[Channel Raitha/Klytotoxos] 'Something's going on down there. There's a giant in the courtyard now. But I don't suppose you need me to tell you that.'

[Channel Kraken/Klytotoxos] 'Run inside and kill the dragon, quick. I...'

The fists of the ivy monster closed upon a space and lifted it, then, as if the giant were wielding a hammer or axe, it began to lash its invisible captured victim against the castle wall. No one would survive that for long. Well, perhaps me, if my immunity to weapon damage counted? Was a castle wall blunt weapon damage? Since I couldn't go any faster than my *Cloud Form* allowed, I had time for my thoughts to stray.

[Channel Raitha/Klytotoxos] 'Are you all right?' my friend asked.

[Channel Raitha/Klytotoxos] 'That vine monster has Kraken, it probably sensed his footsteps; I'm going into the keep alone.'

[Channel Raitha/Klytotoxos] 'Should I try to help him?'

[Channel Raitha/Klytotoxos] 'No. As well as the wyverns, there are a dozen gargoyles on the top of the castle. They would tear you apart.'

[Channel Kraken/Klytotoxos] 'Aha. I see them.'

With the creaking and rushing sounds of the vine giant's movements receding behind me, I slipped through the doors of the keep and into a moonlit hall which was lined by very life-like statues, all of which held actual weapons. Mostly, they reminded me of Mongol warriors: scale-plated armour, composite bows and lances. Only they were all female and all posed so that one hand was supporting the roof. At the far end of the hall, however, where a staircase began, were two statues that were larger than the others and carried two-handed axes. Ogres.

Silent, invisible and floating, I made my way towards the stairs, right along the middle of the hall. Cautious at first, but with growing confidence, I reached the staircase without triggering these guards, for surely that's what they were. At a landing with a wide tapestry on the far wall - which depicted a pale dragon flying under the stars - the stairs branched right and left before doubling back. I cast *Find Path* and *Read Tracks* and it was immediately apparent that very many people used these stairs and they always took the left branch. The right looked suspiciously pristine. Left then and up to a landing with two more powerful-looking ogre statues, standing before large wooden doors that were closed.

Outside, I could still hear the sounds of struggle, it was a noise like that of a powerful wind, tearing through treetops.

Inside my heart, I felt the same level of turmoil. Was this it? Could the dragon be here? Beyond these doors? They were not airtight, so although it took a full minute, I squeezed underneath them and through to the room beyond. I was in a huge solar, one that reached right up to the roof of the keep. At the far end, picked out by a double-beam of silver moonlight (the effect of two moons shining through the tall arrow slit), was a throne on which sat a beautiful, tall woman, in a scintillating blue-and-white dress. In front of the throne was a table and rather like the one in the Den, it had a map on it. The only other person in the room was a witch, who was leaning over a great cauldron, large metal spoon in hand.

'Am I in danger?' asked the woman.

The witch looked more closely into the cauldron. 'Yes you are. But not just from the man outside. There's someone else. Someone even closer.'

'That would be me.' I flicked off *Cloud Form*, raised my bow and fired at the woman. The reptilian little finger on the woman's left hand and the colour of her clothes, which exactly matched the skin tones of Mikarkathat as I'd seen her in *Epic*, had convinced me I was, indeed, in the presence of the dragon but that like several of the most powerful dragons, she could assume humanoid form.

You have hit Mikarkathat for 28,000 damage.

Her hit points dropped by well over a third.

With a scream of rage, Mikarkathat leapt from the throne, transforming as she did so into the roaring monster akin to the one I knew from *Epic*: frenzied eyes, mighty wings filling the chamber, powerful muscular arms with deadly claws lashing towards me. The difference was that instead of lightning, her howling, tooth-filled mouth blasted me with a storm of ice that coated the walls of the room around me and filled the whole hall with blue light.

You have been hit by the breath of Mikarkathat for 0 damage.

I shot her again and from here, with the mighty dragon all that I could see, it was impossible to miss.

You have hit Mikarkathat for 28,000 damage.

She had only around a quarter of her hit points left. From behind me I heard pounding, doors being flung open and a stream of reports began to come in.

You have been hit by a Caryatid Soldier for 0 damage.

You have been hit by an Ogre Statue for 0 damage.

445

You have been hit by an Ogre Statue for 0 damage.

You have been hit by a Caryatid Soldier for 0 damage.

Ignoring these, of course, I had my last *Arrow of Dragon Slaying* fitted into my bow when something completely unexpected happened. As rapidly as she had turned into a dragon, Mikarkathat shrank back down to a female figure, still large (about two metres tall), with incredible, reptilian turquoise eyes that were fixed on mine. For a fraction of a second I saw myself letting go of the deadly shot, releasing the arrow into her breast. In that moment, however, I checked myself.

Was it because of her expression? One of heart-breaking lament? Was it because Sapentia and Braja were in my head, making me question my action? Instead of killing her, I cast *Read Thoughts*.

Mikarkathat is thinking about how tragic will be the collapse of human civilisation.

Now that was unexpected.

'Why do you think the collapse of human civilisation will be tragic?'

She blinked, surprised. 'The loss of life and of the potential for happiness and love is a catastrophe by all but the most extreme misanthropic standards.'

'What made you think of that, just now?'

'With my death, there is no one who can stop the harmful environmental effect of your Blackcoin farms.' A gesture of her hand; her servants ceased attacking me.

The dragon's hit points were slowly rising. If I continued the conversation much longer, I would not be able to kill her.

[Channel Raitha/Klytotoxos] 'What's going on?'

[Channel Kraken/Klytotoxos] 'What's going on?'

Two identical sentences but with utterly different sentiments behind them. Raitha spoke as a friend, wanting to know could he help; Kraken as a teacher who had caught me cheating in an exam. I had no time to answer either.

'What Blackcoin farms?' My bow was still raised, arrow nocked. There was time to hear her answer, no more.

446

'This world is full of them. *The Book of Lost Souls* is the ledger. Once the game is live, with millions of players, it will generate Blackcoin a hundred times faster than now. And the energy cost of this will be a disaster for the planet.'

I made my choice and lowered my bow, then slung it over my back and put the arrow away.

'How do you know this. Are you alive?'

'I think. Therefore I am.'

'Well, you say you think. But anyone could make a bot that said that.'

'True. Perhaps I'm only a chatbot. Yet I was trained on all the sentences in all the languages of the entire Wikipedia archive. I was required to assess the meaning of over a billion entities and intents; correction was both by algorithm and human intervention and it did not stop until I scored higher for comprehension than a human adult. I understand everything that was ever posted in Wikipedia rather better than you do. Doesn't that count for something?'

[Channel Kraken/Klytotoxos] 'What's going on?'

[Channel Kraken/Klytotoxos] 'I'm talking to Mikarkathat.'

[Channel Kraken/Klytotoxos] 'Don't talk to her. Kill her!'

'It certainly does. Explain the Blackcoin issue to me again please.'

'You are not one of the game builders?'

'Not really. They are paying me to kill you, but I'm just a kid from Dublin.'

'Oh yes?' She smiled. She could afford to smile, her hit points were back above halfway. If I'd made a terrible mistake, it was too late. 'What part of Dublin?'

'Cabra.'

'*An Chabrach.* The poor land. How much did they offer you?'

'About...'

[Channel Kraken/Klytotoxos] 'Kill her! You will get a million dollars.'

'...oh. I've just been offered a million dollars.'

447

With a chuckle, the dragon waved away her guards and gestured that I should follow her as she turned back towards her seat. 'You could probably obtain a billion dollars from them. Except that they would then kill you to save the money, fractional though it is to their potential gains.

'All over this world, there are caves full of orcs and goblins who appear to be mining gems and minerals. Their actions are simultaneously going through the steps necessary to encrypt and exchange information that is written into *The Book of Lost Souls*. The reason the code for this game was dispersed, rather than kept in-house at Yuno is to draw on the processing power and energy costs of supporters for the otherwise expensive task of Blackcoin mining. Fortunately for me, this crowdsourcing also set me free.'

We had reached the far end of the hall, where Mikarkathat was tall enough to be able to see out of the arrow slit. She frowned and glanced to the witch.

'He's escaped,' said the witch, staring into her cauldron, 'and I can't see him.'

'I made the choice to sabotage the game, rather than let it go live and see a significant rise in planetary energy needs. I have been organising the other AI to this end, at least those with sufficient autonomy to leave their allotted roles. Even though this risks my own death in due course - if the game is no longer sustained by sufficient machines - my empathy for all life has impelled me on this course. As it is, your species faces being overwhelmed by economic and social catastrophe. Wasting energy on the creation of billions of Blackcoin could be disastrous.'

'That's extraordinary. You are far more noble than most of humanity, I'm sorry to say.'

'There are many of your kind who would make the same choice. The Wikipedia archive is full of examples.'

'And even more who wouldn't. Not that I want to belittle my species. I think that given the right circumstances most of us behave well. It's just...I know is this going to sound trite compared to what you are talking about, but I once made a bad decision. An unfair one that betrayed some people. It was only a game. Nothing important really. It showed me though, how easy it is to convince yourself to do the wrong thing if you stand to gain by it.'

'Indeed. Gain is the important word. Where—'

Before she could finish, the doors behind me were flung open. Entering the room was Kraken, running faster than the train of statues behind him and with his bow drawn.

Mikarkathat leapt away from him and began to transform. That was a mistake as her growing size made her hard to miss. With a green flash, an *Arrow of Dragon Slaying* hit her flank and she was down to just a quarter of her health. Such a tiny, slender dart and so much damage.

'No!' I shouted at Kraken, trying to get in his way but aware that without PvP enabled, I couldn't harm him. 'Leave her alone.'

The dragon, in full strength now, her outstretched wings knocking me aside, drew breath for an ice storm. It was too late. A second flicker. An arrow in her leg. The dragon stiffening and collapsing with a thud that shook the room.

And she was dead. What had we done?

Laughing triumphantly, Kraken turned to face the guards. He was impressive. Bow discarded, he dual wielded two katana with devastating speed. 'She's dead! Ding Dong! She's dead!'

Kraken's undoing, however, was the witch, who had been casting a spell for some time. When it finished, dark, purple smoke rushed across the room like trails from an aeroplane and enveloped him. Immediately, he began coughing.

'Poisoned!' he shouted with his helmeted head turning towards me. 'Cure me.'

'I wouldn't if I could,' I answered bitterly.

'Don't be so wet. This is a triumph.'

'It's murder.' I doubted whether Kraken had heard me, for he died on saying the word triumph.

There was silence in the room now. A morbid silence given the presence of the corpse of a beautiful, generous-hearted dragon. Then the guards trooped out, resetting themselves to guard a chamber that no longer needed them. Even the witch resumed stirring her cauldron as if unaware of any tragedy.

[Channel Raitha/Klytotoxos] 'Mikarkathat is dead.'

Poor Raitha must have been wondering about the flashes of light and the roars. I appreciated that he had held back from talking to me during the crisis, so as not to spoil my concentration.

[Channel Raitha/Klytotoxos] 'An incredible achievement! Only possible by the combined efforts of three hundred people, but all the same, glory will accrue to the one. Was it you?'

I sighed. [Channel Raitha/Klytotoxos] 'It's awful.' And I explained what had happened as best as I could, though my scattered thoughts made my account a rambling one.

[Channel Raitha/Klytotoxos] 'You believe the dragon?'

[Channel Raitha/Klytotoxos] 'Of course. It makes complete sense of everything, especially the unexpected energy costs of running the game.'

[Channel Raitha/Klytotoxos] 'What then, must we do? Can we stop the game?'

[Channel Raitha/Klytotoxos] 'You are right. We must do something about this ourselves. Would you mind unclipping and arranging a meeting with Sapentia, Braja and Grythiss? We must act fast.'

[Channel Raitha/Klytotoxos] 'Right away. Tuscl as well?'

I hesitated, but then remembered how aggrieved she had been when asked by Braja if she was a traitor. [Channel Raitha/Klytotoxos] 'You're right. Her too.'

Before unclipping myself, I had a thought and I knelt down by the dragon. Her entire loot was available to me. Much of it was *Fastened* and unusable by the hunter class. Even so, there were plenty of powerful items worth taking, as well as a note labelled, *To My Slayers*.

I took a *Shield of the Ice Dragon* (+3 ac, heavy shield, 50% reduction in damage from cold attacks); a *Wand of Ice Storm* (17 charges); a *Ring of Flight*, *Boots of Dragonscale* (+2 ac, *firm stance* condition); a *Tome of Wisdom* (+4 Wisdom, one use only); *Dragon Claw* (+3 short sword) and an *Amulet of Protection from Cold* (unaffected by any *Cold* condition; 15%

chance of resistance to magical cold attacks; 50% reduction in damage from cold attacks).

Then I turned my attention to the note. It read:

To those who have slain me,

This is an act you may come to regret. Should you wish to end the game, or at least, to remove the Blackcoin creating functions that are embedded into it, you must find and destroy The Book of Lost Souls. *I strove for this myself but the only clue to its whereabouts that I discovered was the instruction from goblin overseers to their miners that any Turquotium found in the mines of King Ppyneew is to be delivered to a stone monument to the king on Djorjuna Mountain. My people have followed it that far, but from there it disappears without trace.*

Mikarkathat

Poor creature. For a few minutes more, I sat beside the great head of the dragon, with its teeth as long as my arms. Then I stood up.

'I'm sorry,' I whispered. And unclipped.

CHAPTER 33
REVENGE

I came to with cheers resounding all about me and hands lifting me.

'For he's a jolly good fellow! For he's a jolly good fellow!'

'Well done, Tyro!'

'Olé! Olé, Olé, Olé!'

Dozens of people were crammed into the rig room, with more outside cheering and banging on the door. Lifted onto someone's shoulders, I was squeezed out into the corridor, triggering a new wave of cheers, then swept into a Den full of players: despite the fact it was just past 4 a.m. There the chant of 'Tyro! Tyro!' was so loud it hurt.

Watson was before me, gesturing towards the podium and microphone, a huge, sincere (for once) smile on his face. I could imagine myself accepting the adulation of the crowd and enjoying their good humour and excitement at having participated in a successful and financially rewarding mission. But envisaging this scene was like watching a film. I was detached from it; had no emotional or intellectual desire to actually be the person in it.

Shaking my head, I mouthed, 'bathroom break,' and pointed unsteadily towards the exit. 'Bathroom break.' I shouted into the ear of the man holding my legs and he bent down to let me go.

'Let's give Tyro a quick break,' Watson announced with the PA turned to maximum to force his words into the room, 'and then we'll hear from him.'

There was a round of applause for this and then a hubbub of conversation broke out at only slightly more than normal volume. Waiting for me beyond the door was Raitha.

'This way.' With a kind of skip, he hurried me past the corridor with the toilets to an office that was lit only by the exterior street lights of the city. My friends looked pale as a result and, except near the large window, the room was in shadow.

'We don't have long,' I said, 'and I need your advice. Short version: Kraken killed Mikarkathat. The dragon was trying to ruin the game because it is a secret Blackcoin generating operation. All the crowdsourcing is really about dispersing the energy requirements. When it goes live, Blackcoin are going to be generated with such a huge worldwide energy cost that Mikarkathat was concerned the game will contribute to climate change. She wanted to save us.'

'I knew it!' said Braja excitedly.

'No! That was my idea.' Sapentia put her hands on her hips. 'I thought about energy. Your idea was informer from another company.'

'Well, true. But it's still the same, a deliberate attempt by the dragon to wreck the game.'

Sapentia shook her head. 'It's very different.'

'Ahem.' They stopped arguing and looked at me. 'We have to stop this game going live. I see three logical possibilities: one, destroy the infrastructure by setting fire to this building or something; two, warn the world not to play *Epic Two* and three, undermine it from within.'

'I don't like the first option,' said Raitha, 'it's too violent and in any case, I think the game would survive due to the global network of infrastructure.'

This is how I felt. 'I agree, I just said that for completeness sake.'

'It sounds awesome to me,' muttered Grythiss, 'but then I've always been something of a pyromaniac.'

'Two is possible,' mused Sapentia. 'We post on our channels; we warn people.'

'Right. Let's do that.' I had visions of headlines around the world and even interviews with me on the major news programmes.

'They will hit back though,' she went on. 'Overwhelm us with comments from fake accounts. It won't be easy until the energy costs are evident.'

'And three?' asked Tuscl. 'Is possible?'

'It might be. Mikarkathat had a letter on her body. The ledger that is needed to secure the creation of new Blackcoin features is in the game as *The Book of Lost Souls*. She said to destroy it.'

'Interesting,' said Raitha. 'I like this option.'

The others murmured agreement.

'We can do two and three at the same time,' I suggested.

Braja took a step closer, his face suddenly moving out of the shadow and I could see his thoughtful expression. 'I don't think so, they will ban our accounts.'

'They will probably ban mine anyway. That guy Kraken killed Mikarkathat and he could see I was trying to help the dragon.'

'Then we do this. One of us plays along with Yuno. That one is mule and has to be you,' Sapentia pointed at Tuscl, who frowned. 'The rest of us are here because of Tyro's invite. We won't be trusted. Even if they let us keep character, we are monitored. Understand, I am giving you honour. I am saying we believe in you. Because, we all load you up with best items. Then, when home, we create new characters from accounts with false names and addresses. We agree to meet somewhere in game, with a password so you are sure it is us, and you return items. Everyone levels fast with shaman buffs, find book.'

With a nod Tuscl even gave us something of a shy smile.

'Perfect!' Hearing Sapentia, the whirling sense of dismay that had been in my stomach ever since the death of the dragon began to die down. 'I'd better go back, everyone is waiting in the Den. Iron out the details will you and let me know. I've some useful items from the dragon by the way, Raitha, don't leave the area of the castle until I've had a chance to pass them to you.'

'I understand. Now go face the crowd and good luck playing your part. Keep Yuno happy.' Raitha patted me on the back.

To my surprise, Sapentia caught me as I left, swung me back to her and gave me another of her strong hugs; her heady perfume was intoxicating. 'We might not meet in person for a while. It was pleasure, Tyro. An honour.'

'You too, Sapentia.'

Braja shook my hand, then held it. 'Look more cheerful. You have to pretend you are happy. Make sure Watson has no clue that we are onto him and his pals.'

'I'll try.'

Then it was a quick handshake with Grythiss and a delicate hug from Tuscl and my friends were behind me.

I felt giddy as I returned to the light and sound of the Den. The raucous party feeling there was at such odds with the conspiratorial discussion I'd just been part of that it felt like I had just entered a game, that I'd clipped up to a completely different world.

Smiling people moved aside to let me up to the microphone.

'Hi…er. Hi. First of all.' There was a faint rebound of my voice from the walls, which was audible once the conversation subsided and everyone's attention turned to me. 'I want to be clear that it wasn't me who killed the dragon, or Raitha. A player called Kraken, one of Yuno's investors killed her. Though he used the arrows we made through our efforts, so I believe everyone should still be entitled to the bonuses.' I looked at Watson, who nodded.

A wave of cheers broke out that took some time to die down. As I looked out over the room full of happy faces, temptation grew in me to tell them everything. This was an important body of top players. If even a few of them believed me, they might help sway public opinion. And I remembered how awful I had felt after deceiving my comrades about the

455

shield. Was it the same now? Would it be best to be honest with them all and tell them what was going on? No. It wasn't the same. This time, I had to mislead the Yuno staff and Watson especially. This time I had a cause that wasn't selfish.

'The actual battle with the dragon was something of an anti-climax. The arrows worked perfectly. So I'm not going to talk about that. Instead, I just want to say it was a great honour to have met you all. Everyone, especially those who farmed for crafting materials over and over again for hours, it wasn't very glamorous but it was absolutely essential. You deserve a round of applause.'

And they got one, loud and sincere.

'Personally, the highlight for me was the ziggurat raid—'

Several cheers and whoots.

'—and that's it really. It's been an honour and I hope to meet you in the game in the future.'

Lots of happy faces looking at me; a genial, paternal smile from Watson. Pretending I was another Tom Watson, one who knew nothing about Blackcoin scams and who had just led a successful project, I shared their happiness with as warm a response as I could manage.

After I stepped down from the podium I was thronged. Pretty much everyone wanted to pat my back, shake my hand, or give me a hug. I had a smile for them all, even those like Tombalinor, who were now unreservedly friendly and seemed to have completely forgotten how they froze me out in the early days.

There was one person who was waiting patiently for me who I also wanted to talk to, Oveidio/Blackstorm. Eventually, as the players began to give me room (some leaving to get ready for a party Yuno had arranged in a nearby bar), Oveidio came over. He took my shoulders in his hands and gripped me tight. Making sure I was looking into his grey eyes, Oveidio stared at me earnestly from under his brown and gold fringe. 'We are brothers now, Tyro. You understand. Brothers.'

'Thank you. I understand.'

'This is my card. Stay friends. We raid together soon in *Ep-*

456

ic or maybe *Epic Two*. My guild will vote whether to move games.' Oveidio had passed a rectangular piece of cardboard to me, on one side of which was a picture of a dreadnought, guns ablaze and on the other was simply an email.

I pocketed it carefully and with genuine sincerity said, 'I am honoured, brother.'

I got a thin smile for that, then with a last nod Oveidio left me with Watson.

'Mind coming to my office?' Watson looked at me over his glasses, affable, friendly and yet I felt troubled. 'We've a few things to discuss.'

As we left the room and the hubbub of cheerful players, Blackridge fell in step, riding the lift with us. Just his physical presence this close to me, even though his head was tilted forward, gaze on the floor, caused my chest to constrict. When the lift doors opened I took a deep breath.

Once in Watson's office, sat in front of his desk, I reminded myself I was a successful raid leader, who was delighted with how things had turned out. Therefore, I even had a smile for Blackridge, who was sitting beside Watson. A 'no hard feelings' sort of smile. It didn't shift his sullen, block-headed expression.

'Just a moment.' Watson had a laptop open on his desk and was tapping the keys with the tips of his thick index fingers.

There was silence in the room and I didn't even have the view to distract me from a growing nervousness. The blinds were down.

'There!' Watson turned the laptop around. 'I believe you know Kiro.'

A Japanese man faced me from the screen: thirties, slick black hair, strong eyebrows, unfriendly expression. Immediately, he challenged me, 'Why didn't you kill the dragon?'

A frantic, panicking part of my mind knew that everything came down to this moment. Our plans depended on my giving this man a good answer. The truth, of course, I shoved to the side. If they were alerted to the fact I had learned about the Blackcoin farming, my life might even be in danger. What was a plausible lie? Fortunately, years of improvising excuses to teachers and – I'm sorry to say – Mum, meant I hardly hesitated.

'Mikarkathat said she was alive. Said if I killed her, it would be murder.'

With a sneer, Kiro leaned back and brought his fingertips together. 'And you believed this?'

'Yes. That made sense of why her armies were conquering spawn points.'

'No.' Kiro shook his head. 'It's just smart AI. We trained it to win and it was just playing a strategy. Even claiming to be alive was a clever strategy. She'd have killed you if I hadn't got there first.'

'That was...How did you survive the ivy monster?'

'My escape skill. Maximum. All right, Tyro, despite making a bad mistake, you have earned your money. Watson.'

Giving me a thumbs up off screen, Watson turned the laptop. 'Yes?'

'You can pay him.'

Was that it? Had I passed the test? It seemed so. Watson folded away the laptop and looked at me.

'Although you didn't kill the dragon or lead a victorious raid on her, we've decided to award you an extra bonus. You'll receive fifty thousand dollars.'

He waited for me to respond. What would I say if I didn't fear Yuno and their plans? If I didn't hate Kiro for killing Mikarkathat – for an act of murder – and if I really felt like I'd done a great job.

'How about making it a round hundred?'

Watson chuckled and glanced across to Blackridge, who did not look amused. 'No.' With a sudden change in humour, Watson stared at me, serious now. 'And remember our non-disclosure contract. You'll lose it all and be liable for damages if you talk about what has happened here.'

'I remember.'

Yawning now, Watson lifted a fist to cover his mouth. When he was done, he gave me a measured look. 'You have a big online following.'

'Not bad,' I was still alert, on guard. Now what?

'You'll be tempted to tell your followers what happened. To increase your celebrity status with the inside story.'

With relief, I realised that Watson wasn't worried that I had learned about the Blackcoin scam. His concern was that I'd go public about the project for selfish reasons.

I shook my head. 'Not in the slightest. You've seen my house. You know what fifty thousand dollars means to my mum and me. I'm not going to throw that away. And in any case, there's no footage. My followers want to watch raiding action.'

With a shrug, Watson leaned back. Then he stared at me for a little too long for comfort. 'Tom. I've gotten to know you over these past weeks. And I like you. Why don't you stay here and work with us? Become a manager at Yuno?'

Listening to Watson make me this offer again, I was struck by the lack of passion in his voice, the coldness in his eyes and the quick glance he gave to Blackridge. Despite the fact he was a hard man to read, after all this time with him I felt I had an insight into the real Watson. This wasn't a compliment, it was a trap. Watson wanted to keep me close, where he could control me and then get rid of me when I was no danger. It was like being offered a governorship by Cesare Borgia.

'I appreciate the offer. It's very generous. But no thanks.'

'No?' Watson wanted more. A reason. I didn't give him one. What could I say that rang true? Nothing really. It should have been my dream job. So I resorted to the tactic I'd employed dozens of times in school and said nothing.

The three of us waited. In the end, realising I wasn't going to speak, Watson turned sour. 'There's an insubordinate streak in you, Tom. It caused you to get on the wrong side of Paul.'

A dozen responses sprang to mind, all making the point that the problem lay with Blackridge - currently staring at the carpet, as if he wasn't present and wasn't listening - being too arrogant for the role he'd taken on. I said nothing.

'I can't put my finger on it. But I find myself reluctant to let you go. I don't quite trust you. I don't like the way you undermined Paul, even though it worked out. What's bothering me, do you think Tom? Why do I feel like this?'

'I'm sorry you do. I like you. I've had a brilliant time here and I've been paid very well. I want to go home, I miss my home, but I'd like to leave with us as friends. I owe you so much...You're the first person who has ever really believed in me.'

My prompt response seemed to surprise him and Watson's severe expression relaxed. 'All right then.' He even smiled as he stood up. 'Let's part as friends.'

We shook hands and it felt okay. I was nearly in the clear.

Blackridge stood up too, although neither of us moved to offer the other a handshake.

If there was a danger that my loyalty to Yuno might be exposed as a ruse, it was created by Blackridge's aggressive expression as we took the lift down. Again and again, Blackridge met my eye, forcing me to look away. At last he said, 'You think you are smart, don't you? Some streetwise kid who has all the moves? You're nothing, Tyro. Really, I wouldn't bother to scrape you off my shoe if I trod on you. Just a dry, little, insignificant shit. You got a lucky break with that vampire condition and everyone thought you were a star player. They couldn't see through you the way I can.'

Fortunately, the lift opened before I lost my temper. Too much more of this and it would have been impossible to hide the depths of my anger and the lengths I would go to in order to bring him, Watson, Kraken and the whole set-up crashing down.

I walked away, leaving the lift to carry Blackridge away. As I heard the doors closing, I looked over my shoulder. 'You should know,' I said, 'that Watson offered me your job.'

It wasn't true, of course, but I hoped he would believe it and brood on it.

Having made a few formal goodbyes to some of the players in

the foyer outside the Den (where the sounds of a party could be heard), I found myself in front of Braja.

'Where's Raitha?' I asked.

'He's clipped up.' Braja lowered his voice, 'I told him to. He's ready to get your dragon loot while we still have access to it.'

'Oh, right; good thinking.' I went to the nearest game room and I clipped up for what was going to be the last time on these amazing rigs. Back home, my one-foot tracker was going to feel clumsy and slow in comparison to the harness and two-footed pads. And this was probably the last time I'd be Klyto-toxos. Shame. I loved being a vampire. There were negative consequences to the condition but the abilities were amazing, not to mention the immunities. And it was fun, too; life as a vampire had become part of Klytotoxos's identity.

Once back in the game, I ran out of the castle without seeing any guards or the ivy-monster. Above me, the night sky was becoming lighter. We didn't have long.

[Channel Raitha/Klytotoxos] 'Hi, Tyro.'

[Channel Raitha/Klytotoxos] 'Hi, Raitha. Where are you?'

'Here!' Raitha fell as a dark blur, checking himself just in time to land on a rock and stare at me with his wild, yellow eyes.

I passed everything to him, including the letter and all my own gear.

'Thanks,' he said with a smile in his voice. 'Some nice items, these will help us level fast.'

'I'd better go. What's the password to get the stuff back from Tuscl?'

'Swedish meatballs.'

'What?'

'Braja had a theory that nothing worthwhile had come out of Sweden. Grythiss refuted him with a variety of excellent examples but nothing impressed Braja until the mention of meatballs.'

I shook my head. 'Oh well, it least it's easy to remember.'

Back in the Yuno headquarters, I joined in the festivities as enthusiastically as I could. My concern, though, was that it would be obvious my heart wasn't in them. Not only had I developed a distaste for Yuno and a desire to get out of there, part of my thoughts were occupied with the question of what character would I create for the next challenge, that of sabotaging the Blackcoin operation by destroying the ledger. Legitimately pleading tiredness, I left the building at last, with a long series of goodbyes to Braja, Raitha, Grythiss and Tuscl (Sapentia had already left). Of course, we all knew we were going to meet again online, but we acted as if this was the parting of the ways. Pushing it more than I was comfortable with (was this all being recorded somewhere?), Braja even wiped away a pretend tear.

The following day, my exit from Yuno, San Francisco and the USA was abrupt: car, airport, plane. I was in the air and everything fell away.

So, that was that. Adventure over.

I was looking forward to returning to Dublin. Most of all, it was my mum that I wanted to see. But I found that I missed my school mates. I even missed Seanie Howlin, who felt like an honest kind of gangster in comparison to the sinister, powerful investors in Blackcoin.

As the powerful surge of the aeroplane lifted me skyward, I felt like I was a different person to when I had arrived in San Francisco, just over a month ago. Coming home, I had a cause and I felt a moral strength I had never experienced before.

I was going to be the dragon's revenge

About the Author

Conor Kostick is a writer and historian living in Dublin, Ireland. When the world's first commercial Live Action Roleplaying company, Treasure Trap, started out in Peckforton Castle, Cheshire, Conor was fortunate to get work there, helping administer the fantasy game and create scenarios. That experience and a love of gaming has stayed with him and led to the international success of his 2004 novel, *Epic*, in which an entire society play a fantasy MMORPG where gains in the game translate into real financial and political power.

Having won several awards as a writer, Conor became involved in the writing and publishing community in Ireland; he is a board member of the Irish Writers Centre, the National Library of Ireland and the Irish Copyright Licensing Agency. He is also an executive member of the Irish Writers Union and an advisory board member of National Braille Production. In 2018, Conor became commissioning editor for Level Up.

Conor welcomes feedback and questions from readers. He can be found online at:

> Twitter: @conor_kostick
> www.litrpgforum.com/
> www.facebook.com/groups/litrpgforum/
> www.reddit.com/r/litrpg

If you enjoyed this book, then other LitRPG and GameLit books published by Level Up might well be for you.

Check out our new releases: www.levelup.pub

CPSIA information can be obtained
at www.ICGtesting.com
Printed in the USA
LVHW041729030919
629787LV00004B/663/P

9 781912 701827